THE BEST OF *LIBIDO*

Travel sex . . .

"Freud, Cavafy and the Comforts of Civilization"
by Richard Collins
A couple arriving in Vienna from Bucharest finds that a bath, a visit
to Freud's house, and a stop at a sex shop are wonderfully
stimulating experiences.

Extramarital sex . . .

"R & D in Suburbia" by Arlett Kunkle
After fifteen years a wife's sex life has gone on automatic pilot—
until she decides to live out her fantasies with a cop out of uniform
. . . completely out of uniform.

Strange sex . . .

"Performance" by Melissa Moore
An affair featuring a string of pearls, a seedy hotel room, and a
nameless man for a little S/M in the afternoon.

Dangerous sex . . .

"The Remover of Obstacles" by Frieda Madland
Turnabout is very unfair play when a lover gets out of hand and a
woman plots her revenge.

**AND DOZENS MORE
HEAT-GENERATING, THOUGHT-PROVOKING
STORIES AND POEMS**

THE ECSTATIC MOMENT

The Best of *Libido*

◆

Edited by
MARIANNA BECK
and
JACK HAFFERKAMP,

editors and publishers of

Libido:
The Journal of Sex
and Sensibility

◆

Delta
Trade Paperbacks

A Delta Book
Published by
Dell Publishing
a division of
Bantam Doubleday Dell Publishing Group, Inc.
1540 Broadway
New York, New York 10036

Library of Congress Cataloging in Publication Data

The ecstatic moment : the best of Libido / edited by Marianna Beck
    and Jack Hafferkamp.
        p.   cm.
    ISBN 0-385-31586-4
    1. Erotica.   2. Sex customs.   I. Beck, Marianna.   II. Hafferkamp, Jack.
III. Libido.
HQ454.E27   1997
810.8′03538—dc21   96-49404
                                                                  CIP

Manufactured in the United States of America
Published simultaneously in Canada

August 1997

10 9 8 7 6 5 4 3 2 1

BVG

CONTENTS

◆

◆ **v**

Satine caloris tibi est?

IN PRAISE
OF LIBIDO

◆

Mysterious are the ways of libido! Both those of libido proper, that force whereby the world is granted being, and those of *Libido: The Journal of Sex and Sensibility,* which is one of libido's grooviest receptacles and channels here in Norte America. *Leigh-BE-dough:* It rolls off the tongue like a perfumed ball of attar-dipped hashish. As well as the malleability and molding of Princess Leia in, let's say, a hayloft. I don't know what "libido" was called in English before some neo-Latinist Freudians let us have it. The Puritans might have just called it "the urge" and fought it with cold compresses and valerian root. But it was Rabelais who said it best: "Pantagruel lay on the river bank and let the moist beast lie on top of him, filled with compressed lust, sure that when he rose up to it, the river would carry him off by his, how shall we say it, mountain-sized organ of inquiry." Not only did Rabelais say it five hundred years ago, but he delighted both in it and the happy poetry it evoked, just as the editors of *Libido* do. Marianna Beck and Jack Hafferkamp are two neo-Rabelaisians in fin-de-millennium America, loose in a world of playful lusts but also of dogged Helmsians and Christian rottweilers. The playful lusts drove them to cull these delicious pieces from their pollen-heavy publication, while the snarl of the Christo-Helmsian attack dogs makes them fighters in the pursuit of happiness.

What's in *Libido*? There are stories by women who can and do take pleasure in the surprises that willingness and practice can bring about. Johanna Baird, for instance, in a gustatory romp titled "B Is for Béchamel," merges the ways of *gourmandise* with those of lust. The result is what every writer drools about in his or her dreams of glory: a poetic tone that murmurs simultaneously to the gustatory and incantatory centers.

There are stories and poems praising the mystery of sex. In "Cock & Balls" by Laura Rosenthal and "Tit" by Annie MacNaughton, the colloquial is rendered in song. But humor is present because the world surrounds every gesture. One of the salutary constants of this collection is the grown-up wonder of it all. There are smiles here and belly laughs too, which prove that joy is the true medium of Eros.

These are stories, poems, and art about the difficulty of maintaining the sacred simplicity of Eros in a world full of impediments. Stories and poems about the erotic charge of impediments. About the ironies of arousal. Stories and poems about the untamable fantasy of humans aroused. The range of possibilities is played by the writers here like the keys of a fabulous piano. Lovers watch, are watched, aroused, awakened, called to the flesh. All the classical motifs of Eros are explored, from pain to pleasure to sexual gymnastics and gender-bending masquerades.

The convergence of the senses is another of this *festschrift*'s constant veins. The body is constantly seeking multiple pleasures while awash in multiple ironies. The lovers in Richard Collins's "Freud, Cavafy and the Comforts of Civilization" are ecstatic to discover hot water in the afternoon in a Viennese hotel, after having spent grungy months in Bucharest. Their delight in hot water and soap turns quickly into an intellectual and sexual adventure that exemplifies another of this book's veins: The body and the mind are each other's catalysts and blossom bearers.

The editors are erudite. They have gathered here a book of the best of contemporary erotica but they have also given us a comprehensive and unpedantic lesson in the rich history of the genre. You will find Victorian, Edwardian, and Sadian echoes in these pages. Oscar Wilde, Aubrey Beardsley, Henry Miller, Alexander Trocchi, and William Burroughs watch over this book. Let the Robertson-Helmsian mastiffs come: They have the lights of literature shining in their eyes.

Andrei Codrescu
New Orleans

INTRODUCTION

Welcome to *The Ecstatic Moment*, the best of *Libido: The Journal of Sex and Sensibility.*

The book you hold is a compilation of the best written, most provocative, humorous, and thoughtful stories and poems we have published over the first half-dozen years of *Libido*. We think it is a remarkable collection, an engaging, revealing, and hot set of insights into the sexual state of the union. If you want to take America's real sexual temperature, forget trash-talk TV: Read this book instead.

The Ecstatic Moment has two goals: massaging the primary sex organ—the one between the ears—and stimulating thought and discussion about sexual issues. These pieces travel all over the sexual landscape, exploring the ins and outs of sexuality from many compass points. They play with the conventions of sexuality and the writing about it. We like to think there is probably something here to shock almost everyone. And yet these stories and poems finally underscore the community of sexual expression in all its diversity.

And that's just as it should be.

Marianna Beck and I started publishing *Libido* in 1988 because we believed there was value in creating a literary magazine of erotica. Our aim then—as now—was to put out a sexually positive publication for literate, independent, adventuresome adults. We chose to aim at what we saw as a large yet mostly ignored audience of people, male and female, gay and straight, who are turned off by the stupidity, homophobia, and misogyny of most popularly available sexually ori-

ented publications, yet who remain open to the possibilities of eroti-
cally charged expression and who are not intimidated by the cultural
thought police.

What our remarkably loyal readers get in each issue of *Libido* is
fiction, black-and-white photography, poetry, historical reflection, and
journalism that are not hung up on the dualities that so plague the
American discussion of sexuality: gay or straight, male or female, black
or white, good or evil, and on down the line. *Libido,* we like to say, is
all-embracing in its approach to sexuality. Save for the violent and
exploitative, we appreciate all the stops along the spectrum.

We also think this book is proof that standing up for tolerance
doesn't have to be preachy or dreary. It can be quite pleasurable. And
funny. In putting this first collection of *Libido*'s best together, we were
pleased to rediscover the darkly droll humor of much of the work. Sex,
after all, is an amusing business. At *Libido* we say that if you don't
think so, you're missing the joke.

We hope you'll find *The Ecstatic Moment* an antidote to the omni-
present depictions of sex as banal, sleazy, or full of angst and pain. We
believe you'll find this book a heat-generating and thought-provoking
refuge from the pressures of daily life. We hope you enjoy it.

And if you do, please share it with a friend.

Jack Hafferkamp

A-B-C

◆

A Is for Arab, Anthurium and Autonomic

B Is for Béchamel

C Is for Closet, Crevice and Colossus

Three Stories by Johanna Baird

A IS FOR ARAB, ANTHURIUM AND AUTONOMIC

♦

The woman next to me from the United Arab Emirates, the dusky, older one with the magnificent nose and large, faintly hennaed hands, suddenly turned to me and whispered, "You must be like hot sweet tea, the kind that first burns the tongue."

"Excuse me?" I said, apparently to no one, for she turned away quickly and resumed her conversation with the fossil sitting on her left.

What do you say to something like that? I admit that her words registered quickly beneath the silk chemise I wore, even while they continued to ricochet inside my brain. Have you ever had just one nipple grow erect? Oddly enough it wasn't the one closest to her that stood at attention, forming a tiny solitary tent of indigo, but rather the other, the more distant and apparently contrarian one.

She leaned even closer to the ornithologist, the shrunken professor emeritus whose bobbing white nest of hair gave him the appearance of an excited cockatiel whenever he spoke. "Yes, yes," he said, "toxoplasmosis. You probably won't get it from canaries."

As it was, she was simply buying time. I resumed picking at my fennel and shiitake salad when her hand executed a perfect Esther Williams swan dive under the tablecloth. It was a triumph in physics Busby Berkeley–style but I suspect an accidental one, for in one swift motion her fingers had overcome all sorts of sartorial barriers and managed to slip into my warmest recesses unimpeded. The joke of it all was that I had unwittingly engineered this feat by choosing—at the precise moment of her maiden voyage—to cross my legs.

I don't know whether or not she'd meant to have it happen quite so effortlessly but there we were; an octogenarian ornithologist, a diplomat's wife and me with an autonomic nervous system in overdrive. I glanced at my husband across the table, his face obscured by a large blood-red anthurium lurking in the floral arrangement between us. Sometimes an anthurium is only an anthurium, I mused, but this was botanical mockery of the highest order! What would he think of her fingers trapped in the humid crevice of my thighs, one of them moving ever so slightly against the thin membrane of cotton? Would this prandial *pas de deux* irritate, amuse or seduce him? Would I tell him later that her finger stroked slowly, methodically, as if she needed to satisfy an imperceptible but lingering itch?

I sat welded to my seat, beyond conversation, drinking sips of water as if that alone would cool the hot little trough her finger had formed through the thin cotton. My breathing grew more concentrated, more shallow, and I wet my lips, this time with my tongue. Sooner or later, someone would notice—or worse, I'd be swept away by some banality like, "What is it that you do, again?" And I would utter some non sequitur and say that I was amazed, astounded really, how my dinner companion could perform such profound and relentless digital movement beneath the table without having anyone notice her upper arm be anything but perfectly still. At any moment, she was capable of magically holding me aloft for all to watch, squirming and undignified at the end of a single finger.

And then, as deftly as she'd slid into the dewy warmth, she retreated. She threw her head back and laughed deeply, bringing her hand from under the table and extending it out for the ornithologist to kiss.

B IS FOR
BÉCHAMEL

She finished licking the last of the *béchamel* sauce from his armpit and looked at him, sadly. In his horn-rimmed glasses and thick uncombed hair sticking up in large kinetic clumps—no doubt a result of his chef's hat—he reminded her of a crazed-looking James Joyce. She moved to cradle his head, pulling him closer to kiss all the large parts of his face—his jutting brow, his aquiline nose gone German, his Dudley-Do-Right chin. Ursula was about to tell him it was curtains, *finita la musica.* Since hiring him as her *sous chef* six months before, she had put on twenty-seven pounds.

The problem was food, naturally; specifically *his* food. He kept insisting she eat it, lick it, nibble it—off his body. She ate knowing he was bad for her.

"Here, my ramekin," he'd order, "lick this!" And he'd drop his white pants, invariably covered in flour so that a small cloud of white dust enveloped him, giving the illusion that he was some sort of genie rising out of the white-tiled kitchen floor. He would pour some delicious elixir from a small silver pipkin over his mandrake root and, well, it was difficult to deny him.

Ursula didn't necessarily want to give up the wild, and at times capillary-bursting, sex, but she faced two dilemmas. As owner of a small restaurant in the Village currently blessed by the trendy, she feared looking like the Venus of Willendorf in relation to the fashionable, stick bodies who swallowed fistfuls of antioxidants for breakfast and fasted until dinner. Secondly, she needed to make a living. She was dependent upon Wolfie. His culinary genius had catapulted her restaurant from a little-known bistro to "a gastronomic nirvana," where one critic wafted: "It's manna for Everyman!" Unfortunately, in order for Wolfie to both create *and* rise to the occasion, as it were, he demanded some sort of oral approval from Ursula.

He forced her to repeat the little gratified noises she made every-time she sampled his cuisine, her tongue swirling in and out of any number of crevices. "Do you think it needs more saffron?" he'd sud-denly ask about the sauce he'd slowly poured in a thin stream from his chest to his now slowly rising *baguette.* Ursula lapped ceremoniously, then stopped. "I really can't taste the saffron. It's something more subtle, more aromatic. Did you add basil, my concubone?" He grew more excited. "Of course! Yes! Yes? And what else? Can you guess?" After three or four more such exchanges, he grew as hard as a marble rolling pin and she straddled him for the roiling romp that inevitably followed these culinary forays.

For her birthday, he actually wore a *schwartzwälderkirschtorte.* Ur-sula had just closed the restaurant and gone to switch on the alarm system when she found him in the nearly dark kitchen, reclining on one of the prep tables, a miniature cake impaled on his penis *complete with candles.* Nobody had ever done anything like this for her before.

"Now, come here and blow them out and tell me if there's too much kirsch," he commanded. How could Ursula resist such atten-tions? Despite her fatigue and the late hour, she found herself moisten-ing at the prospect of taking her first, tentative nibble. Her nipples hardened in the wet, warm air blowing from the three nearby dish-washers.

"I thought about a pistachio *soufflé,* but then changed my mind," he whispered. Ursula bent over him to make a wish and blew out the candles. He took her hand and drew her closer. "Or would you have wanted a delicate *crème anglaise*? Or perhaps a penuche icing instead?"

"No, my sweet, it would have fought the cherry taste. This is perfection," she said, pulling out the candles and allowing the aroma of chocolate and cherry to permeate her nostrils. From what she remembered now, she ate until she found the tip of his penis; shiny, taut and ready to be sprung from its gooey prison. It was the first time Ursula remembered eating an entire cake. She wasn't sure whether she'd enjoyed it because it was good or because she suffered from false consciousness.

But now, six months later with her triglycerides at an all-time high, enough was enough. No more scurrying her tongue over his well-defined gluteals and down his crack in search of that last little taste of clarified curry butter. Or lapping the remains of *babas au rhum* from behind his knees. Or foraging for the lobster *rumaki* he claimed to have buried inside his tiny Calvins. Or nibbling from the *Königsberger Klopse* he'd so carefully arranged between his thighs.

Ursula needed to find a way to loosen his gustatory grip and stop feeling harassed by food. *His* food. She stroked her puffy mons, contemplating a bleak return to boiled chicken breasts. With her thighs around his neck, she watched him gazing at her quim just inches away from his nose.

"Wolfie," she began, "I've been thinking about the menu. We should spice it up and add some Thai and Szechuan dishes. We could start out with that dish called Tiger Cries." She had suddenly remembered reading how red pepper purifies the blood and removes toxins. If she suddenly adopted a diet high in capsicum, telling him she needed peppers to stimulate her metabolism, he might relent. Perhaps the thought of a peppery epiphany in his tenderer parts would send him scurrying in search of some other woman's arteries to occlude.

Wolfie traced the outline of her jade grotto. "Maybe I should just go back to watching *those* videos," he sighed. "You know the ones. It's just that . . . well, I lose control when I see that much of . . . Julia Child. I act out in profoundly dehumanizing ways. I end up not caring *who* I cook for." His voice was as thin as rolled-out phyllo dough.

Ursula shifted her upper thigh so as not to cut off too much blood flow from his carotid artery. "Society is obsessed with food, Wolfie. Everybody eats. Some more than others. I know you think it's only food. It's just that you don't have to turn *every* woman into an endo-morph.''

In Only Words *procensorship advocate Catharine MacKinnon argues that pornography harms women. Why, then, should one not look at food as yet another example of linear causality?*

C IS FOR
CLOSET, CREVICE
AND COLOSSUS

Amicule, deliciae, num est sum qui mentiar tibi?*

Yesterday, I had lunch with a man who confessed that he liked to lay on the floor beneath a woman while she dresses.

"Yes, of course I know, it's utterly puerile," he said, quickly, "but the excitement it induces in me is nearly indescribable." I found this statement quite disconcerting. After all, I didn't know him that well and I was put off that he'd casually drop a line like that and not expect me to stomp out or hurl some shriveling feminist invective at him. In these cases, you either choke on your food or you keep moving, so I said, "Really? Why's that?"

He actually blushed. I didn't think Republicans blushed. And that brought up another, more pertinent and irritating issue. What was I doing out to lunch with a Republican?

I remembered. Now that he was no longer in politics, my acquaintance—he certainly wasn't more than that—had gone into international consulting and hired me for one of his Washington-based projects.

"Sure, there's more to it, but why would you care to know?" he asked.

* *Baby, sweetheart, would I lie to you?*

"I'm big on original sources," I said, trying to sound as flip as possible.

"Well, I suppose, more than anything, it had to do with my favorite German grandmother, Lili. She's the one who slept with her head at the foot of the bed," he began. "She'd started sleeping like that because her husband had nightmares. My grandfather would wake violently and flail his arms, and twice had inadvertently broken her nose. Not one to move to another bed, Lili decided to sleep with her feet next to his head."

So maybe this explained how he'd gained a reputation for often bizarre, sometimes topsy-turvy management style. Still, it didn't explain how he acquired the predilections of an eight-year-old boy.

"After my grandfather died, Lili moved in with my parents and me and I ended up sharing my room with her. There were twin beds, and she slept with her head at the foot of the bed just like she always had. With my room crammed full of a lot of her junk, I retreated to the floor of my closet to play."

Oh, here it comes. The closet. I should have known. He probably likes to wear garter belts under his Brooks Brothers suits.

"For hours, I lay beneath a full rack of voluminous housedresses, infused with the smell of rose water, liniment and the rancidy odor of her clothes, and played with my toys.

"One afternoon, I was in the closet carefully constructing a battle zone with her shoes when she opened the door and rummaged for a hanger. She stepped right over me, naked except for her brassiere, and provided me with a direct shot of her furry cleft. I froze. Up until then, I'd only heard about these things. My mother had once referred to a woman's *schmuck kästchen*—little jewel box—in relation to some neighbor who was pregnant. So I naturally thought that females possessed something with a lid which they regularly flipped open to have children.

"What I saw was decidedly much different, something considerably more alive, forbidden, mysterious—something I wanted to touch. I wanted to know what those puffy banks of hair felt like and where that thin dark crevice disappeared to between her legs. Although I spent every day in that closet for about six months hoping to catch another glimpse, I only saw Lili's furry patch maybe a half dozen times. She never seemed to notice me and I never got caught. Then, we moved to a bigger place and I got my own room again."

He paused for a moment. He'd answered my question, but I admit I wanted to hear more. His answer had seemed honest to me, if not a little touching, and it all seemed rather innocent.

"So that explains it all?" I finally said. "I mean, this is why you like to—" I suddenly realized I was asking for more details about a subject I hadn't initially wished to touch with a barge pole. I felt like crawling under the table from embarrassment. But, clearly, he needed little encouragement.

"I don't know that it explains anything other than it provided an impetus for more. Of course it all had to do with those early feelings of seeing something I wasn't supposed to, the fear of getting caught, eyeing the forbidden—all rolled into one thrilling, tidy package. The fact is, I never consciously incorporated any of this into my fantasy life until my first lover, who was a philosophy major, read Nietzsche to me while kneeling over my face and wearing no underwear. I remember gazing at her lips just inches from mine, close enough so that I could see through the tufts of her red-tinged bush and observe the changes in color of her lips—from dark brown at the edges to that lighter, pinkier hue they take on when excitement causes them to part all on their own. It was intoxicating, like the aroma of sycamore trees in full bloom or that tingle you get when you walk into a warm Chinese restaurant and a delicate sweet and sour piquancy finds its way to your nose and makes your eyes water."

He stopped to take a breath and I ceased eating.

"I admit there haven't been that many women, including both my former and current wife, who've indulged me in this capacity. I don't exactly understand this because, after all, it seems fairly innocuous. Anyway, I've experienced the whole gamut from one woman who wanted to turn me in to the police—this after we'd been sleeping together for four months!—to another who threw a drink in my face and called me a pervert.

"But then there was Jan, who took it to a whole other level. Jan was working on her doctorate in Mycenaean anthropology and was studying up on this whole woman-as-earth-goddess schtick long before it got to be a trendy Book-of-the-Month-Club topic. While she wasn't exactly what I'd call a lesbian, men to her were basically carbon-based life forms with a dildo attachment. Her line, I might add.

"One night, stretched out on the floor with a glass of wine at her place, I asked her if she would stand over me while she dressed. She had just gotten out of the shower and was toweling her hair dry and the look that came over her made my Boy Scout compass point magnetic north."

Nice touch, I thought. At least he's being subtle when it comes to body parts.

" 'Sure, I will,' said she, licking her fingers and sliding them between her legs. 'But you keep your pants on and I'll just pretend you're not here.' She walked over and stood directly over me, and I felt I was looking up at the Colossus of Rhodes. Jan was taller than me, probably six one or two, and her legs seemed to go on forever. Her tiny pointed breasts seemed to be somewhere in the stratosphere. While her fingers danced a slow rhythm in her pubic hair, she talked to herself. *Probably won't get laid tonight better get myself off now loves to finger me but haven't seen his, nice feelssogood I think I'll wear no underwear tonight see if he notices he probably won't likes to discuss finance a lot.* She talked like that and it made me crazy. Still standing over me, she bent her knees slightly and began to rotate her three middle fingers in a furious circular motion. I swear I had never seen a woman masturbate before. *He likes this I think wonder what he sees if my cunt is bigger to him swollenred can he see inside I'll put a finger in and show him.* Jan slid a finger inside herself and for the first time I noted how red her pudenda was, as she called it when she was being coy. Fra Filippo Lippi opened and bowed in a wet oooooo and then stretched back into a vermilion slit as she spun her fingers at an increasingly furious pace. Every now and then I caught a whiff of her sex and it was all I could do to keep myself from pulling her down and washing my face in all that warm musky dampness. But I decided to play by her rules for as long as I could stand it. As it was, she fell to her knees over my face at that moment and made this preternatural noise that emanated, I thought, from somewhere deep between her legs.

"Okay now, baby banker, lick me dry as if you were a mama cat." She lowered herself over my face until I was barely able to breathe, let alone get my tongue out of my mouth. I slid around and for the first time felt her pleasure button with my tongue—the size of a big spring pea I might add—from underneath. I stroked and played with it because that's all I could do given that she had me locked in her favorite Mycenaean goddess submission hold and I was trying to make the best of it. If she wanted me to dry her, whatever I was doing wasn't working because everything was feeling considerably wetter. But it didn't seem to matter. Whatever I did manage to do made her whole pelvis grind into my face so that I could feel her labia in all their slipperiness wash my nose like two little tongues. She pulled away slightly, let me breathe for a bit and then used my chin to get herself off again. Finally, she stopped, sat back on my chest, and gave me a look that indicated she was extremely pleased with herself. If you can believe it, she actually reached back to feel if I was hard. Apparently, I needed only the slightest touch because when she pressed me there I was screamingly erect, and I did what I hadn't done since high school, which was to come inside my pants.

"Hard to believe, isn't it?"

"No!" I said, more vehemently than I'd wanted to, stunned that I'd answered at all.

"Well, that was Jan for you." He stopped talking. What else could he say? For that matter, what else could I say? We weren't exactly going to start discussing profit margins. He sensed my embarrassment and said, "Sorry, I didn't mean to make you an unwitting voyeur, but I guess I have. Let's skip the business stuff and meet up again tomorrow. Same time, same place?"

Without waiting for my answer, he stood up from his chair, paid the waiter and left. I finally made a motion to leave some ten minutes later, but only after I'd made sure no one saw me flip the cushion over that I'd been sitting on.

DESIRE

◆

Communion
poetry by Marael Johnson

Freud, Cavafy and the Comforts of Civilization
by Richard Collins

Milk, Butter and Eggs
by Jane Underwood

The (Sex) Lives of the Great Composers
by Dennis Bartel

Pianist at the Colonnade Hotel, Boston
poetry by Michael Warr

COMMUNION

I have my best orgasms
when in near proximity
to a religious shrine.
It doesn't matter which religion,
I'm an easy convert
pinned beneath some lover
like Jesus to his cross
or, perhaps, poised
in tantric bliss
fucking those steeples
and spires
moaning like a Baptist
at revival
gnawing ravenously on flesh
drawing blood in ecstasy
glowing like a thousand
votive candles
in a tribute
far more intoxicating
than stale wafers
and cheap wine.

Marael Johnson

◆

FREUD, CAVAFY
AND THE COMFORTS OF
CIVILIZATION

◆

By Richard Collins

We arrived in Vienna from Romania, my wife Lelika and I,
like refugees on a first visit to a Western metropolis. How bright the
streets! How quiet and shiny the automobiles! How they purred at the
stoplights, these reflective machines, waiting for the light to change! It
had been almost two years since we'd been in a country where the
drivers didn't jockey for position, or use their horns as a sonic prod.
After Greece, Turkey, Egypt, Bulgaria and Romania, Vienna looked as
slick and orderly as Disneyland, the capital of hygiene and good clean
family fun and entertainment.

We settled in at the Pension Bosch. Its name conjured up images
of Hell and electronic parts. It turned out to be like neither. In our
spacious room the decor was Hapsburg kitsch, with its striped wallpaper and blown-glass hard-candy light fixtures. A languorous painting
of blond girls in Fauntleroy frills hung over the fluffy four-poster bed,
where Lelika said she expected to have truly Boschian nightmares.

"Of electrical systems gone amok?" I asked.

"No," she said. "Of cannibal orgies, hacked limbs and excremen-
tal streams. That sort of thing. That Bosch."

"Sounds like Romania," I said. "Where you always dream of fresh
fruit and guacamole, cappuccino and fresh cream."

"Wish fulfillment or anxiety," she said. "I guess you always want what you can't get."

"I guess you're right," I said. "In Romania I dream of electrical systems that work."

We opened the taps and filled the enormous tub with steaming hot water, got out of our clothes and jumped in for a long soak.

"Imagine that," said Lelika. "Hot water in the middle of the afternoon. A miracle!"

"Just one of the comforts of civilization," I reminded her.

Slowly the grit from the train ride from Timisoara to Vienna began to melt from us, turning the water gray. For months we had been washing our clothes in just such gray water, when there was water and when it was hot. We drained the tub and filled it again, marveling at the endless supply of clean hot water.

In the metal rack above the tub there were huge bricks of snow-white soap. We played with these, made them our bath toys, sinking them with force and trapping them between our legs, only to have them escape and breach the surface like the white whale coming up for air, or floating them back and forth to beach them on our bellies.

I soaped Lelika's neck and shoulders, sliding the white brick over her arms and around her teardrop breasts and belly. How smooth her skin was, how white! So much whiter and smoother than the soap itself. She was all slippery-sleek like an albino seal. Her slipperiest parts I lifted up in the palms of my hands and gravity did the rest, re-arranging them to perfection. She stood in front of me, allowing me to shampoo the wild tangle of pubic hair, to sculpt an old man's beard out of the foam and then blow it away like the head on a mug of beer. Using my forearm as a loofah, I reached between her thighs and let her ride there as on a banister from elbow to wrist. I drew my fingers forward from the small of her back, along the dark and tender hidden flesh, delving the smooth shadowed fjord, and grooming her anus with my fingertips until the puckered kiss grew as relaxed and slippery as the rest of her body.

Dipping my hands into the water, washing and soaping them up again, I sent my fingers back to work (and to play) massaging the fine silken lining of her cunt (just like a little dug-out canoe!) until it was slick as a slice of guava. Then I rinsed her body down with a lush sponge, squeezing it over her breasts again and again. The water cascaded along her breasts and belly like the drapery of some gorgeous caryatid pissing in the rain. From her pubic hairs, now twisted into a pointed curl like a Freudian goatee, the water ran in a clear filament.

I kissed the slight swell of her belly, burying my nose in the tiny basin of her navel where the streaming water caught and swirled. Then dipping my head lower I made an urn of my mouth to catch the filament as it flowed from the curl, a little turning drill bit of holy water. I drank deeply and long, paying my respects.

"This," I said—I was thinking of (among other things) how we had to boil the water before drinking it in Romania—"is surely one of the comforts of civilization that I miss most."

Continuing the massage downward, I took care not to neglect those parts of Lelika that over the few years of our marriage had become like extensions of my own body. I take joy in releasing the tension from her thighs and muscular calves. I like to massage them gently but deeply and to concentrate on the nodes of energy that collect in her feet. Her poor, lovely feet. I am particularly fond of my Lelika's feet. Not as a fetishist might be, although I find them erotic enough. My fondness for Lelika's expressive nether extremities is almost purely sentimental. Deformed in their childhood by the rigors of ballet, her feet possess the charm of being flawed, her toes gnarled by standing on point. She no longer dances, except for me when I ask her in the privacy of our bedroom, naked at the foot of the bed, where she needs no atmospheric light to limn her curves. Her body glows, a phosphorescent wave. Whenever I wash her feet, I think of her damaged toes bearing up the weight of this dancing light. And I think of the girl, even lighter, more glowing, and still there, gazing out the windows of her eyes, in her mature body.

When I tell her this in the tub, she tells me a story.

"Did I ever tell you about the first time I decided to lose my virginity?" she asks. "I was sixteen."

She's lying against me now, the small of her back pressing my erection to my belly. I have never heard this story. I've heard the true one about when she did actually lose her virginity at eighteen to her boyfriend in the backyard under the swing set, at her instigation rather than his. I've heard about how she played doctor with her cousin Marie, the one nursing her baby with a fragrant, swollen breast at our wedding reception. (Also true.) I've heard any number of her erotic stories, most of which turn out not to be true, but I can never tell when she's telling them whether they're true to fact or only to her vivid portrayal of how fact might have been. It doesn't matter because both have the desired effect, the desired effect resting at the moment on the erotic region at the base of her spine.

"No," I say. "I haven't heard this one. But let's get out of the tub. I want to appreciate it."

So we're out of the bath now, both still damp and red and glowing. She's settled in a fluffy bed, and I'm giving her the treatment as she tells me the story of how she might have lost her virginity. I'm drying her feet with the soft white towel, sucking her toes, licking between them until she's squirming and screaming for me to stop because she can't go on with her story with me sucking her toes like that. So I get out the clippers and trim her toenails, file them carefully, and buff them on my eyebrows.

"So anyway I was sixteen and there was no one at home," she has been saying. "My father was at work and my mother was somewhere, and I was looking out the window at the street, afraid that I'd never have sex. I don't remember why I thought that. Maybe I thought the world would end. I didn't want to be an old virgin. I didn't want to be a dead virgin, even less. I was looking out the window and thinking that I would ask the first man who came down the street to come in and fuck me. I was so lucky no one happened to knock on the door. Can you imagine someone coming to the door, a salesman, or a relative or something?"

"Or a garbage collector or somebody selling cable TV?" I offered.

"Or something, and little me with my tits newly formed, and my pubic hair just past the stage of a duckling's down."

"Or Bambi fur."

"Or something, and me dragging him inside and forcing him to fuck me? Can you imagine?"

I tell her that I can imagine. I am imagining in great and vivid detail, but I control myself. I give her middle three toes one last quick suck, darting my tongue among them, and then let go of her squirming foot. I also let go of myself with my other hand. We are tourists, I remind her, and have sights to see. The bed would be there when we returned. I finished drying her with the towel, consoled by the fact that she was still warm and wet and glowing inside, and would be for quite some time.

As she began to dress, I delayed the process as long as I could. I nipped at her breasts as they disappeared under her shirt, the nipples puckered and hard against the T-shirt cotton. When she pulled out a fresh pair of cotton panties, I intercepted them and tossed them onto one of the hard-candy light fixtures. Our sightseeing would be more enjoyable, I suggested, if she didn't wear any. As she was pulling her skirt on, I wagged my cock on her thigh, still imagining the strange man—me—obliging the hot, impatient sixteen-year-old standing on her tippy toes at the window. It was winter, but her stockings came up to above her knees, her skirt came down to below her knee, and the soft leather coat fell to her ankles. I tried to convince her to discard everything but the leather coat, but she was sensible.

Freud's house was first on our list of things to see. It seemed a pilgrimage every civilized person should make. In the two years since we left New Orleans, we'd made our way to other erotic wonders of the world. The Erechtheum on the Acropolis with the sturdy and forbearing caryatids still lithe and youthful after centuries of abuse by the Turks, Napoleon, and other unappreciative philistines. (It was the caryatids' drapery, I realized, running the length of their bodies that I was reminded of while admiring Lelika in the bath.) The Madonna of Ephesus in the museum at Selchuk was another erotic wonder, with her mysterious buckler of breasts, rows of nipples exposed to excite or to suckle the hordes. (The Madonna reminded Lelika of her college boyfriend, the basketball player with the three nipples that she would often dally with and suck, she said, although she never slept with him.)

The Temple of Whores was another, at the site of Ephesus itself, with the slab of marble in the walkway, an advertisement and a road sign pointing the direction of the temple with the impression of a foot in the marble. (Seeing it, I recalled how when I lived in Hollywood I would often pay homage to the fragile imprint of Garbo's toes in the courtyard of Grauman's Chinese Theater.) And yet another erotic wonder, hitherto uncharted, that we found on the island of Santorini last summer, a great crumbling sandstone phallus. Lelika made me strip naked and stand, making obeisance to the thing that was twice my size (twice the size of my entire body, that is), so that she could take a photograph. This was her way of reminding me, I suppose, of my mortality. For soon this brave erection thrust proudly from the belly of the earth would go the way of all ithyphallic columns, man-made or earth-inspired, self-made or Lelika-inspired, once time and the elements had gone down on it and worn it out.

Freud's house was a haven of sanity in that sanitary city of sausages and caffeine, Schnitzler's *fin de siècle* and Hitler's *fin du monde*, Vienna. We lingered there, rambling from room to room. We appreciated the Victorian sensuality of the paneled walls, the dustless atmosphere of velvet and damask. Examining what was left of his library, we pored over the great man's letters and manuscripts, and stood in silent awe at the foot of the infamous couch of recited dreams. Whatever you think of Freud and his theories, modern sexuality is unthinkable without him. With his little penlight, the Great Spelunker went deep to reveal the erotic subscape of the brain. What he envisioned in those hidden convolutions may have been half-hallucinated, but his hallucinations were more plausible and vividly imagined than most people's home videos, which is what contemporary psychology reminds me of most.

I have a reaction to museums that is not uncommon I find, at least to men. It doesn't matter what sort of museum it is, I get a hard-on. I have the same reaction when it's a gallery full of nudes, like the Schieles and Klimts we found in the days to come, or a hoard of Persian armaments, like those we saw at the Topkapi Palace, or the warehouse full of mummies, like what we saw in Cairo. So it wasn't

Freud's well-worn couch, nor the cocaine spoons the master used to kick-start his imagination, nor even the erotic statuettes and drawings he'd collected from all over the world, that caused the particular quality of erection that sprung up that day in Freud's house in Vienna, the quality of which can only be intimated by the word "prong." That's the kind of hard-on it was, the kind that, once it raises its shiny bald head, won't be denied. With a weight and will of its own, part flesh and part dildo, it is a not-too-smart, heat-seeking ballistic missile. It wants cunt, the living texture of dripping cunt, the achingly alive fragrance of panting, parting cunt, as the natural consummation of the seductive atmosphere of the museum. As Freud might have said, it makes sense: a museum is, after all, a monument to death. Death is art. The still life which is no longer life, reminding us to live.

I had the same reaction a few months before when Lelika and I visited Cavafy's house in Alexandria, now a museum, with the same result. We'd made the pilgrimage to Egypt partly for this, because she is from Alexandria, Louisiana, and I had long ago memorized Cavafy's "Ithaca," with its unforgettable beginning:

> *When you set out on the voyage to Ithaca,*
> *pray that your journey be long,*
> *full of adventures, full of knowledge.*

It had stayed in my mind, tantalizing me halfway around the world, and bringing us finally here, where the poem had been written.

We were the only ones visiting the creaking house that day. It was really a third-floor flat, overlooking the marketplace. On the ground floor, where there had once been a brothel, there was now a furniture workshop where couches were being reupholstered. Our only company in Cavafy's flat was the caretaker, a smooth Coptic youth, a student perhaps, who alone guarded the first editions, manuscripts, furniture and memory of the dead poet of Greek Alexandria.

Maybe it was in the room with the editions of Forster's and Durrell's books on Alexandria—or maybe it was Cavafy's bedroom with his holograph poems in his long, effeminate hand—but I remember how the floor creaked when I brushed the inevitable museum-inspired prong against the rounded curves and shadowed fjord of Lelika's firm ass as she bent to decipher the Greek, French or Arabic of the display case legend.

Lelika tries to humor me in these situations. At first she acts shocked or surprised. (It's the Southern girl in her, I guess.) Then she invariably does something amazing. This time, I was leaning with her over one of the display cases, containing first editions or manuscripts—like I said, my memory is blurry on this—but my arm was definitely draped over her shoulder. My hand had definitely plunged, more or less discreetly, into her blouse. I was caressing her breast, rolling the right nipple between my fingers, when she reached behind her and without looking or giving any other sign of naughty behavior, grabbed the prong for a quick squeeze. The caretaker's head happened to be turned toward us at that moment, as I saw in the reflection of an etching's black matting. But in such situations Lelika doesn't bother with such piddling details. That too is the Southern girl in her that I love.

The prong thrives on this kind of encouragement, whinnies and romps and snorts. Ah, yes. I remember now what it was we were reading. It was Cavafy's description (in a journal? a letter?) of the view from the windows of his house. From these windows he could, he said, see at a single glance: a church, a graveyard, and the whores walking the streets below; was there anything more to life to know?

At one end of the entrance hall there was a bathroom behind a curtain, Cavafy's bathroom, only slightly refurbished for the visits of his posthumous public. I told Lelika to go in the bathroom. In a moment I would follow.

"But the boy," she said. "He'll know."

"So?" I said. "It'll give him a thrill. His job must be a bore. A privilege to baby-sit Cavafy's ghost, an imaginative gold mine, but a bore on days like today when business is slow."

She made her way to the bathroom, pretending to glance at the framed newspaper clippings along the hall on her way. I followed her without waiting for a discreet interval. I smiled at the student on my way. He smiled shyly back. The door was unlocked. Lelika was waiting with her blouse provocatively half-unbuttoned.

I threw her against the wall. The force of my body caused her to grunt. I pinned her hands above her head with one hand, which brought her breasts out of her blouse and her nipples pointing at the ceiling. Then I was gentle. With my other hand I lifted her dress, quickly for the first half of the journey, then slowly as the hand made its way into the heart of darkness. My hands love this journey up from the cool bare flesh at the top of her knee, along her warm thighs to the humid juncture where the hairs begin, shyly at first like the fringe of foliage separating the desert from the Nile, and then wild and verdant and lush as you reach the wet flow between the slippery mud banks, where the growth is good and tangled. It's here at this junction whence the rich fragrance emanates. I did not touch her cunt, though, not yet. Only every bit of flesh around it in which the ripe fruit is packed tight.

"What if the door had opened and it hadn't been me?" I said. "What if it had been the smooth boy outside? What if I'd sent him in instead? To give him a thrill. To give you a thrill."

This caused her to close her eyes, to imagine the scene better I suppose. She moaned. I ducked my head down and urged her breasts free of her parted blouse, sucking the nipples already hard as nuts, distended as cashews, puckered as almonds.

"What would you have done?" I insisted.

"I guess I would have . . ." she started to say. She caught her breath as I bit down, my sign that I wanted the truth, or if not the truth if the truth was too tame, then something made up and nasty. "I guess I would have known that he was a gift from you."

"What would you have done?"

"I would have pulled his pants down and sucked his cock."

Now was the time to touch her cunt.

"He would be," she said, catching her breath. "He would be terrified." Her knees buckled. She spread her feet for support. "But I would have made him feel better."

Now my fingers were well up inside her, sliding in and out, extracting the juices to spread evenly over the lips of her cunt, parting the hairs and allowing her clit to feel the air.

"Fuck me," she whispered.

"What?"

"Fuck me," she said, a little louder.

"What would I be doing while you were sucking his cock?" I asked her. "Greeting the customers, giving the tour? While you were making him feel better?"

"Fuck me," she said loud enough for the boy to hear.

"What would I be doing, eh?" I whispered hard. "What if a girl came in and I knew that you were in here sucking a strange boy's cock? Do you think I would just let her wander around with her tits covered and her cunt empty, knowing you were sucking and fucking a stranger?"

"You'd fuck her," she said. "Fuck her." It was an order.

"No," I said, rubbing the smooth cup above Lelika's clit with three fingers so that the flesh stretched her clit smooth. "No, I wouldn't fuck her. I'd send her into the room with you. You and your boy with the smooth dark skin, brown and smooth as the skin of the girls on the walls of the tombs at Sakkara. His belly hard, his cock hard as a little mummy case in the nest of his silken hair, hard and bulging around the center from you licking and biting and sucking and wanting it in your hot cunt."

"Fuck me, goddamnit!" Lelika said, forcing me to do as she said.

Now the prong was free to plunge and plunge, pumping the sweet juice of Lelika, nectar dripping to the base of my cock and down her white thighs. Where her dress was pinned against the wall, it was getting wet. My pants, which I had not bothered to take off, were sopping wet with her. She gripped the shower curtain with one hand and bore down on me as she came, a desperate throaty grunt, as her face became a beautiful grimace. With her other hand she beat the wall. I lifted her up on my hips, wrapped her legs around me, and slammed her against the wall. Now she was borne up on my prong, as I thrust, as Europa was borne up on the distended belly and earth-shaking balls of the Bull. My hands explored under her dress, gripping her ass and pulling her against me, again and again. (Later, I was halfway thinking, she would have along her cheeks and throat the telltale spots, broken blood vessels like wildflowers, of having been well-fucked.) Suddenly the curtain came away from its hooks as she tore it away from its mooring.

We groaned together as she came again, as she often does in multiple, uncountable spasms. We shuddered there against the wall awhile. And after some throbbing moments in which she drained the last, subsiding spurts of my diminishing virility, I pulled away, groaning again, this time with the pain of separation. The prong, shiny with her and still bobbing, I tucked away, leaned it against my abdomen like a surfboard at the end of the day, and tied it fast with zipper and button and belt.

"He'll smell us," said Lelika, breathing hard, pulling her dress demurely down. "We reek of sex."

She squatted on the toilet and rolled toilet paper around her hand. She gave me a significant look. I nodded, knowing what she was thinking. In Romania we would have had to bring our own toilet paper. Even here in Egypt, which any Romanian would call the end of the world, there was plenty of toilet paper to spare. But then this was the house of Cavafy, a Greek, a civilized man, after all.

"The comforts of civilization," she said, contracting her cunt to expel the handful of semen I'd put there, and then wiped herself with dignity.

When we emerged from the bathroom together, Lelika and I, the student caretaker was blushing. The blood had turned his ears the color of fired clay. I guess we'd been making quite a bit of noise, quiet as we had (or hadn't) tried to be. I doubt that the boy knew about his part in our little fantasy, but then I'm sure he had his own fantasy going based on the programmatic sound track.

Upon leaving we bought a copy of Cavafy's poems in Greek. After handing over the money in exchange for the book, I reached surreptitiously between Lelika's legs, dipping my hand into her canoe, so that when I shook hands with the boy, I left a generous swab of our blended perfumes on his palm like frankincense and myrrh for baksheesh.

◆ ◆ ◆

I've often wondered since that hot, sticky day, whether the smooth student who stands guard over Cavafy's memory thinks back fondly on our interruption of his meditations when we disturbed his equilibrium with our fucking in the other room. I've often wondered, too, how long he stood there sniffing his palm and recalling the sound and smell and shape of my young wife (closer to his age than mine), and whether he realized that only the sense of her touch had been denied him. After we left, did he go into the bathroom and take care of the sense of touch with his own hand, using that perfumed palm to jerk himself off? And afterwards, did he wash his hands? Or did he throughout the day continue to raise his hand to his nostrils and breathe the mixed scent of the three of us on his innocent hand, there in the house of the poet, who wrote of finding "voluptuous perfumes of every kind" on the journey to Ithaca? Did he think to recall how Cavafy ended that poem by saying: *"Poor though you may find her, Ithaca has not deceived you. Now that you have become so wise, so full of experience, you will have understood the meaning of an Ithaca"*? I know I would have.

◆ ◆ ◆

The caretaker at Freud's house, too, was apparently a student, attractive in a lanky, bespectacled, scholarly way, in his turtleneck sweater and tweedy coat, but in his Austrian air of decorum he inspired no exotic fantasy. There was a crowd in the immaculate museum, and the day was dim. The prong, old but faithful, materialized, as usual. Lelika went into the bathroom, and I followed. But when we came out, the bespectacled boy gave us a frown instead of a blush. Maybe it was because he knew he had played no part in our fantasy. Maybe it was because we indulged, oddly enough, in no fantasy at all. Unlike Cavafy's house, which still seemed like a house, Freud's former residence, his home and office, had been turned purely into museum, a mausoleum for his memory. The bathroom was squeaky clean, no shower, no curtain, the bathroom was a museum. When I followed Lelika there, she was warm and willing. She was as enticing as any imaginable contrast to the stainless steel fixtures and baked tiles, especially with her skirt pulled high to expose the white flesh between the black skirt and stockings, framed in the enveloping soft black leather of her ankle-length coat. But I was content to kiss her belly and thighs and to breathe the warm woody fragrance of her cunt, with just the flick of a tongue to seal the pact, just a taste to confirm the agreeable memory, and then to let it go at that.

We had paid our respects, in our way, to the memory of Freud. Maybe Freud's spirit was tired, having been bandied about for so long, his theories having been formerly so controversial, so fashionable, so lionized, now in such disrepute, and yet so diligently and so begrudgingly respected. Fame for Cavafy, who with his contempt for theory had never cared about fame, was nothing if not theoretical. Shunning fame like some rich or religious lover, Cavafy had immersed himself in experience, with the result that he was, though impoverished, still inspired and inspiring. I only know for sure, the evidence being personal if anecdotal, that there are empirical differences between the erotic charge in the house of a dead psychologist and the house of a dead poet.

◆ ◆ ◆

At the Hundertwasser Haus we wandered among the shops tucked into the brightly imagined mosaic curves, the wedges of wood painted in primary colors, and the refracted slices of mirrors. We drank mulled wine in the coffee shop devoted to preserving his memory in the quotidian seduction of bodies moving toward each other among his designs, and talked about all the cultural offerings we were missing in Vienna at the moment, the opera, the ballet, the symphony, et cetera. "But who cares," I said, "when I've kissed your hand in the Hundertwasser Haus and your cunt in Freud's house?"

These were indeed the comforts of civilization. And though we didn't speak of Cavafy, he was there, waving a benediction with his long, effeminate hand.

Afterwards we found the Danube and danced. Not a waltz but a minuet.

Near the Prater we found a sex shop. It was easy enough to go in. I struck up a conversation with the guy behind the counter, while Lelika browsed the sex toys.

"I used to have your job," I said.

He looked at me. His spiked hair was a comment.

"Not here of course," I said. "In Hollywood."

End of conversation.

We bought a vibrator, a silver one, and tested it on our way back to the Pension Bosch. But the tram was so smooth—the wheels really made of rubber?—and so quiet that our new toy called attention to itself as I pressed it, my arm draped over her shoulder, to Lelika's breasts inside the leather coat. Heads began to turn and I was forced to shut it up. (So much for advanced electronics.) In the following days we found, as I've said, the magnificent Klimts and Schieles in other galleries and enjoyed the comforts of civilization in other museums. Before we boarded the train for Timisoara, we bought a liter of olive oil, our favorite salad dressing and lubricant. As for the vibrator, we smuggled it across the border in a sock.

◆

MILK, BUTTER AND EGGS

◆

By Jane Underwood

Milk

"Milk," reads Lenore, when she looks down at the back of her hand.

Lenore often writes such notes to herself, on the skin under her knuckles, because she often forgets to look at the lists she makes on notepads. This way, when she waves her hand in front of her face, or just happens to casually glance down at it, she sees the list and remembers.

Like now. Lenore is remembering that she has no milk for her nine-year-old-son Mack's cereal in the morning. She will try not to forget to stop at the corner store as they drive home from his acrobatics class after school. With both hands almost at eye level on the steering wheel her chances of success are good.

"Milk," she reads again. But what comes into her mind this time isn't cereal. It's the image of her breasts leaned over Neil's chest and of his fingers coming up to squeeze her erect nipples until something happened that was, for Lenore, entirely unexpected.

As he kneaded her right nipple between his thumb and forefinger, a drop of milk blossomed there. Lenore, who had of course stopped breast-feeding Mack years ago, was astonished.

"Good girl," said Neil with a pleased smile. "I knew we could do it."

Then he reached for her left nipple and (as Lenore felt her hot little vagina pulsate and drip with its own milky wetness) coaxed a drop out of that one, too.

As Lenore moved down toward her lover's mouth so that he could taste these tiny, quivering drops poised on the tips of what she considered to be a pair of disconcertingly unpredictable breasts, she felt flushed with amazement.

Lenore thinks now about how she never knows quite what her own body will do on those rare occasions when she gives a man free rein to roam about on it. Desire, she muses during this brief moment of reflection in the middle of a busy day, is a never-ending mystery and delight.

Then Lenore grabs a pen, scrawls "Bread and juice" underneath "Milk," and dashes out the door.

Butter

As Peter left the tip for the waitress, I recalled our half-hour wait for a table. The line had gone out the door, and as we dawdled on the evening sidewalk along with other lovers of Vietnamese food, he obliged me. That is, he acted upon a recent request of mine.

It had been a simple request. I wanted him to caress the crack of my ass in a public place—while standing, for instance, in a restaurant or movie line. I wanted him to discreetly but firmly slide his finger down my most private crevice and press it against that hidden but pulsing place beneath my skirt.

I wanted, I said, to be made to remember the last time he had entered me there. I wanted to be reminded that he planned to take me, in that special way, again.

Peter looked across the table at me now and said, "Ready to go?"

The car was parked four blocks away, in one of those quaint, quiet city alleys that still exist in some of the more charming neighborhoods. At six o'clock, it was barely dark, a warm October night.

Peter again positioned his finger, per my request, as we strolled, and I felt that familiar confused combination of feelings—embarrassment, desire, powerlessness, power, fear, and anticipation.

When we entered the alley, he pulled me over to a parked car, one partly hidden by a hedge, and told me to lean over the hood. I did, until my erect nipples were touching the metal.

He slid his hand up my thigh, pushing my skirt up to my waist, and I could feel him staring at my bottom. I knew he was going to pull my panties down, but after what seemed like an eternity, he only said, "Would you like me to pull your panties down now?"

The waiting had made me feverish and restless.

"Yes," I admitted reluctantly, "but someone will see us, Peter!"

"Just answer the question nicely," he commanded.

"Yes, please, I'd like you to pull my panties down now," I managed to whisper.

But Peter can be merciless. "How far down, honey? Just past your cheeks, or to your knees, or all the way down to your ankles?"

"Don't make me say anything else," I pleaded. "Please, Peter."

"You want me to decide for you?" he said. "All right, sweetheart." Then he pulled my panties down to my ankles.

"Step out," he said, and I obediently lifted each foot as a slight breeze tickled my exposed cheeks.

The alley remained miraculously empty. I've got a lover who knows how to make my heart pound.

Then I felt the softened pat of butter from the restaurant. Peter saw to it that I had the creamiest orifice ever about to be fucked.

"Relax," he said as he kissed my neck. "Take a nice deep breath, count to three, then let it out slowly."

As my breath went out, Peter pushed his finger in and began to probe me.

"That's it," he said tenderly, when I gave a little gasp. "Good girl.

"Now let's really open up that sweet buttery little bun," he said. "I feel like dessert."

Eggs

Paul and I would never have become lovers if it hadn't been for my eggs.

We had only recently met, and I was working late trying to meet a deadline when the phone rang one night. It was Paul, and when I dutifully told him that I was chained to my desk for the evening, he replied, "That's too bad. I was going to invite you over."

Well, I just happened to be ovulating that evening, and when my eggs drop, I descend into a brainless hormonal frenzy that lasts twenty-four to forty-eight primitive hours.

Even as Paul and I spoke, I could feel the heat of my eggs as they wiggled down my fallopian tubes, igniting all my hormones into wild flames of fantasy.

"Where do you live?" I heard myself responding uncoolly. "I'll be over in fifteen minutes."

Paul and I ended up making out to the point where my button-down-the-front dress was all the way unbuttoned, and my breasts were unleashed from my little black bra. Paul, a virtual stranger, was sucking and biting with abandon at my unashamedly erect and begging nipples, and his hand was happily inside my panties finger-fucking me as we kissed—and egged on, I might add, by my undulating, uninhibited hip action.

I did manage to control my behavior to some extent, however. At my request, Paul kept his pants on and zipped, so I didn't get to see his cock that first night. But I could feel it, hard and ready as he swirled his tongue around in my ear.

My eggs are amazing things. They make me sexually brave. They turn me into a wonderful whore. You can even see them in a man's smooth-shaven balls, if you're looking for them.

More Eggs

The last time Paul came over he said he had something to show me. He stood up, took off his pants, and lay down on my bed wearing only a pair of scanty bikini briefs. Then he pulled down the briefs, took my hand, and placed it on his luscious balls.

I felt the difference right away. They were uncharacteristically smooth—like two hard-boiled eggs, I thought—and they felt very, very naked.

I cupped them in my palm, savoring their new texture. I stroked them. I slid my fingers over their silky baldness.

"I just read a sex column," said Paul, "and some guy wrote in and was talking about shaving his testicles. So I was sitting in the bathtub and thought, why not?"

After I stopped touching his newly smooth balls, and after Paul urged me to undress, we fucked.

It wasn't until the next day, however, that I realized how much I'd been affected by his shave, and how much more now I wanted to lick those balls and suck them into my mouth.

I began to be obsessed with the thought of Paul's balls. I fantasized pushing my breasts against them. I imagined sliding my wet pussy gently over those beckoning, fleshy sacks.

Then I began to visualize Paul touching his own balls. I began to think about Paul's erotic mind—I imagined him thinking about shaving his own balls and wondering how it would feel afterward, not just to him but to his lovers.

Did he pick up the razor absentmindedly, simply exploring a new sensation?

Or did he fantasize a scene in which a woman crouched between his legs and slid the sharp edge of the razor against the vulnerable curve of him as he lay helpless under her hand?

Or perhaps he lied to me, and was in fact not all alone in his tub, but with another lover, someone who laughingly lathered his balls in her hand, then placed the razor beneath his hard cock, slowly maneuvering it over and around and under his eggs, undressing him so that she could then swoop down and kiss her handiwork.

Then again, maybe he imagined that I was watching him as he shaved, and touching myself between the legs at the same time. Or maybe he saw a dozen naked demon goddesses dancing seductively, and all moving toward him with but one collective goal: to take turns sucking his cock 'til kingdom come.

The possibilities, of course, are endless, which is exactly why I like eggs—until they are hatched, they leave everything to the imagination.

THE (SEX) LIVES OF
THE GREAT COMPOSERS

By Dennis Bartel

Let's not be too serious. There was no great flash of recognition here. It just happened. Over time. At first he felt it mostly in his stomach, like the sensation of suddenly descending in an elevator. Everywhere he went he thought he saw her, but it would never be her, and when he saw that it wasn't her he wouldn't be interested. He felt enchanted, in Nadaville, then purposely fought it off, brought himself back to earth, because that was the clear-headed thing to do. But she would not leave his thoughts, and he had to admit he didn't want her to. For a while, he wasn't sure what it was, then his initial sexual imaginings dissolved, and in a moment alone he allowed himself to speak freely, aloud for himself to hear. "Am I in love with you?" said he. "Have I really made this awful mistake?" And why was it an awful mistake? Why was it not a glorious awakening? He didn't know that either. He knew only that this had happened. Now what?

At dusk they would often go walking, holding each other around the waist, siamesed at the hip. She had a new-tennies bounce in her walk. He caught it.

He told her of Schumann's walks with Clara on a forest road near their home in Leipzig. "Schumann would look at the sky as he walked, and just talk away. He said there were a lot of 'useless stones' lying around in the middle of the road. So to keep him from stumbling

Clara would walk behind him, and pull on his coat when she spotted a rock. So Schumann says, 'Meantime she stumbled over them herself!' "

They would walk past the baroquely ornamented iron fences and confident lawns of the Pasadena elite. "Where the lawns are more fertile than the imagination," said he.

"What's that?" said she.

"Just something I read somewhere."

But she didn't abide with such arrogance. She loved the smell of the lawns, and the patterns on the Spanish-style roofs, and he would think, *"How can I possibly be more in love?"* The next day he would meet her at the co-op when she got off work, and they'd walk back home where she would fix some delish tempura vegetables, and sure enough he would find himself *more in love.*

She felt the same. It showed in her face. She said she loved the stories about composers he told her, no matter if they were heroic or ugly or silly (or bad) or whatever. She said that telling a story was "magical."

Some of the best times came during her *kundalini* yoga class. He worked hard at it, and he knew she knew. Though she spoke to the entire class, she looked right at him. "Keep your legs up! Keep centered at your Third Eye! Hold the pose to your maximum! Come on, you're great! You can do it!"

And he would do it.

Together they went on a week-long wheat berry fast. He made it through four days, but he couldn't go on for the headache, so he started eating a few bites of salad secretly.

The first signs of early summer were splintering through Pasadena. They heard them in the clear, ratchety, Saturday-morning sound of the lawn mower pushed by Mr. MacDowell up on Rose Villa. They heard them in the well-heeled two-piano music the venerable Cal Tech music teacher Mrs. Schonbach and her daughter practiced every morning over on Sierra Bonita. They heard them in Emily's kitchen—in the snap of fresh broccoli, in the crackle of *chapatis* frying in *ghee.*

One evening she cut her finger while chopping carrots for a curried vegetable medley. "It's only blood," shrugged she, seasoning the medley with *chyawan prash* and droplets of blood. A few days later it was "only mold" on the rennetless cheddar she melted over their steamed zucchini. And after that it was "only tears" that dropped onto the onions which she added to their baked potatoes. It was all organic. It all tasted good.

Out walking one evening she started talking about John Cage. She said she liked the things John Cage said about creating and teaching.

"John Cage?" said he, amused.

"Ji," as she respectfully called him instead of his name, "I'm allowed to know who John Cage is too."

"Sorry. I'm just surprised. Pleasantly."

"Condescendingly."

"Is this our first argument?"

She kissed him. They were always childishly shy after they kissed, unable to look at each other, but unable not to look.

"So," said he, "John Cage."

"John Cage has this poem that goes something like, 'I have nothing to say and I'm saying it and that's poetry.' It's totally egoless. It's like the piece of music of his that's silent."

"Four Minutes and Thirty-Three Seconds."

"I knew I could count on you for that."

"Always there to help."

"Well, it's like he's trying to get you to listen to something that you wouldn't listen to otherwise."

She asked him to start growing a beard. Cutting your hair, any hair, wrecks your energy, explained she. That Samson myth has truth to it, even if people today can't feel it.

He decided he'd grow a modest, trimmed beard. He didn't want to look like a Sikh. The itching at first was fierce, but he kept up, for her.

She showed him how to grow wheat grass in his apartment. With the help of a two-by-four-foot plot, a little water, a little sunlight, and a nineteen-dollar blender from Monkey Ward's, he produced twelve ounces of wheat grass every day at 7:00 A.M. Wheat grass was luminous green. It tasted like electricity. It woke him up. According to Emily, wheat grass cleansed out his something gland.

He burned incense in his apartment to cleanse it of old dope.

Some mornings he got up at 3:30 and joined her at the *ashram* for *sadhana*, sweating through the yoga, meditating deeply, till at the end of three hours he was super-charged for the day.

They listened together to *Kreisleriana*.

They did *karma yog maga* meditation together:

Sit in easy pose. Raise your arms over your head, wrists together, palms spread as if pushing against the ceiling. Facing forward, open your eyes very slightly and peer at the top of your nose. Inhale. Chant rhythmically with the exhale: Sat Nam, Sat Nam, Sat Nam, Sat Nam, Wahe Guru. *Continue for eleven minutes.*

He always made it through *karma yog maga* meditation without succumbing to the pain and lowering his arms, but only because she refused to succumb.

They went together to one of Yogi Bhajan's classes at the *ashram*. He had expected *Yogiji* to be smaller in person than he appeared in photos. But Yogi Bhajan wasn't smaller. He was larger. Yogi Bhajan was a big guy.

Next to all the white-clad *Khalsa*, Emily, wearing a blue scarf as head covering and gray sweatpants, looked like someone who had only one foot in the *Dharma*. But once Yogi Bhajan began speaking Emily was in the *Dharma* body and soul. He felt invisible sitting next to her. This so bothered him that he didn't hear a word of the lecture, and was happy to get to the yoga and sweat out his tension.

Back at her apartment she didn't ask what he thought of Yogi Bhajan, but as they were cooking he started to say something about how much he enjoyed Yogi Bhajan's talk and she stopped stirring the sauteed onions and turned full to him and watched him carefully, then after he fumbled around for words and finally came up only with "I liked it, it was really interesting, he has a powerful presence," she nodded and turned back to the sizzling onions.

They cooked together a lot, and she indulged herself in what she said was her long-cherished wish to explain to her true love everything that happened in the kitchen. As they sat down on the floor to eat, they tuned in by chanting *Ong Namo Guru Dev Namo*. After all this time, he still didn't know what it meant, and by now he felt awkward about asking.

They professed to each other that they loved being with each other, and loved doing things together, and would love to do everything with each other.

There was only one thing they did not do.

Then one night, after *falafels* and *tahini* dressing made with spicy New Age verve, she presented him with a small, saddle-stitched book. *Kirtanam: The Enlightened Road Through Sex.*

He took it home and read through it twice. It was great how his concentration had improved since he stopped smoking dope. How long had it been? Six weeks? *Six weeks?*

◆ ◆ ◆

Next morning, Schumann is back. And here's what he's saying: "Most assuredly, *mein Freund.* Their fire stopped not at the double bar."

"They *all* did?" says he.

"The great ebb and flow is hardly confined to the Liszts and the Wagners."

He grabs a Schwann from the floor and flips through the pages. "Everyone?"

"Ja, even Bruckner. I think. Once at least."

"What about Brahms?" says he, knowing that Brahms had his prostitutes, but it's not prostitutes they're speaking of here.

Schumann guffaws. "You wish me to leave?"

The dawn has barely broken, spilling its yellow yolk between the blinds of his bedroom window. He's been lying on his bed with a hard-on powerful enough to save his soul, but not wanting to go groping because he's saving up for Emily tonight, and feeling that anything less than all he can give her would be a betrayal of some kind, and Schumann has stepped out of the kitchen. All of Schumann's previous visits have been nocturnal. This is his first daylight look at the

Great Composer, but there's no mistaking him. Wide face. Tiny pursed mouth. Strong double chin. Oily brown hair matted to his brow. Small gold earring in his left lobe. Frayed silk cravat. Mildewing frock coat. It is really him, Robert Schumann, smiling *Hallo*. Only one thing seems different. The Great Composer's eyes are abnormally large. "*Güten Morgen*," says Schumann, his pleasant tenor thickened by years of beer and whiskey and cigars. He swings a hip up on the table and sits there like a slumped-over bear.

In the next incredible minutes, Schumann tells of how some of his Great Composer colleagues conducted themselves in the sack.

"Take as an example Rossini," says Schumann. "You know that *William Tell* was his last."

"Sure."

"*Nun*, by the time of *William Tell*, when Gio was thirty-seven, his career was at such a height . . . nothing less than operatic. Then, without forewarning, he ceased. Quit. *Kaput*. No more opera from Gioacchino Rossini. *Und warum?* There was but one unsavory explanation. His was an unabashed sloth. He cared not what people wanted nor what people said. He was in Paris, which no doubt contributed. He stayed in bed for days, slopping down *coq au vin*, devouring Balzac, burping up some such piddling salon pieces he called 'Sins of My Old Age.' And when he stirred down deep he would summon his *valet de chambre* to fetch a tart Parisian mezzo to come straddle his considerable *phiz*. Rossini's love of cunnilingus came to be legendary in High Parisian Society."

Schumann tells the story of Edvard Grieg and his wife/cousin Nina. They would hibernate belly to belly in their mountain villa, *Trollhaugen*, high above the village of Bergen. "Far from the world were Grieg and Nina," says Schumann, "and being thus isolated they rutted *molto adagio* all the long Norwegian winter." He takes on a storyteller's tone of mock wonderment. "Then spring would come and the craggy fjords would thaw and the tundra would creak and the white walls of the firmament would turn again to blue skies, and down in the valley, Bergen would come picturesquely back to life. Church bells would ring out. Peasants would break merrily into rustic song-

and-dance. And up in *Trollhaugen*, for the first time since the October haddock catch, the bushy elegiac eyebrows of Edvard Grieg would peer out the bedroom window." He bites off the tip of a cigar, lights up, and puffs contentedly, stinking up the place. If Emily smells this she's not going to understand.

He wants to know more. "Any of them do anything weird?" says he.

"There was Ives. *Ach! Herr Ives!* He had a license to iconoclasm. Charles Ives used to climb atop his wife Harmony and cry out verses of John Greenleaf Whittier. 'How the belfries rock and reel! How the great guns peal and peal!' "

Schumann has a mischievous grin behind his cigar. He continues, "And Chausson. I recall hearing once of Ernest and a boy and a bicycle."

"I don't believe that," says he. "That's a cruel joke."

"So be it. There was no bicycle. But isn't it pretty to think so?"

"I'll bet Satie was something."

"We can but speculate with regards to Satie," says Schumann. "Over the years there were espied many a hastily clad *jeune fille* fleeing Satie's Montmartre *appartement mystérieux* into the night."

"Tell me more."

"Your appetite is *fantastique*. *Nun*, Shostakovich did not move about greatly, but of what consequence is that? Paganini was all fingers. Debussy would often pursue his *proie* by teaching her *tai chi*, then once in the throes of bliss he became a frantic biter."

"Was Debussy really the son-of-a-bitch everyone says?" says he.

"One can find fault for only so long with Debussy," says Schumann. "Then there is the music."

"You're a German sentimentalist, Schumann."

"And you, *mein Freund*, you listen to me."

"Yeah."

Schumann slaps his thigh. "Surely the most *wunderbar* fellow in regards to the amorous was a favorite of *mein*, Franz Peter Schubert. A typical Schubertiade would conclude with dear Franz in the chamber of some charming *Fräulein*. And if the stories be true, Schubert was a wonderful tickler. There is one account I have heard many times that I wish fervently to be true, and if it were not true I would choose to believe it still. It took place years before the illness that would claim him prematurely, on the evening that he was introduced to the dark and vivacious Anna Frohlich, who taught singing at the Conservatorium of Music Lovers and hosted musical evenings in the rooms she shared with her three sisters. Indeed, that first evening Anna sang 'Erlkönig' to Schubert's accompaniment. *Nun*, upon the conclusion of the musical evening, Schubert stole away with the young hostess, and it seems that when they arrived upstairs at her chamber, whom did they behold but Barbara, Katharina, and Josefine, the three Frohlich sisters, each of whom was richly endowed with feminine charms. Barbara was a noted painter of flowers, Katharina was not as much possessed of talent as of beauty, and Josefine eventually toured as a concert singer. This night, each had yen-yen in her eyes."

"Really. I like this."

"Remember, Schubert was barely four foot ten, and cut a most pudgy profile. He had the eyesight of a mole. He was but in his early twenties, and already nearly bald. And that atrocious dimple. Schubert was not a handsome man. Indeed, his good and dear friends call him *Schwammerl*. Little Mushroom. But he was a most imaginative painter, whose pencil was steeped now in moonbeams and then in the full glow of the sun. To the Frohlich sisters he was utterly Apollonian. With the sunrise, Schubert and his four new friends could be found in Anna's great bed enjoying the fresh stirring of a rising breeze trickling through the window. They remained thus throughout the morning, as Schubert composed a *Lied* for each sister. A *Lied* and a gitchee. A *Lied* and a gitchee."

"Wow," says he. "What were those songs?"

"*O weh!* No one knows. They were lost. As were so many others. This is why Schubert left behind such a volume of quote and unquote unfinished works. Often he would delight his little *Liebling* with a movement, say from a string quartet or a piano duet fantasy, then with another evening and another *Liebling*, he would write the next movement, and with it proffer his love to her. These works were not unfinished. Their parts were merely scattered throughout the bedrooms of Vienna."

He couldn't stifle a giggle. "So the little mushroom sprouted a lot."

"*Ja*, but you must not conclude that Schubert was unfaithful to his loves. While with a *Fräulein*, he was ever-faithful, and when parted from her, oh, how he would send his heart in a letter." Schumann quotes from memory: " 'I am alone with my beloved, and have to hide her in my room, and in my bosom.' Some days he would write seven such letters to seven different *Fräuleins*, and all seven would be heartfelt and true."

"He was so prolific," says he.

"His is such a sad tale," says Schumann.

In the broad daylight of November 19, 1828, Schubert died of syphilis at age 31. His last words: "Here, here, is my end."

So next they were to have the magic moment of lovemaking. With other women, he'd envisioned it so many times before it happened, it would never quite happen the way he'd envisioned it. Not so with Emily. With Emily he had no idea what was to come. A little timidity? Lots of eye contact? He was in the dark here as everywhere else. He loved her for that.

Her bedroom was lined with books. The shelves were improvised concrete blocks and two by twelves. He scanned some titles in the shine from the night-light. Most he'd never heard of. Psychology books. Yoga books. A few novels. Two thick books by someone named Shi Nai'an. Three in a row by Jane Austen. He'd never been in here. Until now she had always steered him clear.

Her bed on the floor was two sheepskins, a pair of sheets, and a cotton blanket.

Waiting for her, he sat in easy pose in front of a small low table with daisies. He inhaled deeply and held in a seven count and pulled *mul ban* and exhaled. All this regime felt deliciously excruciating, a wonderful game. Minutes ago he had drunk a cup of milk so that his *ojas* would be replaced more easily, and he'd cracked open a cardamom seed and chewed the grain to sweeten his breath. Now he was becoming centered.

All day he had been conscious of his *kundalini* moving throughout his body, from his lower *chakras* into his throat, into his arm, back down to his lower *chakras*. At times, the urge to masturbate had been tremendous.

Now he was at his heart *chakra*, the highest *chakra* at which he ever rested. (He would occasionally have flashes at his Third Eye, but they never lasted.) Nothing was stirring, as Schumann said, down deep. He wondered how he would function if his energy remained in his heart *chakra*. That would be odd. He'd never had trouble before.

Her head was uncovered, hair loosely tied on top. She wore a hibiscus-colored robe, linen. She paused in the doorway, not uncertain of entering, but to be longer in entering, to linger with this moment that would never again be, then she went to the far corner and lit an incense stick.

He had forgotten to light the incense as she'd asked. She smiled to show it was all right, and sat in easy pose alongside him.

She led the way, first pressing her thumb to her left nostril and breathing deeply, and finding the rhythm when he joined her, then switching nostrils after a few breaths. She smelled of musk. She rested her hands on her knees and inhaled deeply and chanted long *Sat* short *Nam.*

After a few minutes, she slowly stood and looked at him. "You know how you can feel," said she, "when you don't know what to do next?"

He came around behind her and slipped the robe off her shoulders. She crossed her arms over her breasts as he held her and kissed her ear. Look upon her, the book, *Kirtanam*, had said, "as an unsullied treasure house of beauty, the embodiment of all bliss." That was easy. He believed he worshiped her. And she was beautiful, her pale skin lightly freckled, her breasts perfect, Mozartian, the nape of her neck pure vanilla. She was very thin but not brittle. She was strong as a colt. Long and powerful legs. Boyish hips. Hair blackish red in the dim light.

They sat together in easy pose on the bed. For a long while he touched only her knees, then reached out and lightly touched two fingers to her heart, making a slow circle. She was breathing steadily through her nose, her eyes cast upon him. He began breathing with her. He touched the hollow of her throat. He longed to kiss it.

He ran his fingers over her eyebrows and across her temples. He caressed her earlobes. He had never moved so slowly with a woman, but he wasn't bounding to go. They were still breathing together, a little heavier now. He ran his hands down her thighs and caressed her knees and kissed them, and clasped his hand over her toes and pressed the sole of her foot then her other foot.

She lay back and began chanting *Sat Nam*, not powerfully, not like a meditation, but as if the mantra were simply the sound of her breath. His fingers trickled up and down her arms and encircled her navel. Her nipples were like boutonnieres. He softly sucked them.

He removed his clothes without getting up, and lay on his side, very close to her but not touching. They looked at each other a while, sometimes kissing lightly. "Are you still with me?" whispered he. Her eyes were submerged, her mouth open in an astonished oval as if it had taken on a life of its own. She managed a nod, then caught herself and focused her eyes on his smile and said, "Yes."

Then it was she who moved them forward, raising her knees, touching his leg, inviting him to move into her. He lifted his leg and rested his genitals on her. She lowered her knees.

He felt he would burst. His breath grew rapid.

"Ji," whispered she, calling him to look in her eyes. Her breath was steady and easy. He found the rhythm and began to relax.

They lay a few minutes, then he gently parted her labia and entered, not deeply, partially, daring not to move the slightest.

At twenty-eight minutes, as the book said, there will come an abrupt spasm throughout the body, and this will be the hardest time, the time to struggle and not let the orgasm take him. But the spasm was onrushing fast now, long before twenty-eight minutes, perhaps it had started the moment he entered, and it was about to shatter him.

He concentrated on the chaos down there and sought to raise his energy up out of the second *chakra*. To his surprise, he did.

Then they clung to each other, motionless, as the energy between them rose and fell and swirled through the delicate curls of incense and settled somnolently upon them.

True to the book, his body began to convulse after about a half-hour. He held his breath, curled his tongue as far back as possible and contracted his anus. His face convulsed in pain. She held his face in her hands. Their eyes locked.

Then his body relaxed. He had made it. They rested with their faces touching. He remained inside of her for over an hour.

This was the *samarasa*. With every passing moment they sank further into one another, with no breathless orgasmic onrush coming to explode between them and send them reeling. In the end he withdrew without having come. They got under the blanket and fell asleep, his face tucked into the curve of her neck.

He did not know what Schumann and Clara did in bed, and Schumann that morning hadn't given a clue. Schumann once had a wild reputation, thanks to his thrashings about with Ernestine von Fricken, Agnes Carus, Meta Abegg, Liddy Hempel, Nanni Patsch, Henriette Voigt, Fräulein von Kurrer, Countess Franziska Ernestine von Zedwitz, enough whores to pack the *Gewandhaus,* and a few the memory of whom had been washed away in a great eddy of beer and cum.

But that was all before Clara. Whether Schumann took his frenzy with him to Clara's bed, he did not know. Before tonight, he might have said Yes. Now he wasn't sure. Hadn't Schumann told Clara his love for her was like "a pilgrim thinking of the distant altarpiece"? And in Schumann's letters, written during the long years that Wieck was preventing their marriage, hadn't his love always sounded chaste and reverent?

"My last request before you go away from me—give me now what I have sometimes had from you in our hushed moments—the *Du* that unites us more intimately. For you are my ardently loved betrothed, and once latter—one more kiss—*Adieu.*"

That was not the Schumann who sent asunder scores of *Fräuleins*. But it may have been the Schumann who went to Clara.

They woke in the sunlight. There was to be no *sadhana* today. They stayed in bed all morning. They played and tickled and kissed. His erection was all the more fervent for the milk he'd drunk last night. Piss hard was his term for it. But she had a better name: Morning Glory. She loved being touched, and for long stretches simply lay back and enjoyed his hands upon her. This time they were moving with the urgency he'd always known sex to be. She held his head tightly between her thighs, pressing against his mouth, his beard prickly, letting her hips rise and fall with his steady probing and lapping. Then Morning Glory sprang forth and fucked her. Behind her eyes was a blaze of swirling light like the inside of a great spinning pearl. He remained fixed to that light as he came with such force he felt as if for an instant his soul had surged from his body, only to just as instantly surge back.

PIANIST AT THE COLONNADE HOTEL, BOSTON

Patrons ate something
Mixed with remoulade
As the pianist played
Liszt on the Baldwin.
During soft passages
She threw her hair back
Leaning with legs
Angled as if in the
Inopportune darkness
Her unknown throat
Gasped for the air
Of a stranger.

Possessed by Gershwin
She stared at the stranger
For an eighth note of time.
He was supposed to believe
She exorcised Summertime
From the ivory teeth
Of her wooden beast
Just for him.
Switching from Carmen

To Porgy and Bess on sight
Of his jazz-coated exterior.
But every lobe with a menu
Had access to her repertoire
That night, gang banging her
Inventions, preludes and fugues.

When she massaged
The pains of the *Kreutzer* sonata
Out of the keys' hardened ligaments
Her neck swayed like some
Aristocratic, tuxedoed giraffe.
Her hands spanning octaves
Her mind spanning walls,
Satellite moons and windows.
When she gets home
Round midnight
She screams
Turning Aretha up
To the top of her lungs.

Michael Warr

PAIRING OFF

◆

The Mating Habits of Armadillos
poetry by Anna Mortál

Afternoon Special
by John Goldfine

Decorum
by R. M. Vaughan

A Private View
by David Vineyard

Partners
by Terry Marshall

After a Birth
poetry by Carol L. Gloor

THE MATING HABITS OF ARMADILLOS

Seven pebbles snouted into a circle.
Blossom of red bougainvillea indicating point-of-entry.
Nearby anthill, for afterward.

Wistful moon, epiphanous breeze, rap music on
the boom-box.

Two bottles of Armor-All.
A crowbar.
A funnel.

Anna Mortál

AFTERNOON SPECIAL

By John Goldfine

Heat. Heat can never torment new lovers, naked. We were in the rosy stage—flapping a sheet over our flushed skin, more to click on/off/on/off the visual charge of our still mysterious bodies than because of the temp.

"Stop," she said in a squeaky voice. "Stop, stop, you beast. I'm totally nude under here." New lovers sharpedging their dyad against the chaos, jokes no one else would ever share.

I snapped the sheet up again, and she twisted in the dimness like crumpled paper folding and unfolding, miming agony, as fire catches and kindles.

"Let's take a bath," I said.

"No."

"A shower?"

"I want to keep you on me. Your stink." Her voice was sleepy.

"Nice talk."

"You know what I mean. The spoor of you."

Where had she heard that, read it, stolen it from? She was a great magpie of emotional effects, taking from anywhere what she had none of—probably recycling the spoor bit from some old lover's sweet talk. Even though her nonsense about my spoor made me swoon with delight, even a-swoon I could imagine greater pleasure: words straight from her heart, welling in response to me.

"I'm going to shower," I said.

She said, "Beast."

Her curls disappeared under the sheet. Her body described a shallow S-curve, the precise line Hogarth claimed was the key to all beauty in the universe. Did she take that pose purposely to intrigue? I touched the sheet where it hollowed into her back, but she twisted away, as though piqued. She might have actually been angry, it was hard for me to say or for her to know.

She was lost—molested by her brother, possibly also by her father—so much lost that now she had to create the world *ab nihilo*. Her dislikes in bed were all she could really be sure of.

When I came back from the shower, the nap of the motel shag dug into my feet, insisted on itself. Today, even if I'd been blind, today my soles and all their nerve endings were raw and excited enough to read the indeterminate motel color—somewhere between beige and teal. Her effect on my senses from crown to sole: she made the blind see.

She was still out of sight under the sheet. I had piled my clothes on a round table with a ceiling-hung lamp, a poker table for visiting salesmen. Now I scrabbled through my stuff, hunting my underpants.

"Beautiful view," she said. "Nice buns." She had a little peephole at the edge of the sheet just below the pillow.

"Are you spying on me?"

"No, certainly not. What kind of girl do you think I am?"

That I despaired of ever answering. I said, "Have you got my underpants?"

"No. I just told you I'm not like that."

"I don't believe you."

"Tough." She curled her hidden self into a ball. "If you don't believe me, check it out."

I flipped the sheet: curly hair, bony shoulder blades, vertebrae, then the unshadowed beginnings of the nameless furrow between her buttocks—more truth, there alone, than is dreamed of in all *your* philosophy, laddie! No underpants visible.

"Turn over. I want to see the whole of you."

"You've seen the whole woiks awready, buddy boy, the whole schmeer."

I kneeled on the floor by the bedside, leaned across, and touched her shoulders. I said, "Come on, give them to me. I have to go."

She rolled over like I had prodded her with a pin. "Fuck you," she said. My underpants flew at my head. Her feet flurried for a second and then the sheet was again tight in a ball, she nowhere to be seen.

"Hey, he-yyy," I said.

Muffled: "I don't want you to go. I want you to stay forever."

"Hey, come on. Come on."

"Why? You say you love me, so why won't you stay?"

I felt like I was sucking on lemons. I said, "I can't. You know why."

"I know what you say."

"Please, I do love you, I really do."

Suddenly the ball flew apart into arms and legs and hair and lips and tears. I was back in bed, where I had started twenty minutes before, wrapping her in me.

After a minute, she strained away from my chest and said, "No, this was a mistake. I want a bath after all."

Lying beside her, I deepened my bear hug, forearms happy in the indents above her hips, knuckles riding light over her kidneys. I said, "Tease me and live to tell about it? No, I don't think so."

"I wasn't teasing. I'm really ready for a bath now if that's what you want."

"That's not what I want." I ratcheted on a tiny bit of pressure.

"Let me go. I'll scream." Her voice sounded like Christmas morning, the biggest present of all saved for last.

"No."

Her muscles gathered; everywhere I could feel the tiny dancer heft of her collect itself for the breakout, but I squeezed hard, nipping rebellion.

"Uh, unhhh, uh . . . ." she said.

"Won't work, won't work, wo-wo-won't work." She stopped fighting, her tongue touched my ear. She blew gently. I said, "Is this a trick?"

She whispered, "Lift yourself up a little so I can slide my leg under." Her legs scissored around my middle. She said, "Talk about tricks—what's this supposed to be?" She half-lowered her rump so that it bumped the tip of my high-riding prick, then she bumped it a second time. Twenty minutes ago, I had thought myself all fucked-out.

" 'Supposed to be?' That, m'dear, is the reality principle in the flesh. It *is*, sweetie, no 'supposed to be' about it."

" 'Reality principle?' You Freudian pig."

I twisted us up in the sitting position, holding her a-straddle my lap and flopping our combined weight back against the flimsy motel headboard, then humped a little to position my prick for a gentle probe of that nameless cleft. The moment it slotted in, she rolled up onto her inner thighs just enough so that it sprung loose again. Her pubic hair started flossing the soft area around my belly, her legs splitting a little wider, as only a former ballerina's can—opening to extrude her clitoris, I supposed. During intercourse, she'd shimmy into a long slow-burning Brillo grind, pubic bone to pubic bone, to stimulate herself.

The first time I had tried a diddle she grabbed my wrist, pried my finger away. "No, please," she said. "I don't like that." The look on her face was the one she usually reserved for mentioning her big brother, not a look I would argue with. She was age eleven when big brother started cornering her in the bathroom or her bedroom, and he—the many things she disliked in bed I assumed were his pet wrinkles. Not a look I would argue with.

Now I reached down and repositioned my prick at the very base of her tailbone. "Is that okay?" I wasn't sure if she had wiggled loose and begun flossing my belly because she didn't like my prick sliding around her rump or if the quick dismount was just incidental to the self-stim.

This was only our second trip to the motel, our fourth time

together. New lovers invent their own universe as they go, until all the details are filled in. And then—nothing left to create—part. We were just a few nano-seconds past big-bang.

She didn't answer. Instead, she slid down and off me, onto her back—my prick springing free yet once more, this time raking its dorsa through her pubic hair and vagina as she shed herself.

"Let's," she said. Evasions and elisions were the preferred mode for this girl whose brother had begun by saying, "I want to show you how much I love you."

A little pre-come lubricant seeped onto the head of my prick. I kneeled between her legs and bored the head's ventra in toward her clitoris, packed it right in between the exterior lips with a generous squeeze of my hand, and hovered on my knees and forearms, waiting to see if hand-aided dick-to-clit rubbing was forbidden. Apparently not.

As the head of my prick pressed against her clitoris, suddenly her eyelids fluttered like those counterweighted plastic lids on my kid-sister's blue-eyed, favorite Barbie. Don't ask how I happen to know that the lids are counterweighted inside Barbie's cute little skull.

Despite the out-for-the-count eyelids, after a few seconds she slithered her legs around my hips and locked her ankles in the small of my back, so that the nice tight hot-dog-to-bun fit I'd just achieved was jarred loose.

"Mmmh, mmmh," she said, hinting: enough fooling around, do the deed. Foreplay was not her strong point. I entered; she was a little dry, as usual.

Her strong point was something I've been told by a feminist friend is an aspect only men care about: the appearance of her body. My feminist says: "Do it in the dark. Trust me, it's nature's way."

But my ex-dancer's body was meant for light, for close examination under bright lamps. Ah god, she made me jealous describing her visit to the gynecologist. When the nurse left the room, the lucky doctor said to the inside-out of her riding high in the stirrups, "Alone at last!"

And she, the faithless creature, laughing, playing with fire, she said, "At last! I thought she'd never leave."

Now she said nothing. After a minute, she came in little jerks: "Unh unh unh unh," and I began a quick run-up to my own climax.

I rolled onto my back, pulled her on top, and bent her left leg up to my chest, folded like a grasshopper's. Then I turned ninety degrees so that she was half-kneeling and I in a half-situp, entering almost from behind. Her bent leg was thick with muscle earned at the *barre*: a bread loaf swell of quad, twinkling jeweled knee, her calf the curve of a breaking wave. Her toes, as ever, dancer-pointed—pointing eternally out to some ideal place and solution—their cascade of tiny curves reminding me of chiseled moldings—*cyma recta* and *cyma reversa*—on some antique temple.

I tried to hold the image in my mind. I said silently: "Remember, remember. There will never be anything again as beautiful as this. No other woman will ever take you so hard." The arc of her buttock as it rounded away from my prick!—for my sins, I had fallen in love with Euclidean truths manifest in her flesh, but her geometry, alas, only an idea, ultimately not demonstrable.

Despite the impossibility of proving this woman according to theorem and rule, I came, and although it's vulgar and reductive to scale things or even characterize them adjectivally—the thusness of the orgasm should be enough for anyone—I came a twelve on a scale of one to ten, I blew off like Moby Dick surfacing after a lifetime hiding from his Ahab. I came way bigtime, Old Faithful geysery.

And in the midst of my dance in the dark with myself, from a far distance I heard her: "Unh unh unh unnnh!"

After a bit I said, "Did you come again?"

"Twice."

"Ah," I said, cheerful, not wanting to preen.

"You," she said, doing it for me. "Only you. Never ever has anyone ever made me . . . do that three times. You're amazing."

"*You're* amazing."

Long pause. She named her ex-husband and a former lover. "They both said . . . I wasn't a good lover. They said I wasn't imaginative."

I hugged her, kissed both her closed eyelids. "Fools," I said. "This isn't dance, it isn't a contest, it isn't a question of technique. It's about wanting to be nowhere else in the world than the place you find yourself. It's about merging oceanic and at the same time feeling overwhelmingly yourself. That's what you do for me as a lover, and you came three times because you love me, not because of some trick." Big speech, but I meant it.

We hugged, all sticky with sweat.

"Let's take a bath," she said. She pounded fists gently on my pectorals: "My beautiful Jewish Adonis."

Her Jewish Adonis? Another magpie collectible?

I laughed, unsure, a-swoon again with her and her words, secondhand or not. Then, clinging together, we stumbled between our bed and the bathroom, breasting the dense, hot air with our exhausted bodies.

But heat, heat can never torment new lovers, naked.

◆

DECORUM

◆

Dedicated to Andrew Mullin

By R. M. Vaughan

Where does it begin? The eye's path, the travel of a gaze?

I suppose, like most orderly things, it starts from the top, works its way down.

From, say, the top of the bookshelf, a mantel. A mantel of light, bleached wood; vaguely tired-looking, overstained and once a week, maybe twice, wiped flat until it is without texture. A mantel like tanned skin, taut with effort.

On the mantel are two photographs, a lacquered box, and seven or eight pieces of cut rock, purple and green.

He will know their proper names—you need only ask, or pick them up, turn them in your hand.

The photograph closest to your eye is framed in plain black wood. A tall man and a shorter man hold each other, side by side, on a crowded beach. The photograph is in colour. The taller man, his breasts beginning to droop with age, rests a brown hand comfortably on the low center of his companion's hip. Old friends, perhaps, they are easy in each other's grasp. Their bare legs and chests sport deep, lazy tans—the dark, layered browns of long holidays and money.

I recognize the affection, this quick and harmless coupling a thousand miles from home. I am no taller today than I was then. This is an ordinary snapshot. I can't dwell on it.

A second portrait, in browned black and white. A woman, all alone, singing in front of a stand-up microphone. It is unclear whether or not she has an audience.

Heavy curtains and a square of plywood, painted with the call letters of a radio station, open behind her—placing her, locating her activity. She is a performer, a professional. It is 1940, or maybe later, 1950 or so. She is wearing, I think, navy blue with white piping. Her hair is modish but sedate.

She is his mother, long since dead. She is a star, a memory of knowing his mother was more to the world, briefly, at least, than simply his mother.

Deep down, this still scares him.

He will be running from this, and toward it, back and forth, until he drops. Her stardom compensates for a lot of missed time. He has come full circle, from missing her to glamorizing her, to simply seeing her, every day, framed in silver—a reminder of the glamorous phase in their relationship. But he cannot replace it. She has acquired rights and privileges.

She will never be demoted to the bookshelf, never asked to stand in front of the titles of unfashionable novels or bridge a space where paperbacks mix unevenly with hardcovers. She will always be front and center, as she was then, in that blast of carbon and treated paper.

(2)

As often as he can, he puts fresh flowers in the mauve stem vase next to her picture.

Once, an iris bud turned black, dropped off, and stained a top corner of the silver frame. It had to be cleaned. Dismantling the heavy backing, pulling out the glass, the reek of oxidizing film filled his nostrils. He has been very careful ever since.

Except with me.

The first time we made love he held my penis between his index and second finger, like a cigarette, and told me it was lovely. Not too big, a nice rusty pink. He called it "playful," and licked the bottom rim of its tip with, I thought, a startlingly flat tongue.

Pressed against each other, he told me I was beautiful: no, not too fat. My egg-shaped stomach was endearing.

"It makes you real," he said.

I have never asked for much in romance, except in fantasy. No lover had ever held my slack stomach between his palms and played with it, kneaded it like loved bread. Mostly, my rolled belly merits a quick brush, a glance up, over, and down to the cock. Between men, waists are throughways, meant to be passed over, unremarked.

We could call this Love, this pausing, this holding on to every part.

Later, he would remember my little sites of discontent, spots where my body refuses to please me, and touch them again, call them beautiful.

We could call this hypnosis.

(3)

Decorum dictates that we forgive every kindness we endure. Nothing is done for itself, we see, only for gain. We know this and call it fairness, equilibrium, when it works out for us, or self-indulgence, even cruelty, when it doesn't.

He and I are very decorous.

This evening, he busied himself tickling the bulb of my calf. He tells me my legs are boy's legs—muscled, yes, but undefined, unfinished.

He puts his hands in the hollows under my kneecaps, forcing my legs to bend, and spits on the inside of my thighs, tracing circles between my hair line and the base of my cock.

He presses a wet finger on the hard muscle between my asshole and balls, pushing in until I buckle upwards. With my shoulders pivoted on the bed, I swing forward and back in small, hips-tight thrusts.

Together, we watch my stomach flatten and bunch with each jump.

We call this conditioning.

(4)

Underneath the dining room table he keeps an enormous, oblong faux-marble pedestal. A stage prop, he bought this at an auction long before the rest of us wanted everything to be *faux*, before we paid good money for irony. Because it dominates the room, the pedestal has to be loved and resented equally.

When we have dinner guests, he makes a joke of it, telling his friends to put up their feet, as if he hated it but couldn't find a way to get rid of it.

Alone, we call it The Altar. Pushing back the table, we play Abraham and Isaac—of course, with us, no one intervenes, no god arrives to stop the knife. His limits are his own, and mine.

When the afternoon sun makes its way under the table The Altar reflects, upside down, the left half of the living room; turning over the mantel, the picture of his mother, and, less clearly, the mauve vase. In outline, you can see a high back chair, a book table, and me.

From my chair, out of his sight, I've watched him throw one leg over The Altar and push hard against the rounded corners with his crotch. He always looks puzzled, never satisfied, and then embarrassed. Alone and embarrassed, which is more lasting.

We could call this an experiment.

(5)

"You and I need to talk about the arrangements," he said, last night, before dinner.

By this he means "the future," but he has not mentioned it since. This means the news is not good, this means change. He hates change.

And now, so do I.

I call this negative reinforcement.

(6)

To date, I've bought him three things.

First, a brace of wild irises, which just made trouble all around. But that was early on, before we learned to fight without fear.

Second, a set of dinner forks decorated with fat, lacquered handles. The handles show two red and orange goldfish, fatally caught in a nest of grassy, blue-green spines. It was his birthday, but I really bought them for me. The cheeriness on the goldfish's faces, the round stupidity of their eyes as they swim into the grass, puzzles me.

Why don't they fight? What was in the grass—what food or shiny pebble was worth it?

The noisy glass of lacquer clashed, didn't "work," with the earth-toned flatware he'd chosen for his birthday dinner table. The forks were all wrong for his brown-glazed tea set, decorated with perching cranes and distant pagodas.

"Too zoological," he said.

"Too theme-y, too Japanese," I said.

He kissed my forehead, thanked me, and told me to keep them for myself, which was what I wanted.

Today, I bought him a year's worth of double passes for the cinema.

Again, I really got them for me. They are an investment, a stay of proceedings. Maybe I'll break the curse, reverse the bad news.

Tie us down.

I call this sympathetic magic.

(7)

Pick me up from the floor, by my hands. Pull me across the bed width-wise. Put your foot on the top of my head. Take up my hands again.

Stretch. Till it hurts.

Tell me I'm out of shape. Make a joke about the length of my body.

Set your feet on my shoulders. Spread open the muscles beneath my armpits . . . two open mouths, hollering. Keep the undersides of my arms as tight as sore throats.

You say, "Never fit me properly."

I'll say, "Nothing ever does."

(8)

Wait for morning. Wait for him to shower, shave his face, dress, leave for work.

The weights strapped to my feet make my ankles numb, cold numb. I'll easily untie my hands, let the wrist weights drop to the carpet. After he goes.

He knows this, he expects it, but he does not want to see it done. He hates process, hates to watch the doing or the undoing of events, objects, narratives.

Except with me.

When I hear his car door close, I'll release first my right hand and then my left. He knows I can do this, he tied the knots in shoelace bows. A child could break free from here. It excites him to think of my teeth tugging the knots loose.

When I can feel my ankles again, I will dress and go home. I'll leave the key under a stone by the front door. I'll sleep in my own bed until late in the afternoon.

I'll call him at 6:00. He knows it's me.

(9)

This is how he lives. From memory into pattern and back to memory. The two are indistinguishable.

This is how I live, now, too. Avoiding action.

We call this force of habit.

◆

A PRIVATE VIEW

◆

By David Vineyard

I opened my eyes and looked up to see a column of sun-browned thighs ending in a juncture of thick dark curls. Beyond that, the bright sun slipped around the figure to blind me to the full view.

I didn't need much more. It was the French woman. She was distinctive from the collection of mostly American women gathered on the Pacific shore of the little Mexican resort by two things: her utter disregard for modesty, and the untrimmed hair at her pubes and under her arms.

She kneeled beside me where I lay under the big Cinzano umbrella. Now I could see her flat brown belly deeply cleft by her navel, the slight fold of belly as she bent, and the fat rise of the mons under its curls. The pert breasts were the size of large apples ending in pouting pink brown nipples that seemed to pouch out like the rubber nipples on a baby bottle. She had an oval face with wide cheekbones, a long, almost classical nose, and lips that were too full. Her hair was cut short as a boy's in a tight curled black cap, and her green eyes were hidden behind large sunglasses that seemed too wide for her face.

She was unconcerned about her nudity. Most of the women had succumbed to the lure of going topless after a day or two on the white hot sand, and then finally to the lure of complete freedom—somehow they still seemed clothed with their pubes and underarms trimmed and shaved to perfection. Their very Americanness provided a sort of invincible armor of fastidious invisible plastic molded to their bodies. The French woman seemed all the more naked beside them.

"I noticed your book," she said. I turned my eyes toward the battered paperback lying by me in the sand—*La Maison de Rendezvous* by Alain Robbe-Grillet, a much underscored Grove Press edition I had bought in a university bookstore in the mistaken belief that it was a dirty book a thousand years ago when I was an undergraduate. I had read it a dozen times since.

"Have you read it?" I asked.

"Many times." She let herself down onto her knees so that the sand was pushed up around them. Her legs were relaxed, not held tightly together, so that the outline of the pink folds of her sex was visible where the sunlight made her pubic hair seem almost transparent from the angle at which I was viewing her. "Did you see *Last Year at Marienbad*?" she asked, referring to the Alain Resnais film Robbe-Grillet had scripted. Her English was very good.

"Several times—I even understood it the last time."

She laughed without making a sound. Her teeth were square and white, her tongue the same color of pink as the outer lips of her sex.

"My favorite of his works is *The Voyeur*," she said. I sat up on one elbow, too self-consciously aware of the tightness of the absurd Speedo racing suit that covered my loins and left nothing to her imagination—not even my religion. I had yet to make the transition to the casual nudity of the beach. The tiny swimsuit was a compromise with my all-American puritan passions.

"I think this is my favorite," I said, nodding toward the paperback. "I enjoyed *The Voyeur*, but I think I liked *Jealousy* and *The Erasers* better."

"Do you like other Resnais movies, other than those with Robbe-Grillet?" She had stretched out on the sand by me. One of her breasts brushed the heat of it, and the white grains were pasted to the moist sweaty flesh. She placed one leg forward over the other so that her sex was hidden, and I felt a pang of loss. It was difficult to keep my eyes from straying to the dark triangle.

"*Hiroshima, Mon Amour*," I said leaning a little toward her. I was aware of myself as much as her. Of too much spare tire at the waist, too little hair on the top, and too much everywhere else. She was perhaps thirty-one or -two—where I was beginning to worry more about the gray hairs that were still there than the brown ones that were gone. ". . . and I love *La Guerre Est Finie* and *Stavisky.*"

"A romantic," she said.

"A cynic," I said.

"Aren't they the same?"

"Which are you?"

She rolled onto her back. Her breasts were firm and flattened out to her body only a little. I followed the convex and concave curve of her belly to the rise of the mons where the mass of dark brown hair rose in luxuriant wild curls, neither jungle nor forest, but a sargasso of seaweed concealing the ocean smell of her sex and depths more mysterious than the Marianas.

"It's hot, isn't it?" I said lamely. A drop of sweat fell on my lips and I sucked the salt bitterness of it. There were streaks on her where her own perspiration ran in brown rivers. In my mind's eye I could see a pool forming in the well of her navel, and imagined my tongue sipping its salty tang like some thirst-starved traveler at a blessed oasis. "Would you like a drink?"

"Not here," she said.

I stood up as she did. She brushed the sand from me with a brisk touch, then turned her back for me to provide a similar service. I tried to control my thoughts as I brushed the white grains from her hips and buttocks. The flesh seemed to curve in to my palms and the weight of her ass pushed back into my hand as I brushed a small area that had gathered where her buttocks curved down and in toward her crotch. When she turned back she eyed the slight growth of the bulge in the triangle of my swimsuit—whether with disdain, disgust, amusement, or desire I could not read. I stepped into my espadrilles and picked up the large beach towel provided by the hotel. She went a few feet ahead, paused, and looked back to see if I was coming. Her legs were slightly apart, cocked to one side, and as she turned to look over her right shoulder I could see one breast in half-silhouette. For all her beauty she was not perfect, no goddess. Her hips were perhaps too wide, her ass not as firm as it might have been. There were slight folds and creases across her belly when she turned or bent. I think it was her flaws that made her so damned attractive to me. She was a woman, not a plastic sex doll. She was human. She snored, farted, took a piss, cried at silly movies, lost her temper over unimportant things, and needed a bath as often as any other human. That was what made her so attractive then and there, in that place and time. I might have resisted an army of carefully stamped out California centerfolds—but not one real woman.

Her cabana was well away from the main dining and reception area. Like my own cabana it was small but comfortable, a step down out of the sun into a dark womb decorated with tropical plants and vaguely Spanish style. I wondered if Ravel's *Bolero* would be on the stereo.

Her nudity had been striking, but somehow vaguely asexual on the beach. Here, alone in the room, it was almost more than I could bear. I wished she would put on a robe—or a nun's habit. Anything.

Each cabana had a small bar. She offered me the hospitality of hers while she went into the bath—to change into something more comfortable? She called for a club soda with lime. I poured another for myself. Under the Mexican heat, alcohol sweated out of you with a perceptible stink.

I sat down on the small sofa. I could hear the soft hum of the air conditioner. The cool air was like a razor on the fabric of my nerves.

She returned and sat in a low chair opposite me. She left her legs open so that the view of her sex was unobstructed. The green eyes were level and frank. I felt a yearning for the anonymity of her sunglasses.

"My husband could not come this year," she said. "He is an exporter in Lyon."

"My wife thought I needed to get away early," I said. "She's joining me next week. She sells real estate. There was a closing she couldn't miss." The small talk seemed incongruous, sitting here with a naked woman—naked not nude or merely unclothed—my eyes straying too often to the points of the apple-like fruit of her breast made hard by the cool air and the forested pink sea cave entrance she made no effort to conceal.

"The heat, the beach . . ." she began. She paused, not from hesitation, but to confirm whatever she had read in me out on the beach. There were younger better-looking men who were not married, or were at least equally aware of her sensuality, whom she could have approached. She read something in me—perhaps that I was feeling now a reluctance to carry this beyond flirtation. I wished for my wife, and then was glad she was not here, and I wondered if I would be reduced to the achingly familiar caress of my best-known lover—my good right hand—to relieve the stone ache of her tease. If this was merely a tease. I wanted to stay—to go—to take her violently—to run like a coward—to give in to my body—to stay true to my wife—as if I had not already betrayed her in some way. "My mother was very European, very French you would say. She always referred to it as an itch. She used to say that a man had a fire, a pain, that for a woman was an itch. That a man's fire might bank occasionally, but a woman's itch was always there. She said that the worst thing was to deny it."

"She was a wise woman," I said, feeling at a loss for words and tongue-tied. I sipped at the drink.

"Very wise." She let one hand rest on the arm of the low wicker chair, the other was resting on her belly. Her long fingers lay gently among the pubic curls. She was stroking herself idly as she talked—as yet only abstractly. "Do you love your wife?"

I nodded. "I love my husband," she said. "But it has been two weeks, and in this heat, in this atmosphere . . . You seem to be an understanding man. I hope I have not embarrassed you or led you on. I only wish to be touched . . ." I was surprised to see a red blush spread across the tops of her breasts like a rash. "I thought perhaps . . ."

She stood up and walked over to me. She stood for a moment where my face was even with her pubes and I could smell the fecund sea depths of her and the faint damp hollow of perspiration gathered at the juncture of her thighs. Her legs were open so that I had no difficulty resting my hand between her legs, cupping her sex in my palm.

She closed her eyes and pushed down into my hand so that her sex was pushed open in a wet kiss in my palm and her ass rested on my fingers.

"*Oui*," she whispered, speaking her own language for the first time. "Oh, *merde! Oui, oui* . . ."

I slipped one finger delicately into the crack and began to draw my hand back and forth slowly. She closed her eyes and one hand was caressing one of the nipples so that it darkened and distended. Her other hand rested on my arm, tightening as my stroke became more certain, and then digging her short nails into my upper arm at the instant I slipped one finger between the elastic lips and let it be sucked up into her as she drew her breath in sharply.

I knew what she wanted—needed, and more importantly that I could give it without compromising myself or her. It didn't need words. This was sex, more than masturbation, but it was not betrayal or an affair, or anything so obvious. What I might do for her, and she for me, was out of compassion and mutual need, not simple lust. Each of us was in need of the balm the other could provide, and I knew now that my very reluctance was why she chose me.

She stopped me well short of her release and pulled me to my feet so that she could touch me through the thin material of my suit, and then roll it down from my hips. She grasped the length of me, molding her hand to the rounded helmet and cupping the slip-sliding roll of my testicles, always just beyond her playful grasp, in their hairy purse of tightening flesh. Her hand was warm and dry, like a chamois against the velvet glans. She weighed and measured me with her touch, wondering at the miracle of change that takes place in that part of a man. There was no judgment in that measurement, only awe that it should happen at all.

We never kissed. I took each of her nipples in my mouth in turn and sucked hard points feeling the lengthening nipple against the top of my mouth as I sucked and bit. Then we lay down on the floor by each other on our sides, her feet by my head, and my hand buried in her vagina, three fingers deep in the wetness and heat, her clitoris caught between the deep thrusting fingers and my thumb. Her cunt—there was no other word for it in the circumstance—sucked at my fingers as they played in the spongy elastic folds and moisture exuded by her body, her inner muscles closing down on those invaders. Her own hands grasped my tube of flesh and the hard knot of my scrotum. She stroked the length of me in a tight grasp lubricated by her saliva, alternating long, slow strokes moving the outer skin over the tight inner cylinder, with quickened short jerky strokes near the top concentrating on the glans. When the first drops of pre-come changed the texture of the lubrication of her saliva she began a throttling stroke that ran up and down the length of me while all the time her free hand pushed my scrotum up toward my body and one finger teased the opening of my anus. My own fingers moved faster, trapping the hardened distended clitoris under its hood, so that I felt the little electric shocks it conferred to her body. Even her feet were extended, toes pointed in tension, each one standing apart as if she wanted to grasp something.

She came a little before me, her legs suddenly drawing up toward her, my hand pinned by the firm thighs. Her entire body shuddered, and my hand was soaked in the copious flow of her release. She rocked back and forth and I could feel her cunt trying to push out my fingers even as her thighs trapped them there. She screamed when she came, a short sharp bark like a vixen in heat, and now her head was thrown back, her neck taut, her whole body arched like a drawn bow, and my fingers were pulling the string that triggered her release. The whole time she kept a strangling grip on my cock, her tension and release going into me from her grip. Then she exhaled the breath she had held during the entire sequence of the orgasm, releasing my nearly numb hand from her soaking grip, shivering a little as my hand slipped from inside her. She smiled at me, and it turned into a wicked little girl's tongue biting grin as she seemed to connect me to the object still pulsing in her fist.

She concentrated on me with renewed urgency, until I felt the familiar electric surge run from my spine into my balls like a static charge along the urethra. My entire body spasmed in a sphincter-like grip that lifted my buttocks from the floor and ended only in the pumping of my seed. She brought me to such tension that it spurted several inches in the air and splattered us both with its scald. She had cried out, but I could make no sound other than a stifled groan. I was suddenly aware of the sweat on the back of my thighs and buttocks, of the unsubtle maleness of my smell and the sweet musk of hers.

She continued to pump my dying soldier until the sensitivity was so great I bit back a cry, and then, her hands bathed in the sticky flow, bent her head down, and, in the only kiss we would ever share, pressed her slightly parted lips to the slimy head of that defeated warrior like a benediction. We lay side by side touching but separate, each in an orbit the other was no part of.

My wife arrived a day later, and before she could unpack I took her passionately across the fresh-made bed in our cabana. I don't know if she guessed something then, or simply thought how alone I must have been. Afterward we showered together and then went out to the beach. The French woman was following a boy in a red guayabera and white duck trousers with her luggage. She nodded toward me with that slightness of glance reserved for not-quite strangers.

I never knew her name. I never asked. . . .

PARTNERS

◆

By Terry Marshall

We wind down too slowly, even here, even in the tropics. I do anyway. So does Marie.

Or maybe it's that bedtime falls too quickly. "Night is a roller shade," Marie once joked. "It unrolls to the equator, then free-falls." It is no longer something we can laugh about.

The solution should be simple: speed up the routine—early to bed, early to rise. Tonight, we tried. We sat down at six. Dinner was an executive summary: the day's highlights. We suspended conversation for an evening romp with Suzanne, her bath, a bedtime story. Suzanne was asleep by eight, but the workday continued—a call from the Ambassador, tomorrow's report, notes on my meeting with the Prime Minister. It was ten o'clock before Marie and I took coffee on the veranda.

The islands are magic at night: breeze like a sauna's breath, brilliant southern sky undimmed by electric light. On the veranda, day's frustrations rolled out like the ebbing tide—the Ambassador's latest gaffe; more nonsensical orders from State; hours spent jockeying with the Minister of Natural Resources over our new aid package. No less from Marie—the clinic's daily stream of patients provides grist enough for a week's discussion.

Breathlessly we talked, as if we were still in D.C., racing minds spewing thoughts and words like exhaust from freeway-bound traffic, trying to touch on everything before we fell asleep exhausted. Only gradually we realized our hands were on each other. Night must purge our minds before she restores our senses; only then do touch and talk become whispered foreplay.

Still we had too little time. We wound down too slowly. We rushed the nightly ritual—in mid-conversation we came to bed, talking as we undressed.

Uncovered, we lay now side by side, talking, touching, deliberately trying to overlay these two stages of foreplay so that we will finish in time. We cannot rush it, we know, and yet we do. I hear the clock. My hands fly when they should be dawdling. She strokes me, but I am dry; her spittle-slickered hands bring me to full erection.

Now Marie is above me on elbows and knees. She whispers, "Yes?" Her breath like incense stirs me. She is astraddle, palms on my chest. Chestnut eyes sparkle in the moonlight. A saucy grin appears. At last we escape the day. She floats toward me, lips parted. I take her head in my hands. We kiss through springlets of frangipani-scented hair, and her breasts nestle onto me. She is up again. Her frizzy hair is a feather duster, tickling my face, neck and shoulders. Her nipples graze my chest, but only briefly; the game is hurried.

She squiggles onto me, wet but not lubricious. In a tight minuet we dance until I am fully inside. Our fear recedes now like the distant surf. Slowly we rock. Our bodies respond. The tightness eases. Tightly clasped, our strokes are long and measured. Our gentle slip-slipping serenades us, and in night's heat we enter a musky cocoon of our own scents. We are the ebb and flow of calm sea on the sand. In concert we build. Tonight we will become crashing waves on rock-strewn cliffs.

Suzanne screams, and a demon's curse echoes through our villa. Marie is off me; I wither. We are too late. Damn kid!

Is it beasties? Who knows what a seven-year-old hears and sees in the dark. We thought at first it might be fruit bats. Twice Marie and I posted guard on the veranda through the night. We heard them, wings like clapping hands that never meet, but we never saw them. They dart under the eaves without sound. I don't think Suzanne can see them, or hear them.

We isolated each sound. In heavy winds, limbs moan, kapok pods like pitched stones bounce on the sheet-iron roof, roll, and thud to the ground. Clawed feet scurry in the dark. At times, the flame trees outside our louvered glass shutters glow as if their brilliant red burns from within. They seem alive; might they frighten her? "It's our fireplace tree, Daddy," Suzanne said. "It keeps me warm." Nor do critters bother her. Last week she burst upon a reception wearing a rhinoceros beetle like a brooch—three inches long, coal black, tiny claws gripping her checkered blue and white school uniform. She pranced up to a British consultant fresh off Air Pacific, lured him close, then ticked the beetle into a chattering frenzy. The poor fellow tumbled into the buffet. Suzanne giggled. No, critters don't bother her. We don't know what it is. Neither does she. But it's been three months now, and it happens every night.

Her scream lingers. We hear little feet tearing down the hallway. She flies quavering into our bedroom.

"Come, Suzanne, come. It's okay," Marie coos. Suzanne dives into bed. Marie's arm like a dove's wing gathers her in.

Eleven o'clock. We were too slow. Ten minutes pass before Suzanne's eyes close. Another five before she breathes evenly.

"Asleep?"

"I think so," Marie whispers.

We're wide awake. We don't move; we won't disturb her.

Marie's back and buttocks like sculptured alabaster haunt me. Mother with cuddled child are carved from a single block. Suzanne sleeps lightly, an alarm that will ring at the slightest movement, the softest sound.

Beside them I lie, taunted by the stars: Marie alone is cast in their diffused beams like a featured exhibit in a darkened gallery. I touch her. Both hands. Fingers caress translucent shoulders, hot, pliant. Time hangs still as my fingertips explore her every cell. My hands are a meandering stream, current so gentle it seems motionless. Over shoulders, spine, hips curving tautly into firm buttocks, my hands flow, and flow again. We make no sound, suspending breath. Love expresses itself in touch, scent, sight.

Lubricants flow. My hand between her buttocks slips over a

downy nest. My fingers taste her. They explore the oiled channel and its byways. Nymphs unseen stroke and fondle them. My penis cries in anticipation; it has puddled the bed.

I can wait no longer. My hands on her buttocks guide us. She pushes toward me so slowly there seems no movement, and I wiggle toward her. I arch backward, extending myself to full length as she swallows me. We couple fully.

No violent flailing this; rather, a fusing of our most sensitive selves. We muffle the sounds, groans, sighs, whispers and cries, even involuntary mutterings. No rhythmic slurping of silent thrusts tonight; I am embedded within her, motionless. Through this coupling pass our thoughts, sensations, love without sound, without motion.

Yet we are not still. Marie summons an internal masseuse who kneads, caresses, devours me. She suckles, squeezes, gnaws. From within explodes the need to cry out my joy, to thrust wildly, to buck and snort. Our bodies are exposed nerve-endings, tensed and coiled as we deny ourselves sound and movement. God, how she is at me now, hungry vulva stronger than suckling mouth.

She rakes my penis; her teeth could not mark me as visibly as she marks me now. Coitus becalmed inflames the fire. Without sound, without movement, I boil within. Steam builds; I shall explode. I bite my lower lip. If only Suzanne would disappear, if only for a moment! I ache for an uninhibited night. I ache to thrash about, a wild animal, to expel this emotion.

Marie releases me. My heart pounds. Her pulse beats against me. Bathed in sweat, we lie quiet. Thoughts come again. I've been angry, unfairly so. Poor Suzanne, it's not her fault: she hasn't chosen this nightly terror. How ironic, that this product of our love so constricts lovemaking. Yet, ironic also that she forces upon us imploding rapture that this night propels our lovemaking into a new dimension. Marie and I know each other so well. Our lives are so entwined that we need no words, no wild thrashing to join as one.

"I love you, Marie," I whisper.

She shushes me with a squeeze. She begins again, silent, kneading.

rhythmic. I relax, let her tend me. I kiss her shoulder, lightly like a butterfly. She tastes salty.

Suddenly, it is too late. Have I drifted off? I've missed the torrid rush that explodes from deep within my bowels and charges through my body. Without thrusting I come. No gushing, spurting. I simply flow into her, as if by will alone she has milked me. With a shudder I am drained. From within me, an animal's grunt bursts forth.

Suzanne thrashes about, sits up. "Mommy, I'm thirsty."

"Daddy will get you some water, honey," Marie says. She squeezes me. I'm soft; I slip from her clasp.

Marie turns over. She's smiling and she winks.

I'm up, padding down the hallway. My legs quiver. It's a nuisance; Suzanne will be asleep before I find a glass.

I return quickly. I'm right. But Marie has somehow freed herself from their mother-daughter tangle. Suzanne faces away, toward the doorway; she cuddles her stuffed koala.

Marie is lying on her back. Her right arm stretches across the bed; her hand rests on my daughter's hips. Marie is awake. Head turned, she studies me.

"Face me," she mouths. She lays my hand on her upraised left knee. She is sliding my hand down. Her legs part.

The moon is out, the room well lit. Marie closes her eyes. "We're not finished," she whispers. I'm touching her. She cups me. Silently we kiss.

AFTER A BIRTH

The doctor said no sex
after seven months
and we obeyed.
The baby was born in early March
and the doctor said no sex
for six weeks
and we obeyed
until that early Easter
broke our windows
with sunlight while
I was in the shower.

I remember the smell of
Safeguard soap and the renegade white air
filling the tiny bathroom,
shouting longer days.
I remember my stretch marks
ending in a delta of brandnew hair.
I remember how you met me
in the kitchen and, buffeted
by air and hope,
we lay down.
I remember my fear
of forgetting how, of tearing

I remember how you
whispered oh my love
it's been too long for you,
too, too long,
how I took your words,
distilled droplets of lemon sun,
and held them hard against
the back of my throat,
as you whispered again
it's been so long,
and I formed my lips
around your
thrusting hand.

Carol L. Gloor

MEN

◆

JABBERWOCKY REVISITED

'Twas brillig in that cheap hotel
The looking-glass had cataracts
All mimsy were the bureau drawers
The paper was a glimpse of hell
"Come to my arms, my beamish boy,"
Her scarlet mouth invited him
He felt it to his slithy toves
Now hidden by his jockey shorts
She fell upon the lumpy sheets
And took his vorpal sword in hand
He chortled in his joy.
He found her frumious bandersnatch
O frajous day! Callooh! Callay!
They gyred and gimbled in the wave
Of sweat-stained sheets and coverlets
And burbled as they came.

Ralph Tyler

◆

THE THINGS
I DON'T WRITE

◆

By Wayne Jones

Here are some facts about me that might be relevant in
the story I am going to tell you about breaking up with my girlfriend.

1. I'm really a fat guy. I mean, I'm not the size of the guy in the
Guinness Book of World Records who had to be buried in a piano case,
but my fat is the first thing you notice about me. I have to wear those
GWG work pants all the time because they are one of the few things
that are easily attainable in waist sizes in the upper 40s. I wear XXL
T-shirts all summer, and have only two or three long-sleeve shirts at
all. I own one suit, an outdated pinstripe, the kind all the guys wore at
the high school graduation. It is starting to look a little ratty.

Keep an eye on a fat person for a couple of weeks. Pick one out on
your bus route to work, for instance, and you'll notice they have a very
limited wardrobe. A fat man may have a pair of rugger pants that he
wears more often than anything else, and a fat woman will have something dark and shapeless with thin accessories. It's a sad thing, really,
and you should feel lucky you don't have to live that way.

2. I'm good in bed, especially after I've had a few glasses of red
wine. I have surprised many women. They usually date me for the
most primal of reasons, that is they think a guy my size hasn't been
laid for years and would jump gratefully at the chance. They also date

me because I am pretty easy-going and attentive. I have that character-istic which used to be desperately attributed to those homely girls that no one would *ever* date: "a good personality."

Being good in bed has nothing to do with how beautiful your body is or how long you can last or how many orgasms you can give or have. No. For those of you who like to learn something from what you read, get out a pencil and a piece of paper, and copy down this bit of wisdom from the sexiest fat guy I know: A good lover submits to the wanton integrity of sexuality.

3. I am hard to live with. Just ask my ex-wife. I nearly drove the poor woman crazy. Here's another interesting fact (pencils and paper out again): Fat people are generally not slobs. They crave order in their lives as a compensation for the disorder of their eating habits. I was unbearably fastidious when I married: insisted that all fluids in the refrigerator be on the same shelf, complained when the TV remote was left unaccountably in the bathroom, sighed like a peevish teenager when one of the CDs had been misfiled.

4. I fall in love easily. *Daily,* in fact. It is not large breasts or diamond calves that draw me. It's always a detail, something quirky, something endearing. I tend to admire self-consciousness or non-aggressive self-confidence. Today on the bus, for example, it was her shy glances combined with the way she wore a pleated mini-skirt over an abdomen and legs that weren't designed for it. With my ex-wife it was the nervous playfulness. And with my girlfriend that I just broke up with—well, it was the utter lack of dissembling. That can be pretty sexy.

Marlo. I wouldn't bring her up if it weren't for the letter I just received from her. Try this on for your all-time clichés: She wants us to remain friends. She's living in Toronto now so there's not much chance of a romantic reconciliation anyway. (I'm in Ottawa.) Just exactly what "remaining friends" would entail I'm not sure, but no doubt it would become a correspondence of diminishing intensity in which I would keep her abreast of the latest flare-ups of my tendonitis, she would lovingly detail the mishaps with her Lada, and we would both develop an acute knowledge of how the weather systems move between southern and eastern Ontario.

In order to remain civil if nothing else, I have to reply to her letter. I am uncertain, however, about what to say and how to say it. Versions of several letters have been floating in my head:

> Dear Marlo,
> No.
> Sincerely,
> Jon

This version is harder than I want it to be, especially now that my heart and mind and body and imagination are genuinely starting to recover from the loss of her. It is not much better than "Fuck off and die," which was another version I considered about a month ago when I was even less further along in my emotional recovery.

The other thing about a simple "No" is that the details about how I made it from there to here are missing. There's nothing about those drunken nights of intentional deprivation of consciousness, nights when I drove the car about 200 kilometers an hour with the sun roof open and the cool moist air of summer gushing over my head, nights when I didn't care whether I made it home at all as long as I could plop insensate on the bed if I did, no tossing and turning, no staring at the ceiling at 3 A.M., no rushes of sexual arousal while I lay there reminiscing about pleasure that I could not even hope to approximate alone.

> Dear Marlo,
> Do you remember that weekend we spent in Kingston? I mean not just the lovemaking but also the waking up together, the walking around. Jesus, Marlo, I remember waking up before you did that Sunday and you were lying on your front with the sheets to your waist . . .
> That's why we can't be friends, Marlo. I don't want to be

getting letters from "my friend Marlo." It's too pathetic. There's just too much of a distance from the sight of your back . . . to what? . . .

- "I've got a new office at work."
- "Dorothy and I have discovered a great new Thai restaurant."
- "The car died again."

Sincerely,
Jon

No, definitely not, that version is too close to being out of control. I may be trying to accomplish the impossible here, trying to be civil and firm and honest without detailing my excessive drinking and over-eating. I'm fatter now than I was six months ago, but I am not overly worried about that. I'm not obscenely obese and besides—another lesson—in my humble experience with women, and to their credit, that kind of physical detail doesn't bother them anyway. Women *like* me, fat as I am, and I have consequently developed an enormous attraction to women with a nice earthy layer of fat surrounding *them* as well. They're preferable to those emaciated Paris-model refugee types who are often *emotionally* thin as well. No versatility, no imagination. They're used to being catered to by those hairy-chested gold-chained Camaro studs I see racing down Preston Street with some drug-headed heavy metal nimrod band blaring way too loud on the stereo system. Fat women, fat *people*, are people with appetites for all of life: not only food but also love and lust and art and frivolity.

Her appetites and her honesty are what drew me to Marlo. An example. We meet in Kingston at a conference on history of textual bibliography. I stumble out of a stiflingly hot room and find her standing alone luxuriously sucking a Popsicle. I drop some papers and some books at her feet (accidentally, I swear): some photocopies of the text of *Julius Caesar* from the First Folio, a bit of Johnson's *Rambler*, an edition of the *Canterbury Tales* with Middle English and modern English in parallel columns.

"I like that part in *Julius Caesar*," she says, "that part where Caesar doesn't want Casca around him because he has that 'lean and hungry look.' Great stuff."

"Cassius," I say nervously, regretting it immediately.

"What? . . . Oh, right. Cassius. Do you know how that goes, how that quote goes, exactly?"

" 'Let me have men about me that are fat, sleek-headed men and such as sleep a-nights.' " I am worried that I sound unbearably pompous, but she prods me.

"And about Cassius?"

" 'Yond Cassius has a lean and hungry look, he thinks too much; such men are dangerous.' "

"That's wild," she says, and I am in love even before she starts asking me about myself and my obsessions.

Dear Marlo,

I had an accident last week. Rammed the car into the corner of the library when I was reaching for another donut. It sobered me. I threw the flask out the window. I gathered the rest of the donuts into their box, threw it out the sun roof, backed over it and drove off.

The only other thing I remember is the spinning, spinning totally out of control in slow motion knowing that something awful was happening but not being able to do anything except sit there and wait for it all to be over.

Love,
Jon

JEWISH SEXUALITY, SUCH AS IT IS: VOLUME ONE

◆

By Albert Stern

Around the world, Yiddish is recognized as the international language of love.

The scenario is easy to imagine. A man and a woman embrace in front of a fireplace in a warm cabin that overlooks a sweeping mountain vista. The lovers press together, feeling the heat of each other's bodies as they watch snowflakes pelting the cold window glass. She raises her chin and he moves his mouth slowly down her smooth white throat, alternating soft kisses with playful, gentle bites. She is aroused as he releases the snaps of her black bustier, and as he loosens the garment she digs her fingernails into his neck and moans with almost unbearable expectation: "Speak it! Speak the Yiddish!"

And so he says: "*Hey, shayneh maidel! Ich vel dich kishen, und du vest shrein far fargineegen.*" (Hey, pretty girl! I will kiss you, and you will scream with pleasure.)

She surrenders.

There is a serious problem with the language of love, however, that was revealed to me soon after my non-Jewish girlfriend and I started dating. Amazed by the seemingly endless variety of Yiddish words that designate the male member, she—as I discovered only a gentile is likely to do—asked the word for its female equivalent.

I had no idea. While the Jews have more words for penis than the Eskimos have to describe different kinds of ice, I could not remember ever having heard the term for a woman's private parts. What was more disturbing was that even though I love Yiddish words and phrases and have lived in a sexually open era, *I had never before thought to ask.*

So I went to my father, who is, after all, my parent, and thus the first person to have confused me about sex. Born in Romania and raised in New York City, my father learned Yiddish as his first language.

When I asked him for the translation, a haunted expression settled on his face. He thought for a moment, then told me he had no idea.

I said, "Dad—you grew up on the Lower East Side. You were one of the guys. Surely you talked about it and you knew about it."

"Albert," he answered sadly, "we did not talk about it . . . we did not know."

My father has always been something of a prude, and so I sought help elsewhere. Luckily, I live in Miami Beach, a city with a large population of feisty Jewish senior citizens determined not to leave this world without a fight, or, at the very least, an argument. I began asking every Yiddish-speaker I know for a translation. From the condo lobbies to the folding chairs along the ocean, the reactions were nearly identical. The senior citizens would listen to the questions and then give me a strange, faraway look that said: "You know, I never thought to ask." Many of the older people adamantly insisted, some to the point of veins popping out on their foreheads, that there is no such word.

Several times, I came tantalizingly close to an answer. A friend's grandmother said that she knew, but would not tell him. One porch-sitter said he was certain that there was such a word, but he "forgot it many years ago."

Al Resnick, who is perhaps the greatest of Miami Beach's ocean-side sages, offered a parable to explain why the Word (which clearly warranted higher-case distinction) was not commonplace:

"Harry Epstein has a physical breakdown. Comes very close to death. When he's in the hospital, his doctor examines him and makes a diagnosis. The doctor calls Mrs. Epstein into his office for a private consultation. He says to her: 'Your husband is very sick, Mrs. Epstein. His system is too weak to handle drugs. What he needs is sex to invigorate and relax him—four times, five times a day. As many times as you are able to accommodate him, you must do so. Or else your husband is a dead man.'

"Mrs. Epstein returns to her husband, who is waiting anxiously. 'What did the doctor say?'

" 'Harry,' Mrs. Epstein tells him, 'the doctor says you're going to die.' "

Al Resnick put the word out along his extensive network of contacts among the melanoma set. Within days, he reported only one lead: the word *loch*, which means lock. The person who suggested *loch* admitted that he was unsure of its correctness. Al Resnick advised me to continue my research and collect my findings as part of a book titled, *Jewish Sexuality, Such as It Is: Volume One* and subtitled, *There Ain't No Volume Two.*

Striking out in Miami Beach, I tried my cousin in Israel. He responded that everyone he asked in the Holy Land was, predictably, confused by the question, but eventually he came up with two possibilities. The first was *knish*, after the cement-filled Jewish pastry; however, *knish* sounded too cute to be used by adults in a moment of passion. The second possibility was the word *shmoonke*, which seems more plausible in that it sounds somewhat Yiddish for penis.

My next stop was the library. Uriel Weinreich's *Modern English-Yiddish Dictionary* offers as its preferred definition the transliteration into Hebrew characters of the English word "vagina." This is something of a cop out, and makes me think of my grandmother in her later years, after her Yiddish (and maybe a few cogs in the noggin) had slipped somewhat. We'd ask for the translation of a word, say "window," and she would reply "vindeh!" in a strong Eastern European accent.

The Weinreich dictionary also offered a second option, *mutter-*

scheid or "mother's sheath," an unfriendly word that is not likely ever to have much currency either in the bedroom or as street slang. In any case, *Schied* is the German word for the female sex organ.

None of the suggested words save *shmoonke* have the descriptive and onomatopoeic flair of most Yiddish obscenities. A *shvance*, for example, could be none other than the homely golem hanging between every man's legs. Words like *schmuck* and *putz* have become part of the American vernacular. In contrast, even Jews are not sure of the Yiddish word for vagina.

Obviously, steps had to be taken, the world had to know. And so a plan of action quickly crystallized: start my inquiries with Nobel Prize laureates and work my way down to Joey Bishop.

The questions that needed answering were: What is the Word? Why do so few people know it? Of those who do, why do they?

And so the letters went out. The first response only made things a bit more confusing. Answering on behalf of her husband (who was quite ill at the time), Mrs. Isaac Bashevis Singer politely replied: "The word is s[illegible], I believe. Mrs. Isaac Bashevis Singer."

That the word in question is the only one that I could not make out strikes me as mysterious indeed. It might be *sdword* or *skmmuk*, but not conclusively *shmoonke*. Maybe her hand failed her as she was writing the Word, I don't know. The stage was set for controversy.

In a letter dictated to his secretary, Saul Bellow responded that "the word you are seeking does exist. It is *pirge* (pronounced pir-geh)."

Having already won his Nobel Prize, Bellow felt no need to join the fray and address the deeper questions raised by my inquiry. However, as the author's secretary conveys: "Having answered your question, Mr. Bellow hopes that your quest for enlightenment will not stop."

Well, it didn't. The answers received from the Nobel laureates put the two great novelists at loggerheads. While Bellow says the word is *pirge*, Mrs. Singer believes the word starts with the letter "S." Even if Mr. Singer had not been consulted, wouldn't she have at least heard the Word from him? Wouldn't that word—whatever it may be—exchanged during moments of intimacy with the greatest Yiddish writer be the preferred terminology, or at least the word that packs a bit more punch?

Clearly, I had to press on to Joey Bishop.

Bruce Jay Friedman writes: "I ran into an actress once who, distastefully I might add, referred to the said private parts as her *kugel* (potato casserole). All other references, in my experience, were the traditional ones in English."

Questioning the methodology of my research, Friedman adds: "Good luck as you work your way 'down' to Joey Bishop. I would have thought that was working your way up."

Friedman's contribution vaulted *knish* back into the running by establishing a tenuous baked goods linkage. Linguistically, likening a woman's private parts to a potato casserole is consistent with a frequent tendency in both Yiddish and Hebrew to refer euphemistically or ironically to a distasteful object or place. For example, a toilet would be called "seat of honor." Speakers of both languages did this in order to keep the vocabularies pure.

This was not always the practice, however. The word for "womb" in the direct, vital language of the Old Testament is *raham*, which also means mercy and compassion. More prosaic Hebrew language literature and religious works, however, refer to the vagina simply as "that place." My Israeli cousin pointed to a passage in the *Shulhan Orukh*, the authoritative code of Jewish law, that forbids a man to look at the genital organ of his wife, also warning: "One who kisses that place . . . violates Leviticus 11:43: 'Ye shall not make yourself detestable.' " This prohibition is also elucidated in the Talmud, Tractate Nedarim (Vows).

The Jews have a historic tradition of not knowing exactly what might be the right thing to do with their genitalia, a confusion begun at the dawn of the faith as part of the Almighty's covenant with Abraham. Following the example of Abraham, Jewish law commands that the foreskin of every male child's homely golem be snipped eight days after his birth. In light of the treatment the male organ has received over the millennia, perhaps Jewish women have demurred on naming their organ in fear of calling unwanted attention to it.

As the months dragged on, finding the conclusive definition of the Word developed into a pathological pursuit, a strange obsession—to mix a metaphor, my Moby Dick.

The litany of befuddlement continued:

Mordecai Richler had no idea.

Comedians Jackie Mason, Robert Klein, and Richard Lewis declined to answer. Lewis's agent went so far as to explain that "Richard is trying to get away from his image as a neurotic Jew." (And, from what I hear, Mr. T is moving away from his image as a Negro.)

When asked if he knew the word, Philip Roth confessed: "I come up blank." If the author of *Portnoy's Complaint* never thought to ask, then the problem is truly larger than I ever imagined. "You better ask Joey Bishop," he wrote, an affirmation of the correctness of my initial approach to the problem.

When I posed the question to Joe Nevel, owner of Miami Beach landmark Wolfie's Restaurant, he initially had no answer. Nevel is an amateur linguist who together with his wife translated several of Isaac Bashevis Singer's short stories in the late seventies. He was at first unsure that the Word existed, commenting that "there are no Yiddish words for many things. For example, there is no Yiddish word for 'ceiling.' Why? Because in Eastern European villages, houses never had low-hanging ceilings like they do in America."

Presumably, however, the women had vaginas. "Strangely enough," Nevel added, "there is no Yiddish word for 'disappointment.'"

When presented with the proposition that if a Yiddish word for vagina existed, Jewish men would have coined a Yiddish word for disappointment, Nevel's memory was suddenly jarred. He offered two possibilities — *shmushka* and *shtalt,* the latter translating as "slit."

"I guess there are words," he says, "but since no one ever uses them, we tend to forget they exist. It shows the honor and respect our people have for women."

There are twenty-five Yiddish words for vagina to be exact, according to Dr. David Gold, co-editor of *Jewish Language Review* and a professor at University of Haifa in Israel. I learned about Dr. Gold through an editor to whom he had once written about his two "exhaustive studies on the Yiddish word *shmok,*" both of which were published in that august journal, *Comments on Etymology.*

I wrote to him with a partial list of my own findings, asking him for the definitive translation of the Word. What follows is his response:

> Dear Mr. Stern,
>
>   I can offer you nineteen more Yiddish words for "vagina" (and perhaps twenty)—at $3 per word, payable in advance by check (made out to Elsie Gold).
>
>   Of the five words you give, three are misromanized and a fourth one may be. I can give you the corrections (all of them) for $5.

While I respect Dr. Gold's obvious erudition, I refuse to knuckle under to lexicographic extortion. (For readers who know little Yiddish, here is a word to add to your vocabularies: Dr. Gold's request for money is known as *chutzpah.*)

Mrs. Dee Weinreif, a teacher of Yiddish at New York's Yiddisher Visenshaftlikher Institut (more commonly known as the YIVO Institute for Jewish Research), asserted that she did not know the Word, making it very clear that my inquiry had offended her. She said that the Institute, the principal world organization conducting research in Yiddish, might somewhere possess dictionaries that had various slang words for vagina, but huffily added that she wouldn't look them up for me. (And this prudery from a woman who works at a place that has the word *visenshaftlikher* in its name.)

Yet persistence on my part enabled me to get through to YIVO's director, Dr. Alan Nadler, who, predictably, did not know the Word, but offered a thought about why it was widely unknown: "The word is not a matter of regular concern, because that part of the body is no longer particularly active for those people who still speak Yiddish."

Dr. Nadler, however, referred me to Dr. Mordkche Schaechter, Senior Lecturer Emeritus in Yiddish at Columbia University, who was shocked that I could find so few people who knew the Word. "I could give you the names of hundreds of people in New York who know many words for vagina," he said, "although I guess it wouldn't pay for you to call them."

Nevertheless, after speaking with Dr. Schaechter, I had no need to look elsewhere, for the man possessed a trove of Yiddish knowledge. "How one would refer to the organ would depend on many things," he explained. "A scholar would say *mutterschied* or *vageena*, both technical words borrowed from other languages in the twentieth century.

"However, the middle class, bourgeois Jews—who we refer to as *ballebatish*—would by and large be ashamed to pronounce a word that actually meant vagina. Their preferred usage would be *oysemoken*, which means 'that place.' Interestingly, the euphemism refers only to the vagina, not the penis or anus or any other unpleasant body part.

"Other middle class terms include *dos vayberifher*, or 'the female part,' and *die mayse*, which means 'the story.' As with most euphemisms, it's best not to ask why about that one."

According to Schaechter, *pirge* is the preferred vulgar usage, the equivalent of the Anglo-Saxon word beginning with the letter "C." Of Slavic origin, *pirge* is a centuries-old word that can be used when speaking Polish, Russian, Byelorussian, Ukrainian, and other Eastern European languages and dialects. So rack up one for Saul Bellow.

The Professor directed me to some source material that enabled me to come up with some other words: *beis kibbel* (home of the bucket), *ervah* (an unseemliness), *spiel* (game), *zach* (thing), *dorthen* (there), *shmoiya* (a derogatory word applied to many contemptible objects), and *ainhil* (wrapper) and *byoah* (buoy). Another term is *makom ha-turpah* ("the place of weakness"), which, in addition to denoting the pudenda, is also the equivalent of "Achilles' heel" both in Yiddish and Hebrew.

Finally, two terms that are perhaps related: *shande flaisch* (shame flesh) and *schmandeh*. Yiddish speakers cut highfalutin people and ideas down to size by using the mocking prefix "*sch-*." For example: "Boss, *schmoss*—who is he to treat me that way?" As no separate definition for *schmandeh* exists, it is tempting to think that the word spoofs the mortifying epithet *shandeh*, as in: "*Shandeh, schmandeh* (shame, schmame—I'm kissing that place)."

Dr. Schaechter offered his theory of why I had trouble finding these words. "These people you asked probably knew some of the words," he said, "and I wouldn't be surprised that if you tell them, they will remember knowing. Jewish people, especially of the older generation, tend to be sexually modest, and it's very likely that the *ballebatish* people you spoke to would suppress their knowledge. A woman, in particular, would never use any of these words. It would be an absolute taboo."

He also suggested that since parents were unlikely to have told their children these words, first-generation American Jews and their progeny would probably have no knowledge of them.

Although I was satisfied with both the Professor's translations and social theory, I still somehow felt obliged to press on to Joey Bishop.

As befits his stature as a national treasure, the king of the *tummlers* is not an easy man to find. The Los Angeles phone number in a recent celebrity directory was outdated by several years, and booking agents at the major hotels in Las Vegas and Atlantic City could not remember employing Bishop in more than a decade. The entertainer is no longer listed with the Screen Actors Guild. The Friars Club had no way to contact him, and when I asked their operator if he might be dead, she answered that with Joey Bishop "it could be hard to tell" (ba-dump-ump). I could not even find an agent to tell me that Joey Bishop is trying to get away from his image as Joey Bishop.

So although some questions have been answered, other mysteries remain—principally, why don't people who are not repressed sexually think to ask about the Word (and what does that say about Jewish sexuality, such as it is)? And second, why has Joey Bishop gone underground?

So perhaps there is enough material for Volume Two. But as evidenced by my girlfriend's reaction to my research, I fear that I face a tough road ahead as a Yiddish sexologist.

"All very well and good," she said after reading my findings. "By the way, what's the Yiddish word for orgasm?"

A haunted expression settles on my face.

"There is no such word!" I shout, veins popping out of my forehead.

◆

JALOUSIE

◆

By Dennis Bartel

In recent months, I have been wrestling with questions of jealousy. Naturally, I've wrestled with them in the past (perhaps like you, kind reader), but now to my eye-opening surprise I believe I've begun for the first time to gain the upper hand on this maddening vixen of emotions. Comes with age, I guess, though as recently as my thirties, when many of my illusions faded like steam on a bathroom mirror, I never believed it possible that I could do anything once my balls were caught in the malicious grip of jealousy but flail with instinctive rage. Stop, look, and listen, I now tell myself, there are other ways to respond. Quietness is the master of the deed.

My own quest to conquer the green demon had its earnest beginnings around Labor Day, when my wife and I were eighteen days in Nassau, the turquoise Atlantic twenty feet from our cedar terrace. For two weeks our bodies became saturated with heat and our appetites for debauchery flourished in Nassau's environment of cultivated decadence. There is something about the vast blue horizons, sun-baked salty air, mega-alcohol (mixed with assorted substances), and beaches full of butt-naked young women that will bring out the island dweller in you.

Something wonderful happened. Let me first explain that in the past few years my wife has required a level spoonful of closed-eyed fantasizing and a daub of lubricating gel in order to engage in marital duties at irregular intervals. I'm sure I've showed the same enthusiasm.

◆ **105**

But get this: after two weeks of Nassau's aphrodisiac heat, and a decade of marriage, we rediscovered eating one another, with relish. Imagine that, kind reader. It's the same sort of thing that travel ads try to insinuate but can't quite say outright. My dear wife was juicy as a peeled peach.

The final days of our stay got a little pleasurably warped, which for Nassau, as I suggest, is a *raison d'être*. (It's the "ass" in Nassau!) My wife, a rightly celebrated flirt among all who know her, somehow silently communicated to me that it might be exciting and interesting if I were to watch her be ravished by another man. One time only, then we would flee back to our safe haven of home. Not even an exchange of last names. Just her with a strange and handsome Joe— and then, away!

One afternoon during a passing squall we sat in our favorite thatched hut of libation, Meloy's, when this idea of thrilling badness took root in my consciousness. I had one hand wrapped around one of Meloy's smart-bomb mai-tais, and one hand tucked brazenly into the denimed crotch of my dear wife, who sat upright on the next stool. (Maybe it wasn't so brazen in Nassau.)

"That man you've been flirting with over there," I whispered, holding my gaze on a neutral object, a low-hung, two-blade fan turning leisurely. "I think you should fuck that man, with me watching."

"Funny," she said, elongating her spine like a cat. "I was thinking the same thing."

By mutual agreement we dispatched her to open negotiations with the sandy chap, though from the look of their opening exchanges—as outside in the courtyard rained drummed on the banana leaves—it was apparent to me that negotiations had already progressed far. His hair was cut short like a New Testament convert. My dear wife was wearing, as well she should, shorts cut immodestly up her thighs. (Maybe not so immodest in Nassau.) Just before she brought the long-jaw fellow over to meet me, she took hold of his index finger, which rested on his knee, and ran it along the frayed hem of her shorts, emitting her coquettish laugh, tickling herself with this foreign hand.

The act was enacted in our beachside bungalow, on our round, satin-sheeted conjugal bed, which as I well knew was plenty big for athletic sex. It went much the way we envisioned it at Meloy's, thanks largely to the gentlemanly accommodating manner of our new friend Jan the Norwegian tourist and his condom-equipped stoked stovepipe. And perhaps the point is that as I sat across the room watching, slumped in a bamboo chair and utterly helpless, with nothing to hold on to but my erection, as my own dear wife, her fine legs in a clench, shrieked from the delight of another man, I began to sense the presence of answers to the deep conundrum of jealousy.

We returned home. There may be marriages that routinely operate at such a treacherous level of passion without suffering viscosity breakdown, but I've yet to know one, so over the next weeks, nursing again on our respective routines, our passion subsided to a manageable level. We still banged hard and loud one night a week, or one morning a weekend, but nothing on the order of Nassau.

And yet, while I cannot speak for my dear wife, my senses had been re-awakened. *I wanted.* So I proceeded to—what?—how best to say it? Shall I say it with a shake of *scandale romantique*: "I took a mistress"? Or perhaps the more modern and mundane: "I began an affair"? The faintly criminal: "I engaged in an adulterous liaison"? Let me say it like this: "I was blessed by a casually introspective young woman's interest in learning more about the ways of eros, and who viewed me as an acceptable proctor."

Colette, pronounced not with a long English "o" but in the French manner, as in *calin*. Her gestures are like arcs drawn in the air. There's a high-born quality about her; whether high-class or high-being depends on her mood. A dark-haired beauty with Camp Fire Girl eyes and a trace of Euro-trash in her aura, Colette chose me. It's not that I deny culpability. What I mean is others choose Colette (many others), then she makes her pick. Perhaps they, like I, took pains to disguise the ardor of their yearning. We maintained composed faces and courteous postures. We grinned, though not too broadly, and offered non-threatening endearments. Perhaps. One thing is certain: we all thought that this lovely Colette's *derrière* is nature's most perfect shape.

And she picked me, oh smiling spirits, though why me, or for how long, I don't know. What I do know is that caressing Colette's pale hips as I rock my sweaty cock in and out from behind is akin in divinity to the turn of Degas' wrist as he dabbed a brushful of ecru on a canvas.

Colette lives on a meandering little street on the upper floor of a seventy-year-old rehab, a stone's throw from a coffee bar called The One World Café. Her beamed boho pad is tastefully outfitted, containing the essential audio-video-culinary components. Over the months I have largely absorbed the rent for Colette's chic hideaway. This financial circumstance is not as haremesque as it may appear. I happen to know that Colette does not make sufficient wage for one of her *nécessités*. She has some hype-hawking job at a Society or Association which she invariably belittles, when she speaks of it at all. "Working in an office," says Colette, "it is like being in primary school, yes?" Her job pays hardly more than a child's allowance, so near the end of each month, as she and I are comfortably in a fully clothed embrace, I whisper, "Colette, my sweet, may I help you with . . . things for next month?" She honors me with a small nod. Later, in her presence, I place on the kitchen table an envelope containing money that I have drawn at intervals from an ATM—usually between three and four hundred in all (hardly the monthly for my new Accord), sometimes more. Not another word is said about it.

The drive from my home to Colette's is twenty-five minutes; twenty minutes from work. Consequently, *rendezvous à l'improviste* are rare. But about twice a week we plan it right; that is, my circumstances and Colette's generous graces align and link.

This time, *chez* Colette, I am greeted at the top of the stairs by my stylish courtesan wearing an outfit suitable for in-bed or out—a white cableknit sweater that reaches halfway down her thighs. Her small round breasts have a vigor all their own. Her hair falls lazily across one eye. She welcomes me inside with a look of fetching promise, her lips pressed together in greedy anticipation.

Colette's mouth tastes faintly of the black cigarettes she favors. Kind reader, you may think this unappealing, but in fact the dark taste of Colette's mouth is acutely arousing to me, as if I were eating her very ashes. I want all of her, burnt or raw.

"Today," she says, "my horoscope said, someone of the opposite sex will say to you, you're fascinating but I'm slightly afraid of you. You are afraid of me, yes?"

At that moment I recognize the Debussy *Preludes* on the stereo, the CD of the old Gieseking recording I gave her. "I *am* afraid of you, sweet," I say.

Colette says this time she wants to leave on her baby-blue canvas shoes.

"But I adore your feet," I say.

"Then you should adore my Keds, too, yes?"

Part of Colette's studied coquetry is her way of ending most sentences with the word *yes*. I'm very fond of this little affectation, particularly when she wishes to play, as she calls it, "L'antioch," in which I am to ask her at each critical juncture of our lovemaking if I may proceed.

"May I slip this off you, dear Colette?"

"You may, yes."

"Your nipples, my sweet, they're so erect. May I suckle them?"

"Yes, you may, yes."

Keds or no Keds, Colette's nudity sets off in me a medieval fervor that soon reduces me to a worshiping grovel. Often, as now, I have dropped to my knees before her and mustering all my resources of sincerity professed, "Colette, Colette, you incredible female creature, I worship you," and licked her pale belly. I am hardly ashamed. It is no more than true.

"Dear wonderful lady, may I bite your ass?"

"You may, *oui.*"

A short round of cake-eating leads us to a state of high sixties.

That is, first we get high (as in snow-capped) while listening as Gieseking's fingers run zigzag fillips over Debussy's *Preludes* like gusts of leaves blown along the sidewalks of Montmartre cafés; and second I take Colette to the floor, a black carpet, on my back, my tongue anointing the plush bouquet of my *chère amie,* my nose buried in her dark pungency. Meanwhile, she is holding up her end of matters.

After a splendid few minutes (that will live in my memory like a long soak-it-up stare at a Sisley Port-Marly landscape), Colette frees her lips momentarily, maintaining a steady stroke, and offers this intriguing insight: "You know what I like about you, *Denis?* You fuck me like fucking were invented for women, yes?"

Colette's use of the salty obscenity is *exquis.* She saves it for the moment that most requires it, never during chat, then she speaks it with a casualness that tries with coy futility to mask how badly she wants it.

I take her *bon mot* as an unsolicited vote of confidence and swell with pride. Summoning a response, but unwilling to extract my tongue from my lovely friend's perfumed lubricity, I manage only "Hmmm."

"Tickles," she laughs, and gives me a retaliatory nip with her teeth in a spot that is at the moment unusually sensitive. "Fucking *was* invented for women," she says, making known to me by her tone that she understands hers is not an original thought, only the most *à-propos.* "You think so, too? For the purpose of giving women pleasure. Men are only willing functionaries, yes?"

Reluctantly, I stop licking her, for this is quite a mouthful from my reticent *petite amie* and deserves a response from her proctor. I think a moment. What can I say? Nothing comes to me. I say the only word that my mouth, fixed in a smile wide as three keyboard octaves, will enunciate, sending my voice arching over the crescents of Colette's naturally perfect *derrière.* "Yes."

Colette adds something else, but what I'm not certain. I like to think it is "And you function *très bien*" or something along those lines of positive reinforcement, but, alas, her words are garbled (or perhaps some French I can't understand).

◆ ◆ ◆

But the subject is jealousy, not lust. As you may guess, kind reader, I have my suspicions that Colette enjoys the amorous company of other men who possess equal *désir*. Or perhaps *suspicious* is the wrong word. It smacks of possession. In fact my very lack of possession is one of the things that excites me most about Colette, besides, of course, her fragrant Cézanne pussy.

And why shouldn't she enjoy other men? I can't say the thought is entirely unpleasurable. Nor can I say that I am in any position to ask her not to. She tells me without my asking that she has friends whom she often sees. It's always plural, friends, and non-gender-specific. She goes drinking with friends. She sees movies with friends. She attends poetry slams with friends. She has friends for dinner.

Recently the presence of all these friends began to cause me to envision *les choses négatives*. Needing to know (and, I like to think, as part of my efforts to expunge the blot of jealousy from my being), I edged close to the lip of bad faith. I spied on Colette.

Shortly after lunch, I called her at work. "May I come for a visit tonight?"

"No, I am so sorry," she said. "I have already invited friends over to dine. I am sorry. But I cannot call them all and cancel, can I? It would be rude, yes?"

That evening I arrived at The One World Café, across the street from Colette's. The scene was familiar: black walls, rough-hewn floor, the sort of chunky wood chairs you find in university libraries. The menu was written in colored chalk on a standing sandwich board. The paintings had price tags.

A coolly poised thirtyish woman took my order across a marble-top counter. She wore a dark flowered dress and a lank black sweater. When she turned around to the shiny chrome works to froth up an espresso machiatto, I studied the line of her narrow hips. How natural it seemed to me to picture me working my thumb up this anonymous java lady's anus, my fingers plumbing her unfolding lotus, as I scarfed on her chewy macaroons.

As she turned back I shifted my gaze to the glass jars of coffee beans displayed on the shelves. I paid for the espresso and stuffed a five in the Tips jar by the register, figuring I might be in for a long spell of surveillance. I didn't want java lady to get fidgety about me being here too long. I took a table near the sidewalk window.

For decoy I had brought the Sunday *Times* crossword, but I tried not to take my eyes off my task for long. On the stereo a woman was singing songs of past sins and barely repressed anger, with only her acoustic guitar to accompany her. A billiard table upstairs made itself known.

My wait was not long. As I finished my brew, Colette's friends arrived, pulling up in a simulated combat vehicle, four men dressed in typical hip-hop fashion of choreographed sloppiness, and a woman wearing ridiculous granny glasses with purple lenses, very unColette. Whatever else it may be, I thought, four men and two women is not a sexual combination. (Unless they were to "dine" on club sandwiches tonight, but, really, how likely was that?)

Minutes later one of the men stepped out onto the small balcony of Colette's bedroom and smoked a cigarette as he watched the street below. He leaned with slacker contempt on the wisteria-entwined railing. Something about the man's posture brought me to the conclusion, though it was not without a small measure of disappointment, that for tonight at least Colette's friends were just friends. I left The One World Café for home, where after two glasses of merlot, a demi-jay and the slow onset of tumescence, I sought my dear wife's flesh.

All of which, however dreadful of me, is no more than true. Kind reader, I hereby stand before you accused of fascination with the world. And I plead guilty. Which is how I feel most of the time. Guilty.

But the subject is jealousy, not guilt, and besides I don't feel so guilty as to miss an opportunity the next day at dusk to stand before the large mirror in Colette's beamed bedroom as she takes pleasure in my insistent, digital massage of her clitoris, like a smooth pebble in olive oil. Colette is small in my embrace, and never so *complaisante* to my touch as when she is nude. The white Easter-time sunlight through the muslin-curtained window catches her white throat.

"My sweet, Colette, my precious love, tell me that you fuck the friends who come here to see you. Tell me how you like that man inside you."

Colette speaks not. She is already immersed in the Monet deep greens and blues of orgasm. She comes to the touch, then gasps her breath back, issues forth soft pointillist sounds and is ready and eager to come again. ,

No one is counting, but I estimate that in our hour together Colette's *petites morts* number about a dozen, most of which occur while she is *à la broche*. Afterward, instead of driving home immediately I walk across the street to The One World Café. Sitting alone, my hands cradling the warmth of a tall latte, I muse philosophic on Colette's hypothesis that coit was made for the pleasure of woman. Has my darling *ingenue* provided a primordial clue to solving the mystery of the jealous sphinx?

Doctors agree: "Women are the higher form of the species." Where it comes to Colette, I am *en rapport* with doctors, and so I ask you: Is it not a small triumph over jealousy that I feel no pangs at the inequitable natural laws governing our respective pleasures? I know it's a stretch, but please follow me a moment. If I were lashed to the mast of the dark ship Jealousy, would I not be jealous of Colette's mythic immersion into the open arms of the orgiastic sea? Picture this: I am atop my *blanche* sweetheart, sunk to the hilt, both hands full of her Offenbachian-boppin' butt. Cancan, my *belle-fille!* For me it is *sans pareil.* But Colette! Colette is splashing about in a more unearthly sea of pleasure. Lolling back on her skull, she exposes her white throat to my sloppy tongue. The sounds she makes! "La ilaha illa 'llah." It is as if her conscious self were being bludgeoned by her own body. She seems to lose track of time and space. Kind reader, I don't mean to recite some sort of Watch-My-Brute-Dick routine. I've no doubt that, for Colette, mine could be Everyman's Dick. I only say this because it is no more than true. While I am granted the star-spangled grand finale, the pleasure that Colette derives from my bobbing and weaving prow is beyond my capacity to fathom.

I arrive home to the questioning eyes of my dear wife. "What are you trying to hide from me?"

"What?" I answer promptly. "I'm not hiding anything."

"Don't say no. I can tell."

I've no doubt that from the very start of my *affaire de Colette* my beloved spouse has suspected something was being hidden from her. Perhaps she's suppressed it, or not wanted to investigate. But now I see in her terrible eyes that jealousy has at last seized her. She *will* have an answer.

"Look at me and tell me you're not lying," she says.

I return her glare with my own look of questioning and concerned sympathetic confusion, though in fact the evil green glint in her eyes has sent jolts of arousal through my groin.

"All right," she says with finality. "I *know* you are."

It is time to go on the offensive. "Know I'm what? How do you know?"

"I'm not going to tell you how I keep track of you. Anyway I found traces of powder on the shirt you wore the other day."

"Traces of powder? You went through the dirty laundry looking for *traces*?"

"I was not looking for anything. I was washing clothes. Don't avoid the question."

"What *is* the question?"

"All right, I'll start with this one. Are you buying coke?"

I imagine my dear wife playing Sherlock, rubbing "traces" along her upper gum. "I am not buying coke. That was just from the other evening at work. There probably was a little on my shirt from that."

Having stalled the few seconds needed to develop my story, I explain, "I had some with Lee after work. He was celebrating something, I don't know what, I didn't listen. Things just got a little sloppy. It was the first time in a long time."

Lee, of the snakeskin boots and string tie, of the LEE patch on the back of his hitched-up jeans, of the habitual smirk, the racial jokes and the transparently secretive manner, Lee of Accounting usually carries a little fun dust, perhaps to relieve his deadening routine. My dear wife knows that now and then Lee will share. "That's all there is to it," I say.

"Is that really all?" says my dear wife, who appears to want to believe what I tell her.

And I tell her what she wants to believe.

And you, kind reader, please believe this: Among Colette's many enchanting *caractéristiques* is a guileless urge for unearthing eros, and it is my aim to lead her on all the archeo-sexual digs I can. On this evening Colette wishes to become versed in the double-edged delight of bondage. The moment I slip inside her door, Colette signals to me to tie her hands with a flannel shirt and render her incapacitated.

I help her out of her clothing (except the baby-blue Keds, again!) and tie her hands. Her narrow wrists are tightly secured. She says it pinches, so I tighten it more and this startles her. I take her in my arms and tickle her to see if she can get me to stop. She can't. I bring her to a tickle-scream, for the hell of it. Colette's screams are French and never overdone.

I glance about the bedroom looking for an improvisatory opportunity. There is one: a large satin-covered chair with fat arms, the kind you'd find Leslie Caron sitting in sideways, holding a martini aloft, her famous legs tossed in the air.

"My lovely Colette. I'm not going to ask you if I may do what I'm going to do to you. But I'll tell you. I'm going to turn you over the arm of that chair."

And so I do. Her pale back is curved gracefully as a Fauré *Barcarolle*. I press her face hard into the cushion and work my meat into her helpless pussy with little regard for niceties. "I'm going to fuck you, sweet bitch."

And so I do. Rocking in her cunt, side to side, pulling out, ramming back in, taking her with Berliozesque manliness. I reach and find her engorged clit and rub it fiercely as I pound her from behind.

Colette's muffled sounds are unmistakable. It is as deeply carnal and pleasurable as she's hoped; more, yes?

I withdraw and forcibly pull her from the chair and throw her on the bed and leap onto the bed myself and grab her pale fanny in the crook of my arm and smack it till it turns pink as a Caillebotte sunrise. Colette begs me to stop. "No, no more, please, yes?" I roughly turn her over, pinning her arms awkwardly beneath her. I climb between her thighs and draw her knees to my ears and plunge my Eiffel Tower into her *pièce rosée,* meanwhile plugging her ass with two fingers.

Colette's eyes are agape. She closes them in final surrender and begins a sequence of shuddering, cock-squeezing orgasms, as I fuck her and fuck her.

Later, she wants to go to The One World Café. Colette, who disdains exercise, seems always to walk with enjoyment. The mere action itself is pleasurable to her. We arrive. I am so glossed over from the ferocious cumdom that I take no notice of what *café* delights Colette orders across the marble-top counter from the same chewy java lady. We take a table near the window where she can view the evening's alfrescoers and passersby. At the next table is a woman with Coke-bottle glasses, marking up her Penguin Classics with yellow highlighter.

Colette doesn't say much at first, but prefers to sit smoking one of her black cigarettes and looking on with One World *condescendence.* The stereo drones with a bare-essentials band and its whiny, lit-rock singer. "This guy sounds like he's singing about the death of his grandmother," I say in Colette's ear.

Colette gives my comment the patient smile it deserves. She now re-retrieves the cigarette pack from her tiny bag and places it on the table, on display: Sobranie. Moments later she leans over and whispers, "I enjoy sitting with the man who has defiled me, yes." She shoves the unfinished cigarette into the ashtray with an uncertain hand. "You *are* a filthy man, yes, you."

Sensing a likely opportunity to advance to our next eros lesson, I sip my brew, then whisper, "You know in the *Kamasutra,* in India, they used to do it like they were having a fight. They hit each other.

Not hard, but with fists. And they shouted things. Like, 'Don't do it, you pig!' Or sometimes they shouted praise, you know, for your partner's efforts."

Colette smiles with her eyes, sipping carefully from the white porcelain mug with her very lips.

"And for some reason they also imitated the sounds of birds. Sparrows and doves. Cuckoos, parrots, birds like that. Even a duck."

"I like that. And you can imitate some birds, yes?"

"I can."

"Which?"

"My dear Colette, I mustn't give them away, not until the right moment."

Colette pouts her lips.

"But I can tell you one. I can imitate a little bird called a sora. It's a small piping sound. Very musical. A descending scale."

"What does it look like?"

"It's black and yellow. Actually, only the bill is yellow. But it makes two sounds, really. It also has a sound for intruders."

"Intruders?" Colette says with mock alarm.

"Intruders to the nest. When someone comes poking around, an adult sora stands on the edge of the nest and makes an explosive little *keek*."

"Do it," she commands with affectionate interest.

"Here?"

"Here, yes."

"Which sound?" I say, getting up the nerve.

"The musical one."

Above all else I want to please my *chère amie*. And so I put two fingers to my lips and begin *pipe pipe piping*. Luckily for me I get reasonably close, a soft mid-range sound. It seems not to register much upon others in The One World Café, thankfully. No one stirs. Too cool.

Then I see that my small aviary exhibition has raised another smile from Colette's lips. She touches my cheek with her fingertips. "You ask if I fuck the friends who come to see me?"

"Yes?"

"I now have an answer for you, *Denis* . . ." she lets her voice trail off.

And now I, believing these past months to have gained an upper hand on jealousy (of all things to believe!), must decide whether to ask my lovely Colette to finish her sentence.

◆

THE PHALLUS

◆

By David Vineyard

"I want to fuck you like a man," Lisa said in the darkness.

I lay stretched on my side half asleep, in that endless twilight between the deep and endless REM state and wakefulness. I lay facing away from her, looking at the red glow of the digital alarm through unfocused eyes, my glasses on the night table beside the bed.

I sat up on one elbow and turned. I could make out Lisa, her long dark hair spread out on the satin pillowcase she had purchased to protect her hair from mussing. Her large sloe eyes were half closed, her wide sensual mouth moist and parted. She seemed asleep. I must have been dreaming. I turned back over.

"I want to fuck you like a man, Jason." There was no mistaking the reality this time. She had a low, whiskey kind of Kathleen Turner voice that was seductive as hell whether she wanted it to be or not, a bass *pianissimo* whisper of husky and breathless craving. She put her hand on my naked shoulder. Her long fingers with their short clipped nails were cool on my bare flesh. I felt her move closer, the bed reacting to the shift in weight, her hair brushing my shoulder, her cheek against the point where the triceps joined the shoulder and neck. Her tongue stuck out serpent-like and tasted me. "Salty," she said. "Salty and a little bitter. Like a good gin and tonic, or a perfect martini. I like the way you taste. *All* of you."

I felt the heat and warmth at my core. My cock pressed against the soft cotton of the sheets. There was a pleasant agony in my balls. I began to turn over.

"No," Lisa whispered. "Don't move. Stay on your side like that." Her hand moved over my hip and weighed the shaft of my engorging penis with a gentle stroke that ended with a feather-light brush of the delicate eggs, tight and swollen in their pouch by the position I lay in. I leaned back into her, the points of her breasts against the sharpness of my shoulder blades. She had removed her gown. I felt the soft wiry curls of her pubes tickling the small hairs of my ass, her thighs fitting to me in a sinuous curve.

I let her work like that for what seemed forever. She played with the short hairs at the nape of my neck with her free hand, and then, freeing my penis before her dry-handed manipulation brought me to a climax, she placed her right hand on my hip and stroked my buttocks, ending by insinuating her fingers in the warm cavern of my crack, teasingly missing the deeper caress her touch promised.

She leaned over my shoulder, her lips brushing at my ear. "Jason. Do you think there's something wrong with me?" Before I could answer, she said: "I want to fuck you, Jason. I want to be the man with you. I want to feel myself inside of you, gripped by you. I want you to know what I feel when you take me and . . ." She seemed hesitant to continue, her words poured out in a sort of breathless stream of consciousness. "Jason?"

"Yes?" I felt a curious lightness inside of me, like butterflies dancing or sparrows flapping their wings.

"I went to one of those shops today. One of those places on Harry Hines. It cost me ten dollars just to go in and look. There were all these sleazy magazines, and these funny-looking rubber things, and this one magazine, there was a man who looked like you, sort of, and a woman—not a woman, a—transsexual—they call it TV, isn't that funny, like television?—she-he looked something like me, but she-he had a penis, and you—the man—was lying on his side, and she-he was—was—buggering—is that the word?—you—him—while I—I mean she-he masturbated you—him—it's only—it turned me on so, the idea of somehow being both things with you, and there was this counter, and these—he called them dildos—isn't that a silly name?—under the glass, and—some of them were so big, they were frightening, but there was this one, it was just like you, and this man—just a kid, not cheap like you would expect, just sort of bored—he was reading Henry James—really, Henry James in a porno shop—*Wings of the Dove,* I think—he was gay—Henry James—I've heard somewhere—but this man showed me this belt thing, and how this—this dildo fit in it, and he said a lot of lez—he thought I was a lesbian, I guess—a lot of gay women and men bought them for play, and it was so much like you, and I was—I was wet, just thinking of it—I was wearing my white shorts, and I was so scared a spot would show, and yet the idea sort of—it was on sale, and this man said that lubricant wouldn't hurt it, that it was silicone, and that it would retain warmth just like flesh, and give just like flesh, and—"

I was barely breathing. I felt her hand touch my penis again, and she seemed reassured that I was still swollen with want. All this time she had been moving her open legs against my butt, one leg thrown over me, so that her humid sex was ground against the muscled curve of my ass, and spread a sheen of wetness over my buttocks. Her own breathing was deep and regular.

She moved again, away from me for a moment, and I feared she was embarrassed, and pulling away, mistaking my silence for anger or disgust, but then I felt her against me again. She touched something cold and heavy to my arm.

"Feel it, Jason. Warm it in your hands."

I took the object. I was surprised by its weight. It was a cylinder wider at the bottom as it reached a flat base, and tapering until it flared out again at the rounded pyramid of the head. Was this how I felt to her? Was I so large? I used one of the new, larger condoms, but I never really thought before what size might imply to the person on the receiving end. The butterflies were dive-bombing in the pit of my stomach.

She took it away for a moment, then brought it back.

"Kiss it, Jason. Like I . . . Lick it, please." I could feel the want and need in her voice. Her body against my back was hot, molded to me by our mutual glaze of perspiration, and the flow of her urgency.

I let her guide the thing to my lips. She held my head gently between her hands. I let my tongue run around the point of the rounded head. She had wet it in her cunt, and it tasted of her, the way I must have tasted a thousand times to her. "Oh, Jason, oh, yes," she whispered as I grew bolder, and when I took the heavy helmet of rubber in my mouth she shuddered against me as if it was really her own flesh.

She rolled me half onto my belly, pushing her satin pillow under me, so that my aching prick was caught in delicious bondage by my own weight, in that satin trap warmed and scented by her long hair. I felt like a virgin. I was a virgin. The way she had been a virgin, trembling on the brink of this experience. There would be pain. Could I stand it? Should I let her, she might hurt, tear me, should I stop this now, stop this silly game . . . and yet . . .

She pulled away again, and from her movements, the lifting of her hips, the increased speed of the breathing, I knew she was fitting the harness to her waist. I could see an image of her, with that incongruous erection of sinew marring the gentle curve of her perfect lines, extending from the convex rise of her bush and the fat sweet rise of the mons, and somehow in that vision of her, the thing was part of her, part of some hermaphroditic Lisa, and in that same vision as I lay under her, supplicated, waiting, I was no longer me, no longer *only* me, but somehow part a woman, and open and vulnerable yet beckoning and hungry for the flesh that would impale me—be conquered by me.

Her hands seemed stronger and more masculine than I could ever remember. She spread the cheeks of my ass, and teasing with her finger, lubricated the area liberally before working her fingers inside of me, opening me to her touch, reaching and bringing sensations I had never felt, never explored. It was as if that tender spiral of small brown and pink muscle, those most profane of all lips, had melted and deepened to her caress and probing. As if the pleasure that had always been focused in the erect flesh of my cock, and the weight of my balls, was now moved to a deeper part of me, and yet at the same time as she massaged the oval bean of prostate, sensations of orgasmic release moved the length of me, and drops of pre-cum tears moistened the soft caress of the satin pillow.

I tensed at the weight that suddenly rested at the opening, my cheeks pinching that rounded helmet that seemed now more a part of Lisa than alien and inhuman fiber. She seemed to sense the fear, the apprehension, stroking me and cooing as a rider might a nervous mare about to take her first stallion. I was Jason, but I was also Lisa and Lisa was me, and this link of mock flesh was a tangible living bond between the new duality of our lust.

The pain was unendurable, yet even in that, in that searing fire of undefiled rupture, a great warmth and fullness lifted me beyond the spasm of pain, and try as I might, sphincter muscle screaming, my breath ragged and uneven, a huge hot turd of something tearing apart my secret and shameful mark of vulnerable and forbidden delight, I could only moan, begging Lisa not to move, not to go deeper, yet not to pull away. Above all not to pull away.

Then gradually the pain gave way to a deeper warmth and fullness, and as she moved inside me and began the *faux* dry humping of this androgynous fuck, I was carried away to another space, another level, and when she spread more lubrication on my cock it was again tight and yearning, and we were connected in a single long rubber rod of muscle that ran through her, through me, and was now frigged in the increasingly desperate movements of her hand, so that in that last long moment, when the pressure of that intruding arm of flesh falling away in the tunnel of bowel so teased and abused the prostate at its mercy that a searing prodigal fire ran up from the seminal vesicles and seemed to run from Lisa into me, so that when the flame shot through the length of me, and I bucked against her, and her cupped fingers caught the pearl drop copious jet invoked by her knowing touch, I could feel her, caught in the same orgasmic flash, at almost the same moment, and trembling so that I did feel her woman's orgasm in me, and she too felt the explosive male eruption in me, and I was part of the undertow of wave after wave of pleasure and near death just as she was caught in the epileptic contortions of male release.

Later she applied soothing ointments to the bruised and smarting chaste gate that had been a passage for us both. She weighed my once heavy balls in the palm of her hand, and kissed the still wet tip of my flaccid cock with a gentle brush of lips more affectionate than profane.

We lay like spoons, no longer the two separate entities we had once been, but somehow melded in a more intimate way than before, as if some ancient god of Greek alchemy had appeared and seeing us in our blasphemous embrace had touched us with Apollo's breath or Aphrodite's lips or lame Hephaestus' lightning, and in that instant transformed us into those mythic hermaphrodites who copulated in fantastic rut—less like human or animal than some magic creation of both and more. And when her touch and smell and the memory of our liberation came again, I turned to her, and was again that rutting beast of male seeking the endless solace of her womb, and yet we would both be something more whenever we touched from now on, as if that silly molded obscenity of silicone imposture, that unfeeling and preposterous phallus like the decoration of a Pompeiian tomb, had become an enchanted wand, and we had fallen under its spell. Cursed and blessed at once, by whatever gods of eros might have taken pity and found amusement in our insistent and clumsy coupling.

◆

CHESTER AND THE
CONSCIOUS CUCKOLD

◆

By Spider McGee

"You're liberal Democrats, both of you. I've got your number. And you, you're an auditory voyeur." This from a man I treated for sexual abuse of his daughters. Successful treatment. The kids got through the trauma, the violation of trust, the twisting of physical pleasure and emotional pain. His wife had loved him, and loved him, and loves him. She loves the kids, too, and felt their pain. It was hard for her, and she didn't make it easy on him. There were legal consequences, too, a little jail, a fair amount of house arrest, in a tiny little apartment, of course, since he wasn't allowed to be in his house where his daughters lived, whom he had abused, in distorted parodies of parenting turned lustful.

Treatment wasn't easy. Beneath the perpetrator issues were victim issues, as there often are. His mother had died recently. He cried, later. At first, he just stared. Sat in his rocking chair and stared. Thinking, remembering, trying not to feel.

He was the oldest of four boys. He tried to protect them. His mother tried to protect them all. But if she stepped in to protect the kids, his father would turn on her. She'd catch the beating. And he couldn't stand that, the sight of his beloved mother being beaten. So he did the only thing he could do. When he saw rage, he captured it, gathered it in like a sandwich, and ate it for lunch. What angry man can resist a smart-aleck? Especially one who acts like it doesn't hurt, like he doesn't care? So he had taken his father's beatings, and he had survived, though not unscathed, and his little brothers had survived, and his mother had survived, and now she was dead.

His oldest daughter became a teenager, a young woman almost. She was growing up fast. A varsity cheerleader as a freshman. No one could remember the last time a freshman had made varsity cheerleader. The other cheerleaders liked her, accepted her, treated her as a friend. She was younger, of course, but she fit in well with them, seemed comfortable with the kinds of things the older girls were doing, starting to do the same things, liking it, feeling good, fitting in.

He loved her, he was proud, he was scared, he was hurt, he was not unscathed. He was her father. Some things he knew about, her mother didn't even know about. He just wanted the best for her. He loved her.

He didn't administer discipline the same way his father administered discipline, no. Not the ritual beatings. Not the struggle to see if father could make son cry, if son could defy, withstand, take it like the man he wasn't. But he did administer discipline. He was, after all, the man of the house. It was his job, not his wife's. He loved his wife so much, would never do anything to hurt her, and knew that the one who disciplines is the bad guy, and he would never want his wife to have to be the bad guy. He loved her.

So he administered the discipline, from the very beginning. A spank or two on the bare butt. You don't hit a kid in the face, or the arm, or the leg, or the belly. You hit a kid on the butt, when you have to, because kids need to be disciplined sometimes, as much as you love them and hate to hurt them. Disposable diapers are just too thick; they've got to feel the hurt, much as it hurts to hurt them. Training pants are thick, too, can't have them. Just a couple of smacks on the bare butt, almost seems like the sound of the smack is as important as the sting.

The girls get older, the discipline basically stays the same. Looking back, he could see how it became a ritual, not like the ritual beatings he took, for his brothers, his mother, himself. God no, not like that, but he had to admit, the spankings became a ritual. And the hard part, the part he hated to admit, my psychological treatment of him was court-ordered, but he wasn't court-ordered to find the truth, but he did, we did, at least some of it, and he became more and more conscious of what had been going on, and maybe why it was going on, though who really knows why what goes on goes on? He had to admit that, as the girls got older, it was a benny—civil servant talk for benefit—that they had to bare their butts for his spanking, and it was a benny that they had to strip entirely, and wait, wait, bent over, for him to spank. He didn't spank them for pleasure, just to turn him on, no, he only did it when they needed it; when they needed discipline, he did it to help them, as fathers must administer discipline to their children, to help them. But, he admitted, as the girls got older, it was a benny to see the sweet curve of their asses, the swell of their budding breasts.

And the waiting, waiting, that must've started just after his mother died, when he was spending a lot of time staring, not crying, thinking, remembering, trying not to feel. Trying not to feel lonely, alone. As hard as it had been for him to take the beatings, to take them without crying, he had taken them, and his brothers had survived, and his mother, and now she was dead. It had been worth it, though, hadn't it? What else could he have done? But it wasn't enough. The beatings he took had hurt her, too. Still, she survived. And now she was dead. He loved her, he missed her, what else could he do?

So as an adult he was still the smart-ass kid who diverted his father's rage to himself, and took the beatings, and tried not to cry, and always used smart-aleck remarks to get his dad, and got good at it, got him good. He's the one who told me that all little boys want to be fire fighters when they grow up, and the ones who never grow up become fire fighters. Simple as that. Never grow up. Then the arrest, the jail, the newspaper, the humiliation, the house arrest in the tiny little apartment. A room, a fold-out bed, a rocking chair. Sitting, rocking, staring, thinking and remembering, trying not to feel. And treatment, and seeing, and admitting, and feeling and crying, god-damnit, real man-size crying, and feeling, and seeing, not quite accepting, but seeing, and growing up. And his wife loved him the whole time, tough and tender, and despite what everyone told her, almost everyone, she waited, and worked with him, and he made it, and they built a life together once again, and house arrest was over after a couple of years, and after all the treatment and the family therapy and everything else he had a wife and a family and he loved them, and he'd grown, grown up maybe.

Then today at the stress debriefing I was doing for the rescue personnel involved in that four-year-old boy's ugly death, his name came up, and it surprised me. I hadn't thought about him for a while. And thinking back, how the hell did he keep his job? Must have gone as a misdemeanor, or maybe they withheld adjudication, or whatever. I remembered he'd been on restricted duty, then eventually approved for full duty, probably on my recommendation. And he could do it, I knew. He'd grieved his mother's death, his childhood, his own malfeasance, and he'd admitted things, and grown, and could love people without hurting them. His name came up when somebody said something about emergency workers, how you see something that disgusts you, it does, like it does anybody, but you've seen everything, haven't you, and often as not you make a joke about it, like Jensen, you make a joke of it.

Then on the way out with the other debriefer, seeing Jensen in the kitchen, and Jensen calls out, "You're liberal Democrats, both of you." Still the smart-ass. And I'm thinking, liberal Democrat, like that's something to be ashamed of, and I'm not ashamed. Hell, if I could have thought of something the other side of a liberal Democrat, I might've said it. A card-carrying member of the ACLU. I'd supported the ACLU for years in spirit, though I don't think I'd gotten around to a donation until I heard the phrase about the card-carrying member, and I said to myself, I've got to get one of those cards. Like when I finally got around to burning my draft card, tripping on LSD, listening to Jimi Hendrix play *The Star-Spangled Banner*, and it was gesturing, maybe posturing, because though draft cards were still required and what I was doing must have been a federal offense, they weren't really drafting people anymore, just missed it, and nobody ever asked to see my card after that, I never had to decide whether to say I burned it while tripping on Jimi and blotter, or the dog ate it. But when I told that story to my wife's lover I could see that he, being a little younger and not getting a draft card to burn, had missed something.

She said something, "I burned my bra at . . ." or "I burned my bra while . . ." Something. It was clever, I think. Though I don't remember. Maybe it was the beers, or the distraction, sitting and drinking and shooting the shit with my wife and her lover, and maybe with his wife, too, though I think she came over later.

A liberal Democrat, a card-carrying member. Okay. But, an auditory voyeur? What was that, a Listening Tom? What was he saying? That while I was treating him, helping him, getting him to look at all that stuff honestly, to learn and grow, and maybe grow up, to learn how to love without hurting people, that hearing about his daughters bending over, the shape of their asses, the swell of their budding breasts, were bennies? And the beatings his father administered, too, and his struggle not to cry, and his mother's death, and the sitting and staring and thinking and remembering and trying not to feel, how much of those were bennies? An auditory voyeur? Maybe, sometimes. Yeah, sure. Maybe he's not grown up, but I think he's right, he's got my number.

So what about this bit of sitting around with my wife and her lover, drinking beer and telling anti-war stories, making the world safe for hypocrisy? Any bennies here?

She's happy. I love her. I remember times she wasn't happy, took meds for it for a while, which helped, with some not-too-god-awful side effects, but side effects, still, and when she went off of them, thinking about it for a while, would she need to go back on them? What's a bad mood, a bad day, depression? And this afternoon, she says, coming out of the grocery store, some guy asks, "Has anybody ever told you, you have a beautiful smile?" And her thinking, yeah. And thinking about what she was smiling about, seeing her lover for lunch, and me having a date canceled with an is-she-gonna-be-my-lover-someday, and her saying, come along, we were just going to have lunch today anyway, he's got a lot of work and can't take much time off today, and the three of us sitting around, eating and talking about a concert he invited us to, and this time I said no thanks, you guys go ahead, him and his wife and mine, and she said okay, I will.

Dropping him off back at his office, and going to mine, and having some time, and having good sex, and feeling good afterward, real good, all the way through, then working with the emergency workers so the stress of working with that beautiful child's ugly death won't turn into a lasting trauma for them, then seeing her at the bus stop, as we pick up our beautiful child, seeing her smile, and hearing about the guy who noticed her smile, has anybody ever noticed what a beautiful smile she has, and I'm thinking, as she did, yeah, somebody noticed.

So am I a liberal Democrat? An auditory voyeur? A participatory voyeur? Or just a man in love? Like Jensen, I'm playing the hand that's been dealt. And all I know is, she's got a beautiful smile.

SALAMANDER LOVE

If all I had to do
was undulate my body
and rub my nose on yours
and drop my spermatophore
on the floor
and you'd get so hot
you'd go down on it
with your cloacal lips
and draw my sperm cap
up inside
to fertilize your ova
and we had lots of larvae
in the spring
and lived to see them
transform
into adults just like us,
our silent salamander love
would bring us
self-renewing
amphibian bliss
and save us from this
l o n g   d r a w n   o u t
and ultimately
fruitless
fuck.

George Held

WOMEN IN CHARGE

◆

TIT

The breast that wins the prize
in nationwide wet teeshirt contests
is the one that stands UP the most.
That's easy.
It's just a few years old and
hasn't been sucked enough
yet.

She drove her pickup into the station,
jumped down, brushed the dark tail of hair
out of her eyes and slammed the cold nozzle
into her gas tank.

Under the thin cloth of an old white teeshirt
her tits were loose, weighty.
Old tits.
But the nipples were still sharp.
One breast—larger than the other—
hung an extra inch down her arm, almost to the
elbow.

Attendant slides over to her.
You shouldn't be goin' around like that, you know.
Aren't you 'shamed
in public without a bra?

Nah, she says.
I USE these.
Use 'em for what? he asks,
leaning on the pump.

She looks up, stares him straight in the eye.
I put 'em in men's mouths, she says,
to get myself off.

And ever so often
I bleed oceans of thin caramel
into the mouths
of babies.

Anne L. MacNaughton

AT THE THRESHOLD— THREE DIFFERENT BEGINNINGS FOR ELLEN AND FRANK

By Jane Underwood

#1: Decisions, Decisions

One afternoon after she had been dating Frank, her new lover, for two weeks, Ellen found herself in an enviable quandary, trying to decide whether to meet him at the door fully clothed, partially clothed, or totally naked.

"If I open the door fully clothed, the advantage is that he will have to undress me," she thought. "That would be nice. But if I open the door without a stitch on, then he could unzip his pants and fuck me without any preliminaries. Then again," Ellen vacillated, "if I open the door only partially clothed, well, it's hard to predict what might happen. I do like surprises."

She decided to call him up and leave the following message on his answering machine: "Frank, I've been thinking about seeing you tomorrow, and I'm beginning to get very excited. I'm having some, *mmmm*, delicious thoughts.

"I was wondering, Frank, if maybe I should just forgo putting on any clothes at all before you come, so that when I answer your knock, you'll see me naked right away and get a wonderful hard-on. You could unzip your pants, turn me around, bend me over at just the right angle, make me hug the door frame—then reach down and pull my legs apart, causing my pulse to race because of the embarrassment and desire I'd feel, knowing that you were about to fuck me. But I'd only want you to fuck me for a few seconds, Frank—just long enough to set the tone for the rest of our, *mmmm*, lunch."

An hour later, Ellen got Frank's response on her answering machine. (Frank, a real estate agent, always returned his calls promptly. This was good business.)

"Ellen, it's Frank. I think your idea has tremendous potential," he said in his best businessman's voice. (Ellen could hear his employees talking in the background.) "And doing it that way sounds like a perfect beginning. I'll see you tomorrow at noon."

She listened to the message three times. Each time, she imagined their doorway encounter a little differently, and each time, she became a little wetter between her legs.

#2: A Dance for Frank

One night, after she had been dating Frank for six months, Ellen met him at the door wearing her sex goddess mask. The face was white, with features painted in black and red. The expression was impassive, contained. With the mask on, she found it easier to wear her most revealing lingerie—that which usually seemed too exotic for a mousy bookworm such as herself. (She possessed what someone had once called "small, intelligent breasts.")

Ellen loved the look of surprise on Frank's face, mixed, of course, with amusement, when she swung open the door. But underneath the surprise and the smile she detected what she most wanted to see: a ripple of curiosity, a glimmer in his eyes that was a reflection of the mystery hidden behind the mask.

It is always good to remind your lover, after having been lovers for a while, that your layers are infinite—that no matter how familiar you may have become to one another, there will always be more to discover.

She said nothing as Frank entered the hallway. Instead took his hand and led him to her bedroom (where they usually undressed eagerly and without ceremony).

She motioned for him to lie down, and after turning on some music, went to the foot of the bed where she stood facing him. The room was dark except for the flicker of a red candle burning behind her. The aroma of jasmine curled through the air. Her shadow fell onto the wall behind his head, and when she began to undulate, a witchy woman emerged.

Frank had never seen Ellen dance, and the expression on his face was priceless. She grinned behind the mask as her hips swayed in a seductive circle. Then she began with a wicked bump and grind to pull her long satin gown up, up, up.

She had expected him to be shocked, and he was. How could Frank have known that beneath her shy secretarial exterior there lurked an X-rated exotic dancer? Where did she come from? And why had she chosen to reside in Ellen's body?

This was a question they would both explore, later, after the show.

#3: Sneak Preview

The moment she opened the front door, Ellen announced, "I want you to put your cock up my ass before we leave for the movie." Now that he had been fucking her for over a year, Frank wasn't the least bit surprised by Ellen's, well, how should he put it—candor?

"I'll lean over the edge of the bed," she continued. "But we have to hurry—you know how I hate being late."

Before he could answer, Ellen had unzipped his fly and slid her hand—into which she had already poured some warm oil—down the front of his briefs. He wasn't expecting the oil. The sudden sensation of it made him instantly erect.

He followed her into the bedroom, his awakened penis pushing out against his pants, and watched as she kneeled on the hardwood floor, positioning herself over the edge of the bed.

"Could you please pull up my skirt?" she asked, in a vulnerable voice that took Frank by surprise.

He reached over—amazed and amused at Ellen's rapid shift from assertiveness to docility—and tugged her tight leather skirt up around her waist.

"Now could you pull my panties down?" she said in the same submissive tone.

He pulled them down and stared at the white skin in sharp relief against the black garter belt and stockings. Then he licked his finger and reached down to moisten his favorite of all Ellen's orifices.

"Not yet," she protested. "I'd like you to put some oil there first. Then I want to show you something."

Ellen reached under the bedside table where she kept her vibrator and pulled out a small, shiny black butt plug. As soon as Frank had finished lubing her, she reached around and began to push the plug up her ass.

When it was all the way in, she moaned and began to pull it out. "It feels so good, Frank," she whispered. "Whenever I do this to myself, I'm thinking of how it feels when you fuck me up the ass."

He reached down then, clasped his hand around hers, and helped Ellen fuck herself until she let her hand drop. Then Frank took over. When he had her good and excited, he withdrew the plug completely and said, "Would you like my cock now?"

"Yes," she said anxiously, "but just for a minute, okay? This was only meant to be a preview. You know how much I like previews, Frank."

Yes, he thought, as he ran his hand lovingly over her soft bottom. Ellen always makes sure we get the most for our money—first the preview, and then the delightful double bill.

NOT SO TENDER IS THE NIGHT

◆

By Mario Dworkin

It had sounded so easy.

My agreement was that I would be naked and commit to answering whatever questions she asked.

The studio was dark but for the glow of sandalwood candles around her and a canister floodlight that shone down directly on me. I felt like I was sitting in a cage of bright light. I hadn't expected that, and it made me uncomfortable. Suddenly, I was feeling far more exposed than I was prepared for and that alone made me nervous.

I fidgeted on the pillows she told me to sit on, waiting for my eyes to adjust for the light. She didn't say anything for quite a while, and I felt pressure grow around me. How many women were sitting there? I wondered. The room was warm, and within moments I felt droplets running from my armpits down my sides. My feet grew clammy. My stomach felt too big. I could hear whispering and an occasional snort of repressed laughter.

I leaned back and crossed my legs and then hurriedly uncrossed them, certain that that posture must make my balls, hanging down below my leg, look absurd.

When she proposed this night and told me what it was I would have to do, I laughed spontaneously. It seemed so silly. I am a big man, used to feeling in charge, especially when I am naked. The women I know like that. But I had never expected to feel this vulnerable when I'd agreed to do this. Before I could ask her if she was joking, she said, "Are you afraid then?" What could I say but "Who are you kidding? Of course I'm not!"

Instead of telling her to sit on her feminist orthodoxy, I found myself intrigued by the idea—or more accurately I was intrigued by her inner fire. It turned me on. I admit it. I wanted her, and I was willing to act as target practice for her minions.

She runs a theater group that focuses on feminist issues, and is renowned in this city as a woman of some small but significant successes and large appetites. Her pronouncements on men are well known, as is her reputation for playing a female Pygmalion with younger women. Of course this has confused plenty of people. Some claim that she's a card-carrying lesbian while others swear to her clear and unbridled lust for men. But in the lingua franca of sexist verbiage, she was a hot number and no matter which side your chromosomes were on you wanted to dial it.

Working on a rehabbing project for her, I came in expecting to dislike her, to be rubbed the wrong way by her attitude and her dykey little haircut. But I was surprised. I liked her instantly and she seemed to reciprocate. She made it clear that we were working as equals and, after a week of rapid progress, I asked her to meet me for a drink. She looked surprised, peering at me over the top of her heavy art-girl frames, her green eyes wide for a fraction of an instant as she scoped my face.

"Oh yes," she said softly though I caught a bit of a smirk. "That might prove to be an exploration well worth pursuing!"

She insisted on meeting at a quiet bar so we could talk. She looked great, I remember that very clearly, with those great green eyes sparkling. She has remarkable lips, which were very red and very full and despite my best intentions, I was already imagining them feeding on various parts of me. I tried to tell her how good she looked, but she regarded me suspiciously and kept the conversation on me. Where was I from? What did I read? Why wasn't I married? What were my politics?

Each time I began to tense up during this inquisition, she coaxed me back with a joke, a great one-liner or her disarming smile. She invited me for a nightcap at her place. Her tone was effusive and breathy even, and I went fully expecting to explore various and sundry parts of her. I thought to myself, "She's not so tough."

But instead of fucking me she insisted on stripping to our underwear and talking—intensely, passionately—on the difficulties of communicating man to woman. She largely blamed men, which I find really annoying, but she looked so good sitting six inches from me, legs crossed, breasts moving freely beneath silk, I didn't argue too vehemently. Her scent made my nose tingle and run. I could clearly see the outline of her sex under skimpy panties and after a while, I took satisfaction in the fact that I could see the silken triangle swell and dampen. I let go enough to feel myself get hard.

When I finally objected to her line of reasoning, which had her back in time mucking around with the Venus of Willendorf and the female earth goddess, her tone took a sharp turn for the scornful. I found myself on the defensive.

"Men have no idea what women put up with. Women put up with all that male ego and childishness because most of us think we need you. So we serve you, thinking you have the key to our happiness—love, security, family, children, all those fundamental values. We think we'll earn those things by putting up with men, and then providing maid service on top. That's why so many women are glad to act as trophies. Let's face it, sex to most men is the equivalent of squirting jelly into a donut."

I countered that men also have to put up with a lot from women; that we, too, find ourselves pressured by male roles and the demands of the women we choose. But somewhere, somehow in the fog of the wine, the late hour, my desire and her cunning, I found myself arguing that I could handle any criticism a woman could hand out and I could handle any questioning situation she could propose.

"How about nude? An inquisition in the nude. Could you handle that, Mr. Testosterone?"

"You can make book on it," I said, bravado hiding the fact that I was already quite drunk.

"How about if I sell tickets on it? Women only," she said. And when I snorted, she shot back, "You're on, big boy."

"Sure thing," I said, feeling that I was being put on. "I have nothing to hide." We agreed that nobody could touch me, but that I had to answer all questions truthfully no matter how invasive.

And then we put aside what seemed to be our clashing ideals and made deep, grinding love until the sun came up. Then we collapsed into each other's arms.

That next morning she did not let me forget what I had agreed. I tried to dismiss it, but she was adamant. I came up with a compromise. "If I do it, you'll have to provide naked maid service for a whole weekend at my place. No underwear," I insisted. She smiled broadly.

A month later I found myself sitting before her and the others— just how many I couldn't tell exactly, but I don't think it was more than twenty—feeling very foolish and small. I was suffering from a performance anxiety I had not quite expected. I heard light laughter around me, and felt my cheeks and ears flush.

"So!" her voice thundered over an unnecessary microphone through speakers all around the room. "Here we are. Are you ready to begin?"

Looking at my feet, which seemed quite yellow in the light, I stammered a quiet "Yes."

"What!" she roared. "I can't hear you! Speak up or we'll never get anywhere here." She was so loud I felt her voice echo in my rib cage. Every bad interrogation scene I'd ever watched on late-night TV came to mind. Instinctively, my hands crossed over my groin. Rude laughter rose in my ears.

"Trying to hide something? Don't bother, it's almost too little to see from here," she said in the most sweetly derisive voice I'd ever heard.

I looked down, and she was almost right. My balls appeared to have retracted completely and my dick was so shriveled nothing showed but the head. Suddenly I felt so enraged I rose from the pillows, turned on my heels and headed for the exit. "Find somebody else to crucify, you castrating bitch," I murmured under my breath.

But there was something so nasty in the way she said "I *knew* you couldn't take it, none of you ever can," that I wheeled around and stomped back to the little island of cushions in the middle of the room. I sat back down and folded my arms over my chest, glaring out into the darkness.

From then on she was unmerciful. She was expert in pinpointing all my vulnerabilities, cutting them out and laying them out in front of everyone. I was an insipid lover, my ego was as inflated as the Goodyear blimp, and my politics were as anachronistic as the clothes I wore. I belonged in a time-warp—"back in the Summer of Love with your beads and patchouli oil," she added nastily. My concept of women, she cackled, hadn't metamorphosed much beyond Lassie's mother.

"What's wrong with June Lockhart?" I wanted to say but thought better of it.

Furthermore, I had no class and couldn't taste a good wine if it bit me. She then rooted around in my failed marriage and nailed me for all the things I know I'd done wrong. When she got through alluding to my "congenital insensitivities" with all the women I'd ever been intimate with—"no wonder you are incapable of forming any meaningful relationships"—she started in on my thinning hair and the spare tire I'd formed around my waist of late.

"You know you guys really have some nerve. Your physical ideal of women is usually a cross between a fifteen-year-old and Bambi."

"Bambi's mother," I corrected her.

"Shut up!" she hissed. "You don't think we notice your crow's-feet, not to mention your less than Grade-A ass? Women just aren't as bent out of shape at the sight of imperfection as you assholes generally are." I could hear several of them murmur agreement on that one.

"Lucky for you," I managed to say in a small voice that emanated from somewhere in the Lower Caucasus.

"When your dicks don't salute you the way they used to, you go out looking for fresh meat. It's because you guys can't handle the sight of your own sagging flesh. What makes you think we don't notice the effects of gravity either? But then we know what teensy weensy little egos you have. If we *dare* let on that we've noticed you're not quite the

Apollo of our eye anymore, your response is to go find some chicklet who'll barf up the lies you want to hear. And she'll be *so* thankful for the experience of coddling your three-minute egg." From the tone of her voice, she could have talked small animals into vivisection.

"Yeah!" a couple of women shouted aggressively in unison.

"Don't you think the term 'chicklet' is rather lacking political, uhm, correctness?" I mustered, hoping to cut the vitriol. During the last few minutes, my hand had been resting on my three-minute egg as if to protect it from cracking open. She picked up on that, of course.

"Do you play with yourself a lot?" she asked, clearly changing her tack. "Bet you do."

"What?" I was stunned by the question. "Of course not." There was considerable tittering in the room.

"Afraid you'll get hair on your palms or something? Judging from the tufts on your head, I'd consider it. At least you'd have hair *somewhere.*" The glee that erupted made me think she'd scored a field goal in overtime.

"What do you do, pray for deliverance from blue balls?" someone shouted from the back of the room.

"Wait a minute, I didn't say I *never* masturbate. I do . . . on rare occasions." I certainly did it when I felt especially horny, couldn't get laid or had trouble sleeping. But I sure wasn't feeling like making a public declaration.

"You're a liar," she said sharply. She sounded just like the second-grade teacher who had caught me playing with myself behind a bush at recess. I felt humiliated having been nailed for something I obviously couldn't deny. And here I was again with my pants down, only several decades later. Unlike my second-grade teacher, my interrogator's voice took on a honey-dipped there-there tone.

"It's okay, baby, we all do it, don't we?"

"No shit, little beaver," someone shouted while the rest of them cracked up.

"The only difference," she continued, "is that you do it when you want a woman and don't have one handy. We do it to get away from men—to have a few minutes to ourselves or to finish what some dude has started and can't finish."

"It'll keep your coat shiny," heckled another one of my persecutors.

There was more tittering. "In fact, we wish you guys would do it more often. Don't you think that if men beat off more often the world would be a much better place, even if we would find the stuff all over our shoes from having to jump over puddles of it? It would significantly reduce the world's testosterone toxicity. Can I get a witness here?"

Several women voiced their assent. "I'm convinced so many men are violent because they've got testosterone-overload. They think they're born with little steering wheels in their hands or worse—boxing gloves or machine guns. Pump it out daily and this would be a mellower place." The women's laughter was egging her on. "Besides, if more of you did it to yourselves more often, it would make you better equipped to touch us."

The women were laughing and murmuring and moving so much that I could make out shapes on furniture arranged in a semi-circle around me. "It's really not hard to bring most women to orgasm, you know. You just have to *feel* what you are doing when you touch us. Yet men seem to have a problem with simple touch. If it's not too rough, it's too predictable or too soft or too little. Maybe more men would know this if they would play with themselves more often."

She paused to let all that sink in, and I could hear voices whispering behind her.

"So now I'm asking you again," she said. "Do you play with yourself a lot?"

"What's a lot?" That got me a little laugh, and I began to feel a little more relaxed until she asked, "What do you think about when you do it?"

"Lots of things." I was hoping to put her off, but I could not.

"Like what?" she insisted. "Do you have your basic variety pack of fantasies involving cheerleaders without panties, truck drivers with hairy forearms, nubile pole vaulters from Sweden? Do you get off reading stroke books, *The Story of O* or *Little Red Riding Hood*? Do you consult the notches on your bed board and remember how so-and-so's nipples hardened at the sight of you, how one had a vulva that could blow smoke rings, or that memorable butt that hovered over your face until you could see all the way to China? I mean what turns you on?"

Her questioning made them all laugh and it took nuclear-level restraint on my part to keep from making a crack about one of those references. But then I remembered where I was sitting. I cleared my throat.

"I like to think back on women I have known who have taken great pleasure in having sex with me. Contrary to your apparent perception, I happen to greatly enjoy the fact of a woman being turned on and satisfied. I like to think of the way her face flushes, the smell of her excitement, the look on her face when she knows an orgasm is approaching. I can get off just thinking about how various people have looked when they were just about to go over the edge."

"So you like to look?" I wasn't certain how to respond and she read my confusion.

"It's all right to say yes. Women like to look, too. Did you know that? Tell them," she said of the women in the room.

As she spoke, she rose from her chair to walk behind me. I turned to follow her with my eyes, but she indicated I should face front and answer. I said yes, and she stepped close enough to put a hand on my shoulder.

"Yes, we like to watch, too. Do you mind if I touch you like this?" I thought it amazing she'd ask after what we'd been through.

"No," I said, although I had a gut-tightening feeling that I knew we were about to kick this event to another level.

"Good. I for one very much enjoy having a man lie next to me and stroke himself until he squirts. That makes me *very* hot. I especially love to see a strong, self-possessed man feel really vulnerable. Do you understand?"

"Yes," I wheezed. I held my breath.

"I think you should try to make us all see that." Her hand moved up my shoulder and was met by the other at the back of my neck, which she began to massage. She leaned close to my ear. "Show us," she said in a voice that sounded like an almost plaintive command. "Do it for us here and now." Her whisper in my ear sent shock wavelets down my spine all the way to the base of my balls. I could feel myself begin to stiffen.

"Good," she cooed. "I forgot to ask you if you use your left hand or right." She put her tongue in my ear.

"Right," I mumbled ridiculously.

"Go ahead," she said. "Show us." She dragged her nails across my chest and pinched my nipples so that every hair follicle on my body saluted. I reached down and felt my hardness, the contours of my circumcised head. A clear glistening droplet had already made its debut.

"I knew it!" she said louder. "You are a show-off, too! You like to feel on display, don't you?" She passed her fingers under my nose, and I knew they had been plundering in her own luscious parts. I said nothing, but bent to my task. If they wanted a show, I decided, suddenly feeling defiant, I would give them a show to remember. My juice would arc toward them in perfect symmetry and rain droplets of warm come all over them.

I felt a surge of power roll through my body. I rose on my knees as tall as I could get. I wanted them to see it all. I turned so they could get different angles. I was conscious of my eyelids being half-closed, of my chest and leg muscles being taut. I liked how I felt in my hand— long and hard and ready.

When she slid her hand down my back, over my butt and down to caress my balls and gently finger what the Chinese so elegantly refer to as a "starfish," I roared past the point of no return. After a deep intake of air, the seed of a tumultuous orgasm bounced at the pit of my balls and reverberated around the deepest corners of my guts. I heard myself roar and felt my hips rock back and forth to launch a spasm that was far beyond my control. It sent me sprawling backward over pillows as if I were holding tight to a flailing fire hose that rose of its own accord to point at the ceiling. I heard gasps as I flew backward and shot up toward the floodlight.

That was two days ago. I'm still trying to sort it all out. I remember her leading me through a pleasurable gauntlet of cheering women, hands caressing every part as I exited the room. I remember falling into a bed. I remember her kissing me and whispering in my ear that the male sex of the species had hope of evolving.

At this point, I don't know about evolution. I am having vast, quick mood swings. I go from feeling like a satyr on a roll to the biggest twerp in town. But I also know I can't wait for her to fulfill her end of the bargain.

Preferably on all fours with her butt up in the air and me holding the feather duster. It's only fair.

◆

THE REMOVER
OF OBSTACLES

◆

By Frieda Madland

It was the last time she would play around with elephant-headed deities. Calling upon the Remover of Obstacles had been a rather bad idea—at least from the standpoint of invoking gods. But it really had been the fault of the anthropologist. He was the one who had told her of Ganesh, son of Siva and Parvati—"the one formed from the rubbings of his mother's body."

She and the visiting anthropologist from Delhi, had sat next to one another at a dinner given by a mutual friend—a lover she now claimed to "only fuck by phone."

"It keeps us from totally destroying each other," she explained. She could tell he was titillated by the way his earlobes flamed. Clearly, she had provided an oasis from his symposium on Ethnographic Dialectics.

"A vestigial act of your more larval days I presume?" he said, confidently. "Or is this what you Americans call safe sex?"

She ignored the question. "Quick, tell me how to say 'I love you' in Hindi," she whispered, eyeing another across the table from them. For the moment, it chilled her immeasurably to imagine the man with the ponytail across from her, naked and on all fours. He was an arrogant art dealer known to pounce on anything post-adolescent. Anyone like that deserved to be tested—or at least hog-tied, she decided.

"That depends on what you want," said the anthropologist, clearing his throat. "Are you concerned about obstacles?"

"You could say that," she said, looking across the table. "It's always something—blackmailing girlfriends, incontinent dogs, kids who need braces."

"Then you must, quite simply, make a wish and invoke Ganesh. The danger, of course, is in getting carried away and losing your head," he said in mock concern. She watched as he then slipped his card in the side pocket of her blazer.

Indeed, it had been quite a while since she'd visited the dark gods, gone supine, fucked herself into a stupor. It had been a millennium since the last carnal embrace. Almost six months. She stared at the art dealer, closed her eyes, and silently called on the Remover of Obstacles.

When she opened them again, she was met with a wicked smile from across the table.

She got a taste of him all right.

In the elevator, the dark-haired man with the ponytail told her to stay away if she expected "the usual."

"I don't fuck the usual," she said sweetly.

"Who said anything about fucking?"

He was right about that. Back in his loft, it was she who eventually ended up on all fours.

"So, okay, it won't kill me to be a love slave for a night," she said when he told her to remove her clothes. He flung some harness at her to wear—a symphony of leather straps lined with mink. She refused. "I can't deal with furs, okay?"

What she hadn't expected was having to watch him fuck art girls all night. His endurance, she had to admit, was remarkable. Every half hour or so, a new one appeared, wearing the same black leather dress slit down the back for easy access. One, in particular, had gravity-defying tits, legs to her neck, and chewed gum while her priapic prince pumped away. The rest, it seemed, had neglected to wear any underwear, which, in retrospect, she considered a nice touch. He did, after all, collect minimalist art.

But what drove her to distraction, more than the capricious use of his cock, his fingers and variously, a candle and a nozzle from a bottle of Dom Pérignon—all liberally smeared with butter—was the blindfold she'd eventually been made to wear. A man or a woman had then bound her to a chair and stroked the insides of her thighs with a miniature feather duster. Only later, after she'd been made to present herself to him, kneeling and on all fours, did she notice that her inner thighs were wet to her knees.

She was getting rather used to this bondage business, but at dawn, he dangled her underwear in front of her and announced he was calling her a cab. "I don't know about you but I have to go to work in a few hours," he said.

That had killed things, all right. The liar hadn't remembered it was Saturday. Still, the smell of sex tingled in her nostrils—that unmistakable odor of raw dough she had always linked to the smell of men.

"So, do you suppose that was a gift from the Remover of Obstacles?" she wondered aloud in the shower, gently soaping all those tender buttons that had been forced to salute all night long—to no avail. She practically felt ready to straddle fence posts. "This is probably what I get for invoking what's-his-name," she thought, burying an undulating finger inside herself.

Unfortunately, she had forgotten about the piano lesson. She had slept only a few hours when he arrived, punctually at eleven, bearing the two things she detested most—jelly-filled bismarcks and carnations. It made her wish he'd been forced into early retirement, preferably back to Cologne and numismatics. Still, he knew his Kurt Weill and that alone was worth enduring the way he said *liebchen*.

But she should have known things would be different this time when he began with Chopin. She should have guessed because he had once said that Chopin lowered his resistance to women with "smooth, calescent thighs." Hers, she knew, were at the point of grasping and incinerating tree trunks.

And then it happened. Somewhere halfway through a prelude, he crawled beneath the piano and nuzzled his large furry head under her skirt. With his teeth, he tore off her lace panties, and slithered a warm and probing tongue between the soft, persimmon lips of her pudenda, moving with the precision of a metronome.

"This probably means we'll be skipping the Weill pieces," she thought, her cheeks on fire. She continued until she could no longer endure the sound of her fingers on the keyboard.

When he resurfaced and took his place beside her again, his wet lips were the color of fuchsia and his gray and black-flecked beard glistened like the matted muzzle of a damp schnauzer. Even his glasses, she noted, had steamed.

"Ich habe keine Ahnung, Liebchen . . . What can I say?" he shrugged. "The old boy brings me to my knees every time."

"Some piano lesson that was," she said, talking to herself and crawling into bed after he left. "My God, it's as if I have no resistance—no taste. What would happen if someone were to say, 'Have a nice day?' I'm liable to embarrass myself on the bus in front of . . ." and she thought of leather boys with nose-rings and civic-minded socialites on their way to volunteer jobs. She thought of calling the anthropologist to discuss the problem. A nap, however, seemed more pressing.

But her sleep left her little peace. No sooner had she drifted off than she found herself in a monastery surrounded by an entire order of chanting monks. With appropriate instructions from an androgynous movie producer—she couldn't tell if the person behind the dark sunglasses reminded her more of Wertmuller or De Sica—the monks rushed toward her taking great delight in disrobing her.

She had to admit she rather liked the sensation of all those callused hands suddenly kneading her limbs with olive oil. But tying her down on a cold stone sarcophagus with their knotted rope belts was another matter, especially when they began penetrating every orifice with the curiosity of the uninitiated. She felt on gross display, helplessly restrained for the pleasure of a few rabid celibates who wanted nothing more than an earth-moving fuck but hadn't the slightest clue how to do it. An older monk took it upon himself to lick her nipples as methodically as a cat cleaning itself while another crouched over her, his tongue on a crusade to parts usually forgotten. One by one, they climbed on top of her, merely for the sensation it seemed of being inside of her.

They were oblivious of her protests and turned her over to pour more olive oil on her buttocks. Fingers and phalluses probed everywhere, stopping now and again for instructions from the producer who stood high up on a balcony barking orders in Italian. She feared it was something like, "Again! And this time with feeling!"

The phone rang and the monks evaporated. Rather than answer it, she lay on her bed and with cool fingers stroked her pulsating nether lips.

"What am I going to do! I can't go anywhere," she lamented, fearing that Monday would find her beneath the desks of all her male co-workers.

It was clear she needed help, and who else but the anthropologist would know how to undo the powers she'd incurred. She stood up to look through her jacket, remembering the long, delicate fingers that had slipped the card into her pocket. It made her suddenly wonder whether his toes were prehensile. She located the card and dialed the hotel.

"Well," she said when she'd finally reached him, "you've got some talking to do. This business of invoking elephant-headed deities merits further discussion."

"How about dinner? I'm in Room 1302."

"Look, honey, wipe the testosterone off your chin for a minute and enlighten me. Things have been a little problematic around here. For one, I've lost my head and become a runaway train," she said, mixing her metaphors for greater impact.

"Erotomania is curable over time," he said calmly, as if he already knew the symptoms. "Before long, you'll be back to your—what did you call it—telephone fucking? This American form of techno-lust."

"But when? I'm a little nervous at this point about public appearances."

"Enjoy it while it lasts. Ganesh is probably a bit vexed you chose him for purposes of lust. That's generally not his department. No doubt, he prefers to remove obstacles on a grander scale."

"Look, can't I take back what I said—do some reverse chant or something, burn a little incense? It's not as if I'm exactly in control here." She decided to leave out the details. "Know what I mean?"

"We will discuss the antidote. Perhaps there is a way you can pacify. . . . Room 1302." He hung up.

She had to hand it to him. The man was a cocky son-of-a-bitch, but he knew how to get a date.

His arrogance, she admitted, had stepped up her percolating lust even more, and she had been overcome with delicious thoughts of poetic retribution. Alone in the mirrored elevator on the way to his room, she had lifted her dress to her waist and adjusted her stockings. She hated garter belts but she knew how well all that imprisoned flesh could accelerate desire. She smiled and moved her hand inside her panties, bringing out a glistening finger. The more impediments to surrender, the better, she decided and dabbed a little wetness behind each ear.

When he opened the door, she was hit by waves of cologne and clichés. "You are more beautiful than I remember," he said after she'd finished sneezing. "You are a vision. It's no wonder Ganesh takes delight in tormenting you."

She noticed he was only wearing a bathrobe. "The nerve," she thought and blew her nose. "It's not going to be *that* easy."

But it was. When he joked and reminded her that her "febrile state" could be reversed by first straddling his face, she accused him of contradicting himself. Hadn't *he* been the one to invite *her* to dinner? And *what* about this Ganesh business?

"Why can't I put the brakes on my desires or more accurately, why don't I have any taste? And what am I doing here?"

He shrugged. "You invoked the wrong god—who knows?" He looked pleased with himself and poured them each a glass of champagne. "To determine your personal love coordinates is difficult since I don't really know you. Perhaps you are simply—how do you say it?—a bitch in heat?"

Suddenly, she felt imbued with a strange sensation, a kind of bipolar tingling that seemed to be phoning in from both her brain and from between her legs. She refused his glass of champagne and instead, opened the top of his bathrobe.

"In that case I don't want you to forget me," she said as he continued to hold both glasses. She circled his nipples with her tongue and bit them lightly until they had darkened into little erect buttons.

When she'd removed the belt to his bathrobe, she noticed his bronze periscope emerging from between the plaid folds, a glistening bead crowning its tip. She knelt and moved his cock like a lipstick around her lips. "Weren't we going to have dinner someplace?"

For the first time he had been at a loss for words, so she finished for him. "I guess I can wait," she sighed, rising before him. She took the half-spilled glasses of champagne from him and tied his belt around his head, covering his eyes.

"You don't mind, do you? I never fuck on a bed. It's too prosaic." She guided his hands up her dress and along the elastic and lace straps guarding her thighs.

"Why does this Ganesh have an elephant head? You never explained." She moved his hand inside her panties and forced his fingers to read her pouting lips.

"His father cut it off, not knowing it was his own son. Ganesh was guarding the door while his mother, Parvati, bathed. Is this important to you now?"

"Go on or I'll stop and call room service."

His breathing had become almost labored but he persevered. "To console Ganesh's mother, Siva promised to cut off the head of the first living creature that he came across."

"I think I can figure out the rest. But I'm a bit confused. If I'm to assume I've temporarily lost my head, doesn't this mean we have to cut yours off to fix me?"

His fingers ceased their spelunking and he moved his hand out to peek between the folds of his belt. "You are a curious woman. How you entertain me with your conversation."

She slid the blindfold back in place. "I'm also polyphasic—just you watch. I can do several things at the same time. Now before you fuck me," she whispered, sliding his bathrobe from his shoulders, "think of me as some kind of Rosetta Stone. Try to imagine what secrets you're capable of unlocking."

She led him naked to the bathroom, grabbing her purse along the way. "I like to see myself fucking in a mirror. I like to see my face grow flushed and my eyes distant and unfocused. I want to see my back arched and my ass coming to meet you. I want to feel those long fingers of yours tighten around my waist as you grasp and enter me from behind."

She had become, she decided, a regular Scheherazade.

His anticipation was palpable. "Your clothes, don't you remove your clothes?"

"I prefer you see me without my clothes afterward—when we can savor the pleasure of lingering in our juices," she said, quietly removing the handcuffs from her purse and hooking one side to the doorknob.

"As you fuck me, I want you to imagine what I look like. Pretend what it might have been like to touch, to feel, to smell the Dead Sea Scrolls before you were ever privy to their mysteries."

She brought his hand between her humid thighs again and raised a moistened finger to his lips. "A little taste before we start?"

"I must have you," he said, licking his mouth. She could feel his breathing accelerate and his chest expand. All systems were "go."

"And I must have you." She brought his hand down and snapped the handcuff around his wrist. "Foreplay," she murmured, placing a finger over his lips before he could react. "I want you to go mad wanting me." She kissed him lightly and slipped out of the bathroom.

Before she closed the door, she hung out the Do Not Disturb sign and reminded him once again to invoke the Remover of Obstacles.

Outside, the evening sky was as clear and blue as a Turk's Evil Eye. With a smile, she glimpsed the Pleiades and hailed a cab.

PLAYING WITH THE GODDESS

♦

By Sophie du Chien

I don't believe in omens. But all that sunshine and the promise of a break in my routine had me smiling at everybody . . . even on a jammed afternoon United flight into Washington D.C.'s National airport.

Barbara was the first person I saw when I emerged into the terminal. Her big brown eyes locked on to mine like radar.

I have known Barbara since college, when we were very close and about as intimate as two non-sexually-involved roommates could be.

Years, marriages, careers and half-a-continent have opened time and distance between us, but when she called out of nowhere one day, we picked up the threads no problem.

"I read a marvelous story by you and I had to call you up. I found you listed in information! Astounding!" Barbara always has had the ability to charm birds out of the trees. And so persuasive is she that I found myself agreeing to spending the week of spring break with her. Her husband was taking the two kids on a seven-day trek in Central America, and she was staying home for the pleasure of being single.

"So I thought of you," she said. "Please come. I promise it will be even more fun than back then. I want to get to know you again."

And so we did.

Talking to Barbara in person, I soon learned, is as natural and easy as on the phone. So easy that after I rediscovered the charm, my almost-forgotten sense of awe returned, too. Barbara is one hell of a go-getter. She looks great; her kids are fine, growing quickly; her career is still expanding; she loves living in Virginia and most of all she loves being the wife of the kind of man who will stay afloat in Washington no matter who sits in the White House.

"Even Pat Robertson," she says he said cockily.

Underneath it all, however, I detected a sense of anger in Barbara. I've seen it often in women of my generation. The world is their oyster, but something's not right in the sauce. There's an undertone, hard-edged and polished by years of experience, that unexpectedly goes on the offensive. I wasn't quite prepared when she brought up my late marriage.

"I don't know how you stayed with him for so long. I was beginning to lose respect for you. . . ."

Before I could fully register and respond, the warm glow returned to Barbara's tone. She said, "From travail, does experience grow. And in your case it's given you a new voice. A very interesting voice."

Barbara was surprisingly knowledgeable about and interested in my, you'll pardon the term, reputation. She said she was "interested in separating fact from fiction," and that I might just be the right person to help her in a project.

I said, "And . . ."

"A women's empowerment event. I'm still working on how, exactly, it would work, but the idea is to bring women I know, like, and respect together to tap into a deeper connection, to explore our goddess selves. . . ."

My snort was involuntary and she didn't let it stop her.

"Don't laugh, I mean this. I want to reach a new level of group intimacy and awareness. I want us to feel empowered by the realization that we can strip ourselves to our spiritual levels and feel secure, accepted and appreciated. I identify this state with my goddess self. I want to bring women together to experience this feeling. Yes, there is a strong sexual element in this. And I thought that if anybody I know might have some ideas on this, it would be you."

What could I say?

II

As she chopped broccoli, Barbara casually let it be known that she enjoyed her vibrator's company more than her husband's. I poured her a glass of wine.

"Do tell," I said.

"I started using it when we were apart for too long. Dick's work at State is important. It keeps him distracted." Barbara averted her eyes.

"Then I realized I began to look forward to going to bed with my vibrator more than with Dick. We used to have fabulous sex. . . ." Barbara sighed. "But that was years ago. Now what are my choices? I don't want to get involved with someone. With my vibrator I can relax completely, instead of always worrying about whether I am turning him on, or looking good, or whatever. Propped up on some pillows, I can let my mind go. I can go as slowly as I want. I can flip my own switch. This is not easy for me to say, so do you know what I mean?"

Her eyebrow rose in a way that flipped my switch.

After dinner, drinks, and more pointed conversation, Barbara asked me if I would dance with her. I was tired, but I admit it was fun. Especially the tango we did to Piazola. I, for one, wound up not only turned on but sweaty. Barbara had a solution. "How about a bath?" She said it seemed a good way to end a grand day. She presented the idea as a dare.

I unzipped and stepped out of my skirt. "I like the water hot." And at that moment, I noted, I was not clear on who was the spider and who was the fly.

When I got to the tub, Barbara already was in it, buried to her chin in bubbles. The tub was an ancient, four-footed thing, and although surprisingly long, it wasn't so big that Barbara could pretend to avoid touching.

I lay back, bending my head around the faucet handle, washing under my arms and across my breasts in ways I knew would make my nipples harden. This gave me Barbara's undivided attention. Sometimes I am an exhibitionist.

My hands stole down my stomach to the water line just below my navel. Barbara's eyes widened as they followed my fingers below rapidly disappearing suds. I must confess something else. At that moment I became very aroused.

Not just turned on; very turned on.

I lay so I could see her face through my parted knees. I wanted to shock Barbara, but what mostly seemed to be happening was that if I didn't stop, I'd lose control. So I stopped. Her eyes rose to meet mine and she gave me a smile that has burned itself into my brain. It's a late-night vision I trot out often.

I invited Barbara to spin around and lean back against me. "I want to get the kinks out of your neck," I said, trying to keep my game face on.

Wordlessly Barbara turned and scooched back between my legs, and put her head against my shoulder. Water splashed over the top of the tub. The texture of her skin was a surprise. Stroking her shoulder with my fingertips launched waves that radiated across her breasts, creating knobs at their ends.

Barbara's brown nipples. I remembered my secret attraction to her nipples, so full, so brown, so firm, so different from my own pallid, little, waspy pink tips, barely there at the end of my little cone-breasts.

Huskily, I told Barbara that back in school, I wanted her nipples on my breasts. There was an intake of breath when my fingers moved to squeeze a time-ripened nipple. It grew under my pinching and the feeling reverberated between my legs. Barbara made a sexual sound. Her hand emerged from the water to pull on her other nipple. When I stopped to watch, her other hand pushed me away to get to the nipple I had abandoned.

My duty was clear. My hand slid slowly and with clear purpose across Barbara's still-flat stomach. I wanted my fingers to feel like an eel swimming through moss. I resisted landing on the knob I knew I would find there as long as I could.

Objective as I am trying to be now, this moment was big for me. In college, Barbara's natural earthiness was a revelation for the Midwestern Episcopalian in me. She was smart, determined, always in control, and sexual. Many was the night I drifted to sleep listening to her and her boyfriend. I loved the smell of her, especially after sex. I think I idolized her ability to get what she wanted. Now, reading the depth of her need by the quickness of her breath felt very powerful for me. She surrendered herself to me. And she clearly was even more turned on than I was. She was trembling.

In her ear I whispered, "I want you to show me how much you like to show yourself off when you are hot. Lift yourself out of the water so we can see my fingers play with you."

She barely broke the surface, when a spasm took her. Her hips splashed down, rose and splashed down again, fingernails dug into my arm and a most wonderfully moist, guttural gasp passed her lips. A chestful of air came out and her hips undulated in another, grander spasm that sent more waves over the top of the tub. Her eyes rolled up. A note came from her that was so urgent, so compelling that I lost all control. Fingers still in her, I clamped my thighs around her leg, buried my free hand in my bush and ground myself and howled to meet her every note.

III

In the morning we were lazy.

When I awoke, I made as if I should go to my own bed, but I let Barbara talk me into staying put while she squeezed oranges and brought me the *Washington Post* on a platter.

I lay back into the pillows, pulled my knees up and drank in the sweetness in the air.

Next to me, looking at the ceiling, Barbara said softly, "When I came the last time, I was thinking that what we were doing was so good that we can't keep it to ourselves. We have to share it."

I had no idea what she meant, but the way she said it made me wet. It also gave rise to a powerfully aphrodisiac recollection, something that made me feel both aroused and guilty in a way that felt very familiar.

I remembered why. In college, I passed Barbara's bedroom door very early one morning. It was open enough for me to see her on top of her boyfriend, fucking him with an abandon that made them oblivious of me. For a moment I was frozen, then I realized that in their state, even if they noticed me, it wouldn't matter. *It would just make them hotter.* A phosphorescent heat from my pudenda ran up through my body and probably emerged from my ears as blue static. I nearly swooned as I staggered away, rushing back to my bed where I masturbated over and over. For months after, I fingered myself often to that blazing image of Barbara: head back, mouth open, hair whipping, hip-thrusting, bronco-busting, butt-squeezing, man-eating, earth-mothering sex . . .

My eyes must have drifted closed, because I didn't see Barbara's hand move under the covers. I felt them find the wetness seeping from my cunt.

I felt Barbara turn and even with my eyes closed, I could see her eyes exploring my face. She whispered, "I hope you can help me, Sophie. Please help me to prove that women can have hot sex together that is satisfying, renewing and completely safe."

She was toying with me. I knew it. I exulted in it.

"I know this isn't a completely original idea. Other people have done it way before me, Annie Sprinkle, Betty Dodson, maybe even Emma Goldman, for pete's sake. But now I feel it's important for *me* to act this out. I want to create an environment where women can explore their bodies together, celebrate their woman-ness and find our goddess selves. I want a supportive, erotic environment where goddesses can howl together; where we can be the witches we really are; where we can get off together."

Meanwhile, Barbara's fingers stopped their stroking. My hips moved on their own, up after Barbara's retreating fingers. She laughed.

When her fingers returned they landed knowingly. She tipped my head back and stuck her tongue in my mouth as her fingers strummed my clit. She bit my lip and then she whispered, "I want you to help me bring women here and get off together. You would like that, wouldn't you? Think of the energy, think of the exhilaration. Women together, getting off."

I thought and I came on Barbara's hand.

IV

On the morning of the big day a month later, I awoke in Barbara's bed with a knot in my stomach, and Barbara knew what to do. She greeted me with nectarine slices, coffee with warmed milk and a hug—wherein she reached into my robe to pinch a nipple.

Barbara had sent her family to a weekend-long Civil War re-enactment, telling them she was hosting a women's support group retreat. This, after all, was true.

Barbara said, "When we were in school I always wanted to do this to you—to touch your breasts and to turn you on. I thought you needed it. But I was afraid you would think I was gay. Now I say gay schmay; who cares? I'm more into what is inside heads than genders and whether the body looks tight or not. Right now, I want to do this with women, to see if it can be done. I know some great heads here . . ." Her voice trailed off and she laughed. "My God, I do sound like some hippie now! What I mean is these are women you will like. What we want here is a feeling of primal togetherness, the intimacy of eight spiritual nurturers really getting down to it. My idea is simply that the way we're going to get to that level today is through sex. I see all this as a clitoral convergence, a swampy mingling of primal oozings, a harmonic hormonal hoedown that breaks down all the barriers among us."

I laughed.

She said: "It's also going to be the hottest time you ever have had. Forget your short stories, you'll get novels out of this one. You'll be coming in chapters."

Barbara kissed me warmly. "When I ask for a volunteer to take off

her clothes so we can all practice massaging someone to orgasm,"
Barbara enthused, "it will be you."

And that's precisely what happened.

V

I should tell you that the women were an impressive group. The
former model and sometime actress I recognized immediately. Another
is a senior staffer for a conservative western U.S. Senator. One doles
out major arts grants. One is married to a prominent eastern liberal
congressman and is active in the Junior League. One is a nationally
known radio reporter. One writes for *Vanity Fair.* And the last one is a
jet-setting socialite from Chicago who raises funds for Republicans and
writes trashy novels. Sweetness, as I remembered calling her, and I had
met at charity functions many times in Chicago, but I was put off by
the combination of her attitude and her legs—I never felt that she even
noticed me.

Funny how so sophisticated a group could be so nervous. Despite
Barbara's warmest greetings, the initial moments were quite awkward.
The introductions were stiff and postures included lots of crossed arms
and legs. I began having serious doubts, which did not improve my
mood. I stayed away from Sweetness, who was looking positively pallid. But Barbara was ready for us.

She began the process of getting to know one another by asking us
all to change into exercise clothes and leading a series of stretching and
movement exercises to music. Barbara's family room was just big
enough to hold us all. She got us to break the ice among ourselves with
a series of trust-building exercises. We took turns putting on blindfolds
and falling into outstretched arms. We closed eyes and touched faces.
And then we went out for a group run around the university park
nearby as the sun set.

When we returned, the transformation was complete. People took
turns using Barbara's two showers. She put out raw vegetables and dip,
and conversation began to flow. I soon understood why Barbara had
selected these particular women. The oldest was fifty-two and the

youngest thirty-two. They were accomplished, articulate, united by an edginess and obvious interest in pushing boundaries, and once warmed, good humored. I wish I could say much more about them, but I have to be careful about revealing identities and betraying confidences.

Barbara lit candles and burned frankincense and myrrh.

Under Barbara's lead, the talk became quite personal. I was surprised at how easily we began talking about our fears and shortcomings, unhappy sexual experiences, STDs and learning to love latex and Nonoxynol-9 in the 1990s. At the right moment Barbara asked us to move close enough so that we could complete a circle, touching both the person on our right and left. Underneath the talk and laughter, a clearly perceptible sexual tension was incubating. Barbara encouraged us to take turns massaging one another's necks, calves and feet.

Barbara and I were the last to shower and we took ours together. From behind me she soothingly soaped my body and stroked away my final traces of doubt, which seem to have been lodged mostly between my legs.

"These women adore you, Sophie," she whispered in my ear just before she bit it.

Within a few moments Barbara had me lying on a sheet, gloriously naked, aglow in candlelight and surrounded by seven women for whom I knew I was going to have an orgasm. Around me floated the sounds of the Bulgarian women singers, with their endlessly woven harmonies. Barbara invited the women to move in close.

"Sophie," Barbara whispered soothingly. "Just close your eyes and let your body do your talking."

She began to massage my legs with warmed lotion. I lay on my stomach with a pillow under my hips, feeling wonderfully wanton. Barbara said, "In the beginning I was shy about my vibrator. I didn't want to admit to myself that I enjoyed it more than making love to little Richard, let alone discuss it with anybody else. But gradually it came out that a lot of women I know have them. More than I ever guessed—at least until I began finding ways to ask my acquaintances about it.

"Some clammed up, but what I love about you is that you all told me, at one time or another, that you have one and enjoy it and that the idea of being with other women while using them is a turn on. That's why I have invited you all here. I want to turn loose that impulse. I want your pussies to twitch. I want to conjure up primal images of musky amazons in you. I want you to find the goddess in you by journeying up the river of your juices. You don't have to do anything you don't want to do here, and if you feel like touching others, you may, as long as you use common sense. There are gloves and lube and Saran Wrap if you feel like dining in."

As she spoke, Barbara's hands moved steadily north and soon were kneading my butt. I found myself becoming quite aroused thinking about how I must look.

Barbara said, "And to help put you all in the proper mood, I am going to use this vibrator on my oldest friend here, Sophie." Even though I knew it was coming, when the vibrator touched me I jumped. "In college, I regularly fantasized pulling Sophie's panties down and putting her across my knees. I didn't want to spank her, I just wanted to pet her lovely round ass. And now here I am doing it for you all to enjoy. Doesn't she have a lovely pussy?"

I know I was enjoying Barbara's performance. Her knowing hands guided the vibrator around my elevated butt. Holding the vibrator head in her fingers, she let her hand settle for the briefest of moments deep into my parted legs.

It felt so good that when she abruptly withdrew, my rear squirmed. I wanted more. So Barbara turned off the vibrator.

"I get the feeling we're ready to try something a little more adventuresome. I want to invite any and all to begin stroking Sophie. She has told me how turned on she is by the idea of being touched by so many people. So please make her feel it."

In a moment, hands fluttered all over me. I wasn't sure how many. The touches all were different. Definitely exciting. "Good, good, good . . ." Barbara said soothingly again and again.

Then: "Now, Sophie, I want you to show us how you like to play with yourself while you lay on your stomach."

I hesitated; this I had not anticipated. Yet I was too turned on not to obey. I lay so I could bury my face in my left arm and slide my right hand down to press my clit against the hardness of two bony fingers. I held the fingers still and pushed myself against them.

I had a brief moment of self-consciousness then. The hands felt odd in such a personal moment. They were disjointed and separate in their motions. Then, Boom!, all the separate hands came together into one motion. The movement synchronized with mine. Time stopped.

I heard myself singing in a voice I almost did not recognize. Hands lifted me to my knees, pushed open my legs far enough to see my fingers glistening, and began to probe me. When Barbara bent down to put her tongue in my ear, I did not hold back. I had a crying, trembling, dizzying orgasm that stretched on and on and on.

And so began the most remarkable sexually charged evening I ever have spent.

VI

Some time while I was still drifting back to earth, Barbara gave everyone a vibrator and told them to strip to bra and panties. I remember the scene in snippets, women pulling off leotards and sweats. Barbara played gamelan music softly on the stereo and made them all kneel in a circle, left arms over right shoulders, and apply their vibrators. It was electric.

In less than a minute the group began breathing in unison and the sexual tension became palpable. Lying back and looking at them through still-blurry eyes, as spent as I thought I was, I found that the energy vortex they were creating was pulling me into their orbit. I, too, was breathing along. Soon, even without a vibrator, my pussy was calling me again.

The group swayed back and forth a couple of times and seemed to be trying to steady itself when the first woman gave in to the pleasure and began whimpering in a way that amplified the effect of her approaching orgasm.

It set off chain reactions in both directions around her, and the chain broke down into parts. Three women fell into one heap, and after a round of intense eye contact, broke for latex gloves and lube. Barbara came to sit beside me, and Sweetness followed.

I took Barbara in my arms and kissed her deeply. Sweetness spread Barbara's legs and laid a length of plastic wrap between them. As Barbara and I necked, Sweetness went down on her.

Across the room, the threesome was taking turns playing two on one. The other two women, the oldest and the youngest, were sitting on the floor facing one another knees to knees, faces inches apart, their own hands vigorously dancing in their pussies.

I know I'll not soon forget this scene.

I wish I could better describe the sounds in that room. I wish we had recorded it all. With gamelan in the background, female energy was in full bloom, full of chirps and gasps and grunts of individual and synchronous arousal and climax. The smell was unbelievable. The air was ripe with estrus. If a man had walked into that smell, he would have squirted spontaneously.

Barbara's latexed fingers found me and as we kissed we brought each other off. I confess I enjoyed knowing that Sweetness was frustrated because we ignored her, until I reached out my hand for her to rub on.

I am not sure how many times I came before I staggered off to sleep, but I'll bet that if we had been counting collectively we would have a *Guinness Book of World Records* entry.

In the morning there was some initial sheepishness, but then the humor of it all kicked in over our morning coffee and before we quite knew what we were doing, we lay on the floor in a heads-together, eyes-closed circle, skirts up and pants down, vibrators between legs, ohm-ing together with hands-roaming, giggling, panting, squeezing, grunting, and deep-breathing, in a visceral getting of the whole group off together, as one, erupting and cursing the darkness with the primal flame of nine women, together.

What else can I say? It was awesome. We left there feeling as if we had tapped into the electric mother lode. Some of us had more orgasms between Saturday night and Sunday morning than we have had in years. I know I was positively bowlegged when I dragged myself away.

VII

A month later, Barbara called me one morning. She said she was horny and asked if I minded talking to her while she played with herself. I got wet instantly, and I let her talk me into coming. It was my first real insight into why phone sex is as fun as it is safe.

We couldn't help but talk about Barbara's Big Day, as the event is now unofficially known in polite but progressive D.C. circles.

She said: "I love what we did for lots of reasons, some even beyond the obvious. For example, I told my husband, who was so green with envy and so aroused that he came before he even got his pants off. He's been passionate for a whole month. Big whippy . . ." Barbara bubbled. I encouraged her to go on.

"I even toyed with the idea of having a group jerk-off safer-sex session for couples, but fortunately I remembered that when men get off once, they're not worth much anymore. And when they realize their wives are having such a hot time, they'll get demanding like two-year-olds. Men would just spoil it . . ." Barbara's voice trailed off.

"Oh, I don't know," I said. "If they can get past their mine's-bigger-than-yours hang-ups, think how lovely it would be to have half-a-dozen men all squirting at once."

And the next thing I knew, Barbara had talked me into organizing a spermathon. To be honest I'm still not sure exactly how to pull it off. I'm not sure if I know six men who will agree to a circle jerk for the benefit of two curious women. But if I can find them, I know it will be fun.

A FINE MESH

You're with her now,
I see you—
at the movies—
your arm
snakes around
her stout shoulder,
the coarse hair
of her shaved nape
bristles through
your Shetland sweater.
Your jelly stomachs
bounce with each giggle.
You kiss
with pursed lips,
still chafed
from that harsh
Mexican sun,
gaze fondly
into each other's
passionless eyes.
She spits popcorn kernels
into your graying beard,
you drool mineral water
between her sagging tits.

Your bald spot glows,
her bushy eyebrow furrows,
both of your mustaches
mesh.
She hikes up
her pantyhose,
you scratch your balls,
I close my eyes
and yawn.

Marael Johnson

WOMEN
ALONE

◆

The Orgasm
poetry by Janice Heiss

Warm Silk
by Carol Queen

Close Encounters
of the Sophie Kind
by Sophie du Chien

My Life with Mr. D
by Lydia Swartz

THE ORGASM

Vagina lips are goldfish lips
Rising to the top of the bowl.
Shooting
Rising
Up
Unpredictable fish
searching for food.
Opening and closing
for air, for food.
Fat lips
fish lips
stirring out of mud.
Trawling,
taking collections
all the way up.
Gathering.
Old scavenger
of crumbs.
O mouth
Big mouth
Open mouth
waiting with thick, pink gums
to encircle its prey.
Picking it off.

Becoming bigger and
bigger,
breaking the surface.

Then, as easy as floating on your back.

Janice Heiss

◆

WARM SILK

◆

By Carol Queen

My skin feels like buttered silk after I come. I run my hands over my belly, my thighs, which are still pulsing and aching as if I'd run up several flights of stairs, and I swear I've never had anything so wonderful under my hands as this glowing expanse of my skin.

What I love about getting turned on when I'm alone is that it sneaks up on me. I run around all day, busy and maddened. I slump into a stolen few hours of solitude at the end, too tired to return phone calls, much less think about watching sexy videos or open dirty novels or pull the Hitachi out from under the bed. Far too tired to think about sex.

Yet I've been thinking about sex all day.

Every bus shelter poster of k.d. lang or Roger Craig in briefs I drove past today. Every short skirt and every luscious set of buns in bike shorts. Every sparkly-eyed girl or guy I waited on at Good Vibrations; every tattoo, pierced lip (or nose), pointy-toed boot, fishnet-stockinged leg, leather jacket, every tight dress, every pair of jeans faded where the cock rests or rises, every hole in a pair of jeans, especially where the white warp-threads lattice and half-cover the skin underneath; every red-painted mouth, the darker the better, and scarlet-lacquered nail, especially short ones; every curve of breast or curve of muscle under skin, in fact *every* curve; every pair of young lovers or old lovers or any sort in between in any gender combination, with extra points if the gender's indistinguishable; every teenaged boy trying

◆ **179**

to hide his hard-on, Catholic schoolgirl who's hiked her skirt up or put on lacy tights, boy's ear pierced by one gold ring, black lace bra peeking.

And at home! Too tired to notice the piles of books and magazines with contents devoted to sex, lingerie spilling out of drawers like it's trying to come alive, piles of pearly-cunted seashells, scattered around, all these femmy, flowery curtains; four kinds of lube, an antique Rosevill dish full of condoms (four kinds of those, too) and a box of sex toys that'd get me busted in Texas (and lots more in the closet); a set of steer horns, gleaming, pointed and priapic, red candles and ostrich feathers and my old white-enameled wrought-iron bed with enough bars to tie two or three people up, not to mention the big mirror situated next to it, all the scenes *it's* seen.

And all the pictures—of my lover (now and when he was a little boy); of my ex-lover when she was a little girl, holding the stuffed tiger she used to masturbate on; of my adolescent friend who's not old enough to think about (but I do anyway); of a turn-of-the-century dance-hall girl with a big snake; a young leatherman with a snake; Gustav Klimt's "Water Serpents"; two lovers twined around each other like snakes; of Madonna, Marilyn Monroe, the Virgin Mary, and angels with their wings mightily unfurled, and French whores and antique lingerie and old pinup girls; women in sailor suits who look like sisters but were probably lovers, holding hands in 1919; sisters photographed by Imogen Cunningham, which I bought at the art museum gift shop because their small breasts and curved bellies look just like mine though the shutter snapped in 1920, the year my mother was born; Betty Dodson's muscled couple fucking that people always think are both men (that's why I bought it); and of course my Dad, debonair in his officer's clothes and thin mustache who can be sexy now because he's dead and anyway the photo's from fifteen years before I was born.

And somehow it still surprises me when I find in my fatigue that I can't sleep; that the pillow feels too hot on my cheek, that I toss and turn. What I love about this turn-on is how my body won't let me forget I've seen all those things today, a thousand sex-signifiers that my mind has stored and my flesh and blood remember.

So when I finally run my hands over my skin I find I am already releasing into little tension-orgasms, not really comes but little flurries of shaking at the relief of my touch, and if I kept this up I would drive myself crazy: the more I touch everywhere else, the more my pussy wants it. (Sometimes this starts with me beginning to think about, no, just be aware of my asshole, and before long my body is a writhing snake with an asshole as its hungry mouth and nothing will satisfy me except to slide something in and fuck myself as slowly, at first, as I can stand, as hard and fast, then, as I can manage with my hands tense and trembling—but not tonight.)

Tonight my clit is hard already and insistent. My clit wants it. My skin is prickly in a lush way; my body is full of tension, the sex-tension so intertwined with the city-traffic-tension and too-many-phone-calls-to-make-tension and I'm-on-deadline-but-I-can't-think-tension that I can't separate it and all I can do is let it all work together.

I can reach my vibrator without turning on the lamp. Car head-lights cut flickering beams across the wall. I raise my knees under the blanket, make a tent for the Hitachi, switch it on. At first buzz my heels dig into the sheets and the muscles in my arm pump like I'm weightlifting. Then I relax into the vibration, descending into a valley before I start to climb.

The vibrator is on my clit as a tease. I don't come that way; I want my cunt full, if not with a cock or fingers then with a zucchini or a dildo or my dad's old hairbrush handle. I used to fuck the strangest things before I discovered sex toys—protruding knobs on furniture, anything. I love the wave of crazy horniness that washes over me when I'm alone, separate from any love or lusts I feel for a woman or a man, that makes me want to straddle bedposts. I love the frantic attempt to incorporate the whole world into my cunt, a juicy itch that can't possibly be scratched from the outside.

Tonight I fish in my toy box—not moving the vibrator, which purrs mechanically on my clit—and pull out the first cunt-appropriate toy that comes to hand. Two ivory plastic balls, the size of Ping-Pong balls but heavier, attached by a cord. Slicked with a little lube and pressed against my labia, I bury them with twin moans. Hearing my own sounds is more exciting when I'm alone and sometimes, though not tonight, I talk the whole time, at once lewd show-off and *ecoteuse*. But tonight I'm distracted from this—which is sort of a masturbation extra—by this tense and building wave of need.

I get so tense that tugging on the string is difficult, but each tug moves me palpably higher, whether it's rhythmic, as it is at first, or a wild and frenzied yanking. By the time I lose my rhythm it's too late. I am stretched out taut. The flexible neck of the Hitachi is bent nearly at right angles and its purring has changed to a labored, complaining whine because I'm pressing so hard. I hold the vibrator against my clit from the left, with my labia cushioning it. The nearness of orgasm brings my body up like a bow, the arc I learned about from Reich and my first girlfriend, the one who used to rub off on the stuffed tiger. It is an entirely different electrical current than anything else I know. I feel in and out of my body all at the same time. In that second when my body arcs up at its tightest—and only then—I understand what release means.

It no longer has anything to do with tight jeans and pictures of Madonna. I'm not even human, and that's the best release of all. I'm part of the electrical energy of the universe, part of natural laws, one with protons and electrons, one with satellites circling. It's the clear, breathless instant before my cunt starts pulsing stronger than my heart. It's the second I feel my voice get ready to howl. Tonight it's so strong I bellow like the stuck calf of the Goddess, and my whole body is spasming like my cunt—out of control, writhing and snapping, I feel like a necklace of pearls whose string has been cut.

The second time it's even stronger, and with the first squeeze of my cunt I gush scented sex-brine all over the hand that holds the ivory balls' string: the balls come squirting out with the nectar, and somehow, somehow I manage to switch off the hot and throbbing Hitachi. I am flushed pink and panting.

And slowly I come back to myself, begin hearing the sound of cars again, notice the moving shadows again on my wall. My awareness comes back without the tension, like warm liquid filling a hot-water bottle. I know it's been a big one because I feel the sweet muscle-soreness of working out. Best of all is my skin, wrapping me up, holding all the wet loose pearls inside, so alive to my stroking that I almost want to start over again, but no I've had enough for tonight—I'll put myself to sleep stroking this warm, buttered silk.

CLOSE ENCOUNTERS OF THE SOPHIE KIND

By Sophie du Chien

Editor dears,

I know that I am late this issue with my contribution, and I hope you can excuse me for being difficult to reach and for not sending you what you may have been expecting. But since I last wrote you my most significant experience was not with any of the men I have been interviewing. While each of their stories was moving, not to mention lubricating (You know who you are!), for me the most significant encounter was with a lawyer.

And in fact, this attorney is a woman. Since *Libido* magazine played a prominent part in what happened, I think you'll want to hear this story.

Our association began last winter when I received the following E-mail from a law firm that is well known in the East for its work on behalf of women's causes.

Dear Ms. du Chien,

Recently I was given copies of your work by colleagues who brought it to my attention because in the normal course of gathering information on First and Fourteenth Amendment issues they found your work and it thoroughly offended them. They targeted you as an example of the worst sort of selling out of women by a woman. And I must say that I, too, am appalled. Your writing, offered in the name of feminism, is clearly porno-graphic and thus serves only to harm the true interests of women. That it is well-written and funny only compounds that insult by perverting your God-given talent. Don't you know that by going far beyond normal stan-dards of decency with your dirty little stories you not only bring shame to all women, you encourage men to commit sexual crimes against women?

Of course, I have had to listen to this reasoning on so many occasions that it was only with some difficulty that I resisted the urge to drop the note in the round file. And I'm glad I held on, because in the very next paragraph I found what seemed to be an opening. She wrote:

I am sending you this note because I think there is a chance that I might get through to you as a writer, artist and woman of some substance. My head is demanding that you desist, but I know that to yell at you is not the way to reach you. So I simply ask you, as woman to woman, do you have no doubts about what you do? Do you not sometimes feel that your work serves not the liberation of women but their oppression, that what you do adds to a climate of harassment?

I decided I would issue my own little challenge to little miss misguided to see if she was woman enough to meet me halfway. I sent her the following, along with three back copies of *Libido*.

Dear Margo,

I appreciate your compliments on my "dirty little stories" being well written. But I also reject your notion that what I do is somehow anti-woman. If anything is anti-woman, it is the argument that women need to be "protected" from men by a series of laws that curtail freedoms of the press or expression. Your fundamental error is the assumption that women are necessarily victims of sex. I believe that if women are to achieve genuine equality with men they have to be willing and able to assert their own sexual identities.

I appreciate that you—and others—in the neo-Victorian wing of feminism believe you are operating in good faith, but you are missing the point. And sometimes that makes me very angry, because as I see it you are playing directly into the hands of the most regressive elements of our society.

But I am a pragmatist at heart and I also understand that to close this damaging rift in the women's movement we must find ways to talk to—instead of past—one another. I suggest that you reread my stories. But not in your office. My work doesn't read well in fluorescent light. I ask you instead to draw yourself a warm bath, light some candles, burn some incense and generally create a private-space atmosphere. Your goal is to surrender your disbelief. I know this is probably hard for you, being an important, hard-driving feminist attorney and all, but trust me, a little surrender—at the right time and place—never hurt anybody.

P.S. I hope you own a vibrator?

To be honest, I thought I had a better than fifty-fifty chance of hearing back from Margo. She wouldn't have written me in the first place if she weren't looking for something more than to scold me. And I did hear back.

Dear Sophie,

I think I should resent the inference that just because I believe that in the face of inequality women need special protections against unwanted advances from men that I somehow am anti-sex. I have no problem with sex. I enjoy sex. I love my husband. I firmly believe that the problem here is not sex, but the public display of it.

On the other hand, I will confess to you that I did read more of your work, in a relaxed context, and I found it most affecting. And this causes me some confusion. I would like to discuss this with you in a format more conducive to open communication. But before any of that can happen, I have to have your word that this is all confidential. This is a trust situation for both of us. Are you interested?

Sophie does know a pickup line when she sees one, so I said yes. And as it happens when the energy in these things is right, she just happened to have business in Chicago. We met for dinner in a quiet little Vietnamese restaurant I know in an out-of-the-way neighborhood.

Margo was younger than I expected, professional as a tack and generally equally as pointed, a woman on a mission. I was simultaneously repulsed and attracted. The bright, intelligent look in her dark eyes was invigorating, but the vulnerability her note showed was not in the least evident now. She wanted to talk about court cases and she rarely gave me an opening. It took me a while to understand that she was nervous. I did my best to be understanding.

I waited until I was pouring the last drops of wine into her glass before I asked her what the confusion her note mentioned was. I liked that she didn't bat an eye while switching gears.

"I sat in the tub and I pulled out the magazines. I have to tell you that I did this not because I expected to be aroused, but because I was going to convince myself once and for all that this kind of material, which should be repugnant to me, would not and could not turn me on. I started out looking for reasons to hate what you had sent me, and initially there seemed to be plenty.

"Some of the photography was more than I could look at. It was far too intimate. And I hated the first thing I read, which was a poem. But then I started reading a story of yours, 'Playing with the Goddess,' and something changed. I hope I am not revealing too much, but I found that fantasy of women being sexual together in a spiritual setting very stimulating.

"Sophie, I am not used to being aroused by something I read. I admit that I liked the feeling a good deal. And I also tell you that it led to some wonderful sex with my husband. But it also made me feel guilty—an emotion I don't like."

I nodded in agreement. Nobody likes to feel guilty. I asked her, "Have you had a chance to analyze your guilt feelings?"

"Yes, I have. And I think I can say honestly that it wasn't because I played with myself in the tub. I am aware that masturbation can both be liberating for women and probably is medicinally valuable as well.

Once I was turned on, I went back and looked at the photos and realized that my discomfort was in the unashamed sexuality and that in my heightened state, they were stimulating."

"So what is the point?"

"The point is that an enlightened woman simply cannot put her personal pleasures above what is better for the community as a whole."

"How are you doing that by masturbating in your bath? I'm sorry, but I draw the line there. I take responsibility for my own body and that includes its sexual side. And I certainly don't want anybody, man or woman, telling me what I can and cannot read." Again, Margo did not blink.

"My problem is that if that story aroused me, then stories like it must do the same thing to men. And then there are problems. Real problems you can't just wish away. Men are raping women every day, assaulting women, harassing women, demeaning women. That is the problem. And you're just encouraging them." Margo's voice was rising, and I realized that three of the four other occupied tables were listening to our conversation.

I chose my words deliberately. "Your problem is that you are confusing sexism with sex." And before she could respond I suggested that we pay the check and go someplace more comfortable to continue this discussion. In the car she agreed to go to my apartment, where she let me talk her into another glass of wine. I said to her, "So did you show your husband the *Libidos*?"

"Of course not." She said it so sharply I was taken aback.

"Why do you say it so vehemently?" Her smile was the first flash of vulnerability she had shown all evening. I wasn't going to let her off the hook. "Were you afraid he'd be so aroused that he'd jump your bones?"

"Of course not."

"Or that he'd go on some rampage in the neighborhood?"

"Of course not!"

"You know you are saying that altogether too much. It leads me to suspect we're on to something here. Maybe ve haf a problem viss men?"

I was expecting Margo to get mad at that point. But she fooled me. She said, "I didn't show him the magazines because I didn't want him thinking that I might masturbate with them. I didn't know how he would react to that. This is not something we ever have discussed. And I was afraid to ask him." She paused to let that sink in, and then poured herself another glass of wine. "You know, one of the reasons I called you was that I am intrigued by these sessions you have with men. Want some? . . ." she gestured with the bottle. I held out my glass.

". . . I can't imagine what that must be like. They are naked with you. I mean, you're not naked, too, are you?" I shook my head. "Okay, so why, exactly, are they naked? I'm not sure I understand that part."

I explained to Margo that I believe people are the most likely to be completely honest when they are naked. I tell her that, yes, talking about themselves sexually is a powerful stimulant for a man, so these sessions usually turned into erotic experiences and are thus very revealing. Since I began this project, I have now encouraged upwards of fifty attractive, intelligent, powerful men to stroke themselves to orgasm in my presence. And I admitted just how powerfully erotic the experience is for me as well. I told her, "It's tough sometimes, but I never fuck them." It was only a little lie. Margo said, "That's just it. How do you keep them off you? That's the thing about men. If you encourage them they go crazy."

"I see the problem here," I said. "You look at men and you see testosterone dribbling from their macho chins. They're not all like that, you know."

Before Margo could object, I said, "In my case it's pretty easy. I often pick out the men I want for my study, so they tend to be people I know in other contexts and generally I feel I can trust them to stick to their word. Increasingly I am getting strangers but I put them through a screening program to see if I will allow them to beat off in my presence. I do say no to many men."

"So that's it!" Margo jumped in. "You're a dominatrix!"

I laughed and said I'm not—although I do enjoy the fantasy. "I just have a few rules, which the men have to accept. And you'd be surprised. Not all of them do actually become aroused. Some just lie there and talk, which is fine. Some of them cry. Men aren't as simple as you seem to think."

It was Margo's turn to be skeptical. "I may not be talking about all of them, true. But the problem is you can't tell which ones are the dangerous ones. A lot of educated, professional, seemingly enlightened men can turn out to be the worst sort of monsters. I just think we're better off, in that case, keeping them all at arm's length and surrounding ourselves with as many protections as possible."

I shook my head. I said, "That's exactly the wrong approach. I think we're much better off dealing with them as their mothers did. Reward them when they are good. You'd be surprised at how many men like the idea of masturbating in the presence of an encouraging woman. It's very hot.

"If I think I might have trouble with anyone, I have a pair of large, strong woman friends who come with me. I have had them around ten times, and no problems." I paused two beats and added, "Does your husband ever masturbate with you?"

Margo's eyes focused intently on mine for a moment, and then she sank back onto the sofa, where her eyes slowly glazed over. "I was going to say 'Of course not,' but, yes, it did happen once and I remember it very well. It was before we were married, on the beach, just at sundown. We were making out, passionately. It was very arousing, I remember that. Lots of bare legs intertwining and wet bathing suits and wetter kisses. He wanted to fuck me right there, but I wouldn't let him. I remember enjoying keeping him right on the edge for quite some time. Finally, when it was almost dark out and we thought nobody could see us, he took himself out of his suit to show me how aroused he was. I pretended to be shocked for a minute, but when I kissed him and felt his naked erection poking at my thighs, I was very turned on. I was aware of his hand moving between us, but it took me a while to realize what it was doing.

"I was very much into seeing this because I had never actually seen a man do it, so I figured out that if I put my tongue in his ear I could watch him, but he couldn't really see me watching. And what I saw fueled my fantasy life for years. I felt so powerful."

Margo's face was radiant as it broke into a smile. "And you're telling me men do this for you all the time?"

I smiled my warmest smile, and as Margo, beaming, lay back against the pillows closing her eyes, I said, "Not just men."

A nervous laugh escaped Margo, but, eyes closed, she said nothing. I turned down the not-very-bright lights and lit candles. I said, "You'd be surprised at the people who come to me. Now that I have something of a reputation the numbers are almost more than I can handle. But I do it because I think of it all as research."

It was my turn to laugh, lightly. But Margo did not react to my joke. So I moved to pick up her feet and swing them onto the sofa. I sat with her legs on my lap and pulled off her shoes. She said, "I think I have had more wine than I realized. I'm dizzy." I was soothing; I said, "Relax, Margo. You are safe here." I massaged her feet until she sighed.

I said to her, "Margo, I would like nothing better now than to take your clothes off you and encourage you to tell me about yourself. But I don't think you are ready. And besides you're dizzy. So I am going to switch roles here. I am going to take my clothes off and I am going to tell you something about me. Is that all right with you?"

Margo said nothing, but her eyes opened very wide and they stayed on me as I removed everything but my bra and lay down on the small chaise across from her. I can admit to *Libido* that by this point I was very into the prospect of being sexual with Margo. She had so much to learn. So I admit it, I was dying to put on a performance that would literally knock the pantyhose off her. I wanted her to feel something of the power of voyeurism for men. I said, "Margo, I know you know a lot about the benefits of beating off, but do you ever do it?"

"Not really."

"Why is that?"

"I don't know. No time . . . no interest . . ." I could hear irritation rising in her voice. ". . . I'm a thirty-year-old woman. Masturbation is something teenagers do, not adults. I have a husband. We have sex. I don't need to masturbate. Why do you?"

I knew I might lose her at this moment, so I said nothing for several moments. Her eyes didn't leave me, and as I began to stroke myself, her irritation gave way to obvious curiosity. I said, "I often masturbate as a way to go to sleep. Sometimes I use it as a meditation to separate myself from a problem or situation that has me feeling uneasy. To me it's a tool of self-mastery." I paused a beat. "Do you have a vibrator?"

"No."

"Have you ever seen a woman use one?"

"Of course not."

I laughed. "You are about to. I just happen to have one here behind the chaise." If Margo was embarrassed or confused or in any way dubious at this point, it wasn't showing. As the Hitachi worked its magic on me and my eyes lost focus, Margo slid off the sofa and slowly moved toward me. I could see that her mouth was open and her eyes were on fire. I came quickly, even before she got all the way to me.

"Wow!" she said. "That was incredible. Did it feel as good as it looked?"

For the briefest of moments I felt very exposed and foolish. But Margo rescued me. She said, "Do you have another one of those? And I hope you won't take this wrong, but I think I need you to show me how to use it. The one I bought once about ten years ago had batteries in it and it didn't work very well. *That thing* looks industrial grade."

After that, believe me, we had a grand old time. Margo had a lovely, lithe little body, very white and with the pinkest of nipples, which seemed so unused. I loved holding her head in my lap while she had orgasm after orgasm. Unfortunately the next morning was a little strained. Over coffee Margo felt the need to inform me that just because she had let herself go didn't mean that she was changing any of her ideas about men and sex. I tried to tell her that I didn't expect her to change anything, except to be a little more accepting. But she misunderstood, and left in something of a huff.

Yet to her credit Margo phoned me three days later to apologize. She said, "I had to leave you that way because in the morning I was terribly embarrassed by what had happened and I didn't want it to show. Maybe embarrassed isn't the right word. Maybe confused is better. Even more confused than I was before. But now I have had a chance to sort out my feelings, and I want to thank you for being so open with me. And so challenging. I had to give myself permission to admit that I enjoyed myself as much as you seemed to be enjoying yourself.

"Sophie, I absolutely forbid you to think that because I'm saying this that I suddenly am buying your arguments. I'm not. And I think you are dangerous. But I do want to see you again."

So, dear editors, there you have it. I have begun a mutual masturbation affair with a McDworkinite female lawyer, straight and married. It's very hot.

The only hard part for me is that we have seen one another only three times since the first night, always when she has been able to route a flight through O'Hare. Each time she has walked into my apartment, looking like a very cold-fish, efficient professional, all gray suit and her hair in a tight bun. But within an hour she has transformed to Venus on the half shell, her hair cascading down her naked shoulders and a rosy glow on her cheeks. This woman looks very good riding a vibrator.

What else can I say? I'm hooked and I just had to tell you. Oh, and by the way, Margo is not her real name. I did promise her to keep this confidential.

◆

MY LIFE
WITH MR. D

◆

By Lydia Swartz

The Hard Plastic Kind

Vita is young and almost blond and convinced that notches on her belt mean something. It is the Seventies. Notches mean boys. She does boys and dreams about girls.

In the back of a women's magazine Vita sees an ad. Drawings of impossible women: huge breasts defying gravity, tiny round butts and grotesquely elongated legs, petite feet stuffed into high-heeled shoes.

Horrified and intrigued, Vita sends for the catalog, which arrives monthly for the next seven years despite all attempts to stop it.

At first the catalog is useful. She leaves it out and observes the behavior of the latest boy. If he reacts in a way that doesn't repel her, she fucks him.

Eventually, her heart gets in the way. That's when she gives up collecting notches and uses the catalog to send for the hard plastic dildo, not knowing that is what it is. (It's simply the cheapest vibrator, and all she can afford.)

She gets batteries and slides them inside it. She turns the handle and it buzzes. She's not exactly sure where her clit is but soon finds out. She spends hours and hours and hours in her room.

The hard plastic and harsh vibration, in addition to sheer volume of contact, keep her infected all the time. Her cunt oozes. The tissues are inflamed. They rub against her jeans seam and make her even more turned on. She goes home and vibrates some more. Perpetuating the infection, which perpetuates the stimulation, which perpetuates . . .

It never occurs to Vita to put the dildo inside her. (And when boys do, she feels nothing but impatience.)

Cheap Rubber Ones

The hard plastic one eventually expires from overuse. Plus she has acquired a steady boy now, and if she uses the hard plastic one it makes her numb to his indecisive attentions. Without the hard plastic's influence, she settles into what she refers to as gothic friend-ships with girls (who call Vita an honorary lesbian behind her back) and perfunctory fucking with the boy.

Behind the boy's back, on a private trip to a sex toy shop—not like the loud, hilarious such trips with girlfriends—she buys herself a soft plastic dick. It's violet and has a spackled-looking surface reminiscent of a burn victim's skin. It feels ghastly to the touch: slimy, lukewarm.

She doesn't put it inside her. She strokes herself with it, pushes it against her clit, rocks on it and covers it with her juices. When it gets warm and wet, it's even more disgusting: the smell, the texture. It now resembles some hideous infirmity—a mass of stretch marks in a bub-bly, atrophied surface. And stroking herself with it makes her come over and over.

The dildo, when warm, smells so much like the dolls she remem-bers from childhood that it gives her the willies—pleasantly. Vita smugly concludes she is kinky, because of the doll thing. She is, how-ever, truly ashamed of the pleasure the plastic dick gives her.

The boy is proud of himself when he makes her come (which she doesn't have to fake). After she comes, he kisses her passionately while she pushes her pelvis against him. Trying to come again. Then he falls blissfully asleep.

Sometimes Vita ducks out of his arms and sneaks into the other room to pleasure herself with the ugly plastic dick. He never finds out about it.

But when Vita doesn't change her mind about no wedding and no babies, the boy leaves her.

Upgrading to House Power

Alone at last, she buys herself an electric vibrator. No troublesome dead batteries in the middle of a three-hour session! And, living alone, she doesn't worry about the noise.

She's still working for the good of her soul, so the vibrator she buys is a cheap imitation of the major-brand kind with many attachments. No problem, she thinks. After all, there are only a few of the oddly shaped accessories that are useful to her. (The long, narrow one is claimed by the cat for the annoying noise it makes when he bats it back and forth in the empty bathtub.)

She finds a box of lesbian smut in Cindy's stuff. (Cindy, a gothic friend, is taking the grand lesbian van tour of the United States and has left boxes and appliances in Vita's storage locker.) Vita devours the smut while she vibrates.

The metal button that supports the rubber accessories on Vita's new vibrator gets so hot that the rubber tip slips off. Vita has to be very careful. Sometimes she burns herself. The cat, at first fascinated, then eventually lulled by her buzzing and moaning, has been frightened by the smell of burning pubic hair and now runs from the room as soon as Vita pulls Cindy's smut box from under the bed.

Vita occasionally goes out on a date. She fucks the guy and then loses interest in him. She spends most of her time with her gothic friends. By now, it so happens that every one of her friends is a lesbian.

Vita Realizes Something About Herself

One day, when she has been without an orgasm for almost a week (recovering from a particularly nasty vibrator burn), she falls asleep over cappuccino and feminist literature in a booth at the women's bookstore and coffee shop.

Vita has a dream about the owner, a woman she has watched for years. A woman she has felt strangely shy and awkward around. In the dream, the woman is kissing her, tongue-wrestling her, really. Sucking and nibbling on Vita's nipples, running her fingernails down Vita's back, sliding her mouth down Vita's belly, licking Vita's . . .

Vita awakens with a start. The woman is standing in front of her, laughing. "You need another cappuccino. I'll bring you a double," the woman says. Vita is unable to move or speak. The woman's voice slams right into her cunt and somehow paralyzes Vita.

That's not the only dream Vita has. The tattered pile of smut begins to seem stale as Vita's imagination begins to perform amazing acrobatics.

Vita switches to touching herself with her own hand. She tells herself: Just until the burn heals. But she finds her vulva wondrous now. Not the smelly chaotic mess she once refused to touch.

Vita notices how many women are noticing her. Vita notices how many women she has been noticing. Vita can no longer look right into a woman's face. Vita learns to blush. Vita blushes so often that people comment on her sunburn.

Vita mentions to two of her most trusted gothic friends that she thinks she might be, or might be partially, or possibly was in a past life, lesbian. One friend laughs for so long that Vita becomes irritated. Another friend goes on chopping celery, nods her head and asks what time the movie is showing; are they going to be late?

It Will Never Happen

Vita meets many women. They all have tightly bonded partners, or they're long-standing gothic friends and thus off limits, or they find out she's a virgin and run out the back door.

Vita takes to staring at the *faces* of the women pictured in Cindy's smut, something she'd never noticed before. Where do these women live? What do they look like when they're dressed? Do they have dogs? Are they vegetarians? How did they find out how to do these things?

Vita smells her fingers when she's been touching herself and pretends they've just come out of another woman's cunt.

Month after month passes.

Vita loses weight. She grows her hair out a little and bleaches it white-blond.

She begins to think that lesbian equals celibate and decides to fuck a man who's been pursuing her, after all. She closes her eyes when he's going down on her and pretends he's Grace Jones.

It's a Miracle

Cindy comes home. Vita and Cindy go to the movies. Cindy is very popular, since she's single again, plus she's been out of town long enough to be almost fresh meat. So three other women come along. One of them is named Isis. Vita forgives her that indiscretion when she learns Isis was the name given the woman by her parents.

Isis and Vita somehow end up crammed together in the back seat of somebody's new car on a long drive. They talk as part of the group, but soon to each other mostly. Vita's thigh, where it's crushed against Isis's thigh, begins to glow. Conversation flags. Vita wonders how the other women in the car can bear the intense heat generated by the proximity of Isis.

They exchange phone numbers.

Vita leaves a message on Isis's machine. Isis doesn't call back for one day. Then two. Then three. Vita gives up. She accepts another date with the man she's been fucking.

Then Isis calls Vita. They go out for dinner together. Neither of them eats.

Then Vita calls Isis. They go to a show together. Neither of them follows the plot.

Then Isis calls Vita and invites her over for dinner.

They never eat the dinner.

Vita finds out what another woman tastes like. She finds out she not only can manage to stick her tongue into another woman, but that she can pretty quickly figure out how to do it right (Isis coaching Vita) and that she really, really, really enjoys it. So does Isis.

Isis is unbearably wonderful. Her small faults (she has bad skin, she has a nasty temper when she's had a few drinks, her grammar sucks and she can't spell, she has another girlfriend who isn't supposed to know about Vita) only add to her charm.

Isis knows almost everything. She tells Vita she will teach her everything. Vita is flattered and eager.

Isis has a silicone dildo that fits into a leather harness. Mr. Dick, as Isis calls it, is fat and cunningly curved. Isis likes to bind Vita to the bed, leave Vita alone in the bedroom with the VCR, which is playing a poorly made but graphic lesbian porn tape, and go read the paper.

When Isis comes back in, she's wearing the strap-on and a mustache. "What do you want, baby?" she growls at Vita. "I want your dick," Vita has learned to reply.

Isis makes Vita hot and wet with her tongue, then gets on top and fucks her. Vita has a newfound interest in penetration, something she always used, with boys, only as a reward for satisfying her. Something about this woman on top of her, her tits flopping as she thrusts the dildo into Vita, her insistence on Vita maintaining eye contact . . . Watching Isis get turned on by her getting turned on . . .

As a surprise for her wonderful lover, Vita splurges on some hardware. She carefully nails and screws rings and hooks to her bed frame, lays in a supply of rope and handcuffs, and calls up Isis.

Vita leaves a message on Isis's machine. Two days pass, then three, then four. Vita keeps leaving messages.

On the fifth day, Isis picks up the phone. Vita invites her over. Isis avoids replying. Isis briskly fills in Vita on her plans for the next two weeks, none of which include Vita. She complains to Vita for a while about how busy she is, how tired. Vita hears a voice in the background. Isis says she has to go.

Life with Mr. D

Vita calls up Cindy and talks about everything but Isis, Cindy notices. Vita has been talking about nothing but Isis.

The whole story comes out. (Not the part about the mustache. Vita's too embarrassed.) This is what Isis always does, Cindy says. She specializes in virgins.

"Why didn't you tell me?" Vita wails.

Cindy and several other gothic friends point out, unhelpfully, that they did tell Vita. Vita remembers, unwillingly, that they're absolutely right.

Some friends of Isis call up Vita or approach her at the coffee house. Vita is now fair game, and Isis gives them Vita's phone number if they ask for it. Vita talks to them; sometimes she flirts. She takes their numbers, written on napkins or business cards or backs of tickets, then throws them out of her car window on the freeway.

Somewhere along the line, Vita has given up working for the good of her soul. She has a dollar or two to spend when the bills are all paid.

So Vita strolls into a suburban sex toy shop one afternoon, writes a check that barely fazes her account balance, and takes home the fanciest vibrator on the market. Sends in the warranty card. Removes the hardware from her bed frame. Buys her own damn videos.

And lives happily ever after.

TRIOS

◆

Safe Sex
poetry by William Levy

Jurgen's Tale
by Sophie du Chien

Two Divided by Three
by Sophie du Chien

Trio Amoroso
by Gershon Legman

SAFE SEX

I like it, I like it
that my wife is a little bit lesbian:
    it is very droll to watch her
Go down on you
While she's still wearing her eyeglasses.
Although there are times I would
rather find something excellent to read
    than have to make love to
    two women, again.
"You have to be cool with women," she said.
And I prefer to be clean, then mean.
I start talking about simple things,
passionate ideas of the State
Colonel Qaddafi's *The Green Book*;
    its surreal, situationist notion
    that sports, commerce, culture and politics
    are like eating and praying
(Even sex, I would presume)
    something only satisfying when
    done by oneself, not as a spectator
"No witnesses! No witnesses!" I scream
And start mumbling about
    the relationship between
    the ruler and the ruled

the continuity and
the discontinuity of history
When more sensual conjunctions are possible.

More is the pity
there're no voyeurs in
the Colonel's Ideal City.

I like it, I like it
to lash your breasts with
a cat-of-nine-tails while
you masturbate with nail-bitten
fingers, my wife sitting
    in a chair now, watching.
Don't you enjoy being
    supped
    and sucked
    and spanked
    and showered?
When we see each other again
    Like you be the S and I'll be the M
    or the other way around
Like masochism is the word atheists use
    to describe bravery
Like bondage is merely an extreme
    form of fondling
Like if we could only relax
    there would be a revelation in every pot
    there would be two revelations
    in every garage
Like with a confluence of beneficial prerogatives
    we shall be as the sun
Like at some point I'll have elastic
    or Bach, or something
Like I would provide the condoms

and the hashish
If you would bring your violin
    and homemade black leather whip.

William Levy

JURGEN'S TALE

By Sophie du Chien

Jurgen sat across the sun porch in a silk paisley robe, champagne in his left hand, a kif-laced cigarette in his right, his legs sprawled across the arm of the loveseat where he lay. The legs sticking out were firm and tan in the rich afternoon light. A stream of bright sun lit the wine-colored paisleys across his chest.

"I've never told anyone this," he said finally, his face shining through a placid, glassy-eyed smile. "I was fourteen, visiting my six-teen-year-old cousin near Dijon. He wasn't my real cousin, but our parents encouraged us to pretend because they were close. Michel and I went on a picnic to a swimming place he knew in a tributary to the Loire. We drank a sauterne he brought and ate apples and grapes. I remember laughing a great deal. He was terribly funny, telling me stories about French girls he had kissed, and how far they would let him go, how much of them he could touch.

"The day was warm, and Michel said we should swim before we drank too much. We pulled off our clothes and jumped into the cool pool at the bend in the stream. We splashed and wrestled in the water as we had done every time we had gone swimming.

"The only thing different that day was that Michel and I were alone. He had brought me, he explained, to his special swimming hole, a place he showed only to his best friends.

"And it was a lovely place. A bend in a slow, deep channel lined with trees, and with strong sunlight most of the afternoon on the big, flat rock at the edge of the water. Cattle grazed in the meadow around us. A July breeze rustled the leaves above every now and again, breaking up the buzzing of flies and bees. We swam up the river and then floated back to where we had begun.

"When we came out of the water we flung ourselves onto our clothes spread on the rock. Michel stood again to fish out the bottle, which he had wedged behind a rock and left to cool in the water. He bent back to turn the bottle upside down into his mouth. And I can still picture him well, standing there up to his thighs in the water, head back, brown, curly, wet hair dangling off his neck. He had more pubic hair than I.

" 'I've got something to show you,' he said, 'something I bet you have never seen.'

"From a schoolbook he pulled a packet of photographs, then knelt next to me, dripping onto my legs. The photos were terrible quality, grainy five-by-sevens. But he was right, I'd never seen anything like them.

"In the first, a traditionally dressed Algerian woman was on her knees beside a standing, dark European woman who was dressed in an old-fashioned brassiere and those big, old-fashioned panties. Her outstretched arms appeared to be held by someone or something out of the frame. She had a very strange look on her face. It wasn't fear, but it was animalistic in a way that made my groin tingle.

"In the next picture the Algerian woman was hauling down the other woman's panties. Her pubic bush was clearly visible. I had never seen a grown woman's bush and my little penis went rigid. I didn't want it to, of course, and I was terribly embarrassed—on the verge of trembling, really. But I also could not pull my eyes away from the photos.

"In the third, the European woman was leaning very far back with her eyes closed. Her bra was open and two hands had come from somewhere behind her to cup her large breasts from underneath. The panties were gone, and the woman was holding her legs very far apart. The Algerian woman, still squatting, had her hand between the European woman's legs.

" 'You like these, don't you?' Michel asked sardonically. I blushed even brighter red, and turned away from him, my hard young thing pointing so straight that I couldn't have lain on my stomach if I had wanted to. I tried to cover myself, awkwardly.

" 'It's okay,' he said. 'I get that way from these, too. Look.'

"I turned my head, and my young heart leaped into my mouth. His penis, long, narrow and blue—blue and red—stood out from where he sat. 'That's why I look at them. That's why I'm showing them to you. Look at them.'

"I took the photographs in my trembling hands . . ."

Jurgen trailed off. His cross-eyed gaze drifted from the smoking cigarette to Maria. He flicked the ash into the air with a flourish, smiled and handed her the short end of it. She inhaled deeply, and leaned back into the sofa we shared. She handed it to me. I put it to my lips and she turned back to Jurgen. "Don't stop now. What happened next?" she said huskily.

I sat back thinking to myself, "What am I doing here? Are we being seduced by this German?" Yet I was also very intrigued by this blond sensualist. He was just as bad and charming as Maria had said. We had been talking pleasantly about where we each had grown up, the similarities of the conventions of our romances when, into the third glass of champagne, Jurgen began his tale. I was actually getting turned on by it. He knew what he was doing, and so did we, but it was irresistible.

Jurgen settled further into his loveseat, shifting his legs when his robe fell open up to his hip. As he pulled it back together, he caught me watching his hand. I blushed.

"I remember this as if it were yesterday," Jurgen said. "In the next picture the Algerian woman's head had moved to the other woman's crotch. I could see her mouth disappearing into the other's pubic patch. It was more than my young system could handle. I had my first orgasm simply from looking. I wasn't even touching myself. I just shot off into the air like warm champagne. It was wonderful, wonderful.

"And apparently my orgasm sent Michel over the edge. Lying back in a daze, I watched him slide his hands—both of them—up and down his shaft, humping his fists until he exploded into the river and across the rock next to me. Then he fell across me and we lay still.

"We rested for perhaps fifteen minutes, neither really wanting to move. Then he urged me to finish looking at the pictures. I did, and naturally, I got another hard-on. I wanted to put my hands on myself, too, but I was too embarrassed. And then the most remarkable thing happened. Michel put his mouth on me.

"It was electric. I exploded into instant orgasm, and before I could go soft, I became excited all over again."

At that pause in Jurgen's lurid little story, I became conscious of Maria's breathing next to me. It was sexually charged breathing. To my utter disbelief, she had her hand inside her blouse and was very obviously massaging her breast.

She caught me staring, and shot me a look I'll never forget. I felt myself being sucked into something I was not certain I was ready for, but at the same time I didn't want it to stop. I was tremendously aroused. I could feel myself getting wet as I watched Maria. It was so decadent.

I lit and puffed on the nub of kif again, hoping to break the tension in the air and between my legs. I wasn't certain of what was happening in front of me. Or why.

"And what happened to the Algerian woman?" Maria asked thickly.

"In the next to last photo she had a veil over her face, but was naked from the waist down. Her shaved pussy—that's the Arab fashion—was poised directly over the European woman's tongue. That photo gave me yet another erection on my initiation day, because above the veil, in her eyes, you could see her ecstasy."

Jurgen fell silent. He laughed shyly. "I have to confess, telling you both my little secret has aroused me this afternoon almost as much as being there in the first place. But I am also a little embarrassed. I have told you so much, while I know nothing of you two. Nothing so revealing. Please tell me something a little dangerous about yourselves."

He said that looking directly at me. His eyes were so hungry that I felt my resistance melt. But it was Maria who got up, walked over to him, and without warning pulled his robe open.

"I want to see you hard," she said. He was, rising from half mast against his thigh to point straight up from a thick, darker blond patch than the hair on his head.

Maria quickly pulled off her shorts and panties. "I need it now. Feel how wet I am."

And right in front of me, the quiet girl from the country climbed on his lap, took hold of his erection and after rubbing herself with him, ever so slowly squatted on it. She wasn't even quiet about it.

In fact, her animal noises were more than I could bear. I pulled my legs up, spreading them so I could reach up the leg of my shorts, and began stroking myself like a schoolgirl in the bathroom. I found myself wanting to reach out and stroke Maria's tight, round little butt. Jurgen was beaming at me with the sexiest little smile from under her arm. Then she began coming in whoops, and I started coming and coming listening to her. Before it ended, we all wound up coming together in a groaning pile of hugging bodies.

That was the first of many tender evenings for the three of us. We became well known around town that summer as the three musketeers. Jurgen was a real charmer. But as you may also have guessed, he was a very strange one, too. He liked to sit naked between us, jerking himself off while we, usually fully clothed, kissed his neck, licked his ears and pinched his nipples.

But then I especially liked it when he would hold me from behind, kissing my neck and pulling my nipples while Maria on her knees licked me. And I loved watching them fuck.

To this day, twenty years later, the remembrance of those afternoons with Jurgen whets my appetite for that same kind of excitement. I wish I could feel it again, so fresh and so intense. Many's the time I've lain in the solarium in the morning ever so gently tickling myself and remembering how sweet and hot it was.

◆

TWO DIVIDED BY THREE

◆

By Sophie du Chien

Men are not all the same. In midlife, with one child in college and the other at boarding school, I am coming finally to understand this. Although my years in service to one particularly loathsome example of a banker-cum-bully—you know who you are—have prejudiced me deeply, I find I still can be moved by reactions to what I have taken to calling realtime situations.

And here I must confess that while I never personally participated in threesome sex until this spring in Europe, the idea has been darting across my mind for years, usually very near to sleep after unsatisfying sex with Charles. I find strength in the notion that some people are so comfortable in their relationships they feel free to share their partners. I feel a mystical power in the combination of energies when three people are tuned in to and turned on together. I confess, my interest also has to do with the idea of all those hands, so many pleasures at one time.

Yet what of a situation where one partner uses threesome sex as a tool against the other? The idea also intrigued me, because it was something Charles talked about, making it with two women. I assumed this was part of his typically male notion of how to keep me in my place. But as I have been learning, life is never quite so simple.

Just back from Europe, which had been very good for me, I found myself in a peculiarly bored, superior-feeling mood. Circumstances not worth the retelling threw me together with a young University of Chicago humanities assistant professor, recently separated from J., an attractive woman I have known peripherally for years. He was charming enough, but because I was still freshly inflamed from my liberating sapphic spring, he seemed a bore, annoyingly sincere and painfully naive. I was much more interested in her than him. So when, on his third Martel, he began on his marital troubles, I waited for the first opening to wither him: "At what point," I began as wearily as I could muster, "did sex become a chore for J.?"

His defensive "Never!" clued me that I was on to something entertaining. To be perverse I said, "I understand J. is bisexual." He blanched, but this is what he told me, and I confess that it was good enough to get him an invitation to my apartment.

He was well dazed with drink by then, so that while undressing him I made it clear that under no circumstances would I permit him to make love to me. However, lying next to him, stroking his obviously aching member, I was able to tease quite a lot out of him. . . .

"Two summers ago," he whispered, "I went to a stag party, which is an added little twist to my story. I hadn't wanted to go, but I felt compelled by group loyalty, something I weigh more heavily these days, and I showed up for a night with the male half of the crowd J. and I ran with then.

"It was as bad as I feared, lifeless and forced, so there was a great deal of beer swilling in a failing effort to generate enthusiasm. When S. pulled out his favorite super-8 smoker reels and clumsily loaded them into an ancient projector ('Very retro!' he boomed as he fumbled) I thought of leaving. But the *ennui* was a drug, so I did not. Many is the time since then I have wondered where I would have walked in on J., at what state in her arousal.

"The evening was very warm, I remember distinctly, and when I finally did get home, I found J., M. and her lover sitting on the front porch steps. I instantly knew something had happened. Maybe I could smell it. Maybe it was seeing M. in my wife's shorts and little cotton summer top.

"J. was in tiny red running shorts—the ones she didn't wear panties under. And why was he wearing my T-shirt? I instinctively felt on guard against him. Maybe it was the three of them, dressed so casually in *our* clothes, that felt overly intimate.

"In actuality, I can no longer distinguish between facts and what is my imagination. Did J. really loan them the clothes because after a day of work, sitting at an outdoor café, taking a crowded city bus ride and making the five-block walk to our place, everyone needed to change? Or was it that after their wild little scene, everyone's original clothes were so sweaty, wrinkled and sticky they couldn't possibly be worn?

"The three of them met after work. Because M.'s husband also was at the stag party, she felt confident to bring along her lover. J. had met him the week before at a wedding reception, which I had skipped to work on a grant application. Later, she told me about him, but in terms that apparently did not clearly convey her true feelings. He was married. M. was going through some kind of sexual encounter with both him and his wife. M. apparently was feeling very proud of herself, telling J. that he said he wanted to fuck her—*my* wife—as soon as he saw her.

"J. said to me, 'What a cocky son of a bitch he is.' What a *dangerous* son of a bitch is what I thought.

"And then just days later, there was J. with the two of them, sipping white wine, passing pleasantries and enjoying the tension in the air. I have gone over this scene dozens of times in my mind, as I have gone over every other detail I could wrestle out of J. when she was excited enough to reveal details. Yet I still find questions, things that torture me and excite me at the same time.

"Like was she expecting to meet M. alone after work that day? Or did she know *he* was coming along? J. must have found something engaging in the situation, since she invited them home for dinner afterward. I am still trying to determine when J. knew that there would be no dinner, unless she was the main course.

"J. said the physical seduction began when she was sitting on the green sofa. He knelt to massage her ankle, which she had twisted slightly stepping off the bus. M. was across the room on the new couch, sipping more wine and chattering away. Exactly when was it, I've often wondered—usually with my dick in my hand—that J. knew more was involved than a foot massage?

"When did she catch her breath? Was it when he moved to her other foot, and she was glad he didn't stop? Or was it how he put his leg under her foot to brace it and she could feel the sexual tension in him? Or was it when his hand moved up her calf, finding the nerves that vibrate up J.'s inner thighs to melt the ice cap that had been forming between us?

"When was it she got the idea he actually might climb all the way up under her skirt? And when did she decide she would let him? When did she decide she wanted this cocky son of a bitch to feel her up in front of M? Did she really not get it, back there at the outdoor café, sipping her chardonnay so nonchalantly, that he would try to make good on his words? And that M. was in league with him? What did she think when on the bus M. whispered, 'Promise me, no matter what happens tonight you'll still be my friend'?

"Was the idea that the two of them might really try to seduce J. so farfetched that she did not think of it? Or was she secretly hoping they would? Was it all a flirtatious game that got out of hand when she found herself aroused by his fingers? Or was it the idea of having sex with M. there that led J. to cross a line I had never been able to get her to cross? There always had been competition between J. and M., and I can't shake the notion of J. finding it both safe and extraordinarily arousing that M. should be there to participate in this act of marital defiance.

"Were J.'s sighs involuntary as his hands continued their one-track climb up her legs? I think they must have been. But I also know that she understood her sounds were encouraging him, filling the room with palpable sexual energy. Was she passive when his fingers passed to the insides of her upper thighs, or did she slide her hips forward to give him access? I imagine that from the floor his face was very close to her as she lifted up, and that he could not only smell J.'s musk, but when she arched her back, he saw her lips outlined in thin, damp panties, brown hair peeking out the legs. He was hard by then, I know, and seeping into his shorts.

"I see J. struggling to control her breathing, and losing it as M. openly slipped her hand into her top to pull out a breast and pinch a nipple. J. said she heard herself whimpering when she suddenly realized she was afraid he would stop stroking the outside of her panties. But then his fingers moved under the cotton to probe her slick puffiness, and she felt a wall breaking somewhere in her mind.

"I think of this moment as powerfully sexual, as well as pivotal in the evening. J.'s gasp and twitch marked clearly that instant when a sexual bargain was sealed among the three of them. Each knew fully that together they would go wherever this game would lead them.

"J. told me he put his fingers in his mouth to savor her taste. Then he took off her skirt and blouse. She let him do all the work, enjoying completely the feline feeling of being caressed and adored, until she was naked but for her blue lace bra. Her liquid excitement was plainly evident to bright, eager eyes when his hands opened her legs.

"Over his shoulder she watched M. rise to her knees, shove her slacks and pink panties down to get at herself. M. frigged hard, a glazed look in her eyes, grunting to an obvious, trembling orgasm. J. said she came then, too.

"I have always found this image tremendously exciting. I have come to it more times than I should admit. . . ."

My young man smiled a funny little smile at me then that I still remember quite clearly, because it was so endearing. I put my hand on his to urge him to go on.

"When she could focus again, J. saw that M. had moved closer to her lover, pushing his shorts to his knees. He was thick and uncircumcised. J. wanted to watch M.'s hand shimmy on him, but through the dental dam they all had laughed at, his tongue found its target, and sliding down into the cushions, J. had another, much bigger orgasm."

At that point I must confess, I came, too, simply from rubbing my legs together. I tried to be casual, but he, poor boy, told such a good story that I couldn't help myself. And he, feeling my ecstasy through fingers I unconsciously squeezed, splurted into the night, with an anguished cry.

Soon after, he fell into a deep, yet fitful sleep. And I began a long, slow drift to my own rest, turned on like crazy and knowing I had to get the rest of this story!

I waited until the second cup of morning coffee, having successfully resisted his earliest-morning advances by sending him to the shower. When I was ready, I pulled my chair next to his, and asked him to pick up his story while I stroked his chest under my big blue terry robe.

"I admit to you, I want to know every detail. It is very important to me to be able to see the whole incident cinematically, to separate my feelings, which are terribly mixed, from the whole sequence of events so that I can sort them out one by one."

He gazed deeply into my eyes. "Am I being obsessive?"

I smiled. I pushed open the robe to see his flesh rise to meet my fingers. He did have a very lovely penis.

"One problem in getting it all straight is that J. told me she lost track of what was happening, exactly; of who was doing and who was being done; that there was a great wave of intense feeling. She said she can't remember if her eyes were open or closed. But she did become very aware of M.'s presence.

"I should tell you that the thought of M. in arousal has crossed my mind many times. J. and I had talked about my visions of inviting M. to soak with us in a hot tub. J. even agreed it seemed exciting, especially when I said that after massaging M. I would want to make love to J. But it never happened.

"I worked on J. for days to tell me more about M. on that night. But she was reluctant, which only pricked my curiosity. . . ."

I pinched his nipple for that pun. He spilled coffee on his erection. I enjoyed using my napkin on it.

"Several weeks later, late on a Saturday, when J. was remarkably horny, she responded to my first hint of a question by saying that if I were to 'lick her nicely'—those were her exact words—she would tell me what had gone on. This was very unusual for J., saying something like this, so without hesitation, I slid down to put my lips to her sex. I found her wet. I began kissing her cunt lips as if they were her face lips, sucking them and Frenching her. In a wavery voice, she said that after returning to herself, she opened her eyes to see that M. had retreated to the edge of the rug, and was studying her lover's ministrations. She was playing with herself again, in that same hard way, grinding onto a small sofa pillow, her brow furrowed in concentration. J. said she saw sweat in M.'s blond pussy, and she noted how funny M.'s white thighs were, and how red her face was, like her exposed pussy. J. held out her hand to M.

"I now understand clearly that one reason for J.'s great excitement at being in this situation was that it brought together three powerful currents in her fantasy life: her submerged rebelliousness, her desire to get at me by doing something guaranteed to get under my skin, and the urge to compete with M. in an arena of her own choosing.

"This was very subtle of J. and it took me a long time to figure out. By allowing M. and her lover, whose role in this drama was enabler, to take advantage of her, she had a method to gain power over them. She could control them sexually, and thus felt herself freed from M.'s dominance. Do you see?"

I smiled at him. I shrugged. What could I say?

"Even so it took months for J. to admit that what really convinced her to let go all the way that day was the thrill of turning on M. And when she stuck out her hand, she knew she had succeeded beyond her imagination. M. responded almost shyly, inching across the floor on her knees, a deep hunger clear on her face. In her passion J. pulled M. to her breast, and M. obliged by taking a nipple into her mouth. J. dizzily pushed her hand down M.'s stomach, through her sparse blond bush to find the source of her fine, smooth, musky oil.

"J. hesitated briefly, unsure how to address the firm little nub she had found, but instinct took over. She whispered to me, 'It's a good thing I reached down with my knowing hand.' M. pushed her pussy onto J.'s hand, and together they did a dance, M. responding to every lead.

"I could feel J. blush through the darkness when she told me how just at the moment she had M. on the edge, she pushed her down into the sofa, insisted on opening a dental dam very slowly and then buried her face deep into M.'s dusky source, sending M. off onto another spiral.

"And when J. came down this time, she was a changed woman. Sexually M. had become putty in her hands. M.'s lover's eyes were so glazed with lust and his dick was so hard that he was reduced to lying on the floor, one hand holding up his head, the other rhythmically riding up and down his erection. 'Wow,' he said, 'O wow, O wow, O wow . . .' Over and over.

"J. said she felt sorry for him, too. He seemed in pain, she said, so like Florence Nightingale, she sat on his latex-enveloped erection and fucked him into submission. 'I couldn't just leave him high and dry,' J. said innocently enough. But by fucking him, she cut through the muscle in our relationship."

That's silly, I told him, an adolescent response, basic male crybaby-ness in the face of having his exclusivity challenged.

"It wasn't that," he said calmly. "It was a change in J. She realized through him that she didn't need to be so dependent on me, that she could make her own conquests, that I was merely a phase she was passing through. At a very basic level she didn't need me anymore. That's what she found out. That I was emotionally agitated by the whole story only helped to bring to consciousness the feelings she was trying to repress. But I kept bringing it up, so in the end, she decided she didn't need me at all."

When my young man stopped talking, he leaned back wearily and closed his eyes. I was filled with a great tenderness for him. He wasn't a bad man, just out of his depth. Sitting on my kitchen chair, sun streaming in on his firm, nude body, he was a vulnerable creature at the end of a marathon emotional run. The quiet became loud.

"And what do you think it all means?" I whispered.

"I think of lying naked beside J. in the dark, when she first began to tell me what happened. It was not easy for her, I know, to confess. But as she spoke, I could feel the trembling in her body turn to profound arousal. I hadn't seen J. so turned on since before we were married. She couldn't keep her hands from between her legs. It was very exciting. But I also think I knew clearly at that moment what she already knew, there was a permanent rift between us."

I slipped out of my nightgown quietly and unwrapped a condom. I straddled his legs. His nearly chapped, but nicely firm penis slid easily into me. "Keep talking," I whispered in his ear. Then I bit it. He had trouble talking, but I made him continue.

"Later on I felt some resentment that despite clear hints of interest, I could never get J. and M. to do the same with me. So I spent a while feeling the foolish cuckold—not by the guy, but by M., a woman I desired, a woman with whom I had even once made out."

"There, there," I said, settling into a smooth rhythm.

"Even now," he said softly, "thinking about this as much as I have, I don't fully understand why she would never allow the possibility of involving M. and *me*. It was my idea. J. loved for me to whisper it into her ear. We both got off on the idea. We even took a shower with M. once.

"But when J. did it with M. and *him*, she left me behind; she wouldn't include me in. I would have included her. That's what hurt. That's what still hurts."

And when we came, my young man was crying.

Among collectors, certain scholars and a well-read generation of now fading East Coast intellectuals and artists, Gershon Legman is renowned as the world's leading authority on erotic literature and folklore. Among his claims to fame is publishing the first—and illegal—American edition of Henry Miller's Tropic of Cancer. *Legman's own books include:* The Horn Book: Studies in Erotic Folklore; Rationale of the Dirty Joke; Love & Death: A Study in Censorship; The Limerick; *and* Oragenitalism: Oral Techniques in Genital Excitation.

No shrinking violet, the ever-feisty Legman reports that he was the original biographer for the Kinsey Institute, coined the phrase "make love, not war" and is one of two inventors of the vibrating dildo. The pair, he says, did not patent it, thus making it "our gift to humanity."

Legman has lived in France for many years. This portion of his memoirs, titled Peregrine Penis: An Autobiography of Innocence, *takes place during World War II, when he was secretly publishing* Tropic of Cancer.

◆

TRIO AMOROSO

◆

By Gershon Legman

Part I

One of Magdalen's stories, about the legendary Christmas parties at her office, which had been going on for a long time before I met her, intrigued me very much. Almost never having worked for anyone else in so structured a situation as an office, I had never been to any Christmas office party, which seemed to me, from the usual awed or jealous descriptions, to be a real pagan solstice survival, with ritual public intercourse and all.

"Do they really make love all over the office desks, the way people say?" I wanted to know. I didn't add: "And the way I used to do at Fortuny Press with Sonia, though not publicly." I never gave Magdalen—or for that matter any woman I was ever involved with except my Last and Future Wife—any details about my erotic life before meeting her. Until now. Nor did she give me any about hers, at least not verbally, until we had been lovers for several years. As to the Christmas parties at her office, it appears the reports had been gravely exaggerated. But was there really any public lovemaking, I persisted in wanting to know.

"Are you turning into an exhibitionist, darling?" Magdalen laughed. A great question, coming from her, I mused.

No, I told her, I had no real desire to partake of the office communion. My interest was strictly historical. Honest Injun! Centuries of hysterical orgies at the winter solstice, breaking out the strongest sexual magic of the tribe to drag back the dying sun from the maw of encroaching winter, couldn't have been snuffed out absolutely without a trace. There have been plenty of orgiastic secret clubs for centuries in all European countries, if only under the naively religious name of Devil-worship, ending with the various Hell-Fire Clubs and Hell's Angels, and Rasputin's royal entertainment in Russia, and continuing as erotic private theaters since—now democratized for the masses as erotic movies and midnight videotapes for home consumption. It was the public and accepted element that was always the most interesting and significant, as with the Roman and Aztec murder games and spectacles to keep the mob quiet: now enlarged for a worldwide public in after-dinner murder-and-horror movies on TV to get the kids ready for their inexplicable nightmares two hours later. So . . . did they really make love publicly at the office party? Or not?

"No, of course not," Magdalen assured me. "Maybe they pet a little in the broom closet, or even in the john, but nothing serious. Some men will try to push you against a refrigerator door if you're both drunk, but that could happen anywhere."

In the advertising business, she explained rather bitterly, the men who lay their secretaries regularly never really do it behind locked doors in their office. That's just a wishful dream the bosses have. They actually meet them at a hotel, or take them to a highway drive-in somewhere on the edge of town. That way they can rip it off their taxes, as a separate business expense. Who's to know? Like in out-of-town business conventions, and all that. It's very insulting to the girl, because it implies she's even lower than a prostitute and is worth nothing. It also warns her, if she has her wits about her, what kind of a finagling cheapskate she's laying for, and what she can really expect of him if there's any problem later. Her own boss, Magdalen insisted, never touched her, though she admitted that at the beginning she had frankly hoped to make him.

And it wasn't just to climb the rungs of professional success on her back, she said. "I'd just come from Boston, and I didn't know a soul. Anybody would have been all right, I thought. But he wouldn't even look at my legs." Her top boss had this theory, it appeared, that if you play around with your secretary she'll never do any real work after that, and will just sit around and file her fingernails all day, or wander in a ladylike way from the watercooler to the john and back.

"Isn't he right?" I asked. And I told her about Herman Timberg's big-shot friend in Radio City who ended up with three secretaries, none of whom would do any work for exactly that reason, especially not the one who was already pregnant and planning to sue him.

"Well, maybe," Magdalen admitted grudgingly. "To tell you the truth, women aren't always as calculating as men think. I'd work twice as hard for the man I loved. This way I work like a slave all week, and never get a kiss till Friday afternoon at five o'clock."

I kissed her immediately, and told her the definition of a modern business gal: *"She has to look like a woman, talk like a boy, think like a man, work like a horse, and fuck like a mink—and then maybe she can keep her job."* The only change that it needs today is *dress like a boy,* and to add at the end: *"And then she'll have it ALL!"* I told her too that our weekend love schedule must be too rich for our blood if it was wearing her down to no kisses all week. It was true that our first kiss each time when I'd dash up from the Public Library to meet her outside her office Friday afternoons was apt to be pretty ferocious. "Do you remember the time we got tangled trying to kiss in a revolving door, Magda," I asked, "and your heel got jammed? That was a kiss to conjure by."

"Yes, and everybody stared and wouldn't help us! Big-city hicks!"

Disappointingly though, the Christmas party at Magdalen's office on Madison Avenue, where she smuggled me in, was an outrageous bore. Strictly drinking and loud in-group talk, punctuated with over-eager horsey laughter. Sex was apparently the last thing from anyone's mind but ours. If there were any other exceptional horny couples they must've already floated off to hotels together before we got there. One pleasant chap with a loud bow tie and a quiet foreign voice, whom Magdalen called Alex and seemed to know quite well, turned a rueful eye on the purposely proprietary stance I took next to her. If there were going to be any office orgies, I claimed I saw Magda first! Unknown to me then, this easygoing Viennese playboy was none but the marvelous artist Alex King, editor with the German refugee artist George Grosz of the one best ever American satirical cartoon magazine, *Americana*, in the 1930s, which I was collecting assiduously in back copies. But I knew him not then, except as some flamboyant smoothie evidently trying to grab off my girl.

He remarked that he was only visiting from the *Time & Life* office party a block away. And he offered to take us back there with him and smuggle us in, when he heard about my scientific interest in office parties and sex. I didn't catch his name when Magdalen introduced us briefly. His intention of getting her separated into his own branding-pen once he'd got us back to the ranch was so visible that it hurt. But I had a feeling I could keep hold of her—and would—and we were delighted to take him up on his offer.

We ducked out of the advertising place, and he told us wonderful and wildly improbable anecdotes about *Life* as the three of us picked our way across Fifth Avenue, which was beginning to fill up heavily with the holiday crowd as the afternoon wore on. By evening it would be jammed solid. Another solstice ritual—tens of thousands of people milling around in the streets, especially on New Year's Eve at Times Square, with no idea of why they're there or what's supposed to happen except that their tin whistles will all blow at midnight. And on Christmas Eve, Santa Claus with his sled and reindeer in the sky, bringing toys and bonuses for all the good little office workers.

The *Time & Life* party was more of a hate festival than a love feast. No intention whatever of making love in broom closets here. The ritual had already been standardized a decade before by the coldfaced top boss, Henry Luce, a missionary's son from China who had made good in the soulless business world because he had less soul than anyone else. He was chilling even to look at, posing there as we walked in: a sort of White Nazi, perhaps without knowing it, who bragged to his magazine's billionaire advertisers that he was a specialist in delivering over to them his optically drugged readers million-strong, brainwashed and hand-cleaned; titillated, titivated, emotionally overloaded and reeling with mental trivia, trash and junk, and guaranteed READY TO BUY whatever product or mental pose they were chosen by the advertisers to be stuffed with.

The Christmas party at *Time, Life & Fortune* was the yearly ritual brain-cleansing of the office staff, a cross between the Jewish ceremony of emptying one's pockets of all one's sins over running water once a year, and putting a poo-poo cushion on the school principal's chair. Alex the Necktie finally floated away from us when he saw I wasn't about to relinquish Magdalen for even a minute, and he circulated flatteringly beside and behind Luce with some other evidently high-ranking courtiers. Friend Alex's big, unending and delicately ass-kissing smile was just perfection, though obviously totally faked, as though he were continuously saying "Cheese" for the photographer.

The essence of the thing was that Luce, the Big Boss and head of the mammoth firm, stood smiling grimly by an absurd Christmas tree, without even a drink in his hand, as I recollect; and everybody down to the janitor had the right to come up and tell him off, no punches pulled—verbally, that is. Anything was permitted that one day a year except actually slugging him. All Luce did was to smile, to the degree he knew how to smile, and make sardonic remarks in answer, the evident meaning of which was: "Well, that's your opinion, you low, pitiful worm; and you can kiss my Royal Irish ass!"

Nobody was ever fired later for anything they said to the Big Boss at the office party on Christmas Eve. Our free-booter friend Alex claimed that some of the verbal flak also hit several of the lesser straw-bosses too, and they were expected to take it in the same sporting fashion. The whole thing was Luce's own idea, or was perhaps picked up from Briton Hadden, a genially mad former editor who had invented the *Time* formula and generally acted as the cold-fish Luce's mentor. He referred to it privately as his Feast of Fools, which shows he understood historically exactly what he was doing and why. Better one afternoon (per year) reversing the roles and psychological costumes between masters and slaves in self-conscious masquerade than having to deal with silent slave revolt, sabotage and slow-down all the rest of the year.

One of the Japanese factory empires has now vulgarized this to the ultimate turn of the screw, with cloth dummies of the big boss, Mr. Konosuke Matsushita, in the employees' recreation room they are encouraged to beat the stuffing out of with bamboo poles. These are referred to as "Harmony Sessions." The walls are also outfitted with distorting mirrors. The meaning of this last mock-humorous touch seems to be that since everyone knows the seethingly polite Japanese smiles are involuted grimaces of hate, the distorted grimaces in the mirrors as the loyal Matsushita employees beat the shit out of the dummy-boss are doubtless to be understood as the groveling smiles they essentially are. Or, in current gobbledygook (which means fella-tional) upstage English, a Ph.D. thesis for the top personnel office: "How to Siphon Off the Aggressions of the Workers Against the Boss into Bowling." The road that leads to *Fortune*.

I regret to report that the *Time & Life* Christmas party was not only sexless but extremely boring—just as dull as the one on Madison Avenue. Our cicerone Alex, he of the loud phallo-testicular bow tie who got us in, headed away rapidly in the direction of some other unaccompanied girl. Leery of him as I was, I had found him wonderful and would have liked to meet him again sometime when we weren't competing for a woman. And, I did too, but only a dozen years later. I then found out for the first time who he was, and that he was one of my youthful idols. Meanwhile, I had the incredibly boorish but positive intention of staying right by Magdalen's side the whole time—till midnight, if it went on that long—and if necessary standing over any chair she slumped down in. My arms were crossed and scowling, like any bootlegger's bodyguard, to make sure that I-and-only-I eventually celebrated the ritual rebirth of the Sun with her—me and no-fucking-body else! So much for friend Alex.

Everybody at the *Time & Life* party did, as advertised, get a bit spifflicated except maybe me, and then lurched over to insult the smiling, all-forgiving Big Daddy Luce, who was parrying all their shots with fast, dry repartee and rapier strokes worthy of a Cyrano de Bergerac, if the truth must be told. Though his half-drunk wageslaves, wordsmiths, ideamen and picture editors guzzling free booze didn't really seem to appreciate his undeniably strong backhand stroke.

Actually, the insult ceremony made Luce look great, and twice as tough as he truly was, like a big old bull-moose polishing off all the staggering yearling bucks who had the bloody nerve to want to offer combat for the available females. That was doubtless the hidden or unconscious purpose of the ceremony, though the rumor was that his wife, a minor success-bimbo and playwright named Clare Boothe, considered him a clown and confused him thoroughly with various even more minor male playwrights and novelists. Luce was not impressive to look at; medium tall and with an egg head that made him look like a paunchy midwest undertaker and/or divinity student. But the set-up situation flattered him enormously, as he stood there with his puckered half-smile at one corner of a table of drinks; and it gave him a stature he otherwise must have known he lacked.

I naturally filed by with all the others, and not being a bona fide employee I thought I would go a little farther than the boozy, uninspired insults being trotted out, really to flatter him. After all, here was one of the real secret capitalistic anti-kings of Big Business, pretendedly Touching for the King's Evil one day a year, but actually ramming the power position of his evil money down the necks of his willing slaves and paid brains, right to the arse-bone, for all their half-sloshed "You rotten old son-of-a-BITCH!!" line that seemed to be standard.

"When the Revolution comes, Mr. Luce," I said, cold-sober and staring into his cold-lidded reptilian eyes with all the red-necked Communistic fervor I could muster, "this type of mock revolution isn't going to save your dollar-tattooed ass."

"Well! Don't you worry, son," he said, whirling his eyes and pegging me intensely, doubtless to have me fired pronto on January first, despite all management promises, "I've got the words of the Internationale tattooed right here on my cuff." And I believe he did. He certainly knew who to hire and plug since then, in the way of false prophets and fake revolutionaries like Marshall McLuhan and the CIA frontman, Herbert Marcuse. Who remembers them now? As it turned out, much later, I was accidentally being pegged to be hired, not fired, but I had the luck—being dead broke—to be able to afford to refuse both honors.

One thing was sure. With all the drinking, and the galumphing insults like iron pirouettes under glass, no one was anywhere miles near getting laid, neither on the desks nor under them. No ritual sexual intercourse whatsoever took place, not even symbolic, except the ritualized screwing of the employees in the ass by the boss. By the time I got back from my own quick symbolic ritual gang-bang on or by Luce, Magdalen was already slumped in an armchair with a cocktail, waving her knees at all the sightless male brain-flunkeys in pluperfect style. I went over, and gently pried her loose from the herd.

"Let's go," I ordered. "It's a complete fraud. The aggression level is even weaker here than the sex."

"What's that about sex?" cried another girl nearby, swathed hopefully in a tight black cocktail dress. She was obviously tipsy but desperately fast on the uptake. "Sex isn't allowed here, except today," she volunteered. I guess she'd heard the folklore too, and was just as disappointed as I was.

Magdalen unfolded her voluptuous body from the armchair and stood up with a rather pursed smile that I could see meant "Come out fighting!" She took my arm, sliding hers through, and held up all her ten fingers like arched claws. "Hands off!" she snapped at the other girl with her best Boston-Irish rasp. "He's *mine.*"

"Well, ladies," I interposed, very flattered, "if you're planning to fight over me, *Queensberry Rules: All contestants bare to the waist.*"

The other girl intelligently preferred to continue with sex, not aggression. Overlooking Magdalen's claws, she turned her own elbows inward and pressed her arms together, pushing her breasts richly up inside her dress until they nearly popped out the top.

"You're cute," she said. "Are you new here?"

Magdalen and I walked down Fifth Avenue a short way. I wanted to take her home in a taxi to make all things gala, since we generally took the plebeian subway together to save our money. But there were no taxis to be had on Christmas Eve. I also thought the air might clear her head, as she was getting a little drunk. Fifth Avenue now looked like Poe's "Descent into the Maelstrom."

We fought our way down as far as Brentano's at 47th Street, and then turned west. When we passed the lovely tin sign of the Three Wise Fishermen at the Gotham Book Mart, I suggested to Magdalen that I'd like to pop in—they always had a sedate Christmas party too—and pay my respects to Frances Steloff, who was everybody's favorite bookseller-partygiver for decades, though anything but an intellectual herself.

The place was full to the gunwales and spilling out into the street. When we got inside, Miss Steloff hailed us over and introduced me quietly to William Carlos Williams as the new publisher of Miller's *Tropic of Cancer,* on the basis of the Medusa edition, which had just appeared. We told him how Miller had been paid his entire royalty in advance. No piracy here.

"Really!" he said, in a kindly tone. "Be careful about telling people anything. You can get in a peck of trouble over Miller."

"Just a question of sex pride," I assured him, showing off shamelessly to impress Magdalen. "No male publisher in America has ever had any balls. Every single one of the publishers of *Ulysses* was a woman until they made it legal, and printed the court decision right in the book."

"Is that right, Frances?" he asked.

"Of course 'tis," she said. "Margaret Anderson published it in her magazine, and that awful Sumner took her to court."

"Yes," I added. "And the British edition was published by Harriet Weaver, and the Paris edition by Sylvia Beach—as 'Shakespeare and Company.' Except for pirates like Roth, not one of the male publishers got into the act until they were sure there wasn't any danger."

They wandered off. Magdalen was looking around now for another drink.

"Hullo, Legman!" a deep-down baritone voice said at my shoulder. "Introduce me to this ravishing young woman. Never saw you with a woman before. I thought you were married to your work."

"I am," I said. "And so is Magdalen. This is our annual adultery." They touched hands. It was my one-and-only lesbian friend, Irina Naxos, apparently even more mock-Greek and mysterious than usual in a long dark wool cloak like Anaïs Nin's and always at the same undefinable age somewhere between thirty, and thirty centuries. Irina never made any secret about what she appeared to be, though I must have been one of the few people who accidentally discovered her true Jewish name and Philadelphia origin, which she kept fiercely hidden.

She invited us to come upstairs to the real party, as she explained it. I had to admire her neat manipulative tactic. What man would be fool enough to take his beautiful young girlfriend to a lesbian party? But of course, if one were at the party already, who could resist the flattery of being invited into the inner sanctum?

"What kind of a party is it?" I asked, pretending to be suspicious.

"Just all the sad queer ladies in New York, standing around getting drunk," Irina said. "Some of them can waltz a little too. I wish there could be parties like there used to be when the dancers still came over from Germany. And all the mad young girls and boys making beautiful Greek vase designs till dawn." She really meant it too, and lifted both hands angularly in a somehow erotic and fluid gesture more

Egyptian than Greek. Her face froze for an instant, with her nose and chin lifted in a superb rictus of mock ecstasy, her lips and teeth parted in a passionate, soundless snarl. You could see her taste the flowing pussy juice and jism of the dancers' daisy-chains she was remembering, when she too was a mad young thing.

"It sounds marvelous!" said Magdalen in her most liquid voice, as impressed as I was by Irina's erotic ballet pantomime. Irina was great.

"Absolutely! Let's go," I agreed. "We'll stay till the first Greek vase imitation. Then we'll do one of our own."

"It's all too late now," Irina admitted, full of Weltschmerz and self-pity. "You had to be in Germany ten years ago before the Nazis came. Now everything is gone—here too. But at least we can all get drunk." She fluffed her short-cropped hair pensively and led us out.

The party was in fact next door and upstairs, in Irina's own big studio where she did gleaming calendar posters of clean American girls in tight bathing suits. Irina was only downstairs by accident, getting more liquor, when she spotted us in the bookstore. Upstairs it was just as she said. All the sad queer ladies standing around getting drunk, talking in refined undertones. A few of them dancing together. Lesbians have this tradition about being real gentlemen—where male homosexuals adore camping and screaming in mock femininity, like shopgirls on a roller-coaster. Or, even less real, too-macho masculinity.

Lesbians can really stash away the hooch standing by the fireplace, until they suddenly keel over into the ashes like true British country gentlemen. Stiff upper lip. I always wished I could have seen Amy Lowell operating with that cigar of hers. Gertrude Stein completely lacked class, with that bowl haircut, toad-like face and pose, and insulting gobbledygook that fooled no one at all but my wiseacre friend Joe Bernstein, now Barry.

To avoid having anybody invite Magdalen to dance and then absconding with her, I steered her to the nicest armchair and got Irina to give her a small drink, while I stood guard. Irina's drunken girlfriend-in-residence immediately created a diversion by spitting large mouthfuls of whiskey into the burning fire, while orange flames leapt up marvelously like a witch's cauldron. Magdalen and I drank and watched. Almost no one spoke to us, though a number of the women floated by to get a sharp assessing look at her—and at me. One very young dyke with beautiful aquiline features and jet black hair, but an angry look that never changed, stayed near us staring unabashedly at Magdalen. At a certain point I leaned over the arm of the chair to hear what Magdalen was saying. She was drunk, and speaking too low and deliberately slowly for me to be able to understand it at first.

"Take me to the bedroom, darling," she repeated, very slowly, "before I wander off and rape somebody."

I piloted her into the next room, where the coats had all been thrown on an enormous bed, clearing the way for us out of the studio by means of the never failing subterfuge of looking panic-stricken and as though I needed to vomit, whispering loudly, "Bathroom! Bathroom!" as I pushed Magdalen along before me. Now it turned out she did really have to go to the bathroom, but only to pee, and I went right along with her and drove two lesbians out who were mushing it up against the sink. I put Magdalen down on the seat while she peed, and even stood there like a patrician butler and tore off toilet paper for her, but she waved it grandly away and did a little hula-shake instead to dry her pussy off—an evident impossibility with a juicy female like her.

We stumbled back to the big bed. There was only one floor lamp burning and I yanked out the cord with my foot as we fell on the bed together. Someone went into the bathroom and closed the door. Magdalen started pulling open her shirtwaist and pushing her nipples into my mouth with both hands, rubbing her breasts against each other and against my face while she licked and bit my hair and forehead and the air. She was smothering me with her breasts, so I pulled her down further until our mouths met, which I figured was what she really wanted. People kept going back and forth to the bathroom, and I waited till the room was dark again to put my hand into her crotch. Her river was now running at flood, and she began making little wordless noises and promises. I was making a few pantomime promises of my own too.

"My turn now!" she muttered huskily, and began opening my

shirt-buttons and licking my nipples, and kneading my prick and balls through my pants, trying to struggle my fly-buttons open too. I helped her. Mercifully, no one opened the bathroom door again, and Magdalen crawled up onto her hands and knees and began devouring my prick right to the hilt, never stopping making her little animal noises. I tangled my hands in her hair and tried to help her with my hips, as I knew we could never get laid really, in such a place, without being interrupted.

Magdalen became wilder and wilder as she sucked me, and her teeth began to bite and hurt me. The fortunes of war. I opened my eyes to see if I could roll her over onto her back on the bed, and saw what was making her so wild. The little dark-haired dyke had crept into the room behind us, and she had taken Magdalen's upraised buttocks in both hands and was sucking her, I'm sure, just as wildly as Magdalen was sucking me.

"I'll bet that flood surprised her!" I mumbled to myself, and then let myself go, coming violently into Magdalen's throat. She kept shaking her hips, and obviously coming several times herself, but the little dyke never stopped sucking, and the way her long fingers were kneading Magdalen's big luscious buttocks was really a study. I was sorry it was so dark, I could surely have learned something. Finally Magdalen slid over onto her side, and the little dyke extricated herself, darting then to kiss Magdalen and rub her mouth back and forth over her lips to share the juice.

"I love you," she babbled. "Oh, I love you!"

"Wait a minute," I expostulated, "that's going too far!" I pushed my arm between them and rolled forward so I was levering the little dyke off, and landed lying on her own tiny hard breasts instead. She did not fight me, but pulled away and sat up staring into my eyes with the same angry expression she'd had in the other room. Her dark hair was all disordered, and her whole face gave off the most wonderful pussy odor of pure Magdalen imaginable.

"Please let us alone now," I said, trying for dignity. "We have to leave. This is no place . . ."

The little dyke and I both got up. To my astonishment she stayed and helped me roll Magdalen up to a more or less decent sitting position. Still no one went into the bathroom, and I was glad. I could not have stood too much more company then.

"It was beautiful, beautiful!" Magdalen murmured fuzzily.

The little dyke bent and kissed her on the mouth again before I could stop her. I grabbed her.

"Listen, you little fool," I snapped, "let go of my woman before I cut you to bits!" Of course I didn't mean it, but I felt I ought to show some proprietary emotion at least. She said something I could not understand, and left. Magdalen and I agreed in murmurs that it was time to leave, and we retrieved our coats.

The little dyke was waiting for us at the door, staring greedily at Magdalen as we left, and licking her lips with her mouth open, probably not as any signal but just still savoring her taste.

At the corner of Sixth Avenue we did find a taxi this time and went straight to Magdalen's apartment. Her head had cleared, and we made coffee and ate something out of the icebox to sober us both, a little bit anyway. I made some remark about never having seen anyone with more nerve than that little dyke.

"She's a real madwoman," I said.

"Oh, I loved it, "Magdalen cried. "Every end of the spectrum! I wish we'd brought her back with us."

"She'd never have come with us," I said, "unless she could have thrown me out of the taxi on the way."

"It was beautiful!" Magdalen repeated. "Let's go to bed—I want to remember it some more."

"Well, that's frank," I said. "I'm just lucky you don't know her address."

"I do know her address," said Magdalen. "She works for one of the agencies. Oh, darling," she laughed at my vexed expression, coming over to me and rubbing her breasts into my face, "it's only another girl! A lot more than that happened to me in Girl Scout camp." She brushed her silky red hair away from her face and laughed again. "Orgies are very educational," she said, yawning, and turning both her fists out, her breasts rising promisingly toward my face like howitzers, "but so unsanitary." We went to bed. It seemed to me ironic that I had gone to three different Christmas parties, if not four, looking for folk traces of ritual public intercourse, and in the end had to supply it myself.

Part II

I can't say I was really surprised the very next Friday, only a few days later, when I went to pick up Magdalen at her office to go to dinner, to find the same little dark-haired dyke sitting calmly with one hip on Magdalen's boss's desk, while Magda was making up her mouth to leave. The girl was very young, probably eighteen or nineteen (now that I looked at her), and just as striking as I remembered, with almost the same proud, angry look—but not quite. She must have known she was winning against my private patent on Magda, just by being there—aside from everything else at the Christmas party—and couldn't really be all that angry. She was unforgettably dressed now in dark blue British Air Force coveralls, tightened at the waist with one bright green scarf and another at her open throat. In a day when you never saw a woman wearing even slacks, that was really throwing her lesbianism and male-protest in your face. I liked her style and I liked her nerve.

Magdalen introduced her to me as Susan Aguerra, a fashion artist. I held out my hand to her, and she held out hers but looked at mine quizzically, as if for a knife, before she took it. "You still going to cut me to bits?" she asked, mocking me. She had a strong Spanish accent, or rather New York Hispanic.

"Be nice," I said. "You're winning on points." We shook hands. Magdalen wanted me to look at Susan's fashion drawings before we left, and the girl set a big portfolio on the desk and pulled out some sketches of women in the little jackets and calf-length flared skirts they all still wore. It was perfectly workman-like but nothing of interest to me. I was mostly studying her, not her sketches.

"Susan models for your Irina," said Magdalen, "but she really wants to break in as an artist. Take a look at these drawings."

Now the girl took out some larger boards, the whole size of the portfolio, and fanned out three of them on the desk-top like maps. I actually gasped. They were superb black and white brush drawings in the style of Beardsley, wildly overcharged with sweeping backgrounds of great black masses against which women floated into the air in diaphanous white robes and trains with enormous shoulders and balcony-size peplums. It was right out of Beardsley's *Salomé* drawings, and aping or even topping his every trick, especially in the power of the surging shapes and masses of black. The drawings reminded me, more than anything else, of Harry Clarke's illustrations to *Faust*, especially in the tremendous excess of detail. And it was perfectly incredible that it could be the work of this slender young girl.

"Jesus Christ!" I yelped. "Is this *your* work?!"

She held out both hands palms up. "My work," she said. The expression on her face was still angry and intense, but I suddenly realized that not very far down, she was ready to burst into tears and was holding herself as stiff as a gallows.

I took her hands in mine and pressed both her palms up to my lips. "Aguerra," I said, purposely calling her by her family name, "you are a great artist: Please cut me to bits."

The steel bent. I saw she really was going to cry, and I turned at once to Magdalen, pouring out words noisily about Beardsley reborn, to give the girl a chance to put her tough guy mask back on. She pulled another layer of drawings out, and I absorbed them greedily with my eyes, shaking my head and gesturing my appreciation, and pointing wordlessly to stylized cats and goblinesque details she'd thrown in here and there, in careful balance, but always artfully evading any static symmetry, the mathematical curse of European art. The black masses angrily soared and plunged like scudding thunderclouds, the whites streaking and striking angularly through: the play of the concomitant lightning.

What a feast of imagination and dramatic brushwork that little Spanish girl spread out before my goggling eyes! The goblins, often boldly colored entirely in green, were evidently herself, and appeared in unlikely spots as signatures in every drawing. Each time in a different pose; sometimes upside down and hanging from branches from a prehensile tail like a monkey, and in one drawing presenting its asshole cocked out defiantly to one side, as though to say, "You can kiss this!" That detail made me certain she did erotic drawings too, and I made a mental note to ask her about it at the first diplomatic moment.

Magdalen was enjoying my stupefaction over the art of her friend, whom both of them correctly assumed I had thought of until then as merely some perverted little cunt. I held the big portfolio open for her as the girl began sliding her drawings back in. I even felt a sudden disloyal rush of emotion—that I wished this boiling little genius were my girl, and not big sexy Magdalen's. But there I knew that I was just overidentifying. This girl was really a boy, and a boy that could easily have been me, except that I couldn't draw a straight line with a ruler. Her put-on angry look was not in any way different from my own, when I felt small and alone and terribly ambitious and unappreciated in an uncaring world. My tone changed, and I addressed her respectfully and even tenderly, as I truly felt she deserved. I said I thought we should all go out to dinner and celebrate her wonderful art, which is what we did. I tried to avoid acting as deferential as I really wanted to, holding open doors and snatching chairs and all that, as I could see Magdalen would soon start feeling jealous, and all the more surely in that no one could mistake how sincere I felt.

We ate in a pleasant little Armenian restaurant down on Lexington Avenue as I thought it would be too patronizing to ask her where to find a good Spanish restaurant. Another time. She went to the washroom—in that restaurant there was only one, for both men and women, as often in Europe—and she was gone a long time. I imagine her jumpsuit was pretty hard to get out of, or to twist halfway out of, every time she had to take a leak. Magdalen and I talked enthusiastically about her, and as she was really quite long coming back, we went out into the kitchen to watch the owner whirling his long sword-shaped skewers threaded with shish kebab. This was for someone else and nearly ready, and the long flames of the brazier were licking up snakelike, and charring the meat like a tiny corner of Hell. Susan came in and watched with us.

"I suppose burnt meat like that is bad for the health," Magdalen said thoughtfully.

"Yes, but good for the soul!" I assured her. "I'd love to be a phoenix and eat in flames."

"The phoenix doesn't eat in flames," said Susan. "It dies in flames."

"You're right," I said. "I'm thinking of the albatross, that bites its own breast open to feed the little albatrice on its blood."

"Albatrice!" cried Magdalen, applauding by slapping her hand lightly several times on my arm. "Score one for you!"

Susan told us a lot about herself at dinner, in response to a little diplomatic questioning during the usual endless wait for the rice and lamb and tomato dishes. We all ordered shish kebab, of course. Well burnt! It appears her name wasn't really Susan, but Inez, but she was trying to become Americanized. She had already been in America three years. I complimented her on how well she spoke English. Her family were refugees from the Spanish Revolution and had left at the out-break, four years before. They had been quite rich, and really sided with the Loyalists, not with Franco, intellectually at least; but the father had assessed the situation as very explosive and decided to emi-grate to South America. All their property was liquidated rapidly, and the funds were transferred to Argentina.

When their ship arrived in Argentina, they found that the Argen-tine banker had flown the coop with their money—along with that of a lot of other Spanish refugees—and they were penniless. Friends now just as poor as themselves were able to put them up, but they felt very humiliated, like beggars. Her older sister told Susan they would proba-bly both have to become prostitutes to support the family.

Finally, a political friend of their father's in North America grub-staked them to tickets to New York, and used his influence to get them entry permits. After that they felt too indebted to him to accept any-thing further, and everyone in the family had to go to work. Susan-Inez's first job was in a shoe store, where she was driven crazy by the floorwalkers trying to look up her skirt every time she squatted to pull a box off a shelf or to fit the shoes on lady customers. She had an unusually liberal education for a young Spanish girl of good family, and was not a bit prudish, she said. But she could not endure men trying to exploit her body without her permission, not even by looking at it. She now worked as a nude model for Irina Naxos, and another woman artist in an advertising agency that Irina had introduced her to. She always wore the blue-dyed British jumpsuit in the street, and low-heeled Cuban shoes, and didn't give a damn what people naturally thought. However, she had never cut her beautiful black hair short, dyke-style. Her father liked it long.

"But where did you learn to draw like that?" I asked. She told us that her gift had been discovered when she was about ten years old, and she was given lessons from then on by an elderly artist who was her mother's uncle. He lived mentally entirely in the 1890s, and dressed to match with a white-piped weskit and pearl-gray spats. By the time she was twelve he had her making colored sketches of Gaudi's insanely baroque Art Nouveau church in Barcelona where they lived, and gave her Beardsley's drawings to study and copy. The day he gave her the folio he also gave her a little lecture about the duty of the artist to see beauty bare and pure and to be shocked at nothing. He also suggested she shouldn't let her parents see her copies. When she ran out of Beardsleys to copy she began inventing her own, usually much wilder and sexier. She was already plagued by sex-dreams. When she was fourteen her uncle told her there was very little more he could teach her, and that she must now go out and throw herself into life and nature instead of trying to learn art from books.

"Nature is wise," he said, "and will teach you all the rest." She had already begun sketching herself naked in the pier glass on the door of her mother's armoire, she said, and was in love with her own body. She did not show her uncle her nude sketches of herself, because they showed her budding pubic hair, about which she was somewhat shy.

"Did you ever have a boyfriend in all that time?" Magdalen asked.

"Of course," Susan said. "I only found out how I really am when I was fifteen. I was already a woman and I knew all about men. We lived in the country four months of the year. There were rivers, fields, animals—I had my own horse. I swam naked with my cousins who were boys. I knew everything." She paused and then added, "I don't hate men. I just like women more."

I looked at Magdalen. As far as I was concerned, everything was going very differently from what she had certainly planned. I could see there were lots of things politely missing from Susan's story—just as there are from mine. Such as the inevitable girl cousin or art student who had doubtless taught her to be a lesbian at fifteen, if not with her sister earlier. I was seriously considering whether I ought not to sacrifice my affair with Magdalen, and bow out in favor of Susan, at least for a while. Genius has its rights, I felt. Insane me. However, logic triumphed over gallantry, and I realized it wouldn't work, anyhow. What Magdalen was after was a charming threesome—with her in the middle—"Every end of the spectrum!" just as she'd chortlingly said. She wasn't planning simply to have a lesbian affair, no matter how talented the artist. If I knew Magdalen, that would leave an aching void in her, as they say. Maybe several.

To tell the truth, I thought an erotic threesome would be wonderful too, especially with a female wildcat with the artistic and erotic imagination of Susan Aguerra. I assumed I would probably end up getting scratched but I figured it would be worth it. Her remark about not hating men made the whole thing perfectly practical from the permutational position, so to speak, just as she had intended. How was it done, I wondered? Maybe you went at it just uninflected and simple, as I had, years before, with Merry and Sherry, when we were all eleven. You just laid them out in a row on the bed and dipped your wick into each of them alternately, like Saturday night in the harem. Unsanitary certainly, but damned hot-making for the macho male.

And then let them fight it out for who got it last, so you could lay soaking in the winner up to your balls for the rest of the night.

No, that was too childish. As I'd already done just that with Merry and Sherry when I was a kid, this should be something more complicated and refined. Besides, both these women were experienced physically, surely in every way—she'd just said so—and both had the temperament of sexual artists. What they were after in the threesome we were all preparing, mentally and verbally, with big aphrodisiacal mushrooms and sides of sweet pepper like roasted human hearts between the chunks of shish kebab, was clearly some crazy emotion, or psychological thrill they expected to feel, and not any mere physical sensation. I felt somehow relieved at the thought.

We had great gooey desserts that looked like shredded wheat puffs dripping all over the plate with honey. Magdalen had the waiter take hers back and put a slab of stiff cream on it too. She ate it slowly, unable to repress little lascivious gestures of anticipation with her tongue tip as she licked up and toyed with the mixed honey and cream. When she saw us both watching her, she only laughed.

"Well, you know me," she said. "I want everything."

Yes, and what was I after, I wondered? I looked at intense little Susan, who was even more intensely watching Magdalen's tongue-tricks with the dessert. I was the damn-fool cuckold now, wasn't I? Taking my neurotic wife to the elegant whorehouse to taste new and unedited delights: lesbianism, trios and beyond, doubtless in rooms lined with mirrors and wainscoted in gold. What would come next? Think ahead. Negroes, no doubt, and surely many other men. How many? Three, five? Separately? No—too obvious. All together, to be sure, and attached to her at every aperture and her armpits, like a great gloriously maternal passive queen bee. And then what?—Whippings? Puppydogs? Where would I draw the line? Where would she draw the line? I'd draw the line tonight, goddammit! Why was I doing this at all? I didn't want Susan, or, if I did, it was for what was in her head, not her tail.

We walked arm-in-arm to Magdalen's apartment, which was close by, near Gramercy Park. We said nothing. Magdalen walked in the middle, linking arms with us both. Well, I decided out in the cool air, there was nothing to keep turning around in the barrel about. I'd fuck them both. It would surely be great fun. Why lie about it? Lesbian stuff too? Of course. Let them satisfy me! I didn't have any two pricks, did I? Maybe that was what was really worrying me. None of us could deny that we'd already all made love together, and so very satisfactorily too, on Christmas Eve, though we carefully didn't mention it.

Had Susan come then, I wondered? No one had even touched her, and both her hands had been working like the pistons of a trumpet voluntary on Magdalen's bottom. I was only suffering from buck fever—my first real trio, and with two beautiful women. The red and the black! Gorgeous too. No dogs, y'know. Dammit, it wasn't my first! What about Merry and Sherry? I'd just have to take things as they came. I'd be like Sir Epicure Mammon in Ben Jonson's *The Alchemist*, whom I discovered when I was studying the problem of Pietro Aretino's *Sonnets* and the lost illustrations of the sixteen positions:

> For I do mean to have a list of wives and concubines
> Equall with Solomon, who had the Stone
> Alike with me; and I will make me a backe
> With the elixir, that shall be as tough
> As Hercules, to encounter fifty a nighte . . .
> I will have all my beds blown up, not stuft;
> Downe is too hard: And then, mine ovall roome,
> Fill'd with such pictures as Tiberius took,
> From Elephantis: and dull Aretine
> But coldly imitated. Then, my glasses
> Cut in more subtill angles, to disperse
> And multiply the figures, as I walke,
> Naked between my Succubae.

When the three of us got to Magdalen's apartment and she locked the door behind her, we simply dropped our poses. We all understood perfectly why we were there, and we all wanted it. As usual, my mind was racing along on the problems rather than the pleasures: on how to modulate from sitting drinking sweet wine on the sofa, as we were, into the next room and onto the bed. I guess women are more practical. After refilling everybody's glass just once, Magdalen simply acted as she would have acted if we two were alone. She put down the wine bottle, stood there smiling in front of us in the lamplight, reached down with her hands crossed and pulled her dress off over her head. Her petticoat came next, and she stood in front of us in nothing but a white garter belt, stockings and shoes, with her magnificent red-gold pussy hair shining like Heaven's highest light. It was a great scene. Beside me, Susan was taking mental pictures of her with intensely staring eyes. *Magdalena Triumphatrix*, floating over the shish kebab flames, would surely be her next Beardsley drawing.

Magdalen stepped forward out of the puddle of her clothes, like Venus rising from the foam of Jupiter's semen, and gave each of us one of her hands. She canted her hip to one side, and swaying her big white breasts she said: "Do you want me? Here I am." It was indeed a great scene.

I wish I could say that in a moment we were all rolling together on the floor, but it wouldn't be true. There's often a hell of a lot of awkward fumfuddling about in a situation like that—even with all the realest passion and the most sincere enthusiasm. The best solution would be if the participants or contestants or you-know-what-I-mean could all arrive stark naked together at one central arena, from three separate well-heated undressing rooms or wild animal runways, to circus calliope music of "The Entry of the Gladiators." Or at most wearing just a velvet cape attached only at the neck. Allez-oop!

This would give them a chance to get out of their clothes as gracefully as a born immoralist like Magdalen, who came into this world without panties and bra and stayed that way. With men, however, there he is at a certain point balanced on one foot, trying to get his other leg out of his goddamn pants, and cursing the light he's left on; and he also has some pretty well-twisted underwear and socks to squirm out of too. While the girl is standing or lying there in tableau, panting with willingness. If his shoelaces refuse to come open fast at that point, or his pants-zipper gets stuck, he might just as well have stayed home, or go home. I decided instantly not to bother about undressing. If Sir Beerbohm Tree could play Iago in modern clothing, I could do Tiberius and Aretino with my pants on. I pulled Magdalen down across me onto the sofa and seized her closest nipple with my mouth. Her legs trailed open and Susan fell forward on her knees and began kissing her red-gold bush.

Magdalen was not willing to give up the stage-setting, however.

"Please, darling," she said, pushing Susan away gently, "take off that ridiculous bearskin. It's scratching me. And I've never even seen you naked."

Susan tugged an instant at a tuft of pubic hair with her bared teeth, as though planning to refuse, and then stood up, kicked off her shoes, and shrugged herself out of the jumpsuit. All she had on underneath was a long chemise belted in silk, with a few simple embroidered eyelets at the bosom, and a pair of little green socks. She did not look as though she was willing to take off the chemise, and Magdalen let us all off the hook by jumping up then and running into the bedroom, losing her high-heeled shoes in the process. She tore open the bed—covers, sheet and all—one motion, and flung herself down plumb in the middle with her arms over her head, waiting for us. Susan ran after her fleetly, and was kneeling between her legs and sucking her when I arrived a moment later, undressed. My shoelaces had come open like a charm. There was no light in the room except that of the lamp in the parlor coming through the door, which was just right. Anyone who tells you it isn't exciting to see two women making love is lying to you. I had a hard-on like a primitive Greek statue. I admit I never heard a woman say seeing two men make love excited her. See the Vaertings' *The Dominant Sex*.

As Magdalen was occupied, you might say, and I didn't just want to repeat our Greek vase fresco of Christmas Eve, I sat down on the bed behind Susan's uplifted buttocks and began toying with them, tossing up the back of her silk chemise, which had no crotchpiece, and tucking it under the slender little silken cord that served as a belt. Magdalen's eyes were open and she held out her arms to me.

"Darling," she crooned, with her mouth all inviting, "are you abandoning me?" I wasn't, but there's something about a *new woman* that's hard to resist. Ask any bull. "Soon," I said. "Soon."

I stood up so that I could reach Magdalen's breasts with one hand, but kept playing with Susan's bottom with the other, finally running my hand down the crack and dipping my fingers into her cunt, which was already juicy as I knew it would be. What she was doing to

Magdalen would surely be exciting her too. Otherwise, why would she be doing it? I tried to pull Susan up, not roughly, by her shoulder, and she lifted her head unwillingly.

"No, no," she implored. "Let me! Let me! You do anything you want! Just don't give me no baby!"

"Yes, darling," Magdalen crooned almost maternally, to me I guess, "I'll drink all the babies."

I surely wish I could remember the rest more clearly, but I can't. In those days I kept morning-after sex diary notes, crazily, sinfully, ungallantly—and most unendurably of all, on three-by-five-inch index cards! But there were times like that when I must've been suffering from Dr. Alzheimer's Input Overload, and unfortunate great holes dropped out of my memory. I'd love to have them now, but I've lost them. All I know for sure is that I made love to both women in turn, first to Susan from behind—I mean vaginally, no matter what she might have said or really wanted—and then to Magdalen as she lay there. Meaning that it's perfectly true, as many men believe from having experiences just like this, that being a lesbian is largely a state of mind. And that it can be set aside by many a purported lesbian who wants to set it aside *ad usu delphini*, for some special evening or in a trio where a man is needed or all that's present. I have had a couple of experiences like that even with rock-hard lesbians and avowed man-haters too, when the wind was south-southwest and you couldn't tell a hawk from a handjob.

Later, everything was reversed in our presumed "king trio" with me in the middle. Both Magdalen and Susan were frankly using me as a sexual beast of burden, or copulative coupling-link between them, and they were eventually wearing me down to a phallic nubbit. "Lucky I'm alive today!" as the music hall romantic hero observes in a lewd aside. No man can keep up with even one woman who feels like making love all the time; and when there are two. . . ! The harem-dream we men have is a lot easier to live with than the reality of it. After a couple of nights of making love to both women together, I didn't even try to come any longer. In fact, I tried not to, and was basically hoarding my sperm already like any Hindu practitioner of

Tantric magic. I also didn't bother to worry anymore whether both or either were coming or had come through anything I did. But if the two women were sometimes—often!—too much for me, they were somehow always enough for each other, and showed marvelous erotic patience and *longueur*, especially Susan. She and I both understood sex the same way: as a prolonged nursing at a forgotten mother's breast; a long-lost, almost sacred communion. As a man for them, I tried to act like King Prick. But I was only pretending.

In our nights together, I was simply taking possession of them with my penis, like the cock of the walk, enjoying my self-bestowed right to push anybody out of my way and dip into anyone anywhere I wanted. I did not try to make Susan suck me, as I saw perfectly that the price of her total willingness was to let her keep her mouth fastened for incredibly long periods to Magdalen's cunt, or breasts, or mouth. When her mouth was busy on the mother-body she wanted, Susan was wholly excited and willing to be fucked.

Mostly out of curiosity I guess—does sucking a lesbian feel any different from sucking any other kind of woman?—when at a certain point I found us all in a kind of open triangular ring, with Magdalen sucking me and Susan sucking her, lying across her belly, it seemed the most natural thing in the world for me to curl forward in a circle and suck Susan as well from behind. Childhood memories! She came up onto her knees at once, springing her thighs open frankly and excitingly, to let me in deeper. I concentrated on her clitoris and inner lips with my mouth and tongue, sucking at them deeply and mouthing her flesh in and out. Susan came to her orgasm rapidly, her muscles clutching at my thumb and forefinger, which I was plunging in her, front and back, in a solid but not-too-deep bowling-hold. Everyone was toppling over by then, me especially, and I tensed up and allowed myself finally to come too, so Magdalen could drink her babies.

All the rest is something of a haze. It's not that I don't remember everything we did, but I can no longer remember just which night we did it on. We repeated the whole thing with undiminished enthusiasm and delight every weekend for the next three months. In those months I made a great many notes on what the three of us did together, and know in some detail what I was feeling subjectively. Since nobody wanted my semen anyhow, except orally, and it was a bother and a danger to them vaginally, I continued hoarding it or at least kept slowing down on throwing it around, just the way the Hindus say they do or don't, with the superstitious idea that it lengthens the man's life. In those three months I learned to do what became a habit for the rest of my life: not to make love for my own orgasm—which of course I'd always have at the end anyhow, or more than once—and not really for the woman's either, but to savor the marvelous touch and grip and sensations of the tissue of the inside of the woman's body, in all her ways and places, and times of the month too. I drew no "aesthetic" lines.

The only thing that I remember certainly about the later hours of that first night, and a number of others, was that I somehow jealously resented and tried to prevent the two women from sixty-nining with each other. They occasionally fell into it anyhow before I could interpose my body artfully among or between them, and make one or the other of them suck me instead. *Naked between my succubæ*—and will my publisher have the guts to let me use that for my book title as I want?—took on new meanings for me, that I hardly think even Sir Epicure Mammon really meant. Though obviously when he says that the beveled mirrors will "multiply the figures" of their intercourse as he walks, he does not mean walk but fuck.

Why I was so prudish about the sixty-nine, which other people say and I admit is so decorative and exciting to watch women doing, isn't hard to explain. Especially since Susan would rise often with her mouth dripping from Magdalen's vulva, when she knew Magdalen had come, and they would rub their lips purposely together to share the taste of her cyprine liquor. Some sort of female version of "licking off that first snowball," with the man's semen. I guess I felt it important for Magdalen not to become too convinced a lesbian experimenter. I feared I'd lose her then without any doubt to this indefatigable Other Woman. Because very soon Susan had moved into Magdalen's apartment with her, where I came only weekends. Also, though Magdalen and I didn't realize it at first, Susan was really and authentically in love with her.

That made my jealous proprietariness wrong and irrelevant, I knew, but I continued anyhow. The best way I found to get between them, as it were, was by joining into their now frequent sixty-nines myself, whenever I was in bed with them and no matter who was topside and who was on bottom. I would kneel or lie behind them, whether they were piled on each other or side-by-side, sinking my penis into Magdalen slowly and powerfully—masterfully, I'm trying to say—at the same time. If I had horns I'd have doubtless done a bit of goring and bellowing into the air at the same time, to mark off imaginary property lines on my woman. Of course this is all improperly macho, illiberal, immoral, wrong and very ridiculous, but that's how I felt and don't doubt that's how I'd still feel if it came up again. You might yourself. The liberation of women is a great and noble struggle in which I believe firmly, in the front of my head. But in his prick and balls every man including me is a rutting, rotten chauvinistic goat, or would be if he could and that's all to the good. You can count on it, God knows.

Magdalen had told me half a dozen times or more that she deeply needed to have something—anything—inside her when she came. Even on the rising slopes of her excitement when she would be sucking me, I would always somehow twist her around, on all fours or on her side, to keep two of my fingers plunging delicately or twisting inside her vagina, plus my thumb at her clitoris. If I couldn't twist her, or myself, that far, I would use my arched instep, or my big toe, just as I did when I came in her mouth. I didn't try to excite or help Susan in this way often, since I found very soon that all her sensation was in her clitoris, plus of course the emotional excitement of sucking the other woman. She didn't really care whether or not there was anything in her vagina or anal muscle when she came, or maybe didn't even consciously want it, though I knew that her muscles opened and closed delicately like a clutching mouth at her orgasm.

I guess I must be more feminine than the average lesbian, because

I certainly found it tremendously exciting when Susan would drive a thumb or finger into my anus when she knew I was coming. The power and the ripping intensity of the orgasm, when I had something inside me too, was enormously greater, just as one assumes it is for a woman. It could make me shudder and feel weak, my arms falling limply to my sides. I almost became hooked on that way of coming, especially after Magdalen learned from seeing Susan do it, and also began favoring me that way. At first I felt extremely shy about it, though they were not. I imagined it made me seem somehow homosexual to them—as if that mattered! It certainly at first made me seem homosexual to me. But the sensation was always so overwhelmingly better for me than orgasm ever was without it, that I took my chances on having my conscience call me names, ever since I had learned about it years before as a hopelessly masturbating dishwasher in an Adirondack vacation camp.

Later I also found that having a woman beat me wildly on the loins and upper buttocks with her heels at the moment when I was about to come had almost the same effect, and is easier for her to do in most positions. Women seem to enjoy this charming little demanded violence or erotic revenge. However, it's also a very good way for them to get pregnant accidentally. There are times when any man forgets himself. Everybody forgetting themselves is a population explosion.

PLAYING ON
THE EDGE

◆

In English the Korean Word
Bahp Means "Glutinous Rice";
or
At the Women's College

poetry by Robert Perchan

Yum Yum

by Larry Tritten

Cock & Balls

poetry by Laura Rosenthal

Fantasies Impromptu

by Mario Dworkin

R & D in Suburbia

by Arlett Kunkle

Performance

by Melissa Moore

A Night of Dark Intent

by Larry Tritten

IN ENGLISH
THE KOREAN WORD *BAHP*
MEANS "GLUTINOUS RICE";
OR
AT THE WOMEN'S COLLEGE

Can't stop messin' with the danger zone.
—Cyndi Lauper

Halfway through the semester
finally
they stop asking me
How old are you?
Don't you miss your home town?
How much do you drink?
Is it true you're not married?
and we go on
to deeper things
What, sir, does
she-bop mean?
Good question
I wouldn't've known
except I read *Time*'s
Music Section
to keep up with
my race
It means, I say,
authoritatively
Female Autoeroticism
Blank stares

all around
exotic frogs
on lotus pads
gazing up
into the light
so I say it
in Korean
yoja jah-wee haeng-wee
and I sense a ripple
in this placid pond
of Oriental souls
How does he
know that bad word?
they whisper
quite rightly
given my struggles
with their tongue
but at least I've
let them know
what we sing about
back where I come from

Robert Perchan

◆

YUM YUM

◆

By Larry Tritten

Having an affair, Tafler realized on the first night he cheated on his wife (he accepted the term "cheated" because his incipient mistress, a writer of melodramatic romance novels, savored it, but he used it ironically because he believed that not cheating on his wife would be cheating on himself and therefore potentially more troublesome to his marriage than if he bottled up the temptation and became disagreeable), would be like being a double agent: the essence of the situation was a furtive shuttling back and forth between two powers, in one case political, in the other sexual. Tafler suspected that he would be good at having an affair because he *was* a double agent (of a sort) and consequently experienced at subterfuge. A high-level executive with a company that manufactured state-of-the-art running shoes, Tafler met once a month in Central Park with the representative of an emerging nation whose citizenry was in the process of becoming universally shod and was paid well for the latest footwear secrets. The latest payment from his source would allow him to spend more leisurely on his mistress, who was, incidentally, his wife's best friend and confidante. Which is how Tafler happened to know that his wife was on the verge of having an affair with her psychoanalyst. Of course, Tafler was jealous. A woman's extramarital affair, he believed, was less necessary than a man's because women were more abstractly sexed and not ruled by phallic urgency like men. Tafler had once heard this very point expounded at a party by his wife's psychoanalyst, Parti, a beautiful lesbian who he had subsequently failed to interest in an affair with himself (she had responded to his pass by telling him coolly that she knew from his wife that he was too dangerously romantic and not her type anyway, although she had had a sexual dream about him after hearing from his wife about some of his erotic techniques).

Now Tafler was having lunch with his mistress, Francine, at an Italian restaurant in the Village. In the wake of having told him that his wife was contemplating having an affair with her psychoanalyst, she had also divulged that she was making good money on her own by working part-time days for an obscene phone call service, news that had further astonished Tafler, who had always believed that she had been anesthetized from the need to work by his executive salary.

Tafler, naturally, was jealous. He had always thought of his wife as being almost militantly monogamous. These new developments startled him.

"Oh, she *is* monogamous," Francine said, adding, ". . . more *or less*," with a deadly smile. "I mean, Tanis is only insubstantially interested in sexual adventure, which shows in her abstract choices—metaphoric phone sex and a possible dalliance with another woman, who is just a sort of erotic *surrogate*—I mean, Tanis is resolutely heterosexual . . . more or less."

"How do you know that?" Tafler asked.

"Well, we fooled around a little once, dear—I tried to seduce her, but it wasn't really very . . . successful . . ."

Tafler supposed that he was turning the color of his spinach fettuccine. "You . . . tried . . . to . . . *seduce* her?" The words were like stones tossed one after another into a psychic pool, their splashes radiating consecutive circles of dismay in his consciousness.

"Yes, of course . . . for research on a character I was working on as well as to give her a different kind of perspective that might result in providing you and I with more time together. You *are* the first man to touch my G. spot with the tip of your nose, darling."

Tafler smiled, more or less.

"But I'm really a bush league lesbian," Francine went on. With the tip of her tongue she retrieved a strand of pasta that had draped itself over her lower lip and tucked it into her mouth, smiling damply. "Even at Brandeis I preferred a vibrator to freebies from a dykey friend who was so jealous she always swore she'd steal the batteries." She sighed reminiscently. "But your wife's shrink is really gang busters in this area, honey—I mean she could give Sappho a jump for her money, and I suspect that even Tanis might really get with it with her—you know, orgasms that start out like wind chimes and end up on the Richter scale! She *is* a fast learner, you know . . ."

"Tanis is not gay," Tafler said stolidly.

Francine's laughter, dissonantly musical, tinkled in Tafler's ear. "But, darling," she said with characteristically wicked emphasis, "you don't have to wear a costume to the ball to get confetti on your shoulders."

Tafler sighed, and Francine playfully probed his genitals under the table with a fork. "Relax," she said.

Tafler tried to look as sophisticated as one of the imperturbable cocksmen who appeared on all the covers of Francine's paperback novels. He was wondering just how jealous he should be in a quantum sense of an affair that didn't involve phallic penetration when Francine said, with the deadly grace of a true psychic marksman, "You know, Parti is a writer, too. She wrote something called *Sappho's Scepter: An Informal History of the Role of the Dildo in Tribadic Romance*. It's a sort of a salacious textbook written in a humid academic style that seems calculated to seduce the reader into prurient consciousness."

"Wait a minute," Tafler objected, startled by the news. "Is this the same woman who agreed with me that lust is more characteristically male because of the nature of the dick? She's also an apologist for penis envy?"

Francine smiled semi-sweetly at him—two sugars in a cup of hemlock. "Not really, lover. The point she makes is that women are more sexually imaginative than men because their sexuality is more thoughtful and less physical. She draws an analogy between the male sex drive and demonic possession. She refines the concept of penis envy into something she calls penis pensiveness and concludes that a surrogate penis is better than the real thing for the same reason that diet soda is better than one full of sugar."

"Un-fucking-believable!" Tafler exclaimed. The old familiar suspicion that women were extraterrestrials loomed larger in his mind. He tasted his wine and said, "What do you think of Parti?"

Francine said quickly, "You're a better lay, although she does know how to use a surrogate cock with great expertise."

"You mean. . . ?"

"Yes, of course . . . It was *I* who referred Tanis, remember?"

"*Why* am I a better lay?" Tafler asked in words that sounded remote and frozen to his ears.

"Because I'm basically heterosexual, baby. And I like my cocks with something in 'em. When the oscillating is over I want the *piñata* to break. I want molten lava to run down my slopes. I want the dam to break, *comprende?*"

Listening to her, Tafler felt the warm flush of lust begin to inhabit his blood. Women! Without looking one whit less cool and composed than a model musing somnolently under a Cinzano umbrella, she touched the tab of his zipper under the table with a forefinger. Her smile deepened with slow, subtle force. Tafler visualized *The Birth of Adam.*

"*Where?*" he asked hoarsely.

"The john," she said.

"H-here?"

"Oh, yes!"

"Men's or women's?"

Francine smiled. "Your choice, sweetie." She gave him a look that reminded him of a black cat on a Halloween party invitation he had seen years ago. "There are lilac rain clouds gathering over my libido, lover. The oven is full of compote. The tide is coming in." She shuddered delicately and, bending forward, licked his hand.

"Jesus," Tafler breathed. *Writers!*

Back in his office, Tafler languished in his leather swivel chair. He mopped beads of sweat from his forehead with Francine's canary yellow panties and put them in the Bloomingdale's shopping bag in his desk drawer with the other twelve pair, locked the drawer, and reclined back in the chair. He thought he was in love. But where did one draw the line between fabulous sex and love? Fabulous sex had to be at least two thirds love, he decided. He opened the desk drawer again and ran his hand through the exquisite collection of nylon and silk panties, looking in and marveling at the wonderful blend of lime green, pink, turquoise, taupe, ice blue, lilac, platinum, white, black, purple, zebra stripes, and shimmering gold. He sighed deeply and put the bag away again.

The phone buzzed and Tafler answered it. "A Mr. Realgar," Liz said.

Tafler took the call. "How are things?" he said.

Realgar spoke slowly and with an undertow of melodrama. He always enjoyed this. "Will you meet me on Thursday?"

"Tomorrow?"

"Yes."

"The usual time?"

"Yes."

"Yes."

"Bye bye."

Tafler hung up. Now what? he wondered. Was he being upstaged by someone at Nike? He made a face, took the phone number Francine had given him out of his pocket and dialed it uneasily.

"Hi," a woman said.

Tafler gave her his credit card number and asked to speak to Felatia.

"This is Felatia," Tanis's voice said a moment later. It was low, warm, smoldering with hot possibility. "What would you like to say to me?" she went on, each word like a sweet bite of a dirty confection.

Tafler had always had an entertaining facility for doing accents and voices when he told jokes, and now, talking through his fingers and being careful not to overplay it, he plunged ahead. "I want to make love to you."

"Oh . . ." The word was like a coital sigh. "Sure, honey. Go on. What's your name, lover?"

"Max."

"Max, are you hot for me?"

"Yes."

"I'm hot for you, too, Max. I'm *really* hot. I want it *all* from you. Tell me what you want me to do, baby. You can do *anything*. Are you hard?"

Tafler realized abruptly that he was, although it was ancillary to his motive, which was maddening curiosity.

"Tell me what you want to do to me, Max. What do you want me to do to you? Every part of me is hot for you, lover. I want to hear some hot fucking talk from you. What do you want to do. . . ? *Come on . . .*" It was the same sensual tone she used in coaxing him to eat broccoli, a little joke between them, because she loved it so much and he had vowed eternal detestation of it. *"Come on . . ."* This time it was a hot whisper, a verbal sirocco stirring through the wires.

"I want to make love to you," Tafler said.

"Oh, that's *nice,* Max," Tanis said, easing up on the slut approach, which made Tafler feel giddily respectful. "But don't you want to talk dirty, Max? I'm here for you, and I'm ready for you. Don't you want to use the F word, Max?"

"I—I'm a little shy."

"Here's a nice word, lover. Say *fuck.*"

"Fuck," Tafler blurted, rigid with horny confusion.

"Fuck *who,* Max?"

"Fuck . . ." His mind went out on the high wire of the concept, balanced but frozen in midair.

"Me, Max. *Fuck me . . ."* She made a low throaty purring sound. "You're shy, baby. I like that. But let's relax, okay? I'm so hot for you. Do you like me?"

"Yes. Yes."

"Tell me exactly what you want to do to me. Take it easy. We're going to make great love, Max. Shall I take my panties off now?"

Tafler became speechless. "F-Felatia, can I call you back?" he said.

Tafler hung up and sank back in the chair, dazzled and simmering. That afternoon Tafler left work early and went to a nearby bar, secluded himself in a corner booth with a Zombie, and reflected. He was, he decided, in love with Francine. Was there some quantum difference between being *in* love with someone and loving someone? Being "in love" implied an emotional transit, with an undertone of implication that the condition might be ephemeral, and that was given credence by the fact that he loved Tanis but was no longer "in love" with her. Their love, obviously, had found its destination—marriage. He supposed that being in love with someone was largely a matter of sensual imperative and that monogamy took the edge off of that feeling through familiarity. And monogamy was clearly sexual imperialism—it even came with a proprietary affidavit! In the eyes of society his love for Tanis was supposed to preempt his loving anyone else. It was that Aristotelian either/or, this or that bullshit. This *or* that. He was supposed to feel either this way *or* that way, sans nuances. *They* would have you believe that love was a linear path, with no detours, side roads, or off ramps. Moreover, they expected one's Platonic love and love for humanity to be universal but conjugal love and sexual love in general to be monopolized by a single partner. They would have you buy the attitude that the love that originates in your mind is supposed to be illimitable and pervasive but the love that originates in your pants is supposed to be confined and restricted. In the Judeo-Christian sexual ethic, Tafler concluded, Eros is given a one-way ticket to ride steerage on the Love Boat. Tafler leered into his Zombie. He was much more emotionally versatile than the conventional rules allowed for. He loved his wife. He was *in* love with his wife's best friend. And, the more he thought about it, the more he wanted to fuck his wife's psychoanalyst . . . and that had nothing to do with love . . . although given a chance, he knew the contagion could spread. Tafler simply loved women. The nature of the dick. Nobody expected a gourmet to go only to French restaurants, without a thought for veal parmigiana, sushi, or bacon cheeseburgers. And what was love but psychological gastronomy?

Suddenly intoxicated by the power of both love and lust, Tafler went to the phone booth in a corridor at the back of the bar. He dialed Dr. Dolmen's home number. The phone rang once before a relay clicked and a voice came on the line. The message was brisk and formal. "This is Dr. Dolmen. I'm not in right now, but please leave your name and number and I'll return your call." It occurred to Tafler that a lethal amount of the woman's sex appeal was in her voice— gardenias on the rocks. A velveteen ferret slinked through the psychic underbrush in his libido. Excited, Tafler dialed her office. He was in luck. Her secretary (a man) answered, "Dr. Dolmen's office."

"Is Parti in?"

"Who's calling, please?"

"This is an obscene phone call. She'll want to take it. It's good."

"Hold on, please."

A moment later Parti's voice asked tentatively, "Yes, who is this?"

Tafler shuddered lasciviously. He didn't attempt to disguise his voice, not bothering to wonder if she might recognize it, not caring, going with the momentum of his desire. "Think of me as a voice whispering up from the cellar of your libido, Parti. I love you. I want you. Why should your beauty be monopolized by women? I want to taste your mouth, your cunt, I want to feel my cock pushing lovingly inch by hot inch through the soft channel of your pussy until its tip kisses your cervix and the plush nook starts to get all sloshy. I want to lick your mouth and suckle your tongue and fuck you until we're slippery with each other's sweetness . . ." Tafler paused, enraptured by his carnal eloquence. "Do you hear me, doc?" he croaked.

"I hear you." Her voice wavered.

Tafler forged on, "My tongue is licking the mouthpiece, I wish I could taste your ear. I want you, *want you*. Will you touch your pussy for me, baby, will you, please?"

He heard her breath, measured but audible, on the other end of the line. *"Will you?"* he asked rigidly.

"Yes," she said in a low voice whose single syllable throbbed with the force of her surrender to overwhelming impulse.

"What color are your panties?"

"Pink."

"Pink! Oh, wow, the color of your cunt! Are they wet, Parti? Is your cunt leaking?"

"Yes, yes, yes it is. I'm soaked, lover, drenched."

"Put your hand in your panties, baby, and ease one finger, your middle finger, into the shoal of your pussy and then deep inside until the knuckles of your fingers are pressed into the curls of your thatch. It's *my* hand, baby, *my* finger. Stir yourself up and then take it out and lick the nectar off our finger, lover. Do it, and tell me how it tastes."

"It tastes *good*," she murmured after a few moments. "I'm so wet. So hot." Her breath panted into the receiver. "Fuck me, I want you to *fuck me*," she gasped.

"You want cock?"

"Yes, yes, goddamnit. I give in. I want your cock!"

"And I want you, Parti."

She murmured. "Would you . . . like to fuck two of us?"

"Two?" Tafler was stopped abruptly.

"Jeff, I know it's you," Parti said. "Tanis confirmed it. This call is coming over the speaker. She's right here. She's taking my panties off right now—ohhhhh, she just eased the tip of her tongue into my pussy. She agrees, and I agree, if I'm ever going to try cock—and she's told me again and again how good it is!—your cock is the one, and you can take me at the same time she gives me her pussy to ease me into it. . . . Are you game?"

Tafler was momentarily speechless, and before he could formulate a clear thought or say anything, Tanis's voice whispered into his ear, "Darling, get right over here! Parti's giving her secretary the day off. I know you've made a pass at her. I want you to fuck her. I want you to fuck her while I watch. Then I want you to fuck me while she watches. Then her and I are going to fuck while you watch. Your wife has been changing lately, you sleaze, but I think you're going to like a lot of it . . . *Maybe.*"

There was no doubt about Tafler liking what subsequently happened to him in Parti's office. It was a sexual fantasy beyond his wettest dreams. Sex reduced to its lascivious nucleus. Hot blood and hot pants—sexual passion refined to pure aphrodisiacal craft—fucking, but fucking with a psychological patina of love, love for his wife who in her startling new role as bawd coached him through the menage as one might teach someone an exotic dance, and love for Parti because there is no love quite so exhilarating as that distilled from an inimical relationship: as mutual libidinal heat miraculously replaces the coldness a kind of super passion is generated by the disintegration of antipathy, and it becomes incandescently romantic. He would remember later fragmented mind-bendingly erotic images of the three of them improvising an iconography of passion punctuated with caresses and kisses spiced with the flavor of fresh ardor, a sweet sensual taste. In the end the three of them, glittering with primal brine and giving off a soft heat like that from a bed of cooling embers, sagged happily in each other's arms, Tafler the nexus of the affectionate fusion.

At home that night, in bed with his wife beside him in contented sleep, Tafler wondered what it was all about. Were they swingers now? He felt a little twinge. Sex might become an adventure in statistics. That didn't necessarily appeal to him, although it was certainly the flip side of a proprietary relationship. Surely there was a balance to be had. Tafler sighed. He realized that while he was not resolutely monogamous, he was not necessarily hyper-polygamous. No, just give me a *few* good women, he thought. He looked at the bedside alarm clock. It was midnight. All over the country, hundreds of thousands of people were not fucking (or making love) because of the *Tonight Show*. He got up and went into the front room and dialed Francine's number.

"Hello," she said.

"Hi, it's me."

"Oh, hi, babe. What's up?"

"I just wanted to tell you that I love you." The words had the magical quality of an incantation. Did it matter that the statement was indefinable?

There was a moment of silence, then Francine made a sound like a cat purring with a lump of ambrosia stuck in its throat. "Do you really love me, hon, or are you just in love with my blow jobs?"

"Both."

"If you were here I'd give you one."

"Parti and Tanis gave me one earlier."

"If wishes were horses, baby."

"I want to make love to you."

"I want you to fuck me."

"I will."

"I can't wait."

"Good night, Francine."

"Good night, lover."

That night Tafler dreamed that he had to move and he found himself inside a cunt, appraising it. The walls and floors were floral pink, the rooms furnished with plush pink couches and chairs that were all covered with lustrous white satin pillows. Alabaster tapestries shimmered liquescently on the walls. It was as warm as a summer in Kansas and the floor yielded resiliently with each step. An ethereal fragrance, somewhat reminiscent of bakeshop aromas from his childhood, suffused the air. "This is a nice place," he decreed, ". . . but I wonder how much the rent is."

A pink telephone on a pink quartz table rang, and he picked it up. "Hello," a voice said, "this is the landlady. How do you like the place?"

"I think it's terrific," he said. "I want it."

"There isn't much of a view."

"But it's cozy. I love it."

"It's very expensive."

Tafler felt sudden apprehension. "H-how much is it?" he asked, moving with slow steps across the viscid floor, dragging the pink phone cord behind him. He waited expectantly for an answer that never came, and that was how the dream ended.

The next day Tafler met his man on the bench in Central Park. They sat side by side for a while without talking, then his contact, who wore a conservative business suit with a native cap that looked like a mutant fez, said, "Do you have something for me? I have something for you."

Tafler passed him an envelope. "Some interesting changes in lacing going on," he said.

"Ah."

"How have you been?"

"Millions of shoes are in the works. You are helping my country take one giant step toward urbanity. In a few years we will all be yuppies."

"Good luck."

The contact passed Tafler an envelope with cash in it, then said, "I have something else for you."

"What else?"

"In this business we believe in staying completely informed. In having the eyes of the eagle. Please relax, but do you know that your wife is having an affair with her head doctor?"

"Yeah, I know," said Tafler.

"Ah. Do you know that your mistress is having an affair with your wife?"

Tafler was silent. "What?" he said, finally.

"A word in the ear. Things you should know."

"Well," Tafler said.

"Do you know that your mother is having an affair with her pool cleaner's assistant?"

"Wait a minute," Tafler said. He held up his hands more or less in protest.

When the contact had gone Tafler sat on the bench by himself for a long while in a musing daze. He had been around long enough so that nothing really surprised him. He had learned long ago that even the zaniest satire was consistently being upstaged by reality. He envisioned a world in which science fiction and fantasy magazines were outsold by a new genre of thrilling magazines with titles like *Credible Realistic Tales*.

Tafler found himself, as he often did, watching the women passing by and sifting out the lookers from the others in a typical sexist fashion. He frequently watched women with the same sense of wonder with which he had contemplated a vast assortment of penny candy as a boy, marveling at the infinite variety of them. Over the next fifteen minutes or so he enjoyed with stone-faced appreciation the sight of: a new wave blonde whose hair looked like a corn field after a napalm strike, wearing icy blue lipstick and violet eye shadow, voluptuously dowdy in a black leather skirt and matching jacket; a gamine with unlikely but superb large breasts enhancing the front of a blue sweater, a pink cigarette trailing azure smoke in one hand; a woodsy blonde with cataracts of bright yellow hair splashing down on the shoulders of a plaid shirt, her hips sharply accented by faded Levi's with multi-colored arabesques on the back pockets; a stunning Latin woman with a black skirt swirling around her hips, unhaltered breasts rolling with peaked nipples against a shining blue satin shirt, an ebony tress twisted down in a sexy scallop to partially hide one of her gleaming dark eyes; a cool-looking gum chewer (Tafler had had a weak spot in his libido for gum-chewing women ever since grade school when he sat behind one of the prettiest girls in the class and caught a beatific waft of her chewing gum) in gray jeans, an old Levi's jacket, and white running shoes with red hearts on the laces; a misty blonde wearing white sweat pants, with lavender leg warmers bunched at their bottoms over white running shoes, and a pink T-shirt emblazoned with the word WINO; a voluptuous Asian sprite in white shorts and a huge red T-shirt that enveloped her body down to her hips, a tuft of frizzed hair spilling like a *tsunami* wave down over her eyes; a narrow-eyed mankiller with a long ponytail of wheat-colored hair wrapped around her throat and resting in the cleavage of a black satin blouse, her black leather pants accented by blue high-heel baroque tapestry boots with a floral design; a numbingly aristocratic brunette with a fringe of auburn bangs peeping out from under the hood of a lipstick-red cardigan coat worn over a matching T-shirt dress, a dazzle of black and gold lacy-patterned nylon showing between the dress's hem and her glossy flat black shoes; a post-holocaust Lolita in tight jeans and a T-shirt with the message LOOKING FOR MR. BIG HUNK, an ice-cold glare preceding the tips of her clunky platform shoes.

Before long Tafler felt intoxicated with beauty. He left the bench, went to the nearest phone, dialed a florist and had a dozen roses delivered to his mother, who he thought had given up sex during the Carter administration. He asked that a note be included that read, ENJOY THE ROSES AND RAPTURES OF VICE—JEFF.

He called Francine and asked if she could have a drink with him after work. She agreed and at five-thirty they met at a bar near her apartment. She was in a booth waiting for him when he got there. He slid in, kissed her full on the mouth, tasted her tongue, and said, "You're having an affair with my wife."

Francine looked at him squarely, her gaze tangentially troubled for just an instant before her lips curled up in a small wry smile. "I'm doing it as research," she said defensively.

Tafler's voice was taut. "I don't get it. You said you've tried to seduce her but it didn't work out."

Francine tasted her drink, at the same time gesturing for a waiter. "I lied to make you feel better. She seduced me. It was, and is, heaven."

A waiter appeared and Tafler ordered a screwdriver. "Heaven?" he said. "What is it with us? *Limbo?*"

"Heaven with thunder and lightning."

"Francine, you make my hair stand on end."

"I'll make your tortoise do a double-back flip, too, honey. While we're on the topic, we might as well get with it. Would you like to have us both? We've talked about it, but purely as fantasy." He felt her hand on his thigh, her thumb and forefinger converging on the tab of his zipper.

"Does she know about us?"

Francine smiled. Her fingers stroked him and he pressed himself against her, wanting her. His mind spun. He would never understand the nature of sexual relationships, he thought, because there were no definitive answers. It was like trying to find the gift of truth in Chinese boxes, with each box revealing another and so on, presumably *ad infinitum*. And if one did find the final box it would surely contain a paradox that could itself be endlessly analyzed. Emotion and instinct can't be graphed. You can't have a dialogue with desire, which is impervious to the niceties of language.

"This is going to be good," Francine said. She showed him the tip of her tongue, and she said wickedly, "Yum yum."

Indeed, Tafler thought. I've unmade my bed, and now I'll have to lay in it. Francine's tongue left a sort of sheen of light on the pad of her upper lip as it retracted into her mouth.

Yum yum, Tafler thought. Yum yum yum.

COCK & BALLS

the scariest thing I ever saw   have ever seen   I was
six & it seemed like   it was   it was like   it was
just a flash   a meaty tube of skin black
hairiness between my father's legs   it was
MY DADDY'S THING & I did not want to think
   about it
I thought   so that's what it is   underneath the tweed
lap   I lay my head on   THAT   I lamented the
   deception
which is dog   in man   & paid the boy next door
   M&M's
to show me his   sweet toy-like-penis   scar still pink
balls hairless   he named the thing   & spelled it
PENIS   I smelled it warm like a cookie   sour
like a baby   that scent stayed with me   it was memory
seduced me at fourteen   when I succumbed   to the
   sweet
dirty perfume of a boy   whose cock was so hot & hard
inside his sweaty jeans   it hurt he said & would I
kiss it   please   he came instantly   young sperm
yeasty like fresh bread   later I met a lot of pricks
had sacramental sex   had sons   & in a sense   got
   balls
of my own   but somehow   aroma was gone from the

world
there was no   turn on   no sweet & sour electrons
bonded sense to sense   my sense of the absurd was
    boundless
my sense of decorum grew   dim   I did not know these
    things
I sensed them   I recognized a stranger   in a bar
in my mid-twenties saying   hello   I am a famous poet
can I come   in your hair   BOY POETS are bred in
    MOTHER'S
POT   I hollered   UTOPIA is a cock in every kettle
first   let me   smell you   I breathed in   dog & mountain
leather   wool   & bourbon   there was matzoh ball
    soup
on his breath   I fell in love with the stench   I cook
politically & he makes sense   his penis when erect
is distinguished   by an expressive scar   cut by a canine
tooth   we fuck like wolves   in certain phases
of the moon

Laura Rosenthal

FANTASIES IMPROMPTU

By Mario Dworkin

In her mid-30s, Erin Daniels moved to Chicago from a college town in Ohio. She wanted to get away from people who "couldn't react to either heat or light."

Within six months of moving to the Windy City, which she has since come to regard as an odd combination of sophistication and stupidity, Erin was introduced to Billy by his cousin, a woman who like Erin worked as a medical writer. Billy is a well-known Chicago actor/comedian with a gravelly, stentorian voice who can as easily do Mikhail Gorbachev as Jesse Jackson. It was a case of curiosity at first sight.

What attracted Erin most to Billy was his compulsion for drama even when he wasn't performing. The first night they went out, he picked her up in a limo after his show and they drove around drinking Roederer champagne and fucking until three in the morning.

From Ohio to Billy's limo was quite a trip, very flattering. But what really won Erin over began when she told him no man could possibly compete with her fantasies and he said, "Bullshit, I can make anything happen." That's when Erin began to grasp that dating a case of galloping ego might have its perks, and that her fantasies need not necessarily stay inside her head.

A week later, Billy sent Erin a red leather blindfold with a note indicating he was ready for her to order up her first fantasy. Even now the memory of that note speeds adrenaline through her veins, sending a wavelet of pleasure and anxiety that makes the fine hairs on the back of her neck salute.

Actually, Erin never thought analytically about her fantasy repertoire until Billy. Her first flash when pressed to verbalize her private erotic thoughts was that bringing these personal "stories" to the surface would somehow expunge the powerful pleasures they had always provided her. But as she recounted them, what she felt was an unexpected embarrassment over how all the stories seemed to have the same theme: how a savvy, highly educated, independent woman whose idea of a really good time was a Saturday tour of a sub-atomic particle accelerator could get off being turned into a little pleasure slave, so willing to be subjected to a grab bag of sexual humiliations.

There was something hugely exciting about revealing herself. She also admitted she liked the way Billy pleaded with her to give him the chance to bring her fantasies to life.

Erin compromised with herself by revealing one of her simplest scenarios. She half hoped Billy would laugh it off and tell her to come up with something more sophisticated—her other half wasn't sure how she wanted Billy to react. So as she swallowed the bottom of her second glass of wine, she said she'd always felt aroused by the prospect of being a harem slave about to be sold against her will to a more fearsome master. Erin winced at the cliché, but she held her composure.

Billy laughed. "Well, that's easy enough."

Erin found herself overwhelmed with a desire to fuck Billy right then.

Nights later Billy showed up unannounced around eleven. He told Erin to throw on something simple, and then gently he removed her glasses and told her to get the blindfold. "Now do as I tell you," he said in a way that actually caused her pussy to tingle.

Billy said no more until they reached the car. Then, as if flipping a switch, he began haltingly in a Middle Eastern accent. "Call me Nessim," he said convincingly. Matter-of-factly, he said he favored her enormously and wanted to keep her, but there were unfortunate realities to consider. Oil revenues were down. He had received an offer for her he could not refuse.

Erin couldn't decide whether to laugh or to tell "Nessim" to stop because she had chickened out. But then with perfect clarity she realized that to stop meant she and Billy really would have nothing to do but go home and tackle the Sunday *Times* crossword puzzle together. Erin decided she didn't want to stop. "Be *gentile* with me, Nessim," she teased in her best little girl voice.

Windows down to warm summer sounds, they drove for a good half hour, parking finally on a noisy street in a decidedly ethnic neighborhood. Passing a restaurant open to the sidewalk she heard Egyptian—or was it Greek?—music. At one point, Erin thought she could even smell deep-fried *falafels*. Erin gripped Billy's arm, wondering who in this crowd would notice her mask. No one said anything.

Abruptly, they turned into a sheltered entrance. Billy rang a doorbell, and Erin unexpectedly felt droplets of sweat trickling from her armpits. The door opened and a silent greeter led them down a long hallway to a room or an apartment where Erin heard men's low laughter.

Another door unlocked, and Billy led Erin into a much smaller, quieter, very warm room. She thought she smelled clove cigarettes and cardamom. Were they drinking thick Arabian coffee? She thought: *Billy hasn't missed a beat.*

Nessim announced he had brought "the woman" to be tested by the interested party. Erin heard a man grunt across the room. Despite herself, her nipples hardened. Nessim said he wanted a decision within a couple of hours. Then, he kissed Erin's neck, whispered for her to be very, very good and shoved her into the arms of a man who led her into another room. He gently pushed her down onto a bed and then left her.

Beyond the closed door, the language of innumerable glottal stops resumed. Two muted voices, neither Billy's, began to argue. Erin began to tremble. She wanted to laugh at herself. But she could not.

♦ ♦ ♦

Perhaps ten very long minutes later, in which Erin hoped she would expire from an adrenaline rush that left her soaked with perspiration, the door opened slowly. Distinctly she could smell a man, his yeastiness, his warmth. He approached and she could hear his breathing accelerate. Softly, in a voice she did not recognize, he said in tentative English that she had nothing to fear if she did as she was told.

Silently, he took her wrists and bound them in front with a thin, suede strap. He raised her arms, hooking her wrists to an attachment above her, and he stood very close for some moments, inhaling her scent. He did not touch her.

After a time he knelt and removed her sandals. He told her to stand perfectly still. Erin nearly catapulted as she felt him begin to cut away her dress.

Cool metallic blades inched between her thighs and around her waist until he pulled the fabric away, tearing the uncut cloth as he pulled the lower half of the dress to her bare feet, which he kissed.

Next he cut the shoulder straps, carefully gliding the scissors through the thin cotton between her breasts. He severed her lace bra, and the final frontier—her panties—were dispatched with two deft snips. "Better," he grunted, squatting before her and grasping her thighs from behind. "Much better." He lingered a few minutes with his nose about an inch from her pubis. Erin could not control her shivers.

He got up and methodically walked behind her to pinch the flesh on her buttocks, and to slide a finger deftly down her crack. Erin fought it, but a squeaking sound came from her throat when he found her telltale wetness. A voice in her head shouted: *This is too fucking good.*

She felt him reach around to feel the weight of her breasts with his hands, and to stroke the flesh of her sides with his nails. He said nothing as he pinched the skin at her waist. Then he disappeared for a moment. When he returned Erin thought she felt calipers measuring the thickness of her flesh.

He moved around front and knelt again, signaling for her to open her legs more. Again, she felt calipers measuring a fold of flesh behind her knee. Then again halfway up her thigh, and before she was ready, the lips of her sex were separated and pulled back to expose her clit. A warm, lubricated, practiced finger stroked her from the underside. Erin could not help sucking air as she felt her body begin the familiar slide to orgasm. But he stopped, abruptly, rudely. Her wordless noise revealed exactly how aroused she had become.

A new sensation—a beard—made her jump back and close her legs. But then Erin's knees knocked fiercely until he caught her in a hug and steadied her legs. With one hand he began again to separate her cunt lips. The cool points of calipers grasped her pea-sized hard-on. Gently, holding on to her nodule, he pulled and twisted the flesh ever so slightly until she was standing on her toes, buzzing like a bee, and squeezing her buttocks and praying that he'd do it long enough for her to come.

But he stopped again. He stood up and unhooked her arms, massaging them as he brought them down. At that moment she was so close to orgasm that she vibrated in her frustration. She thought: *This is all Billy's doing! Damn him. I'm going to give him the worst case of blue balls he's ever had.* Then she wondered where he was: *Does he even care what's happening to me?*

With his hand against the small of her back, the man guided Erin across the room, to push her on her stomach on the bed, onto a mound of pillows. They had been arranged (*When did that happen?*) to prop up her butt to some ridiculous height. Before Erin could comfortably adjust to this new humiliation, warm oil cascaded over her cheeks and between her legs. Without delay, latex-gloved fingers began to explore, venturing with great enthusiasm in and out of her various ports of entry, inserting penis-shaped objects into both her openings.

This was humiliating, yes, but also very hot.

When he caught Erin surreptitiously moving her own fingers between her legs to relieve the fierce ache in her swollen pudenda, he vigorously swatted her backside. "No! Not until *I* am ready to release you." Roughly he turned her over, spread her legs and buried his bearded face between them, nibbling at her with such deftness that she imagined he removed corks from champagne bottles for practice.

But each time Erin seemed ready to shoot off into the stratosphere, he found a new place to put his tongue. *He is playing with me! He is playing with me!* She felt an urge to rip his head off. But at last he completed his round-the-world trip and returned to her clit. This time, just before she went off, Erin noted a strong familiarity in the way this tongue licked upward from behind her baby boner. Why did it seem so familiar?

Then it all became clear to her why this man hadn't fucked her yet. Beard or no, it had been Billy all along. The realization sent Erin roaring heavenward in a spasm that took her out of space and time.

Later—from somewhere outside her consciousness—a knocking and an impatient man's voice interrupted her post-orgasmic trance. Billy rose from the sea of pillows and opened the door. Erin heard voices, but felt so blissed there was no need to cover herself.

A champagne cork did pop. There was laughter. Erin heard Billy toasting: "My fellow thespians . . ."

That was the start of Erin and Billy's fantasy enactments. She gave him a plot and Billy made it happen. Billy took these assignments seriously and more often than not, the scenes involved costumes, dialogue and Billy's friends—who were as hot for an appearance in one of Billy's erotic numbers as they were about scoring bit parts off-Broadway. Sometimes he has participated, but mostly he has simply watched. He says it pleases him to observe her ecstasy.

Erin acknowledges that in the last year, Billy has been responsible for choreographing the most extraordinary sex she ever has had. But when pressed, she insists that the one enactment that continues to remain her secret favorite—because it involved a woman—was the one she did not initiate, and which ultimately required the least of Billy's organizational skills. It's a story she calls "Madame and Monsieur."

Unexpectedly one evening Billy called late to say that there was a party he wanted Erin to go to. She protested the hour, but he insisted.

In the car he turned to her with a new blindfold and said, "I'm loaning you to a friend for the evening. Take off your pantyhose." When Erin complied, awkwardly for there was little room in his car, he reached over to touch her bare cunt. "You'll enjoy this," he said so sensuously that in a moment she began to seep onto his fingers. He licked them and smiled.

Every other time he had given Erin ground rules for the evening events. She came to rely on these as hints for what to expect. But this time he said nothing. She found herself becoming anxious. Images from *The Story of O* kept popping to mind.

She felt better when she remembered Billy hadn't read it.

The car stopped and Billy put on the flashers. As he got out, someone opened the car door on Erin's side. A hand slid up her bare thighs dangerously close to her pussy before pulling down her skirt, taking her arm and guiding her to the sidewalk.

"Do I need my purse?" Erin asked foolishly. Billy said, "No, no . . ." and a man's voice said in a distinctly French accent, "Ah, very nice. She is delightful." Billy's deep, rich laughter filled Erin's ears. "I'll come back for you later."

The strange man wrapped his arm under Erin's to guide her. Keys tinkled and a heavy iron gate creaked. Once inside, a second pair of hands, much cooler, came from nowhere to put a collar around her neck. Erin found herself tightly restrained. Later, in her notes, she wrote about this feeling, *I bristle at the restraint, its silent command more powerful than words.* Billy had hit upon her deepest fantasy—and her deepest fear.

"Call me Madame," a woman said curtly. "He is Monsieur. Understand?" Erin was led, awkwardly, up a steep, wooden staircase. Maddeningly, the man and woman spoke quietly in French, a language she did not understand. She could not tell exactly whose hand guided her legs while resting on her butt.

Entering a room through a heavy door, Erin found her other senses working overtime to make up for her lack of sight. The air was fresh but sweet with a hint of incense when she did not feel the breeze from a window. Somewhere Bach's Brandenburg Concertos played.

"Take off her clothes," said Madame firmly. Monsieur knelt to take off Erin's shoes and then removed clothing as he moved up, commenting in French on what he was uncovering. Erin could smell herself. She smelled like sex.

"Come, I will bathe you," Madame said, and she pulled Erin by the leash, moving too fast to walk comfortably. The man and woman laughed as Erin awkwardly waved her hands protectively in front of her. But they stopped when she knocked a glass or bottle off a counter and it broke on the floor.

Monsieur carried Erin into a small bathroom with a tub full of warm water. "Kneel on all fours," Madame commanded.

Warm water cascaded over Erin's back, and the feeling of it running down her arms and thighs, over her butt and between her legs opened wide made Erin feel suddenly free. She had felt this exhilaration during some of the other dramas, but for the first time she understood it: She could completely enjoy what would happen here because the situation was completely out of her control. Whatever happened, she was not responsible. She thought: *In a few hours I will return to my apartment, to Billy, to my life, but right now I am captive to Madame's whims.* And it made her very excited.

Madame's hand, holding a bar of soap, slid across the taut flesh of Erin's rear end. *"Elle est belle, eh?"* Monsieur said. *"Oui,"* Madame replied, as if weighing the word very carefully. *"Elle est aussi très petite. Sa con est comme une fille,"* she said as her index finger made a first probe of Erin's cunt. Shifting gears Madame said so Erin would understand her completely, "Your body is like a girl's. Your skin is so very soft and pale. Your nipples are pink and unused. I shall enjoy pinching them." Which she proceeded to do.

When the bar of soap splashed into the tub, Madame's fingers moved to expertly soap and stroke Erin's exposed posterior, from her anus to her clitoris. Erin wondered, *Does she know that her fingers have me as glistening on the inside as the outside?* She caught her breath. Madame had found her swollen clit.

Then abruptly Erin was ordered to stand. "Dry her," Madame

said gruffly. Something in the woman's tone made Erin tremble. Monsieur wrapped a towel around her and gently rubbed her dry. "All is well," he said soothingly, "let yourself go with the excitement now." Erin leaned against him. Her head fell against his shoulder. She knew instinctively that this man, too, was Madame's slave, and that he would not hurt her. Later, in the notes for her therapist she wrote:

> *"He knows me as he knows himself.*
> *His voice touched my heart.*
> *Her voice touched my soul.*
> *Together they held me captive.*
> *I have both a master to command me*
> *And her slave to soothe me."*

Monsieur led Erin to a big, raised bed and whispered for her to lie facedown. Madame ordered him to tie Erin's wrists, and he complied gently. Then he tied her legs, opened wide, and Erin felt deliciously helpless. Hands—she was not certain whose—oiled her back and her buttocks. Fingers lightly teased her anus, which she raised to meet them.

"She is not excited enough for release," Madame said. "She must be wetter than this. *Whip her.*"

The words sent a chill through Erin's body. For several agonizing moments she held herself stiffly, waiting for the first blow. And for a moment after it landed on her butt, she was not certain how to react— to cry out or to writhe in pleasure. When it landed again she realized that this whip made considerable noise, but did not hurt much. Rather it seemed to make her skin glow. She imagined a rosy red that spread with each swing. Between swats Madame rubbed the spot with her warm fingers. Erin realized the game had become one of anticipation, especially when Madame caressed her tender and glowing flesh with what felt like a riding crop.

Later she wrote: *The whip wraps itself around my body, again and again, always in a different spot. Then I hear the whip but feel no pain, and it is Monsieur who groans. I am strangely excited by the thought of his reaction, a reaction we now share. But all too soon she stops.*

Erin was left alone to savor the warmth on her skin and to silently grind her pubis into the bed. Down the hall she heard Madame and Monsieur talking in mixed English and French. She wanted desperately to know what they were saying, but she could hear only snatches of the conversation: "She is too quiet." . . . "I want to make her moan." . . . "anal penetration." . . . "She doesn't like it." . . . "We'll soon see what she likes."

Madame's laugh was positively manic. A momentary panic seized Erin. She struggled vainly against her bindings as the sounds of Madame's high heels approached.

But it was Monsieur who stretched out on the bed beside Erin. She could feel he was naked. He caressed her face and neck. He said: "Would you rather be fucked by me or Madame?" Erin felt such confusion she could not speak. His gentleness gave her courage. But it was Madame who excited and frightened her at the same time.

"Madame," whispered Erin in a voice so small, he had to put his ear next to her lips to hear it.

What happened after that, Erin cannot remember exactly, not at least as a linear series of events. She remembers twenty fingers touching and teasing, then one finger probing her anus, then two fingers gently squeezing the engorged lips over her hard-as-a-pebble clitoris. She remembers thrusting her butt as high into the air as she could squeeze it. She remembers grunting as something too hard to be human entered her. She remembers being cut loose from her bindings and spreading latex across Madame's furry and very wet cunt. She remembers tonguing Madame into an orgasm, and feeling very powerful. She remembers taking Monsieur's condomed cock into her mouth and making him croon. She remembers Madame and Monsieur fucking on top of her. She remembers thinking that her body had become her sex, and that she could not quite tell where her body ended and theirs began. She remembers melting into a huge liquid pond of sensation. She remembers lying with them for a long time, still uncertain who, exactly, these people were, yet feeling so close to them that she wanted the moment to last forever. She does not remember getting dressed.

When Billy came to pick her up, Erin could hardly speak. She was exhausted, but still very much into her body, which she could feel glowing. In the car Billy tugged at the collar Madame and Monsieur had left on her, and he laughed his deep, rich laugh. "Well?" he said pregnantly.

And she couldn't wait to get Billy home to tell him all about it. She wanted to see his thick penis swell and harden from envy.

◆

R & D IN SUBURBIA

◆

By Arlett Kunkle

Chapter One

Boredom made me do it. And, boy, oh, boy, after fifteen years of fucking the same, straight-arrow man, I was well and truly bored, just about bored to death. My husband's a nice man and all, but, as he so readily admits, when it comes to sex, he's a very "vanilla kind of guy."

If I do say so myself, and I will since it's my ink, I think that phrase is kind of cute. He invented it after a skirmish with a J.C. Penney salesman over some size 42 boxer shorts in a particularly putrid, light ocher color. Since then, "vanilla kind of guy" has become part of our family-speak, but that's another story altogether.

Anyhow, vanilla certainly fits his M.O., because, by perversely keeping his heinie out of my reach when we fuck, he consistently thwarts my attempts to probe, with a wanton, wandering fingertip, his sweet patoot.

I'm talking about a sex life that had succumbed to automatic pilot, with some mechanical farting around in there too; sort of like the official timetable for a bus company: totally predictable arrivals and departures. Before climbing aboard, we sip Stoli in the breakfast nook and stare into each other's eyes. Shucking out of our clothes faster than a body can say "snakeskin," we hot-foot it down the center aisle to the bedroom, sit on the edge of the mattress and tongue each other's oral cavities. He nurses my nipples, always the right one first then the left. I lick his Popsicle for a mile or two. He eats my jelly roll for the same distance. With my legs wrapped around his waist, he fucks me past a few interstate exits. Then it's my turn in the driver's seat. I slide up and down on his dick until he moans for me to de-bus so he won't come to a premature full stop.

Back on my back, thighs spread wide, he pushes a couple of fingers up my twat, grabs the vibrator, electrifies my clit and I come like Evel Knievel rolling over fifty-four barrels and a rusty old Edsel. While I catch my breath, he finagles his putz into my pussy, pistons in and out, puffing and groaning, until, thirty seconds later, he stalls out permanently. Battery dead, he lays on my belly till I push him back into his parking place next to me.

In the twenty minutes it takes us to get from here to there and back again, we motor along the same roads, through the same towns, year after year, right on schedule, and, like I mentioned before, vanilla is the only flavor available at rest stops.

Folks, before I go any further with this memoir, I want to make something perfectly clear. If, as part of some Mickey Mouse Masters and Johnson survey, they asked me a list of wacky questions about my sex life, I could truthfully answer that, using whatever method got the job done, I'm a one hundred percent orgasmic gal. See, my husband is not an insensitive guy, just a boring one.

Chapter Two

So I cruised. I searched our suburban village for a man who would light my fuse, re-ignite my body's banked bonfires, spread white-hot heat into every nook and cranny of my currently listless, but still lusting life. I was looking for a man adventurous enough to help me bash sexual boredom back to Bataan.

I looked for him in all the everyday places, places readily available to me: the dry cleaner's, McDonald's, Dunkin' Donuts, the post office, supermarket, video store and the library.

Ah, the library. Bingo! One day there he was, the man in my

dreams, the man I planned to proposition, ASAP. Comfortably sprawled in one chair, his feet, crossed at the ankles, on the seat of another, he lounged beside one of the half-dozen, long, polished, golden-oak research tables.

"Arlett," I said to myself, "Arlett, this isn't just Avon calling here, you know, so don't you dare screw it up by arguing with God's design. Things will work out all right, you'll see. Accept this gift, Mrs. Kunkle. Take it off the short-term rental shelf, lug it home, sample a few pages to see if it appeals to you and, if it does, accept it graciously with a polite 'Thank you, Ma'am.' "

Chapter Three

I recognized good advice when it slapped me upside the head. I trusted the advice even more since it came from my own self. Watching him study the ups and downs of the stock market in *Crain's Chicago Business,* I realized in the first few seconds of my circling surveillance, I'd seen him before, in a navy blue uniform with a gun on his hip. My dream boat was the new village police officer, a recent escapee from the city that works—some of the time. While all the good people got fucked and tucked into their boring, suburban beds, he patrolled our quiet, ever-so-proper, tree-lined, pond-studded, neighborhood streets, keeping danger from strangers at the far end of the long arm of the law.

With a profile straight off a Greek coin, my pinup was classically handsome. He had the kind of face that would stop your heart, if you let it; Crater Lake–blue eyes, lashes long and thick enough to die for, what I'd always believed to be a perfect Mediterranean nose of patrician proportions and lips that looked as though they'd been stained by pure pomegranate juice.

Brawny, tawny and long-legged, with a flat belly and muscular thighs, his bare, elegant feet were strapped into black sandals. I was especially entranced by those narrow, high-arched tootsies. I'd always considered feet like that the mark of an aristocrat. Dressed in white slacks and black, short-sleeved polo shirt, he wore his curly, dark and glossy hair just long enough to brush the back of his collar. To my greedy eyes, he looked like a Greek god who, due to some inexplicable, cosmic snafu, had become stranded in the suburbs on the western shore of Lake Michigan.

I sat down across the table from him, and, when he glanced up from his reading, I flashed my best Mona Lisa–like smile. At first he looked startled, then a speculative wariness rippled across his gorgeous face. Those few seconds of negatory vibes were quickly replaced by a butane-blue-eyed stare showing definite signs of interest. It high-beamed out of his magical face; a face that drew me to it like a magnet to a refrigerator door; a face promising to fulfill all my forbidden fantasies. I felt this to be my moment of ultimate surrender, the moment when I revealed to him every unchewed mouthful of hidden hunger. So, when he returned my smile, I said, in my best breathy Bankhead whisper, "You are what I need."

He said, "Right."

I said, "Come with me."

He said, "Sure."

When we stood, he reached across the table, circled my upper arm with a giant hand and, in his rumbling, basso profundo voice, asked, "Are you a player?"

I answered, "Why not?"

He said, "Be careful."

I said, "I've been careful all my life."

He said, "You've been warned."

I said, "Let's go."

He said, "Lead the way."

And I did.

Chapter Four

My captive cop followed me home. While I unlocked the front door, he took a black gym bag from the back seat of his Jeep and we walked inside together. He closed the door and turned toward me, studying my face like it might go out of style. Lapis eyes brimming with unfathomable emotion, he read me like the Sunday funnies. Whatever response he was looking for he found because he whispered in my ear, "I'm home."

I stood, quiescent, before him while he pulled my blue silk blouse out of my jeans, rucked it up and over my head, and let it fall to the floor. My breasts, unbound, sprang free, and, although he did not touch them, my nipples stood erect like obedient little soldiers.

Instead, he moved his hands slowly up and down my rib cage, reading a Braille map of my bones, leaving behind feverish finger-prints. He ran his palms along the down on the top of my arms, then nestled those slow hands snugly in my armpits. His actions made me so hot the oxygen in the room caught fire and I couldn't catch my breath. I suffered silently through a major attack of giddiness, but he felt my tremors. Pulling me to his manly chest, he asked, "What else do you shave?"

Chapter Five

"What else do I shave?" I blurted, but after seeing the strained look on his face, I gulped and answered, "I shave my legs."

He took a Fleet enema from his gym bag, handed it to me and said, "I need you to shave your crotch, give yourself an enema, then take a long, hot shower."

I tried to hide my incipient panic, but he saw it and said, "We can stop now and forget about this and each other."

Scared and excited, I said, "No. No, I'm fine. I'll do what you ask. It will take a while though."

He said, "I'm asking this because I need clean and I need smooth now. I worked vice in the city for too many years. Spent all my days and nights slogging through sewers chasing perps of every persuasion who left behind a deadly stink and me without a gas mask. It almost killed me, but I was too stubborn, or too stupid, to admit it."

I said, "Okay. I'm on my way. I'll call when I'm finished."

As I left him, he whispered, "I'll be here. I'll be waiting. We have things to do."

Chapter Six

Police assignments completed, itchy and uneasy about the newly naked pudenda I now owned, I called down the hall to the Fuzz. When he walked into the bathroom, gym bag in hand, he, too, was naked as a jaybird. Sitting down on the toilet-seat cover, he pulled me close again, kissed my hip bones and belly button, then carefully eyeballed my newly shorn pubes.

"Good job," he said. "Perfect. The way they're supposed to be; hairless and smooth, like a newborn babe. So clean, so healthy and wholesome." He moved closer to my crotch, sniffed several times and said, "Delicious. Maybe I could get used to something smelling like Ivory soap."

After my heart completed a triple gainer, a wave of desire burned across my skin. My knees went watery. Dripping wet and shivery with anticipation, I tried to conceal my problem, but couldn't. So, I said to myself, "Arlett Kunkle, you are the Grincher in search of adventure, but, please, put a cork in it. Chill out. Hold your horses, honey. Good things come to those who wait." Needless to say, I was having a whole lot of trouble with the waiting game.

My splendiferous shamus unzipped his gym bag, pulled out a red, rubber enema bag and a tube of K-Y Jelly. Psychic pain radiating wildly from his sapphire-blue eyes, he looked deep into my amber ones, saying, "I need this, too."

That's when I realized his pecker had yet to join our party. "No problem," I said, "but first may I ask a question?"

"Depends," he answered.

"What should I call you?" I asked.

He nodded his head. After filling the enema bag with warm water and hanging it from the shower rod, he said, "Call me Max."

Chapter Seven

Max draped a towel neatly over the edge of the bathtub, then said, "I've been a cop for twenty-four years. Half my life. I've seen every shred of maggot-infested human garbage, every form of feculent human debris a city like Chicago can throw at a man. Those years, my life was a cancer running amok. They messed up my head. Control is the only way I can play now."

It was my turn to nod.

Max handed me the K-Y Jelly and ordered, "Coat the nozzle."

While I got in the mood to squeeze the tube, Max bent over the edge of the tub, resting his weight on his hands and knees, snugging his hips tight against the towel, he spread those patellas wide so that every inch of his bottom line was exposed for the whole world (in this case the whole world was me, Arlett Kunkle) to see.

Max had a limp prick, balls as big as Braeburn apples and, like a dear dream of mine come true, an adorable, tightly puckered bumhole. I very much wanted to interrogate that scrunched up and secret brown button, but figured, since it was his game, I'd play it by his rules. I stood behind him, waiting for further instructions.

"Stand between my legs," he said. "Insert the nozzle as deep into me as it will go, then slowly release the clip. Hold the nozzle in place until the bag is empty. Don't worry. It won't hurt me. I want this. I want to be clean and pure again, like a regular citizen."

I drew a deep and ragged breath, then stepped between his widespread nakedness. Even before I touched him, I saw his cock come out of its coma, stretch a little and begin to take an interest in the goings-on.

Slowly, gently, but with determination, I stuck the sticky nozzle deep into his innards and asked, "Are you okay? Am I doing this the right way?"

A muffled moan was my only answer. I felt empowered. If I wasn't doing it wrong, I must be doing it right, so I relaxed and, as they say on MTV, got into the scene. I loosened the hose-strangling, metal claw and watched the rubber bag wrinkle when the warm water rushed down the tubing and into the tightly clenched rear portal of my prisoner, Mr. Clean Cop.

As the enema bag emptied, Max whimpered and groaned and humped his lengthening, hardening prong against the towel's rough terry fabric. Holding the nozzle firmly in place, I bent down to bounce his balls, but in between panting, grunting and gritting his teeth, Max managed to choke out, "No, don't! Finish the job and get out of here."

Chapter Eight

Not knowing what to say or how to feel, I simply obeyed. Slinking out of the bathroom, I went into my bedroom and sat on the bed. For a snack while I sulked, I reached into the pity pot and devoured despair. Then, glancing down in wonder at my newly shaved pud, a flash bulb popped in my head. I got the picture and said to myself, "Hey, Arlett, you dope. This ain't so bad. Get a grip, girl, get with the program. Go with that flow everybody's always carrying on about." After thinking all that, an internal dam burst beneath the pressure. I felt my lubrication flow even more freely, saturating the sheet bunched beneath my backside.

I was still hot and wet for Max after all. How hot was I? My insides were so hot they'd melted into something resembling butterscotch pudding. I was ready, ready for anything. I wanted it, whatever it was going to be.

I waited out his enema event and shower. Even after my short detour into soul-searching, I admit I wasn't particularly patient about the pause in the action. But, when my cop came out of the bathroom nude, damp and smiling triumphantly, I forgave all.

I saw that the previous shenanigans, no matter how bizarre, were well worth the time and trouble. His was a magnificent schlong, lusciously long, thick as my wrist and arrogantly hard. It stood at attention, straight out from his belly, saluting me as stiffly as a Marine in a May Day parade.

Max knelt between my buttery slick thighs, tenderly kissed the corners of my eyes and whispered, "I'm not a face-to-face kind of guy. Can you handle that?"

Chapter Nine

I coughed to cover my confused delight, but realized several dozen of my most frequent and impassioned prayers were soon to be answered. Even so, my vocal cords contracted so tightly I was only able to squeak out one tiny, strangled, "Yes."

Max asked me to climb onto the bed and lie facedown. I scrambled across the mattress and stretched out shivering, not from an autumnal chill, but from my needs.

He dipped into his goddamn gym bag again, taking out polyester-sheepskin-lined, caramel-colored, Corinthian leather cufflets. He gently tied my wrists into them, pulled my arms above my head and fastened the cuffs' delicate gold chains to the corner posts of my headboard. He positioned two pillows beneath my hips, then laced my thighs into much wider leather cuffs, chaining these to the footboard.

My fantasy fanfaronade had become fact. I was, indeed, a policeman's prisoner and, with thighs pulled so wide apart, the tender flowers of my heretofore secret garden were subject to whatever obsession my gardening gendarme chose to cultivate. I was hanging, spread-eagle, from my own bed, much like a spider caught in the middle of a web it had spun between the thorny stems of two roses, and just as vulnerable.

After Max finished tethering, he massaged spicy-smelling oil into the muscles at the back of my neck, my shoulders, the sides of my breasts and down my spine. He hummed a definitely weird, high-pitched, tuneless tune while he worked. As he shifted his attention to the lower half of my body, rubbing the spicy oil into my hips and buttocks, thighs and calves, even between my toes, he chanted, "Pure baby. Pure Ba-Beee," in that same, screwy, sing-song, pseudo-Brothers-Gibb, soprano-style voice.

And then, out of the blue, a stranger knocked at the door. What I'm saying here is that Max, suddenly, very suddenly, switched back into his normal, everyday, deep and mellow Max-voice. His flip-flop scared the hell out of me.

◆ ◆ ◆

One is now obliged to ask, "Had the scripts somehow gotten mixed up? Instead of a busty, lusty, amber-eyed, auburn-haired, modern-day-Gothic-romance heroine getting exactly what she wanted from the man of her choice, was Arlett Kunkle, our woman of courage, doomed to be just one more dreary, captive female character fighting for her life, while bound hand and foot in a dank dungeon? Was she, in reality, keeping the villain at bay only just long enough to allow the cavalry to arrive 'in the nick of time?' And for a fair-haired, sword-in-hand, derring-do captain riding a white horse to snatch her from the very jaws of a fate worse than death?"

Well, fuck that plot line, Arlo, this is Arlett's story and what she writes is the way the cookie crumbles, or something like that, so . . .

But the change was benign, with no malignant, hidden agenda, because Max immediately began to beg, saying, "Please, may I continue?"

And I gasped, "Yes. Yes. Get on with it. For God's sake, don't stop now."

Chapter Ten

Max began his monotonous mumbling again. He sang his feverish, BeeGees "Pure Baby, Pure Ba-Beeee" song while he spread my tensely protective cheeks, held them wide apart while he filled my unguarded anal orifice with cold K-Y Jelly. Then, my police officer proceeded to delve deep into my derriere. First one, then two, maybe three, maybe more, who knows, cot-covered fingers were twirling and swirling, skating and skidding and slipping and sliding in and out of my rear exit. I could no longer figure out what was going on behind my back. For all I knew, Max was using the muzzle of his genuine policeman's pistol to plumb the strip-searched depths of my piece of ass.

I bucked and jerked, yipped and yelled trying to get away from his rudely romping, ravaging digits, but, at the same time, I tried not to. I guess you could say I tried the "bass-ackward" escape route.

While I begged him to stop, and screamed for him not to, Max, still singing his cockamamie, police-special song, pushed into, pulled out of and prodded every inch of my once maidenly bum. Just at the moment when I believed fainting to be the only reasonable way to escape the sublime torture Max busily inflicted on my fart fortress, he slipped his other hand between the pillows and my hairless mons and, with blind fingers, easily located my clit. He rubbed and circled and tweaked, tweaked and circled and rubbed my release switch until I came so hard I collapsed, hiccupping and shaking, into percale.

Through a delectable haze, I heard him ask, "Please, may I finish now?"

"Just do it," I croaked.

And he did.

Chapter Eleven

Max leaned over my back, his warm breath tickling my shell-shaped ear, reheating the pinpoints of sweat on that side of my face. I felt the head of his rubberized shaft pressing, at first gently, then with more persistence, against the furrowed gateway guarding my now semi-virginal butt.

I sobbed, "No. Don't. It's too big. It won't fit. It will kill me." Hoping all the while that Max would ignore my halfhearted whines and whimpers. And he did, because, by then, for Max, my pleas were a day late and a dollar short.

Clutching my pillow-buoyant hips, wielding the most beautiful truncheon a police officer ever possessed, Max plunged straight ahead, conquering the only body part capable of offering any resistance to his invasion, the circular muscle whose job it had been to defend my innocent innards.

He smoothly, relentlessly pushed his jellied dong to its hairy hilt into my butt, remorselessly, unrepentantly slaughtering the sodomy laws of the great state of Illinois. Pulling halfway out, pushing back in, again and again, my cop advanced ever deeper into enemy territory until, finally, bellowing, "Fuck 'em all," Max banged into my behind and shot me in the ass.

Before the heavy mists of super-saturated, *après*-sex sleep settled on my fluttering eyelids, I vaguely remember hearing him whisper, "I quit. Let the devil sort 'em out later."

Chapter Twelve

Having lost all sense of time, but not the memory of his convulsing cock wedged tightly in my deflowered fanny, I don't know when Max uncuffed my limbs and covered me with tangled, oil-stained sheets. When, through tousled strands of auburn hair, I finally found the strength to look up, he was dressed and holding that damned, delight-filled gym bag in his left hand. He patted me on top my head with his right, saying, "See you in the library, babe," and departed, taking his acetylene-blue eyes and perfect self with him.

After Max exited, I rested and, until a bubble of laughter broke in my throat, I calmly contemplated an aching anus, tranquil clit and the breached boundaries of a country called boring.

Wrapped in an untidy cocoon of linens from my marriage bed, I wiggled, giggled and stretched. Then, into a pillow that smelled of hot sex on a chilly afternoon, I whispered, "Arlett, you harlot, tomorrow is day one of serious metaphysical research into the effects of the cock and bondage market on the ins and outs of your redeveloping sex life. Until then, be still my heart."

◆

PERFORMANCE

◆

By Melissa Moore

She calls him from the train station. Her voice is shaky despite the wine she drank before she left the house. She stuck the rest of the bottle in her bag and touches it now as she waits for him to answer.

Unlike other men, he doesn't bother to let the phone ring several times. He never found it necessary to pretend he wasn't eager to see her.

"I'm running late," she says. "As usual. I'll be there around nine-thirty. Is that all right?" She knows it's all right. He finished his business that afternoon and stayed in town only because of her. Now, he is waiting. Not patiently, but with a single-minded purpose that worries and fascinates her. She imagines him in the hotel room, his eyes narrowing in concentration as he prepares to stage another performance in what he likes to refer to as "the theater of their lovemaking."

"As long as I know you are coming," he responds calmly. "It's on the ninth floor this time. Room 987."

The lobby is filled with people. A group of young Japanese women moves toward the exit, leaving in its trail a thick cloud of duty-free perfume. Midwestern conventioneers, American flags pinned to their buttonholes, have just returned from dinner and march past the reception. The women, oddly confident in their below-the-knee, pastel-colored suits, walk as if they aren't aware that they don't belong in this city of liberals. The men look like chain smokers, their faces gaunt and yellow. Two women, both dressed in tight, black dresses, converse in low voices near the bar. One of them smiles, raises an eyebrow, and picks up her drink. Nicole sees their eyes lock as they make what appears to be a devious toast. She envies their friendship. Wishes she had somebody she could talk to about him.

As always when she slips away to see him, her stomach feels heavy. Nobody knows where she is. She walks toward the bathroom where she studies herself in the mirror. Attractive, sexy, a bit older. It's been eight months. She goes into a stall, pulls out the wine and drinks once, then once more. The bottle is half empty.

Four Midwestern convention delegates ride up the elevator with her. Nicole feels the women's eyes on her bare shoulders and high-heeled shoes. She wonders if they think she's a prostitute. Now that it's too late to go back, she feels strangely confident in returning their stares. "Carrie—proud to serve as Secretary to Christian Brothers," reads one woman's name tag. Perhaps next time, I'll wear one too: "Nicole—proud to be an adulteress" she thinks with a hint of an evil smile. The elevator stops on the ninth floor. Sinning is less than a hundred yards away.

He opens the door before she knocks. Without saying a word, he pins her against the door, pushing a leg between her thighs, and opens her mouth wide with his tongue. He hasn't taken a shower, she registers, as he presses himself into her mouth, between her thighs. His smells, a mixture of day-old sweat and leather, have already penetrated her skin. He thrusts a hand between her legs and sighs deeply. Feeling trapped too soon, she pushes her hands against his chest. He laughs as she stumbles into the room.

She points to a bottle of wine he has been drinking. He pours them both a glass and their eyes meet as they toast. His face hasn't changed much since she met him five years ago. His features are strong, yet the ten-to-fifteen pounds he has gained over the past couple of years have softened the area around his mouth and chin. He looks sensuous in an old-fashioned, indulgent way. King Bluebeard, she thinks.

The room has two beds. She withdraws to the far edge of the one closer to the door, leans against a pillow and stares at him. He needs her so much more than she needs him, she thinks as his eyes move slowly down her body, undressing her.

"Spread your legs and show me your pussy," he says. "I want to watch you play with yourself."

Without looking at him, she pulls up her dress inch by inch until the naked part of her thighs is exposed. She looks up as she begins to unclasp her garter belt.

Leaning against the bed, he appears unnaturally large.

"You can keep those on. But do as I said. Now." His voice is low, but insistent. The performance has begun. She pulls down her panties.

"Slowly. I want you to do it very, very slowly," he demands.

She places the black silk in his palm.

"I love your smell," he says, inhaling deeply. "Now, spread yourself for me. Play with your pussy."

A warm tingling sensation runs through her body. She caresses herself, first hesitantly, then—with her eyes closed—more freely. Her lips are moist and full. She gently pulls them apart, sensing his presence nearby.

"Touch your breasts. I want you to have one finger in your pussy and one playing with your nipples." He is so close she can hear him breathing hard above her. Keeping her eyes closed, she complies.

"Suck the finger that was in your pussy," he demands next. She brings the finger to her mouth and licks it.

"Suck it as if you were sucking me," he demands. She opens her eyes and looks at him, avoiding eye contact. His erection is pressing against his too-tight beige pants. He is still fully clothed and she recalls the time he made her climb up on a table and strip while he, dressed in a business suit and wearing sunglasses, sat in a chair and watched from some distance.

"Now, stick your finger up your ass," he demands.

Nicole keeps playing with herself, ignoring his demand. He raises his eyebrows.

"All right, you know what that means," he says, moving abruptly across the room. "Strip naked and bring your clothes over here."

He sits in a chair sipping wine as she undresses. The tiled floor is hard and cold against the soles of her feet and she shivers as she crosses the room to bring him her clothes. He points to a place next to the right leg of the comfortable armchair and she complies, her back straight, her knees together as she bends toward the floor.

"Now, go stand in front of the bed over there," he demands. "Hurry," he adds when she hesitates.

"The beginning of Act Two," Nicole thinks, biting her lips as her body responds with irrational arousal to the humiliating treatment.

"Stay there until I tell you to move," he says. "Keep your back straight, your arms against your sides," he continues, anticipating the movement she is about to make to cover herself from his scrutiny.

He finally gets up from the chair and walks toward her.

"I love watching you," he says. "Your curves, the indentations, the fine muscles in your legs." He slides a finger between her legs. She pants, wanting him to keep it there.

"You want more?" he asks with a smile. She nods.

"Then you have to turn around," he responds.

He stacks all the pillows in the room on top of each other and pushes her against the pile. She closes her eyes as she imagines him observing her ass, which is raised so high in the air that her legs barely touch the floor.

He spreads her cheeks and she tightens up, knowing what is coming.

"Relax," he demands as he pushes first one, then two, then three fingers through the narrow cavity. She cries out in pain, but he doesn't retreat.

"Come back up," he demands as she tries to pull down and away from him. She raises her behind to take more mistreatment.

"Higher," he whispers. "I like to open you up, you know."

Pearls of sweat are forming on her forehead. She raises her ass again and this time feels the fingers in her pussy.

"You like this, don't you?" he asks. She doesn't answer. He forces his fingers back into her anus.

"Don't you?" he asks again, pushing harder and harder until she nods her head.

"Yes," she whispers.

He takes her in his arms and kisses her.

"I thought about you every day," he says. His erection is pressing against her stomach. When she doesn't respond, he continues.

"All my fantasies are about you. You know that, don't you?" She nods and he draws her closer still.

"I want you to tell me what to do," he whispers.

She empties the glass in one quick gulp then walks to the dresser and picks up one of his ties.

"Tie me up," she says in a voice so soft that it is barely audible. "I want you to tie me up."

He motions for her to turn around and she cooperates as he ties her hands behind her back, pulling the material until it begins to cut into her wrist.

"I'd like to open you up more," he whispers in her ear. "Can I do that?" She nods without looking up.

He unclasps her necklace and dangles it in front of her face.

"Suck the pearls," he says. "Make them wet. It will be easier that way."

She realizes what he has in mind. If she doesn't protest it means that she consents. That's the rule of the stage. She could stop it right now, walk out. But the part of her that longs for this treatment won't let her. She is moist and hot between her legs and knows she's going to stay.

The pearls are cool, and she tries to leave each of them as wet as possible.

"That's good," he says, running them between his fingers. "What do you think I'm going to do with them?" He leads her back to the foot of the bed, turns her around, and begins to kiss the back of her neck.

"Tell me what I'm going to do, Nicole." His voice is low and insistent.

"You are going to stick them up my ass," Nicole whispers.

"You want me to do it?" he asks into her ear. She nods slowly.

The pearls aren't big and the pain is not as great as she anticipated. After inserting half the necklace he asks her to stand up straight.

"I like that," he says. "You've got a tail." He pulls on the necklace and she feels a hot sensation streaming from her anus to her clitoris. She pants and feels his fingers between her legs. She is so wet, his fingers come out with the milky moisture.

"I love your taste," he says. "It's sweet. Strong." He licks his fingers.

She lowers herself into a large armchair and spreads her legs wide. "Fuck me," she says, avoiding his eyes. "I want you to fuck me."

He unzips his pants and comes toward her. His cock points straight upward. Holding her legs in his arms, he thrusts himself into her. They cry out together. It has been so long.

Back in the elevator she nods politely at an elderly couple. She is still sore and tingly between her legs and her hair smells of him. She wonders if she'll go back next time he is in town. He never presses her, although she senses that he needs her, that he relives their encounters over and over during the many months that pass between each act.

Is this what draws her to him, she wonders? The excitement of being, in effect, a forbidden sexual fantasy? Or is it her craving for sexual submission, the desire he helped her uncover?

The two women in black are still engaged in conversation. One of them smiles at Nicole as she passes by. The woman knows why she is here hurrying across an empty hotel lobby on a rainy Wednesday, Nicole senses.

She steps out onto the wet street and inhales deeply. She feels purged and energetic and walks quickly down toward the train station. After a few blocks, she turns and looks back at the hotel which in the mist is already becoming invisible. She looks up, trying to count the floors to where he is, but gives up. And in fact, it doesn't matter. The performance is over, the theater closed until further notice.

A NIGHT OF DARK INTENT

By Larry Tritten

Twilight was lilac on Ishtar. In this livid gloaming, on an isolated moor, stood an immense house. Two high towers rose above its series of chimneys and gabled roofs. Their shape was candidly phallic. The rows of windows on both floors held a lucid pink glow all the more warm and cheerful for its contrast with the house's umber wood. The house stood amid drifts of smoke-gray fog. One might have thought that a subtle sound of music came from within, as if an overture to a drama was being heard—but perhaps the sound was only some fanciful trick of the wind.

It was a night of dark intent. From a distance across the gloomy moor a party of six people approached the house in a Jeep. There were three men and three women, though in fact one could not tell one sex from another because of the colorless uniform-like clothing they wore and their identically blank and pale expressions, like those of androgynous manikins. As the Jeep approached the house the expressions tightened, tightened with the rigidity of the final turning of a screw impaling hard wood. Smoke began to curl from the house's chimneys as a man emerged from a cavernous central doorway to greet visitors. He was tall and unsmiling, but there was a fugitive spark in his gaze, and he wore a flamboyantly multicolored neck scarf with his black suit and black boots that were polished brightly enough to reflect the pale light of the yellow moon.

"Hello, hello!" he called as the Jeep came to a stop. "I've been expecting you!"

One of the party, slightly more solemn-looking than the others, stepped forward. "Holland?" he said.

Holland smiled. "Welcome," he said. He half-turned to regard his house proudly, and as he did the gazes of all six turned upward, up to the facade of the house, where now they saw in shameless ornamentation between its rows of softly lit windows a procession of bas-relief satyrs with erect phalli, of huge-breasted maidens with uplifted skirts skipping along and strewing grapes behind, elaborately carved centaurs dancing with naked nymphs and prancing fauns and laughing girls, all in a lewd promenade across the front of the house.

"Good God!" exclaimed the leader of the party, and behind him there was murmurous assent from the others. "Are you *crazy*?" he asked Holland, grieved.

But Holland laughed dismissively, his smile hospitable. "What took you so long?" he said.

"Brassard," the leader introduced himself to Holland, but did not extend his hand to be shaken. "You were *expecting* us?" he added, with a narrow-eyed stare.

"Of course," said Holland. "Evangelistic zeal knows no surcease. Having purified all of Earth, and made it an inviolable sanctuary for the solace of the resolutely untarnished, it seemed certain that you would turn your iron glances toward the heavens in search of whatever libertines might have fled to other worlds, that missionary devotion would carry you to the reaches of the galaxy with your reins and fetters, your taboos and prohibitions." Holland spread his arms theatrically. "You have found me, good people. And you will, of course, destroy my home. Yet first allow me to give you a tour, to whet your appetite for the destruction of a prurience I feel you will find heroic in scope."

The six people, as one, took a step backward. Brassard touched his hip pocket. "Force is an option," he said warningly.

"Force?" Holland asked, and shook his head. He looked surprised. "No need, Brassard. Love is the law!" He turned an intense gaze on the group. His eyes sought those of the women, whose sex was betrayed by a slight curvature here, a convexity there. And his fingers touched lightly, and away, at the front of his pants. Then, even as a collective indignant inhalation of breath followed the gesture, he was turning, beckoning his guests into the house.

"I don't know," Brassard said.

Holland gave him a withering look. "Why not just *burn* it, then?" he suggested in a sour tone. "Why bother with *knowing* anything? Just *burn it* all as all of you white knights of repression have always burned the books written by libertines without really reading them. I know you, Brassard. Chief Magistrate of the Moral Transcendency! I propose that your organization's motto be 'broader horizons for narrower minds!' All of you good people dedicated to the creation of a better society, one in which the mind is not troubled by free thought and the body is not violated by enjoyable sensations."

"Shut up, libertine!" Brassard snapped, his temper igniting.

"*Libertine*? What does the word *mean*, Brassard? It means *free* person!"

"I know all about *your* kind of freedom," Brassard said with measured distaste. "The freedom of a rutting animal. The freedom to treat women, and other men, like so much . . . meat." His lip fairly curled.

Holland touched his heart. "Ouch, sir, that smarts! *Meat?* Your point is moot. Nor does it have much substance as a *mot*. Do you really think I don't know a cunt from a cutlet? It was the precise color of the sky here at sunset that caused me to build my house here—color reminiscent of the cunt of a fabulous Latin pornographic movie star of yore. Where the unsprawled labia majora yielded into the vivid shell-pink of the vestibule of her vagina the inner linings and outer surfaces displayed a range of lividity from lilac through plum to oyster gray to a precise *bice*. A grayish blue with the soul of lavender in it! In closeups one could marvel at the mulberry, mauve, and indigo play of colors in Vanessa's lush and succulent cunt. I am an aficionado of pussy, sir! Of cunt yet unscrolled but limned with a shimmering hint of liquid nacre, of cunt plushly asplay and wetly radiant between hedges of bosky flax or dense ebony curls, of quim brimming with collops of flesh like simmered and sundered rose petals and basted in its own sweet marinade of buttermilk and brine, of cunt whose redolent fetor makes the olfactory neurons in my nose do glissades and my cock perform *entrechats* in my pants!"

Holland's guests all drew slightly back with a uniform expression of disgust. "We've heard enough of that!" Brassard said, fixing Holland with pitying gaze. "We will have a look at your house, and then we *will* burn the infernal place, and take you away in manacles. What do you think of that?"

Holland was placid, smiling wistfully. "Like an outlaw?" he asked.

"Like a pervert, a *deviant* sex fiend," Brasssard said with elaborate disdain.

"Ah, someone who *turns* from the *path*," Holland nodded. "Meaning: an explorer, or adventurer." He smiled and became again the essence of cordiality, extending a hand to bid his guests welcome, opening the great door and beckoning them inside. They hesitated until Brassard nodded, then began to file inside. Holland fell into step beside Brassard, and began to talk in a calm voice. "As I said, Brassard, I *know* you. I know you are a good man, a veritable paragon of redoubtable goodness. I know how you began as a customs official, snooping for pictures and books and movies that showed people enjoying love in exotic and *outré* ways. . . ."

The party emerged in a grand room softly illuminated by a single huge bowl of lucent rose light cradled aloft in a towering metal structure. The floors were of a patterned marble, dusk pink, lavender, and purple. There were a great many voluptuously soft gold and pink velvet and suede chairs and couches, and the walls displayed rows of huge paintings.

As his guests stood regarding his surroundings with blank faces, Holland went on talking. "I know, Brassard, how in the vanguard of all the forces of Puritan rectitude you pressed your pursuit of prurience, slaying the erect phallus and desiccating the irrigated cunt wherever you found them, and this while the wars continued, the guns proliferated, the killing became rampant. And you rose to power, fighting to destroy what you considered the true obscenity in the world!"

Brassard acquired a look of positive loathing, and he was about to speak when, looking down, he realized that the patterned marble floor depicted a kaleidoscopic montage of symmetrically interspaced vaginas, brightly opalescent in their candy colors. Brassard moved his feet uncomfortably like a man who has stepped inadvertently onto a bed of hot coals. He looked at the paintings along the walls and his mouth twisted in more disgust. He knew many of these from his identification books and had sought them, originals and copies, over the years with knife and vial of acid, aglow with an intoxicated sense of righteousness in the fever of the hunt. Here were watercolors by George Grosz in which bulbous phalli showered fat droplets of pale semen upon supine bacchantes. Here were various sleeping or merely languorous beauties—Gervex's *Rolla*, Goya's *Maja*, Titian's *Venus of Urbino*, the odalisques of Ingres, Renoir's naked bathers, the nymphs of Poussin. And there, quintessentially sensual, were Courbet's lovely sapphically entwined sleeping women. There romped anthropomorphic phalli in a bawdy dance, maidens in their boudoirs amorously impaled by lovers on canopied beds, nymphs frolicking with satyrs in woodland settings, Beardsley's heroically endowed amorists of *Lysistrata*, cubist jades with geometrically angled genitalia in happy conjunction.

"Feel free to enjoy a hard-on, gentlemen, compliments of the house," Holland said in a flippant voice. "And, ladies, let the glair sluice freely forth in your channels. . . ."

"Enough, God damn you!" Brassard exploded in a sudden rage. He stepped back, with a fist raised to menace Holland, but even as the fist poised in the air something remarkable happened. An arrow struck suddenly in his chest, transfixing him in that pose. Brassard, distracted in his rage, lowered his eyes to the deeply sunk red-feathered shaft, then glanced at Holland, glowering furiously, and pitched to the floor.

The five remaining guests stood motionless in shock and dismay until one of them received another bolt directly in the heart, crying out in a sigh that seemed almost orgasmic, and sinking to the floor. The remaining four stared ceilingward at the archer while Holland observed their terror with pleasure. They watched helplessly as the archer, a cherub, plump, pink-cheeked and golden-haired, with an erect phallus that would have been the pride of any brawny young man, hovering in midair high near the vaulted ceiling with a beating of flocculent white wings, nocked another arrow to his bowstring. Before the impulse to flee could animate them another arrow was fired, striking a woman in the breast, and she fell, clinging to the legs of one of her companions. Now the others broke for the doorway, but the cherub swooped down upon them, dropping another with an arrow to the heart. The final two hammered desperately at the door, which they discovered was locked. Leisurely, the cherub flew down to alight on the floor. The two remaining victims turned, trembling and shaking their heads, and the cherub dispatched them quickly, then walked over to Holland, making a slight bow and, with a smile, winking.

"Well done, Cupido!" Holland cried. He reached down, picked up the automaton, and hefted it affectionately into the air, the responsive fluttering of its wings fanning his face. As one might release a pigeon, Holland tossed the Cupid high, and watched it fly up, toward the ceiling, then off and away down a hallway.

Holland appraised the bodies, seeing that all six had smiles frozen tightly on their lips. He walked to Brassard and placed the tip of one boot lightly on his shoulder.

"Welcome to the party, Brassard," he said. "I think I can promise you that you'll enjoy yourself. Before the rose light in these windows embraces morning's sunlight you will know every pleasure you astutely avoided all your life. And then some!"

The aphrodisiacal balms and erogenic chemicals were doing their job, Holland knew, suffusing his victims' blood and coaxing sleek beasts up from the remote subcellars of their libidos. There was no time to waste. Holland clapped his hands and six young women came into the room from the hallway. They were multiracial, their flesh the colors of amber, sunlit honey, designer chocolate, rose-hued creamy satin, antique gold, and brushed leather, and their bodies exhibited an exaggerated opulence behind negligees the color of nighttime mist, ferns, and fresh-cut roses. They moved in an aura of the mingled fragrances of perfume, woodland loam, soap, and the subtle olfactory spice of lubricated cunt. Each of them effortlessly picked up one of Holland's prostrate guests and bore them away.

Holland was flushed with delight. Upstairs, in spacious beds awash in seas of colored silk and on velour couches, the automatons would be coming to life, according to a prearranged schedule. Listening, he fancied that he heard the stirring of all the sundry vamps and bacchantes, the intricately fashioned harlots and nymphs, bravos and rakehells, the lovingly re-created screen stars and exquisitely hung satyrs. The automatons were opening their eyes, a host of sea green, feline topaz, anthracite, and blue-gray gazes confronting their surroundings. Breasts rose and fell with a vital resilient warmth, and cocks shifted flaccidly yet with an incipient firmness between thighs. Women with mouths glossed like translucent quartz or cherry red rose up, breasts full and heavy, jutting, cunts primed with noggins of milky spunk, their hair spilling lustrously straight down or styled in eruptions of lush curls, rowdy tufts and ringlets, punkish spikes, or close-cropped furze.

Holland glanced at his wristwatch, waiting. Another ten minutes passed and his guests returned to the room through the hallway. They looked nothing at all like their former selves. They were all boldly and provocatively dressed. The three women, Holland noted, were now lovely and desirable, their uniforms having been replaced with satin and silk dresses with short skirts and deep cleavage, their sensible shoes discarded in favor of shiny boots and golden and black leather pumps. Brassard wore a tuxedo-style jacket with a gold handkerchief in the pocket and a shirt of golden dazzle. He smiled strangely at Holland.

"My fellow, Brassard!" Holland said, and took the other's hand, guiding him forward. "Welcome, welcome, all of you. The party is about to begin."

Brassard seemed abstracted, somewhat bewildered. "Holland?" he asked, thickly.

"How do you feel?"

"I feel . . ." Brassard sought the words.

"Horny?" Holland chucked.

"Horny, by God!" Brassard admitted, grinning.

Holland addressed them all. "The fun commences," he said. "Explore the house freely. You will find a different kind of ecstasy in every room. Brassard, allow me to be your companionable host."

Brassard nodded graciously. More guests began to enter the room as the visitors turned. Music sprang up from some hidden source as the house became wildly alive. There were men in the arriving group, but it was the women Holland was especially proud of. As a connoisseur of female beauty, Holland was a classicist. How very carefully he had studied the old magazines and films to get perfect effects! Dietrich wandered past them in her *Blonde Venus* costume—a dress that shimmered with points of light like starblaze, a great cascade of soft feathers spilling down over one shoulder from her hat. Following her was a stunningly alluring copy of a popular 1950s model, Diane Webber, wearing a pair of tight metallic-threaded lavender, blue and green hopsack trousers, a Goya pink shantung shirt, and cardinal-red stiletto-heeled shoes whose floral-patterned silk printed linings, Holland knew, caressed her lovely bare feet with every step. Behind her was Leslie Caron circa 1955, wearing tight black pants, a striped sweater, and ballet slippers with pink ankle wraps. Holland loved shoes, adored gamines. Waiters also began to appear in the room now, carrying trays of champagne and liqueurs.

Beside Holland Brassard made a subtle murmuring sound, like someone tasting delicious food, and Holland saw that he had noticed Traci Lords. Magnificently young (too young, the tale went), she looked yet lethally adult, for in spite of her sulky moppet's expression and the freckles sprinkled like cinnamon across the bridge of her nose, her body encased tightly in an emerald satin chemise was exquisitely mature; Holland reflected on how he had labored to make her breasts exact, those hefty and protuberant breasts whose distinctive shape he had for so long sought a proper descriptive word for before settling on . . . *retroflexive.*

"She is one mind-rattling hot and melting fuck," Holland whispered to Brassard, encouragingly.

"This is extraordinary!" Brassard said, eyes widening with wonder as Bettie Page circa 1957, pristinely and quite comfortably naked, moved past him toward one of the waiters.

"Let me get you a drink," Holland said to Brassard, and as a waiter passed by he deftly snatched a glass from his tray, handing it to Brassard. The liqueur was green. Brassard sampled it and smiled quizzically at his host.

"Absinthe," said Holland.

All about them the party quickly became lively. There was much laughter and, Brassard saw, an ease of communication he had no familiarity with. There was also, he noticed, touching. He saw two women with their arms around each other's waist, a woman gliding her fingers admiringly through a man's hair, a satyr drawing a smiling girl into a light embrace and open-mouthed kiss.

"The stew is simmering," Holland said. "But, dear Brassard, let me show you the upstairs. We'll return."

Sipping from his glass, Brassard followed Holland into the hallway. They ascended a great staircase along which candles in stone *flambeaux* in the shape of mythological goddesses cast flickering shadows of yellow flame on the walls. At the top of the stairs another hallway stretched before them. There were several doors along it. Music and laughter filled the house downstairs, but if one listened intently one could also hear sounds, muffled and indistinct, from behind these doors.

"Since you are an initiate, new to revelry, and still perhaps a bit *shy*," Holland said, smiling as he emphasized the word, "I advise a premonitory taste of Cimmerian salacity." He guided Brassard to the first door, opened it, and they stepped inside the room.

The room was absolutely dark, with no hint of shape or presence visible. The darkness was a black theatre in which the performances were given by sound and smell. One could hear the shared protracted heavy breathing of some unseen couple, mutual moans softly filtered from ecstatic mouths here and there, the soft buffeting of buttocks and thighs, the fleshy splash of genitalia tautly slippery from their hot and fuck-locked affusions, an errant whimper there, a rippling of breathless sighs. And the air yielded a whole bouquet of varied fragrances: the acerb scent of vaginal brine, sweet savor of girlcream, tantalizing cunty liquors distilled in pink bogs and deep wells of womb, rills of sublime slime, and overall musk like a strong perfume, astringent blends of lovers' sweat, whiffs of the gingery and baked plum aromas of fundaments plumbed and funneled, loamy heats and sweetly reeking leakages.

"Go," Holland said, urging Brassard with a gentle push, and Brassard was away, into darkness.

Holland stood back to wait, listening to the sounds of the room and envisioning his guest's adventure. He could imagine how Brassard would be drawn into the tactile drama, to the buoyant softness of invisible breasts, his fingers made magical by the touch, seeking calf and thigh, and lured finally, as if by sensual magnet, to the irresistible luxuriant clutch and kiss of pliant cunny.

Holland grinned, waiting. Twenty minutes passed, and abruptly Brassard reeled up to him in the darkness, murmuring, "God, *God* . . ."

"Enjoy yourself?" Holland asked.

Brassard had brought with him the smell of an angel's gymnasium. "Oh, *oh*," he repeated.

Smiling, Holland whispered, "Come along."

In the hallway Holland led Brassard to the next door. On the previous door was a plaque that said DARK, and this one held a plaque labeled MENAGE. Holland opened the door and urged Brassard inside, following. They were in a bedroom with a ceiling and walls the color of white divinity, the room dominated by a big candle-lit bed of pink satin, big pink satin pillows against its plush pink headboard. Three lovely women in *déshabillé* and a man lounged against the pillows, smiling expectantly as they saw Brassard.

Holland remained against the far wall, watching with complete interest. Coaxed onto the bed by the sirens, Brassard sank and languished, all but disappearing beneath soft bounties of supple flesh.

It went on, and on, and on, Holland watching with the rapt attention of the seasoned voyeur. Perhaps an hour passed before Brassard withdrew, pausing to awkwardly put his clothing back on, grinning wildly at Holland, who nodded his approval. They were about to leave when one of the women left the bed and moved toward Brassard with a dreamy smile. Shiny tassels of semen were strung in the chunky twists of her short-cut hair, a viscid comma of it punctuating a corner of her smile, which she pressed in a kiss to Brassard's mouth, whispering "Love is the law."

"*Nice*," Holland remarked, urging his charge along.

The sign on the next door said, in golden script, UNDINE. It was Brassard who opened the door this time, eagerly. They stepped inside. In the center of the room a replica of Rome's Trevi Fountain debouched a continuous stream of water upward, the water pale yellow in the jonquil-colored light. More lovely houris waited on a couch whose cushions gleamed like butterscotch. A song was playing, a male voice singing in a suppliant voice:

> "*Pretty maid, pretty maid,*
> *I'll have warm lemonade.*
> *Leave the glass on the shelf,*
> *Let the pitcher be yourself . . .*"

Holland took great pleasure in watching what ensued, and by the time the tableau had unfolded entirely he had a vibrant and enlivening hard-on, which he yearned to share with someone.

But this was not *his* party, he reminded himself.

Holland led Brassard into the hallway. Brassard was addled with joy, closing his eyes and opening them intermittently like someone absorbing a delicious memory and blazoning it in his mind.

"You know, my friend," Holland said as they drew up to another door, "you have about you the look of the apostate. I think I have shown you some vistas you had never really glimpsed. In spite, of course, of your former zeal in censuring them. Brassard, you are acquiring the values of a satyr. My, my. And so very recently you were quite intent on prescribing your rather repressive values for us, ah, *libertines*, as you put it. All we ever wanted, Brassard, was the freedom to enjoy our own pleasures. Yet the act of love, you claimed, was the property of married couples, to want to enjoy love with more than one person an indecency. You called sex an addiction, pornography and its promiscuous tendencies addiction. As if any vital, lively pleasure must be seen in terms of pathology! And pornography degrades women, you said, pornography is misogynistic. Dear Brassard, I submit that tenacious monogamy might more aptly be thought of as misogynistic. By way of culinary analogies, do you think that a gourmet whose passion for food compels him to dine continuously in a variety of exotic restaurants could be said to hate food in comparison with a man who resolutely and with dedication dines nightly in the same restaurant?"

Holland paused, aware that the monologue was scarcely being heard by Brassard, who was abstracted, hazy-minded from the drugs and from his initiation into carnal epicureanism.

"But you Puritans were inexorable," Holland went on. "And therein lies the danger of the self-righteously virtuous. Virtue is not subject to the constraint of conscience like vice. Virtuous true-believers behave as if they had *carte-blanche* cards backed up by divine rights to enforce their way of thinking. So your great crusade, with its legions of white knights, invaded our privacy and pleasures, and you revoked our freedoms, you chased us down—the pornographers and prostitutes, swingers and sensualists, Lotharios and *femmes fatales*, homosexuals and bisexuals, deviants all in your view—and with your pure hearts and immaculate minds you burned our movies and books, sex toys and sexy costumes, our condoms and aphrodisiacs and love manuals. Sappho and Casanova and Vatsyayana were incinerated, their spirits blown away in ashes on a cold wind. You stood Eros in the lineup down at the police station, cautioned Cupid to use no more than a single dart on one person lest his bow be banned as a lethal weapon, and clapped Venus and Aphrodite into chastity belts. The joy of sex became an offense against prudent sensibilities and the libido a sinister animus of bestial urges. Most of all, you made sexual desire seem vulgar and brutish. *Dirty.* As if dirt was contamination rather than, in fact, a chic costume designed by nature for mother Earth! Brassard, Brassard!"

"Shall I go inside?" Brassard asked, hearing none of it.

Holland nodded at the sign on the door: CONFESSION AND PUNISHMENT. "By all means," he said. "Go in. And when you're finished join us all downstairs."

Holland opened the door for him.

Then he returned to the main room, where a spectacular revel was in progress. He had decided to preface his exit by making love one last time to his *pièce de résistance,* the splendid simulacrum of Marilyn Monroe, but discovered that she had become a crucial link in an elaborate daisy chain between two of his female guests, and he chose not to interrupt.

Rising above an elegant background music was a symphony of moans and murmurs, cries of joy and sobs of exultation. Holland stood smiling amid the revelry. Outside an aircar waited. After a few days, he reflected, without service, the automatons would run down and, finally, cease to function, their warm flesh cooling, the light gone from their eyes. When more authorities of the Moral Transcendency came they would find their emissaries going at each other with unregenerate lust. What woe and wrath there would be, and torches lighted and touched to the curtains of the house.

But Holland would have had his small victory. And, like the soldier they had forced him to become, would be preparing for the next engagement.

This story was inspired by Ray Bradbury's "Usher II" from the Martian Chronicles. *The title, "A Night of Dark Intent" is from the Robert Frost poem "Once by the Pacific."*

AFTERWORD

CAN'T DANCE, TOO WET TO PLOW . . .
EIGHT DOS AND DON'TS FOR
SAFE SEX WRITING

◆

By Marianna Beck

Writing about sex is something like hanging wallpaper while experiencing the seven-year itch. It's not easy to do—and even when writers think they've *really* got it down, it usually comes across as something they wouldn't want publicized.

Unfortunately, this hasn't stopped very many people. In fact, it's reasonably safe to assume that just about everyone who has ever taken pen in hand has clandestinely written about *that one experience* that's indelibly inscribed—or at the very least, *that one fantasy* that couldn't possibly occur unless there were a complete breakdown of law and order.

The main problem is that most writers tend to use the same nouns, the same verbs, the same adjectives—not to mention dangling modifiers—over and over. That's probably due to the fact that there are only so many body parts, so many moves, so many bad lines involving *waves of pleasure* that relating an experience *in situ*, not to mention *in flagrante delicto*, runs the risk of sounding like a badly dubbed Japanese western.

Publishing a magazine about sex is bound to make you a little jaded—especially when reading innumerable descriptions of amorous exploits. Having read several thousand manuscripts over the years, my partner Jack Hafferkamp and I admit we've occasionally suffered from the "been there, read it" attitude. So in order to forestall any more poetry or prose in which love objects are compared to either golf games or vacuum cleaners, we've decided to come up with a few helpful thoughts for writing (more safely) about sex. The following rules should help in not mixing metaphors so you don't end up playing the field with a bunch of red herrings.

Rule Number One: Writing about sex and remembering sex are two entirely different exercises. Once you start to describe what *really* happened, you're bound to run into trouble. A peak experience will invariably sound tawdry and full of diphthongs. In this case it's helpful to employ a bit of hyperbole to get a reader's attention. For instance, if you're feeling disappointed that your love-slave hasn't called in several hours, distinguish your emotions from a bad hair day with something like *I felt seduced and abandoned, blown to the ground, and devoured by foxes.*

Rule Number Two: Never, never mimic the style of cheesy bodice rippers. That means avoid euphemisms—all those words and phrases writers generally think sound better than the actual Latin terms. If there is some question about this, check out a grocery store romance novel. For male body parts, for example, it's not uncommon to find words like *man-root* and *jade column*. Women in these books are prone to refer to their *female essence* or *sacred tabernacle*. These always come off sounding like sale items from the back of New Age catalogs.

Rule Number Three: Whatever you do, never, never, *never* borrow or rework lines from books, movies, or other people—unless satire is your game. For example:

- Call me Morrie.

- Hasta la vista, babycakes.

- I haven't had sex in so long, I can't remember who gets tied up.

Rule Number Four: Avoid occupational hazards. Just because you're a dentist by day doesn't mean you need to refer to her charmingly overlapped canines or fawn over her slightly oversize bicuspids or work in lines like *his primary dentition had failed to exfoliate.* Similarly, avoid hardware terms like *petcock* or engineering terms like *shooting a grade off the wing wall.* Whatever you do, don't show off by using phrases like *love philtre.* People will think you either work for a pharmaceutical company or a swimming pool maintenance company, or, even worse, were once an English major.

Rule Number Five: To describe the obvious in compelling new ways, consider unusual words and phrases. But *caveat amator*: Do not compare a hirsute inamorato to a woolly mammoth, or your delicate, ninety-eight-pound girlfriend to a chickadee or, possibly worse, a double-breasted pushover. Don't define someone's love as greater than the gross national product of Togo. And do not reach for a thesaurus either. Stick to everyday references—like food. To wit: *She finished licking the last of the béchamel sauce from his armpit. . . . She ate knowing he was bad for her.*

Rule Number Six: Don't think you'll come up with a new sex vocabulary by perusing a textbook on human anatomy. This may net volumes in obscure terminology, but again, a writer needs to be vigilant. *Her ischial tuberosities made my eyes water* may be another way of saying she has a great bum, but the purpose here is not to make it sound like you're describing the pollen count in late August. Wanting to kiss that lovely shape created by his *alopecia prematura* is also no sexy way to address male pattern baldness.

◆　◆　◆

Rule Number Seven: Remember that the best way to write about sex is to stick to personal observations of real things:

- the way her toes curl during a lunar eclipse.
- the way his bald spot has taken on the shape of Rhode Island.
- how the sound of that voice, feverishly whispering in your ear, reminds you of Linda Blair in *The Exorcist.*

Rule Number Eight: This rule trumps all the other rules because in the final analysis the major event is really about language. In the universe of unrestrained libido, every line you write should sing. For example:

- Her eyes were like the celadon of a late Ming dynasty urn.
- She dressed like a feckless caryatid, but what did I know of architecture?
- He was the high poohbah of my lowest chakra.
- In the lingua franca of sexist verbiage, she was a hot number and no matter which side your chromosomes were on, you wanted to dial it.

The trick is to avoid going over the top polishing one's jewels. You'll know you've gone too far when rather than use words like *hot* or *primitive*, you find yourself describing your honey as the *most febrile carbon-based life form* you've ever encountered.

Of course, when you've hit that level of contorted prose, there isn't really much point in backing down. You might as well go all the way. So when your inner voice and typing fingers have led to thoughts of calescent rutting, rather than uttering that old monosyllabic standby—*Your place or mine?*—you might as well opt for something like *Can't dance, too wet to plow . . . so how's about a little amplexus?*

And, who knows, maybe we'll publish it in *Libido.*

CONTRIBUTORS

Johanna Baird lives in Washington, D.C., where she caters both private parties as well as large State Department functions. Much of her material, she says, is gleaned from eavesdropping at these events.

Dennis Bartel: Among the literary adventures of widely published Dennis Bartel (including five appearances in *Libido*) is reporting from the Israel-Lebanon buffer zone, and going underground to investigate contract killers, for which he received a top press club award. Bartel teaches writing at Johns Hopkins University.

Richard Collins has published fiction and poetry in *Exquisite Corpse, Fiction International, Yellow Silk, Asylum,* and elsewhere. He has lived for several years in Eastern Europe, first in Romania and now in Blagoevgrad, Bulgaria.

Sophie du Chien considers herself a late bloomer who discovered great sex only when she left her husband of twenty-three years. Retired from being a kept housewife, she now makes it her business to live out most of her fantasies and dedicates them to all the faint-hearted women leading lives of quiet desperation in the suburbs.

Mario Dworkin is a construction worker by day and a teacher of creative writing by night at a small city college in New England.

Carol L. Gloor is a practicing attorney, teacher, and sometime writer. Her poetry has been published in many little magazines around the country, most recently in *River Oak Review* and *Earth's Daughters*. She writes to give herself, and you, the courage to have a good time.

John Goldfine's pearl-snap work shirt has "John" stitched in red above the right pocket and "Top Pro Service Since 1945" above the left. The writers in his technical college classes in Bangor, Maine, often ask what that left side is all about. He smiles back—enigmatically, he hopes.

Janice Heiss is a writer and performer who lives in San Francisco. Her prose and poetry have been published in *Jewish Currents*, *Androgyne*, *Herotica 2* (under the pseudonym Daphne Slade), etc. In the early 1980s, Janice performed stand-up comedy at clubs throughout the Bay Area. Several of her performance pieces have been produced recently.

George Held's essays, book reviews, and poems have appeared in a wide variety of periodicals and anthologies. A chapbook of his nature poems, *Winged*, was published by Birnham Wood Graphics in 1995. He co-edits *The Ledge*, a magazine of poetry and fiction. He lives in New York City.

Marael Johnson, infamous poet, orbits the globe accompanied by a crack team of slave boys deft in the art of burning her lips fiery red while spiking her heels to stiletto points. She is the author of one novel, two books of poetry, and is writer/editor for a series of major international travel guides. Her poem "Communion" was first published in *Mad Woman on the Loose* (Paper Dreams, 1986); "A Fine Mesh" appeared (along with "Communion") in *Sin-a-Rama* (Guillotine Press, 1989).

Wayne Jones is working on a collection of stories called *Food Sex Love*. He lives in Ottawa, Ontario.

Arlett Kunkle was born in Hawthorn Woods, Illinois. "R & D in Suburbia" is her first publication and was written in a hotel room in a village one hundred miles north of Montreal while she waited for her "vanilla kind of guy" to return and take care of business.

Gershon Legman has been described as a "combination of crank, gypsy-scholar and pamphleteer, intellectual spelunker and journey-man-philosopher that has always been a native burr under the American Saddle." He no longer collects erotic literature and folklore. His main activity now, he says, is writing desperate books like *Love and Death*, loving fine women even if he has to marry them to do it, and listening to Mozart concertos. He says that for his epitaph he wants these words: "indomitable and fatalistic as a ticking bomb—like Lenin in Zurich."

William Levy, poet, foreign correspondent, publisher, radioist is author of several books, among them: *Virgin Sperm Dancer*, *Natural Jewboy*, and *Is There Sex Over Forty?* An American from Baltimore, he lives in Amsterdam.

Anne L. MacNaughton co-founded the Taos Poetry Circus along with Peter Rabbit in 1982 and has been a poetry activist ever since. She is a teacher, visual artist, a playwright, and a founding member of The Luminous Animal jazz-poetry performance ensemble. Her work has been published in *The Best Poetry of 1989*, *The Rag and Bone Shop of the Heart*, and *New Mexico Poetry Renaissance* as well as in numerous literary journals and magazines. Born in Arkansas and raised in Houston, she lives and writes in Taos, New Mexico.

Frieda Madland lives in Chicago, where she operates as a *laissez faire* mother and free-floating hetaera.

Terry Marshall currently lives in Carlsbad, New Mexico, a far cry from the South Pacific setting of "Partners." Marshall is author of *The*

Whole World Guide to Language Learning and *101 Ways to Find an Overseas Job.* "Partners" is his first published short story.

Spider McGee's fiction has appeared under various names in *Libido* and *Funny Times,* and is rumored to show up in the E-zine *Texas Chainsaw Magazine.* Two novels and a book of short stories await entrepreneurs.

Melissa Moore manages educational and economic development programs in San Francisco. She writes erotic stories and other works of fiction late at night and during the early hours of the morning. Melissa, who was born in Denmark, has a Masters Degree from Harvard University.

Anna Mortál draws inspiration from the spotted fur of bees, the dark pleasure of soil under her nails. Her most recent credits include *The Madison Review, Kalliope, 13th Moon, The Abiko Quarterly* (Japan), *Stand* (England), and *The Santa Monica Review.* Mortál lives in Sylmar, California, and from time to time lectures on contemporary poets.

Robert Perchan, Cleveland-raised, is a professor at Dong-a University in Korea. His poetry has been published in *Exquisite Corpse, Gypsy, Wormwood Review,* and *Chiron Review.* His novel, *Perchan's Chorea: Eros and Exile,* was published by Watermark Press (Wichita).

Carol Queen is an erotic writer and cultural sexologist who tries to describe sex the way it really happens. Her writing has been widely anthologized. Her first book, *Exhibitionism for the Shy,* is available from Down There Press.

Laura Rosenthal is the executive editor of *Exquisite Corpse* and co-editor with Andrei Codrescu of *American Poets Say Goodbye to the 20th Century,* published by Four Walls Eight Windows.

Albert Stern is a writer and performer living in Brooklyn.

Lydia Swartz is an editrix, pornographer, and bigamist who has proof that somebody up there loves her when she considers her wife, Madelyn, and male primary, Rick, not to mention Saran Wrap girdles, perv events in places with wheelchair ramps, and thunderstorms.

Larry Tritten lives in San Francisco, where he crossbreeds the rigors of technical writing with the intoxicated sensibilities of love poetry. He is a veteran magazine writer who has probably contributed to a wider range of publications than any other writer in the Western Hemisphere. His credits include the *New Yorker, Playboy, National Lampoon, Redbook,* and dozens of other publications.

Ralph Tyler is a former journalist—San Francisco, London, Rome, and New York—who also spent six years as Associate Editor of Literature at the Encyclopaedia Britannica. He now lives in New York and writes his own brand of literature.

Jane Underwood is a freelance writer and editor living in San Francisco. She is also a single mother raising a thirteen-year-old son. In her spare time, she is growing a garden and having as much good unwholesome sex as possible.

R. M. Vaughan is both a poet and playwright. He has written ten plays—the most recently produced was a version of Proust's *Sodome et Gomorrhe*. His poetry has appeared in a cross-Canada anthology of young poets called *The Last Word* (Insomniac Press) and *Plush: Five Gay Poets Appearing Nightly* (Coach House Press). His own book of poems, *the sand that is everywhere*, was published by ECW Press.

David Vineyard is a well-known *raconteur,* former private detective, former spy, journalist, columnist, and linguist, portrait artist, curmudgeon, Dorothy Parker fan, Damon Runyon enthusiast, and *aficionado* of bad opera (Wagner). He is forty-five years old, has a useless degree in history and political science (East European no less), and is a native Texan transplanted among the Okies.

Michael Warr's awards for poetry include a 1994 NEA Creative Writing Fellowship and the Gwendolyn Brooks Significant Illinois Poets Award. He is author of the poetry collection *We Are All the Black Boy*, and has been widely anthologized. He is executive director of the Guild Complex, an award-winning cross-cultural center, and an editor at Tia Chucha Press.